FIRE & FRENZY

Tarnished Angels Motorcycle Club Book 6

EMMA SLATE

©2023 by TABULA RASA Publishing LLC
All rights reserved.

No part of this publication may be reproduced, distributed or transmitted in any form or by any means, including photocopying, recording, or other electronic or mechanical methods, without the prior written permission of the publisher, except in the case of brief quotations embodied in critical reviews and certain other noncommercial uses permitted by copyright law.

This book is a work of fiction. Names, characters, places, and incidents are the product of the author's imagination or are used fictitiously. Any resemblance to actual events, locales, or persons, living or dead, is coincidental.

Fire & Frenzy
(TARNISHED ANGELS MOTORCYCLE CLUB BOOK 6)

They say 'where there's smoke, there's fire…'

Well, nothing ignites your rage more than finding out your fiancé is having an affair.

But two can play at that game…

The next thing I know I'm in a biker's bed being worshiped the way I deserve.

When Smoke touches me, I tremble with need and forget all about the man who let me slip through his fingers.

I've never known passion like this, and with Smoke, I'm insatiable.

It was just supposed to be one night…

But Smoke and I can't stay away from each other. Soon, we're sneaking around, our couplings desperate and forbidden.

This is everything you're not supposed to do. Don't take revenge. Don't date the bad boy.

And never, ever fall in love with your best friend's father.

Content Warnings:

Dear Reader,

Thank you so much for reading *Fire & Frenzy*.

Please note, there are content warnings for this book which include:
   1. **Attempted rape and**
   2. **Extreme violence toward a woman**
   Both of the above instances are ON PAGE and not fade to black.

Thank you for taking these warnings into consideration before proceeding.

XOXO,
   Emma

Chapter 1

"This is bad," I muttered.

"It's definitely not the greatest," Tavy agreed. "Am I allowed to be completely honest?"

I looked at my best friend. Her green eyes were glassy, her shoulder-length dark hair was a mess, and she reeked of bourbon. We both did. "I'm not going to like what you have to say, am I?"

"Maybe I shouldn't say it..."

"You *should* say it." My hand settled onto the wooden slat of the jail cell bench. "I'm already at the lowest point of my life. I doubt I can go lower."

Tavy worked her plump bottom lip between her teeth. Her fair cheeks flushed with color as she blurted out, "I've never liked Knox."

"*Never?*"

"I've never trusted him. And he always gave me the creeps."

"Why didn't you say anything?" I demanded.

"You can't tell your best friend you don't like her fiancé. If I'd told you that, you know what would've happened? You would've chosen him over me and cut me out."

"I'd *never* cut you out!" I denied. "Tavy, you're my soul sister. My partner in crime."

"No pun intended," she mumbled.

I tucked my long blonde hair behind my ear and leaned my head against her shoulder. "It's my fault we're in jail."

"Damn right it is," she said lightly. "But getting arrested has always been on my bucket list. I just wish our crime was cooler. Like, if we'd gotten arrested for stealing a diamond and then gone on the run. That's way better than getting caught peeing in an alley and then yelling at a cop. And I thought for sure he'd let us off when you gave him your sob story."

"I think he would've let us go," I said. "If I hadn't also screamed in his face that all men are bastards."

"You also puked on his shoes."

"Yeah, that might've been the thing that pushed him over the edge."

I was sobering up and I didn't like that at all. Sober meant I could feel things. It was easier to be drunk. It was easier to be angry. Anger shoved out the hurt.

"Who can we call to come bail us out?" I asked. "You're the only person I'd call if I were in this situation, but you're sitting next to me. I can't call a colleague. I'm pretty sure I'd get fired for this."

"You could call your dad," she suggested. "Or one of your brothers."

"And tell them they have to get on a plane to bail us out of jail?" I grimaced. "No way. I can only imagine the lecture."

"Your dad would definitely pull the *young lady* card."

"Seriously."

"My dad," Tavy said. "I'm an idiot. Of course, I'll call my dad. He won't mind bailing us out."

"He won't?" I asked. "Really?"

"Nah, he'll probably find this funny." She grinned.

"Funny? My life is funny?"

"No, not funny," she reassured me.

"Pathetic is more like it," I stated with a slump of my shoulders. "Okay. Call your dad."

Tavy's dad was young…and *hot*.

I couldn't stop staring at the man. His angular jaw was covered in dark stubble, a slight smile appearing on generous lips. Ink snaked up his muscular arms and dark hair graced his head.

He wore heavy black boots, jeans, and a leather vest.

She hopped up from the bench and smiled. "Hi, Daddy. Thanks for coming."

"Tavy." His brown eyes twinkled. "Got yourself into some trouble, huh?"

"It wasn't my fault," she said automatically. "It was Logan's."

"Way to throw me under the bus," I snapped, my nose wrinkling.

"Logan." His voice was deep and raspy.

Our gazes locked and I suddenly forgot how to breathe.

"Logan, this is my dad, Smoke."

"Smoke." His name came out more like a croak. "Thanks for coming."

His eyes landed on his daughter. "I was on a hot streak." He cracked a grin. "Your call got me out of there before my luck turned. Thanks for that."

Smoke stepped back and let the cop unlock the jail cell. Tavy bounded over to her father and gave him a big hug. He embraced her in his rugged bear arms.

"You guys hungry?" he asked as we followed him into the lobby of the police station where we picked up our personal belongings.

"I could eat," Tavy admitted.

"Logan?" Smoke prompted when I hadn't replied.

"Yeah," I muttered. "I need food too. Hold on a sec."

I turned around and approached the cop who had arrested us. "Sorry about your shoes."

The aging cop's lips twitched. "Happens more often than you think. Don't sweat it."

I caught up with Smoke and Tavy at the doors of the building. Smoke's brow was raised in a silent question as if waiting for an explanation about why he'd had to bail us out of jail, but I didn't say anything. He could wait to hear about our escapade from Tavy.

We stepped outside into the warm Las Vegas night. I took a deep breath, smelling clean, dry air. It smelled different than The Strip. No urine. No scent of sweat and desperation.

Smoke pulled out his cell phone from the inner breast pocket of his leather vest and began pecking away.

A car showed up a few minutes later. Smoke opened the rear passenger door and Tavy climbed into the back seat. I moved to slide in behind her. As I was about to get into the vehicle, I accidentally brushed against Smoke. A zing went through me, all the hairs on my body standing at attention.

I didn't make eye contact with him as I settled into my seat. He closed the door and then went around to the front passenger side.

My phone chimed in my clutch. I pulled it out, grimacing when I read the text from my fiancé.

KNOX

I miss you so much.

I showed Tavy my cell. She made a noise of disgust. "Piece of shit."

"Yup." I shoved my phone back into my clutch and stared out the window. The ride was silent until the car pulled up in front of The Rex Hotel.

I was surprised that Tavy's dad was staying at The Rex. The Rex was one of the most luxurious hotels in Las Vegas. It wasn't even on The Strip. It was just outside the city, and it was sprawling. It rivaled the Bellagio for elegance.

"Why did you bring us here?" Tavy asked. "You could've dropped us off at my place."

"You wanted food. We'll order room service," Smoke said. "And I'm not sure I trust you criminals to stay out of trouble."

Tavy sniggered.

We walked through the opulent, old-world lobby to the elevators. It was all white marble and gold accents. Our heels clacked against the gleaming floor. Heads turned to survey us, and I quickly realized it was because of Smoke. Tavy and I were dressed for a night on the town, but he stuck out with his leather and ink, heavy boots, and *don't fuck with me* confidence.

The lobby elevator arrived. I went to the back of the carriage, nestling myself into the corner. Tavy and Smoke stepped in behind me. The doors closed and Smoke turned to press the button for his floor.

The back of Smoke's leather vest showcased a skull

with angel wings along with his club name, Tarnished Angels.

I'd known Tavy's dad was a biker. She'd told me the first week we'd met as suite mates during our freshman year of college six years ago, but she hadn't talked about him much after that.

The carriage felt small even though there were only three of us in it. I kept sneaking glances at the back of Smoke's head and neck. He didn't look old enough to have a daughter my age.

I didn't like that I was noticing him. I didn't like that when we'd accidentally brushed against one another, my body had come alive. I didn't like that my eyes kept darting back to him, stealing looks when I thought no one was watching.

The elevator opened and I trekked after them to Smoke's hotel room. He pulled out his keycard and opened the door.

He'd sprung for the deluxe suite. There was a sitting room and full kitchen. Tavy plopped down onto the plush gray couch and reached for the red leather-bound room service menu. She flipped it open. "What do you want to eat, Logan?"

Every calorie dense dessert on the menu.

"Fries," I lied.

"That's it?" Tavy asked.

"That's it," I said. "We had dinner not two hours ago."

"Yeah, but drinking," she reminded me. "Suddenly it's like you have two stomachs."

Smoke opened the minibar and pulled out two bottles of European water. He handed one to his daughter and then one to me.

"Drink," he commanded. "Beat the hangover."

"I don't think I'll be getting a hangover," I replied, even

as I unscrewed the lid. "Once we were in the back of the cop car, I sobered up really fast."

"You sobered up fast because you puked on the cop's shoes," Tavy said.

"Tavy," I groaned.

"It's true," she pointed out.

"Doesn't mean you have to remind me," I groused.

"My dad won't judge. Will you, Dad?"

"No judgment," Smoke agreed, but his eyes gleamed with amusement. "I did worse in my heyday."

"Yeah?" Tavy asked with a grin. "Like what?"

He shook his head. "Those days are in the iron vault."

"Bummer. I would've liked to know." She opened her bottle of water and guzzled a third of it in one go. "Will you order for me? Burger, medium rare, fries, and the chocolate cake with a glass of milk. I want to go shower the smell of jail off of me."

"We were in jail for barely an hour," I pointed out with a laugh.

"Still, I gotta scrub my skin."

She got up from the couch and headed for the bedroom, taking her bottle of water with her. The door closed and then I was alone with Smoke.

"Uh, thanks for bailing us out," I said.

Smoke let out a booming laugh. "I thought her going away party was going to be chill. She said something about staying in and watching rom-coms."

"Change of plans," I said. "Though we would've gotten into less trouble if we'd just done that."

Never go out for a night on the town after you find out your fiancé is cheating. Bad decisions run amok.

"I can't believe she leaves in a few days," I said, wishing she didn't have to go.

How was I supposed to get through life without her?

She was my best friend, my entire support system. And now she was leaving Las Vegas to start a new job where she could live close to her father—the father that hadn't been around for her childhood.

It felt like she was choosing him over me at the worst time in my life, but of course that was ridiculous. It wasn't her fault Knox had cheated on me and that my entire life was in shambles because of it.

"So, what happened?" Smoke asked as he reached for the hotel phone.

"Why did you have to bail us out of jail, you mean?"

"Yeah."

"Because we peed in an alleyway and I yelled at a cop."

"Why did you yell at a cop?"

"Look, this is really embarrassing for me. Can I just pay you back the bail money and we forget about all this?" I asked.

"Don't worry about the bail money." He dialed room service and put in Tavy's order. He looked at me. "You sure all you want is fries?"

"I'm sure."

My stomach rumbled loud enough for him to hear.

"Double that order, please," he said into the phone. "Thanks." He set the phone back into its cradle and then leaned against the couch.

"The fries would've been enough," I protested.

He shrugged. "Eat what you want, leave the rest."

"How do you know how I like my meat cooked?" I demanded.

"Took a shot. You want me to call them back and have them cook all the flavor out of it?"

My mouth flickered with an incoming smile, but I tamped it down. "No. Your guess was correct."

"So you're giving me shit because…"

I sighed. "Because I've had a rough night."

"You from here?" he asked.

"No."

"You're chatty."

"My night sucked. I don't feel like being chatty," I clipped. "Thanks for the bail money, but maybe I should just go."

"Stay," he demanded. "Your food will be here in a few." He tossed me the TV remote and then stood.

"Where are you going?" I asked as he went to the door.

He flashed a grin. "Testing to see if I've still got my hot streak."

Chapter 2

TAVY MOANED in pleasure as she polished off the last bite of her burger. "That was the best thing I've ever had. I want to make love to it. I want to have its babies."

I dunked my fry into a blob of ketchup. "You're a weirdo."

"Pot, meet kettle."

I took a cloth napkin and wiped my greasy fingers.

"So, are we going to talk about it?" she asked.

"The jail thing or the Knox thing?"

"The jail thing happened *because* of the Knox thing."

"I'd rather not talk about the Knox thing. I'd rather burn every memory I have of him out of my mind and pretend he's ash."

She sighed. "What are you going to do?"

"End it, of course," I said, glancing down at the two-carat diamond on my finger. I'd been overwhelmed by the ring when he'd proposed.

Nothing but the biggest and the best for my girl, he'd said.

I never admitted to him that it felt too big for my hand. Like it didn't look quite right on my finger.

An omen, clearly.

The wedding was in three months. There was more than enough time to cancel and alert the guests.

And my parents.

That'll be fun…

"I feel like a cliché," I said to Tavy. "A young, foolish woman who got swept away by a man's charm and muscles."

"Well, he has a lot of them," Tavy agreed. "Being an amateur MMA fighter will do that."

"Why did you never like him?" I asked.

"I don't know." She frowned. "It was just…a feeling. Like he wasn't always being truthful or genuine. Like he was showing us what we wanted to see, not what really was."

"Classic manipulator and narcissist."

"You can't blame yourself," she said quietly. "Not for falling for him, and certainly not for him cheating on you."

"Do you really have to leave?" I asked. "Do you really have to go be an adult?"

"I kinda do," she said sadly. "Plus, this my chance, you know? To get closer to my dad. That's why I took the job in Waco."

"Yeah, I get it. As much as I want to be selfish and demand you stay and be my emotional support animal, I know you've got to go live your own life."

"*Woof, woof,*" she jested. "Just do me a favor. Don't buy a purse dog and take it everywhere with you. A dog is not a crutch."

"What if I get a German Shepherd and train it to go for Knox's gonads on command?"

"I'd pay good money to see that." She gathered the empty plates and put them on the writing table and then adjusted the sash of her robe. "I'm fucking wiped."

"Me too," I said. "I guess I should be getting home."

"What? No. Crash here."

"I can't crash here."

"Why not? I'm crashing here."

"Where? Does this couch pull out?"

"The bed." She gestured to the bedroom. "Dad won't mind. He'll take the couch."

"I don't feel right about it."

"Too bad. I'm not letting you take a cab home where you'll sit and stew over all this. Just stay here."

"Well…" I looked in the direction of the bed. I was tired and the alcohol had long since run its course. "You sure your dad won't mind?"

"I doubt he'll even be back before dawn," she said with a grin. "Not if he's still on that winning streak."

I followed Tavy into the bedroom. She shut the door and then went to the bed. "I have one rule."

"What?" I asked, kicking off my heels.

"Don't try and spoon me. I'm a violent sleeper. I'm liable to hit you by accident."

"Noted."

We crawled beneath the covers, Tavy in her hotel robe, me in my black dress. She hit the light switch and darkness engulfed the room.

"Tavy?"

"Yeah?"

"Thanks for going to jail with me."

She sniggered. "Any time, Logan. Any fucking time."

"Tavy," I muttered into the pillow, wincing at the early morning light. "Tavy, answer your phone!"

With a grumble, she reached her hand out toward the

nightstand to grasp her cell. "Shit, it's my job." She hastily sat up, swiped her phone, and put it to her ear. "Hello?"

She paused for a few moments, nodding along at whatever was being said. "Sure, that's no problem. I can make that happen. See you then." Tavy hung up and tossed her phone aside and immediately crawled out of bed.

"What's up?" I asked her.

"My new boss needs me to start sooner. Someone left unexpectedly and I have to fill in immediately." She hastily made her way to the bathroom. "This fucks up all my plans. I was supposed to ride shotgun in the moving truck with Dad. Now I'm gonna get to Waco days before my stuff, so I can't move into the apartment they're putting me up in."

A resounding knock echoed in the room.

"Come in," I called out.

The door opened and Smoke walked in. He was barefoot, but he wore jeans and a tight white T-shirt, showcasing his muscled, inked arms. His dark hair was askew. He looked both masculine and boyish and my stomach flipped.

"Hey," he said, his gaze dipping lower.

I looked down and realized that my dress was no longer where it should've been—and my black push up bra was exposed. I hastily covered myself, my cheeks suffusing with heat.

Tavy came out of the bathroom, wearing her green dress from the previous night.

"Hey," she greeted her father. "Sorry we crashed in your bed. Was the couch comfortable?"

"It was fine," he said. "Your phone woke me. Everything okay?"

"Yeah. My job needs me sooner. Someone quit last minute so I need to get there as soon as possible to cover."

"So, we won't be doing a road trip," he said. "Damn. I was looking forward to that."

She walked over to her father and kissed his stubbly cheek. "I'm bummed about it too. Trust me. It was going to be fun tormenting you with my choice of music."

"Don't worry about it. I can handle the drive myself. I'll hitch the car up at your place and get out of here this afternoon. We did all the heavy lifting yesterday."

"I'll get to Waco before you—I can't really stay in my apartment without my stuff. I mean, I guess I could get an air mattress and paper plates—"

"You can stay at the clubhouse until I get your shit to town."

"That would be so much easier."

"Hey, Tavy?" I asked.

"Yeah?" She turned to look at me.

"How would you like a roommate?"

She widened her eyes. "You don't mean—seriously? You want to move to Waco?"

My gaze darted between her and Smoke, but I settled on my best friend's face. "I can't stay in Vegas and have everything remind me of Knox. I've got to get out of here. And you moving to Waco... It just makes sense."

"What about your job?" she asked. "You love your job."

"I'll figure something out. I'm not staying here for a job."

A smile bloomed across Tavy's elfin features and she bounded toward me. She all but pounced on me, her brown hair getting in my face and clouding my vision. "Yes! Please, yes! This is perfect." She pulled back but kept her hands on my shoulders. "We can be roomies and you can ride with Dad to Waco!"

"Oh…" I struggled to keep my face expressionless. "I thought I'd fly."

"Why?" Tavy shook her head. "It doesn't make any sense. You've gotta move your stuff and Dad is already driving a moving truck to Waco. Just ride with him. Plus, I hate the idea of Dad driving alone."

"I've only got a few things. I'm not taking any of Knox's furniture."

"You wanna get out of Vegas sooner, or later? Dad's leaving today and you won't even have to pay for checked bags. Make it easy on yourself."

My gaze drifted from her to Smoke. I couldn't tell what he was thinking. Silence permeated the room. Tension swelled as we all waited for Smoke to speak. Finally, he smiled and said, "I don't mind you tagging along."

I gritted out a smile. "Thanks."

"We'll hit Tavy's apartment first, hitch up her car and then send her off, and then head to your place and grab your stuff."

Tavy hugged me. "This is going to be so much fun!"

Chapter 3

THE THREE OF us took a cab to Tavy's place. She changed quickly, grabbed her suitcase, and was back in the cab in just a few minutes.

"I'll see you in a couple of days," she said to me. "And a word of advice…whatever you do, don't let Knox know anything's wrong."

I nodded, sneaking a glance at Smoke. He didn't know the particulars of my dirty laundry, and I wanted to keep it that way.

Tavy waved from inside the cab before it sped off toward the airport.

"Come on," Smoke said. "Let's get the rest of her shit. There's not much left."

There were a few odds and ends she'd left in the bathroom and kitchen, and she'd set up a cleaning service to come in and tackle the deep clean after the apartment was vacant.

Her place had been vibrant, full of personal touches that made it feel like a home, but now it was empty. It reminded me that it was the people who made the place.

I shook my head at the maudlin thoughts. Chapters in life ended all the time. It was all part of the journey.

After we put the rest of Tavy's belongings into the moving truck, Smoke hitched up her car on a car transport trailer.

"Where am I taking you to get your stuff?" Smoke asked, holding a set of truck keys.

"My fiancé's place. *Ex*-fiancé." It was strange to say. Almost like I didn't really believe that the last three years of my life had been destroyed so completely, and so quickly.

We climbed into the truck and I took my phone out to punch my address into GPS. The phone's voice droned directions and fifteen minutes later, we pulled up to Knox's house. It was a two-story, gargantuan abode with a pool and extensive home gym.

I wondered what Smoke would think about it.

Knox loved to show off. Was that why he'd wanted to marry me? Because he thought he could show me off?

"*Fuck him*," I growled as I looked out the window.

"Fuck who? Your ex?" Smoke asked.

Oops.

I hadn't even been aware that I'd spoken.

"Never mind." I reached for the door and then hopped out. I fished my keys out of my bag as I trekked up the stone walkway.

I unlocked the heavy wooden front door and turned the knob. The foyer was expansive and opulent, mimicking the outward appearance of the home. Knox had leaned into the Spanish, desert motif. Bright woven tapestries adorned the walls and clay pottery decorated the heavy wooden furniture. The couches and chairs were made of the finest leather and wood.

"Nice," Smoke said blandly.

"Nice, yeah." I turned to look at him. "I need to shower and pack some stuff. Kitchen is through there." I pointed down the hallway. "Help yourself to anything. I'll be fast."

"You're not expecting your ex to come home anytime soon, are you?" he asked.

"No." I shook my head. "He's out of town for a few days."

I felt his eyes tracking me as I ran up the stairs.

The bedroom I shared with Knox was littered with memories and I had to force myself to enter. I walked over to my nightstand and stood in front of it for a moment before grasping the ring on my finger and pulling it off. I set it on the top of the grainy wood and before I could think too much about it, I went to the closet to grab two suitcases.

I packed quickly, taking only my favorite clothes. Jeans, comfortable sweaters and T-shirts, and my beat-up white slip-ons that Knox hated.

I showered, refusing to linger in what was soon to be my former home. I didn't even get my hair wet, not wanting to waste time blow-drying it after the shower. I didn't bother with makeup. I wanted to be free, unencumbered. I also didn't have the energy for it.

I brought my suitcases downstairs. Smoke wasn't in the sitting room.

"Smoke?"

A moment later, he popped out of the kitchen, holding a sandwich. "You ready?"

"Almost." I brushed past him into the kitchen and opened the door to the garage. I flipped on the light.

Knox's pride and joy of a vehicle—a brand new look-at-me-green Dodge Charger SRT Hellcat Jailbreak edition took up one side of the garage.

I went to the corner of the room and picked up a half-empty bag of Quikrete left over from the landscapers. I turned to head back inside. Smoke stood in the doorway. He moved out of the way as I marched toward him.

Smart man.

I set the bag on the kitchen table and unrolled the top. I took it to the kitchen sink and dumped it down the drain and then I turned on the water to let it run for a few seconds.

"So, he cheated on you, huh?" Smoke asked.

"Yep." I took the bag of high-strength concrete mix around the house and ruined as many pipes as I could until the bag was empty.

I came back into the kitchen. The sandwich was gone and Smoke was drinking a can of soda. "You done?"

"Nope." My house keys were on the kitchen table and I swiped them before heading back into the garage. I went over to Knox's car and gouged the word *cheater* onto the hood and then keyed the car all the way around so every bit of paint would need to be redone.

I shook small paint chips and clear coat off my keys and then looked over my shoulder at Smoke who'd followed me. "Now I'm done."

～

Smoke put my suitcases in Tavy's car, making them easy to get to when we stopped for the night. I opened the passenger side door of the moving truck and tossed my sweater and brown leather bag onto the seat. I'd grabbed us a couple of bottles of cold water from the house and I put them in the drink holders.

"I'm just gonna check the tire pressure real quick,"

Smoke said. "Make sure we're road worthy. Don't need a blowout."

I nodded and settled into my seat.

A few minutes later, Smoke got into the truck. "We're good. How are you? Do you need to use the bathroom or anything before we go? If you do, you might have to use a bush in the backyard now that none of the plumbing in the house works."

He cracked a grin, but when he saw that I didn't smile, his face went blank. "Not even a snarky clap back, huh? You must really feel like shit."

"I vacillate between angry and sad. Right now, I'm sad," I admitted.

"Feel what you gotta feel. You want to listen to angry metal music on the way out of town?"

"Sure. Why not."

"Thank God. I was worried you'd want to listen to some angsty, whiny, girl music."

"Metal for me." A small laugh escaped me. "Thanks."

"No problem."

He started the engine and then fiddled with the radio. A rocker screaming into the mic filtered through the speakers, drowning out the thoughts in my head.

We got on the road. We didn't speak as Smoke expertly maneuvered the huge truck through neighborhood streets and then merged onto the highway.

He reached for the knob on the radio and turned it down. "Okay. I'm ready to listen."

"Ready to listen to what?"

"Your story." He glanced at me quickly.

"I don't really want to talk about it," I admitted.

"I'm driving on a few hours of sleep. You gotta keep me awake. So, you gotta talk."

"Can't we discuss something else?" I asked in exasperation. "I'd prefer not to relive my humiliation."

"Well, it seems like you got your revenge. That car was his baby, wasn't it?"

"Yup. Though now I'm kind of having a bit of remorse over how I handled it."

"Why?"

I shrugged and looked out the window. "He's got a short fuse sometimes. And when he finds his pipes full of concrete and his baby needing a new paint job…"

"Yeah, about that concrete. How'd you know about that little trick?"

I glanced at him and grinned. "My dad is a builder. I spent a lot of my childhood on construction sites. I learned a few tricks."

He let out a laugh and I laughed with him.

"There it is," he said, his laughter dying down.

"What?"

"You're laughing again. That's a good sign."

"Am I allowed to ask *you* questions?"

"Sure."

"You stayed at The Rex."

"That's not a question."

"No. It just seemed…not your style."

"And you know my style?"

"I'm making a muck of this, aren't I?"

He shot me a grin. "I know what you're getting at. Biker at a nice hotel. Out of place. Normally you'd be right, but our club president knows the owner of The Rex Hotel empire."

I blinked. "Seriously?"

My phone rang and I dug it out of my purse. I looked at the screen. "Oh, it's the lying bastard motherfucker." I fiddled with the radio knob until the music died down.

I took a deep breath and answered his call. "Hi, honey."

"It sounds really loud. Are you in the car? You're not with someone, are you?" he asked in way of greeting.

"I'm in a car and I'm alone." I gritted my teeth. "How's the trip?"

"Going well. I miss you, though."

"I miss you too," I lied.

"When I get home, let's go to your favorite restaurant. We'll sit in a cozy little booth, share a bottle of wine and the chocolate fondue…"

"Can't wait. Listen, the traffic is bad and I don't want to be distracted. I'll talk to you later."

"Love you, babe."

"Love you, too."

I hung up and tossed my phone into my bag. My chest was tight and my skin felt hot and prickly.

"Hmm. I think ragey-Logan just came out to play," Smoke said.

"Ragey, stabby Logan."

He fell silent, almost like he was giving me the space to talk if I wanted to. And suddenly I wanted to. I'd spoken a little bit about it to Tavy last night, but we'd quickly gotten drunk and feelings don't get sorted when you're drunk. It was almost like the liquor froze the emotion in your body so there was no way to actually process it.

"I drove him to the airport yesterday," I said suddenly. "I dropped him off at curbside check-in. I was a few minutes away when I realized he'd left his carry-on bag of comfort stuff. Neck pillow. Noise cancelling headphones. Things that make the flight bearable. So, I circled back around through airport traffic so I could give him his bag and make sure he was comfortable on the flight… He was standing next to the porter and I thought he was waiting for me. Nope, *not me*. A redhead walked up to him and I watched him pull her to him, grab her ass, and kiss her. Like, with tongue and everything."

"Fuck," Smoke said softly.

"Yeah. She works in his firm. I've met her actually. At the company Christmas party." I glanced at him. "I never thought I'd be a walking cliché."

"And last night, you…"

"Had dinner with Tavy. We got really drunk and then on our way to another bar, I…"

"You…"

I sighed. "What the hell, might as well tell you the entire truth. I had to pee, okay? I had to pee, and I thought it would be a good idea to squat in an alley. It just so happened that a cop car was slowly driving by and saw what was happening."

"And he took you and Tavy to jail for that?"

"No. You get a ticket and a fine for public urination." I shook my head. "The cop got out of the car and was planning on ticketing me, but I had to open my drunk mouth and start yelling at him and blaming the only man in front of me for all of Knox's transgressions."

"And that's why he took you and Tavy to jail?"

"Oh no, it gets better. I think he was going to let us off with a warning, actually. But then I puked on his shoes." I winced. "And so he took us to jail *for our own protection*. His words, not mine. I think he has a daughter so he had a soft spot for me and realized we were going to get in real trouble if left to our own devices."

Smoke laughed and shook his head. "What a night you guys had."

"Thanks for coming to get us."

He looked at me. "You've already thanked me."

Our gazes locked and something moved in my chest. I suddenly couldn't breathe.

Again.

Thankfully, Smoke turned his attention back to the road.

"Your hot streak," I blurted out, wanting to cover the strange moment between us.

"What about it?"

"You went back to the casino. Were you still on a hot streak?"

"Enough to pay for the gas," Smoke said with a wry grin.

"That worked out well then."

He looked at me again and then paused for just a moment before he said, "Yeah. I think it did."

Chapter 4

With the phone to my ear, I adjusted the air conditioning in the moving truck.

"Don't tell my dad but flying for a few hours versus being on the road for two days is the way to do it," Tavy said.

"I won't tell him," I assured her. "But I think you owe him a father-daughter hang out."

"Definitely. I'll let him treat me to margs and guac to celebrate my new job. How's the drive so far?"

I looked at the gas station that Smoke had disappeared into. The truck hadn't needed fuel yet, but Smoke had wanted an energy drink. "So far, so good."

"Where are you guys stopping for the night?"

"Not sure," I admitted.

"How are you holding up?"

"Okay, I guess."

"You talk to Knox?"

"For a bit. He called. I had to lie through my teeth and pretend to miss him. Left my ring on the nightstand, keyed his car, and poured cement down his pipes before I left though."

"*Oh man.*" She sniggered. "What I wouldn't give to see his reaction."

"I'm glad I'll be far away." I sighed. "You think he'll be more pissed that I left, or about his car?"

"Well, he really loves that car…"

"Yeah. I thought so."

"Maybe I'll treat *you* to margs and guac and we can have a proper deep-dive about this entire thing. We didn't really get a chance last night before the bourbon hit our systems."

The door to the gas station opened and Smoke came out carrying a plastic bag.

"I thought for sure our heavy meal would've soaked up all that bourbon, but I guess not."

"We were doing shots," she reminded me.

"Never again," I said.

"You hungover?"

"No. Not really. I puked most of the alcohol up, remember?"

The door to the moving truck opened and Smoke set the plastic bag on the center seat. "Hold on, Tav."

I held the cell out to Smoke.

He took it from me, our fingers touching. Electricity sparked in my fingertips and crackled up my entire arm.

I clenched my hands and set them in my lap.

Smoke didn't take his eyes off me. "Hey. Raze pick you up and get you settled in the clubhouse yet?" He paused. "Good. Yeah. We're probably gonna stop in a few hours. I'll text you when we hunker down for the night. Yeah, love you too." He hung up and handed me my phone.

He shut the door to the moving truck. "I got us a

couple of snacks to hold us over until we stop for the night. You good with that?"

"Oh, sure," I said. "We got a late start."

"I'm fucking wiped," Smoke admitted, cracking open an energy drink. I rummaged through the plastic bag and pulled out the candy bars.

"Didn't know what you liked, so I got a medley," he explained.

I smiled softly. "I see that."

"Chocolate is medicinal and necessary to healing a broken heart."

I ripped open a candy bar that was crunchy and caramelly. "You are not wrong." I took a bite and chewed before saying, "It's too bad you weren't around during Tavy's teen years. She could've used this." I closed my mouth and blanched. "Shit. I'm sorry. I didn't mean that to sound the way it did."

"Forget about it." He finished the last of his drink and threw the can into the plastic bag. "Let's get back on the road."

He pulled out of the spot and we turned onto the highway.

I ate the rest of the candy bar and was contemplating going for a another. "She never really told me much about you."

"Damn, you're not pulling any punches today, are you?"

"I'm sorry, I just mean, she told me that you were a biker and that you guys were reconnecting, but that's all she said about it."

"She told me her best friend was named Logan, so I assumed you were a dude."

I chuckled. "Touché. My parents thought I was going

to be a boy. I popped out and they decided to go with the name anyway. I like it, though."

"It's a good name." He glanced at me. "You and Tavy met in college, right?"

"We were suite mates our freshman year. Inseparable ever since." I caved and pulled out another candy bar. "You look way too young to have a twenty-four-year-old daughter."

"I was seventeen when Tavy's mom got pregnant. We tried to make it work, but we were young. Too young. We split up and I wasn't there for Tavy's childhood. Not the way I should've been."

"I think it's good that she's moving to Waco to be closer to you. She wouldn't have done well in South Dakota, though. Tavy and winter do not mix."

He cracked a smile. "Never thought anything good would come from the South Dakota club chapter disbanding. The Waco boys and their families welcomed us with open arms. They're good people. Tavy will like them. So will you."

"Me?"

"Yeah, you." Smoke glanced at me. "Tavy's my daughter, so she's family, which means she'll be hanging around the club, who are also my family. And since you hang with Tavy…"

"One big happy biker family?"

"Something like that."

I sighed. "Family's nice."

"You miss your family?"

I nodded. "Yeah."

"Parents still together?"

"Yup."

"Siblings?"

"Four older brothers. Four older, *very* protective brothers. Not sure I want to tell them the truth about Knox. They might fly down from Idaho and pummel his ass."

"I like them already."

"Not worth the drama," I said. "Best to let it go and move on."

"Let it go by pouring concrete down his pipes and keying his car?"

"I had to be petty first," I said with a wry smile. "He hurt me. I hurt his wallet. Seems like a fair trade."

"Not even close."

We fell silent for a moment and then I asked, "Tavy's stepdad...you ever meet him?"

"No. Never got the chance. Tavy sings his praises though."

I nodded. "He's a good guy. Upstanding. Has a good job. Loves Tavy like she's his own."

"Good man," he murmured.

I wanted to ask Smoke why he hadn't been there for Tavy's childhood. Sure, he and Tavy's mom hadn't worked out, but that wasn't Tavy's fault. He could have at least visited.

"Ask," he said softly.

"Ask what?"

"Ask me why I wasn't there to see my daughter grow up. I know you want to know. So, ask."

"Okay mind reader...why weren't you there?"

"The club was involved in a lot of shady shit back then," he said. "So, I stayed away. Sent money, sent presents. Paid for her college. The club is how I paid for all of it. But what we were doing..." He shrugged. "Sending money was my way of doing what I could without pulling her into my world."

"What kind of shady shit?" I asked.

He glanced at me. "You don't really think I'm gonna tell you that, do you?"

"No. But I had to ask."

"We're not involved in that shit anymore."

"Illegal stuff?" I prodded.

He didn't reply.

I realized that Tavy's college education had been funded by criminal activities.

Smoke was a *criminal*.

A modern day outlaw.

It was hard to wrap my head around what he'd said with the picture he currently presented. He'd been teasing me, bringing me chocolate bars, letting me listen to angry metal music to help me work through my fury.

The man was a dichotomy.

"You paid for her trip to Europe," I said in realization.

"Yeah."

"We had a blast," I said.

"Good to know."

I thought about my own father. He was there for me when I fell down. He was there to dry my tears. He was there when I got rejected from my dream college. Smoke hadn't been there for Tavy in the same way, but he'd provided for her in the best way that he could.

It was still hard to process that Tavy's life had been funded by illegal means. Tavy never said anything about what her father did aside from the fact that he was a biker—and neither of us really thought too much about it when we were having fun.

"So, you were suite mates?" he said finally.

"Yeah." I grinned.

"And you were fast friends."

"The fastest. We were going to join a sorority together."

"Yeah?"

"Yeah." I nodded.

"Why didn't you?"

"It wasn't a good fit," I lied.

"Nah, there's a story there. I want to know. Come on, tell me."

I bit my lip, wondering if I could spin the story so that he'd get the idea without learning the full truth. "Okay. But you can't tell her I told you."

"I swear on my life that I will not tell Tavy," he said, his tone solemn in a mocking way.

"All right. Well, I got accepted into the sorority, but Tavy didn't. So I refused to pledge. Tavy just sat on her dorm room bed and didn't even seem like the news had bothered her."

"I'm guessing that's not the end of the story."

"She tracked down the president of the sorority's boyfriend, kissed him, made sure it got committed to photo and sent it to the girl."

"Vindictive and effective." Smoke laughed.

"I like to think I was channeling Tavy when I ruined Knox's plumbing and keyed his car."

"Tavy doesn't get mad, she gets even. I'm proud of her for that."

"Most fathers would probably tell their daughters to rise above."

"I'm not most fathers."

"I'm getting that," I said dryly.

"Hey, do me a favor," he said.

"What's that?"

"Find us a motel about an hour out. I thought I could keep driving, but I'm fucking wiped. And hungry."

My stomach growled and I reached for another candy bar and then grabbed my phone. "That, I can do."

Chapter 5

Smoke pulled into the parking lot of the motel and cut the engine. We were in some tiny town I didn't remember the name of, but the highway motel had vacancy and a diner within walking distance.

After we checked in, we trekked across the parking lot toward the diner. The scent of fresh food hit me, and suddenly the candy bars that had tied me over were no longer fulfilling. I wanted something greasy and heavy.

A middle-aged waitress gave a terse *hello*. Dark roots peeked out of her dyed, brassy blonde hair, and the smoker's lines at the corners of her mouth were caked with pink lipstick too bright for her complexion.

She escorted us to a vacant booth. The black leather benches were worn and cracked in some places, but the table was clean.

I grabbed the laminated menus from the old wire menu holder between the condiments and set one down on the other side of the table for Smoke.

He settled into the booth, and a moment later I felt his large, booted foot graze mine as he stretched out.

I set the menu down, interlinked my fingers, and set my hands on the table. "I know what I'm getting."

He lifted his eyes from the menu. "Yeah?"

"Yep. Chicken fried steak with extra gravy."

"Sounds good." He set his menu aside as the waitress approached our table.

"Something to drink?" she barked.

"Soda for me, please," I said.

"You?" she addressed Smoke.

Smoke smiled up at her, his eyes glancing at the name tag on her faded gray V-neck. "Long day, Sheila?"

Sheila blinked and some of the animosity drained from her expression. "Long day." She nodded. "Working a double again."

"I remember those days," Smoke said in commiseration. "Graveyard shift?"

She sighed. "Yeah."

"I actually liked the graveyard shift," he said. "So many interesting people awake at that hour."

"Interesting." She snorted, but a playful smile appeared on her lips. "Nothing but drunks and lowlifes looking for trouble at night."

"Bet you handle them no problem." He winked.

Sheila chuckled. "I've had practice. A drunk and lowlife ex-husband prepared me."

I watched in amazement as Smoke completely changed Sheila's attitude. By the time she walked away with our order, she was smiling.

Smoke looked at me and raised his dark brows. "What?"

"That was kind of amazing," I admitted.

"What was?"

"You made her smile."

"She just needed a little kindness. A little attention."

I frowned as I looked at the table. "It was thoughtful."

"And you didn't think I could be thoughtful?"

"Not you. Most people. Most people just seem to sail past someone else's bad mood. Or they get in a bad mood too and it just escalates."

Sheila returned with our sodas, a cheery smile on her face. "Food'll be out shortly."

"Thanks, Sheila," Smoke said.

She blushed like a teenager. I didn't blame her. There was something about Smoke. When he turned his attention to you, you felt like he was really listening. Like he really cared what you said.

My phone trumpeted in my purse. I pulled it out, silencing it immediately when I saw Knox's name.

"Cheating douche?" Smoke inquired, reaching for his drink.

"Yeah." I grimaced. "I really don't have the bandwidth to deal with him right now."

"You're not going to tell him you left?"

"Nope. He'll figure it out when he gets home in a few days." I fiddled with the straw of my soda. "Are all men dogs? Why do they cheat?"

Smoke paused. "Do you want the answer I'd give my daughter, or the real answer?"

"Can I have both? But can you be gentle? I'm feeling kind of fragile right now."

"Fragile? Says the girl who poured concrete down his pipes." He flashed a grin. "I can't believe you did that. That was ballsy as fuck."

I bit my lip, but it didn't stifle my grin. "For once in my life, I said fuck the high road."

"The high road is bullshit."

"I'm starting to agree with that line of thinking."

"Getting back to your question." He sighed. "It's really simple, actually."

"It is?"

"Yeah. Men cheat because they can, and because they want to. Doesn't matter what they have at home. If there's available pussy, and if it's easy to get, sex is just sex for them. Nothing more."

"Nice." I rolled my eyes. "I appreciate the vulgarity of your language."

"Do you?

"No."

He laughed, but then sobered. "I know women want to rationalize the behavior somehow. But the truth is, it's not complicated. Men aren't complicated. They're just walking hormones with dicks."

"So basically, you're telling me that no matter how good or bad my relationship is, a man is going to cheat on me."

"I didn't say that."

"Then I'm confused."

"Women cheat too, you know."

"Yeah, I know that."

"Does that mean all women are cheaters? No matter how good they have it at home?"

"We're not talking about women; we're talking about men."

"Not all men are cheaters, but those that *are* cheaters, do it for uncomplicated reasons. Sex is sex. End of story."

I glared at him. "You're ruining my appetite."

"You asked."

"And this is what you'd tell Tavy?"

"Yeah, this is what I'd tell Tavy. If she ever asked my opinion on the subject. And for the record, I know what it's like being cheated on. I know how bad it stings. The betrayal. The lies. The trust that breaks. It's what broke up me and Leslie."

I blinked. "Tavy's mom cheated on you?"

"Yep. I was working two jobs, we were fighting all the time when I was home, and Tavy was a colicky baby." He shrugged.

"Tavy never told me that," I said quietly.

"I don't know if she even knows that's why we eventually split. It was the nail in the coffin for her mom and me, but I definitely didn't tell Tavy about it. Not even when she was old enough to hear it."

"Why not?" I asked softly. "Why didn't you tell her?"

"Because that shit was between me and her mom. It had nothing to do with her."

Shelia brought us our plates of food and I waited until she left before I asked, "Are you still mad about it? What she did?"

Smoke grabbed the salt and doused his biscuits and gravy without even tasting it first. "Nah. It was a long time ago. She was young, I was young. Shit happens."

I sighed. "I hope I get to that place one day. Where I can just say *shit happens* and I don't want to punch Knox in his square jaw."

"His betrayal is fresh. Maybe this'll turn out to be a good thing for you."

"How?" I frowned. "How could finding out my fiancé cheated on me ever be a good thing?"

"Be glad you found out before you tied the knot. Before you had kids. Divorces are usually pretty messy. You dodged a bullet."

"Valid," I admitted.

"And now you're moving to Waco."

"How's that a plus?"

"Tavy's gonna be there," he pointed out.

The steel in my spine collapsed. "Yeah, she's gonna be there."

"Having your best friend nearby while you sort through wanting to kill all men everywhere will be therapeutic."

"I don't want to kill all men," I assured him.

"No?"

"No."

"Well, that's good. I'm safe for another day."

Chapter 6

I couldn't sleep. It wasn't the lumpy mattress's fault, though that certainly didn't help. My conversation with Smoke played over and over in my head. I'd asked him for honesty and he'd given it. It wasn't what I wanted to hear, but at the same time, I felt absolved of Knox's behavior.

I'd hated that I felt at all responsible for Knox's infidelity. But when Smoke had put it so bluntly, that men who cheat are just going to cheat because they can, the tightness loosened in my chest. It didn't matter how available I'd been to Knox, nor how supportive I'd been of his amateur MMA career. It didn't matter how I'd tried to mold myself into the perfect picture he wanted for his fiancée.

His behavior didn't reflect on me.

I flung off the covers and pulled on my overalls. Knox hated when I wore them—he preferred me in heels, a full face of makeup, my hair done. I never realized how exhausting it had been trying to live up to his expectations.

Why had I let him control me?

I slid into my slip-on shoes and grabbed my motel

keycard. The desert night was warm, but the heat of the day had diminished. I walked around the motel to the back and came to the fenced in pool area. I opened the gate and stopped.

Someone was sitting on the edge of the pool, feet in the water, enjoying solitude.

I quickly turned to leave.

"Logan?"

Frowning, I turned back around and approached the figure. "Smoke?"

He raised a bottle of beer to his lips and took a sip. "What are you doing out here?"

"Me? What about you?"

"I thought it was obvious." He gestured to the six pack next to him. "That energy drink fucked me up. I'm wired."

"I couldn't sleep either," I admitted.

He patted the concrete edge of the pool next to him. "Sit. Have a beer."

"You sure?" I asked. "I don't want to interrupt your alone time."

"Interrupt, please."

Excitement rippled through me.

Oh no…I'm developing a crush on my best friend's father.

I slid out of my shoes, rolled up my pant legs, and then sat down and stuck my feet into the pool. Smoke grabbed a bottle of beer and opened it before handing it to me.

"Thanks." I took a long drink. The dark beer was flavorful and thirst quenching.

Smoke had scrunched up his jeans and his feet dangled in the water.

"Been out here long?" I asked.

"About half an hour."

The motel was close to the highway and every now and

again I heard a truck zoom past. Other than that, it was peaceful.

"How'd you meet?" Smoke asked, shattering the silence.

"Tavy? I thought I told you—"

"Your fiancé. How'd you meet your fiancé?"

"How'd you meet Tavy's mom?"

He paused and took another drink of beer before looking at me. "She was a waitress at the country club."

"You were a waiter?" I asked in surprise.

"I didn't say that. I said *she* was a waitress at the country club."

I blinked and then understanding dawned. "Wait. You were a *member* of the country club?"

"Yup."

"You don't look like the country club type."

"I'm not anymore. Obviously. But I used to be. My parents were big into that world. They still are, from what I know."

"You don't talk to them?"

He shook his head. "They wrote me out of the will when they found out Leslie was pregnant and that I was going to stand by her."

"Wow," I murmured.

"Now you," he said.

"Now me. Right." I took a sip of beer. "I got an internship at Brown, Mullins, & Schreiber my senior year of college."

"What is that, a fucking law firm?"

I sniggered. "No. Interior design. Knox is a lawyer. His firm hired BM&S to redesign their firm lobby. I met Knox one day while I was there."

"And it was love at first sight?"

"Not love, but something. Something I'd never experienced before. I was twenty-one and he was older. Attractive. And when he pursued me, I felt special. Tavy never liked him, apparently."

"Apparently?"

"I just found out the truth about how she felt about him. She managed to keep that from me for a long time. Not that I blame her," I said. "You tell your best friend you don't like her boyfriend, suddenly you don't have a best friend anymore."

"Tavy held her tongue. Kinda shocking."

"Right?" I chuckled. "She was right. In the end."

Somehow, under the starry desert night, at a dive motel off the highway, sharing beers with Smoke, I finally realized I couldn't lie to myself anymore. About who Knox really was.

"I might not be the reason he cheated, but I'm not innocent."

"You're not innocent?" Smoke's tone darkened. "What did you do?"

I whipped my head around to stare at him. His jaw was clenched and he suddenly looked angry, but I wasn't sure why.

"I ignored his behavior," I explained. "I ignored all the red flags even when I shouldn't have."

Smoke's jaw slowly unclenched. "What red flags?"

"His temper, mostly. We fought a lot."

"About?"

"My job. My family. Tavy. It got to the point where he never wanted to be around my family when they came to visit. Or Tavy would only come over when she knew Knox was gone or out of town. That kind of thing." I shook my head. "He wanted me to quit my job. He said he made more than enough to provide for me. But I love my work and I wasn't going to give that up. Not for him. Not for anyone. It was one of the few boundaries I really set. Knox doesn't like boundaries."

"I think you're brave," Smoke said after a long stretch of silence. "Brave for leaving a shit situation and starting over."

"Me? No. If I was brave, I would've left sooner. I wouldn't have ignored the signs."

"Not your fault for being an optimist."

"How do you figure I'm an optimist?"

"You stayed with him, hoping something would change, yeah?"

"Yeah, I guess," I admitted.

"You and I have that in common," he said, an ironic smile pulling across his lips. "I stayed with Tavy's mom for the same reason. I didn't want to break up the family. But in the end, it's what needed to happen. You needed to leave, too. Don't punish yourself for your past decisions. Look forward. You'll be okay."

It wasn't just his words, but the tone of his voice, the earnestness of his expression. He wasn't condescending. He didn't make me feel stupid for getting caught up in the lies and manipulation of my ex-fiancé when it was so blatantly obvious what he'd been doing to me for the last few years.

"Thanks," I said, lifting the beer bottle. "For this."

"You're welcome."

We both knew I wasn't talking about the beer.

I pulled my feet out of the pool and stood up. "I think I'll be able to hit the sack now."

"I want to get on the road early," Smoke said. "Like seven-ish."

I nodded. "I'll set an alarm." After I slipped into my shoes, I lifted my hand in a half-hearted wave and then I turned to leave.

It took everything in me not to turn around to see if he was watching me walk away.

Chapter 7

EARLY THE NEXT MORNING, I was showered and dressed when there was a light rap on the door. I zipped my suitcase closed and then went to answer it.

Smoke held a cup of to-go coffee and a paper bag from the diner in his hands.

"Good morning," I greeted. When he didn't reply, my brow furrowed. "What?"

He was staring at me, his gaze trained on my head.

"*What?*" I asked again.

"Your hair."

"What about it?" I asked defensively.

"It's…you've got curls."

I hastily touched my blonde wavy locks in concern. "Yeah. I usually blow-dry and straighten it. Is it bad?"

"No," he said gruffly. "Not bad at all." He thrust the cup of coffee toward me and handed me the bag. "Wasn't sure how you took it, so it's black. Sugar and creamer are in there."

I opened the bag and peered inside. "You got me a pastry…"

"Thought you might want a quick bite before we hit the road."

Pleasure skated through my chest at his thoughtfulness. I immediately squashed it. "What about you?"

"What about me, what?"

"Did you eat? Get some coffee?"

He nodded. "I've been up since five."

"Oh."

Smoke moved past me into the room and went over to the bed and grabbed my suitcase.

"I'll meet you in the truck," he said.

I shook my head in confusion at his behavior.

He'd noticed my hair. He'd brought me coffee and a pastry. But he was clearly blowing me off now.

What the fuck is going on? And why do I care?

I sugared and creamed my coffee to make it palatable, did one last sweep of the room, and then went out to the parking lot. Smoke was checking the tire pressure on the truck, so I climbed into the passenger side and got comfortable.

The pastry was halfway gone by the time Smoke was done.

"You good?" he asked after he climbed into the cab.

I nodded.

"You don't need anything?"

I shook my head.

"All right. Let's get on the road. You can pick the radio station."

"Anything I want?" I asked.

"Anything you want."

"Even angsty, angry girl music?"

"Even that."

"I won't do that to you," I assured him as I reached for the radio button. I surfed and stopped when I heard a radio personality say, "…a special morning treat for those of you in love with ABBA. That's right folks, this morning we're bringing you *all ABBA, all hour long*!"

I glanced at Smoke who was staring out the windshield.

"Even ABBA?"

He sighed. "Even ABBA."

"Will you hate your life if I sing along?"

"Depends."

"On?"

"Whether or not you can sing…"

"I sing okay."

"Prove it then."

"I haven't had a lot of coffee."

"I haven't had a lot of coffee either."

"Fair point. Okay, I'll sit and enjoy, but I won't sing. At least until you've had more coffee. At least until *I've* had more coffee."

"I appreciate your thoughtfulness," he said with a smile as he looked at me. "So, ABBA?"

I nodded. "ABBA."

"You're a little young to know ABBA, aren't you?"

I glared at him. "My parents played them when I was growing up. And the word *love* isn't enough to encompass what I feel for ABBA."

"Explain."

"Explain my love affair with them?"

"You've shown more animation talking about a Swedish music group than when you talk about your ex."

"ABBA never told me they loved me and wanted to spend the rest of their lives with me and then turned around and fucked another woman."

His shoulders lurched as a laugh escaped his mouth.

"You know why I love ABBA? Because every song is

catchy. Every song gets inside of you and makes you want to dance," I explained.

"Dance?" he asked slowly.

I straightened my spine and faced him. "Yes, dance. Do I know every word to *Super Trouper*? Yes. Do I dance to it every single time I hear it? Also, yes. Tavy understands this. Tavy also partakes in this. Tavy understands my ways."

Smoke laughed again.

"Don't laugh at me."

He shook his head. "I'm not laughing *at* you."

"But you're laughing."

"I'm laughing because it wasn't something I expected out of you."

"Expected out of me? Like you know me at all to be able to expect anything from me," I said, disgruntled. I slumped down in my seat like a sullen teenager and crossed my arms.

"Oh, come on. I'm not trying to get under your skin. I'm just saying I judged a book by its cover, and I couldn't be more wrong about it."

I bit my lip. "I'm afraid to ask what you thought of me when you came to bail us out of jail, but I kind of want to know."

"Well, for one, I was surprised to find that Logan wasn't a six-foot three dude, but instead an attractive blonde."

I sailed past the attractive part, not wanting to dwell too much on it. "Okay, what else?"

"I thought you were a rich bitch," he admitted. "I saw your get-up. Designer dress. Designer heels. Flawless makeup. Reminded me immediately of the country club set my parents call friends."

"Okay, but how did you know my dress was designer?" I asked in surprise.

"Because of how it fit you."

"Fit me *how*?" I demanded.

"You can tell when someone is wearing cheap shit. It's not cut right. Bad stitching, low quality fabric. What you were wearing looked like it had been made for you, like specifically for *you*. And those heels… Fuckin' A."

"What about my heels?"

"They made your legs miles long."

Sparks of excitement danced in my belly. "It sounds like you were checking me out," I said lightly.

"Yeah. I was definitely checking you out. And then I saw the ring on your finger."

"And that made you stop looking?"

"Nah. I didn't stop looking." He flashed a teasing grin. "You can check out the merchandise without buying."

My stomach twirled in exhilaration. Smoke was being honest and the fact that he found me attractive soothed my bruised ego.

"Well, for the sake of honesty, you didn't match the picture I had of you in my head," I said.

"No?"

"Definitely not."

"What was your picture?"

"Handlebar mustache. Gray hair and a ponytail. Potbelly."

"Ouch."

"And a bandanna. One of those doo rags the old, fat bikers wear."

"Double ouch."

"I didn't expect you to be so…so…"

"So charming? Sexy?"

"Young."

He was definitely charming, and definitely sexy. But I wasn't going to admit that to him. It was easy to forget he was Tavy's father. And easier to forget about his seedy past. But I shouldn't forget, and I definitely shouldn't be flirting with Smoke.

When the ABBA hour ended, Smoke said, "My turn to have control of the radio."

"That seems fair."

"Would you find me to be a total cliché if I listened to Aerosmith? You've heard of them, right?"

"Dream on," I quipped. "And yes, Aerosmith is okay by me." I threw him a smile.

He glanced at me for a long moment before turning his attention back to the road. "Fuck."

"Huh?"

"Never mind." He cranked up the radio and we fell into silence.

Chapter 8

"You gonna finish those?" I asked Smoke, pointing to his onion rings.

He pushed the basket toward me and I doused them in barbecue sauce.

We'd stopped for lunch at a burger and shake place along the highway. I'd put away an entire burger, my own tater tots and half a chocolate milkshake. Smoke's sunglasses shielded his eyes, but his lips curled into a smile of amusement.

"What?" I asked, grabbing a few paper napkins from the tin and wiping my greasy fingers.

"I'm impressed." He inclined his head.

"Anger makes me hungry," I said with a wry grin. My phone danced across the scarred picnic table, flashing Knox's name.

I looked at it and silenced it.

The phone stopped vibrating and then immediately started up again.

"Persistent," Smoke said.

"Controlling," I muttered. "I don't want to talk to him.

The shock and hurt has worn off. Now I'm just pissed. And if I talk to him, I won't be able to hide it from him."

"Maybe you shouldn't hide it from him," Smoke said. "Maybe you should tell him you left his cheating ass."

"Why do I get the feeling that you want to witness this?" I asked.

"Maybe I do," he admitted. "Anger is better than cowering."

I'd held my peace for so long that I struggled with the idea that I could let my real feelings out. Knox finding out now or later didn't really matter. And the sooner I dealt with him, the sooner I could cut off all contact.

I reached for my phone.

"You want me to give you privacy?" Smoke asked.

I shook my head. "No. I think—I'd like you to stay, actually."

"Okay," he said quietly.

I looked at him in a silent request for reassurance.

"I'll stay. And if you find yourself faltering, look at me. He gets shitty? Look at me. You got this. He can't hurt you anymore. *You* left him. Yeah?"

"Yeah," I said. "You're right."

My throat was suddenly dry, and I grabbed my milkshake and sucked on the straw like my life depended on it.

Bolstered by Smoke's solid presence, I finally unlocked my phone. I didn't want to answer the call, which was why I knew I had to.

Better to take control of the situation.

I pressed a button and put the phone to my ear.

"Why didn't you answer me?" Knox demanded. "I called twice."

Hearing the annoyance in his tone instantly had me retreating. "I—" my voice cracked.

"When I call, you answer, Logan."

I was frozen in my seat; our dynamic was ingrained in me after several years together. Knox criticized and I apologized.

But this time the apology was lodged in my throat, beaten back by rage.

Smoke's hand ventured across the table and settled on top of my palm. I curled my fingers around his and he gave me a little squeeze.

"Are you listening?" Knox snapped.

"No. I'm not listening."

Knox paused. "*Excuse me?*"

"I'm not listening to you bitch anymore, Knox. Contrary to your own beliefs, I don't just sit around waiting for you to call. In fact, I'll never be taking your calls again."

"What? What the hell are you talking about?"

"The redhead can have you all to herself. Have a good life, *asshole*." I hung up and clutched the phone in my hand. My entire body began to shake.

"Fuck, that was amazing," Smoke said, a smile blooming across his handsome face.

"Yeah?" I asked. "Then why do I feel like I'm going to throw up?"

"Adrenaline. I'm proud of you for doing that."

Smoke hadn't let go of my hand and I wasn't going to remind him that he was touching me.

His gesture had given me the courage I needed. And something more. I liked the way my hand felt in his.

We stared at one another and then as if by tacit agreement, we both let go at the same time. My cell screen lit up, drawing my attention from the enigmatic man sitting across from me.

I looked at the screen and sent Knox to voicemail. And then I went into my phone and blocked his number.

"You finished with your food?" Smoke asked.

I nodded.

He got up from the table and gathered our trash while I went about blocking Knox on all my social media—and turning my settings to private. For the time being, I wanted to be a ghost.

And then I sent Tavy a text asking her to block Knox as well.

Her reply came fast.

TAVY

> Did it the night you told me he cheated.

I smiled. If I said the word, Tavy would ride into battle with me on horseback. She'd probably enjoy it, the blood thirsty savage.

"What's got you smiling?" Smoke asked.

"Tavy," I replied. "I asked her to block Knox and she told me she did it the night I told her I found out he was cheating."

"She's a good friend."

"The best," I insisted. "The best of the best."

The best of the best, and yet here I was lusting after her father.

My elation immediately soured. "We better get back on the road, huh?"

"Probably," Smoke agreed.

I finished off the last of my milkshake and chucked the cup into the garbage.

Relief curled through me when I realized I'd never have to talk to Knox again. Smoke was right—I'd done the actual hard part already. I'd left.

Telling my family and cancelling the wedding was the next order of business, but that could wait until I was settled in Waco.

It all sounded so exhausting that I let out a full-on groan.

"Don't tell me you're having regrets," Smoke said as he climbed into the driver's side of the truck.

"About talking to Knox? No. Not even a little bit."

"Then what's the groan for?"

"You ever cancel a wedding?"

"Can't say that I have."

"Well, I have to. Oh, shit, hold on." I opened my phone and made a note. "Sorry, I don't want to forget. I have a wedding dress fitting this week. I need to make sure I call them and tell them that my fiancé is a cheating piece of shit and that I no longer need the dress altered. Might as well make a day of it and cancel everything. The band, the photographer, the caterer, the hall…"

"You just said a lot of words."

"Ignore me."

"Kind of impossible to ignore you when you're spiraling."

"So, you could ignore me if I wasn't spiraling?"

"Don't think I could ignore you even then." He put the truck into gear and we turned back onto the highway.

"Why are you so nice?" I demanded.

"I'm not nice."

"No? Could've fooled me back there." I gestured with my thumb to the drive-in spot as it disappeared in my side mirror.

"That was a fluke," Smoke said.

"Not sure I believe you."

"Why not?"

"If we'd called my dad to come bail us out, we would've gotten a lecture that had the words *young lady* and *disappointed*."

"The reason you guys were in jail was hardly a reason. I've done way worse."

Oh, right. The criminal thing.

I wondered about his past, but I knew he wouldn't share it with me.

"You really think your dad would've been disappointed in you?" Smoke asked.

"I think so. Yeah."

"Even if he knew the circumstances and *why* you got carted off to jail?"

"You mean the peeing in alley, getting belligerent with a cop, or puking on his shoes?"

"I was going to go with Knox cheating on you, bringing out a side of you I don't think you normally allow to run free."

"I never let that side rule the roost," I said quietly. "I've always done the right thing at the right time. I've never had big emotions."

"Why not?"

I shrugged.

"Not even when you were a teenager and hormones hijacked your brain and body?"

"They didn't hijack my brain or body," I said.

"No?"

"Nope. I didn't even have a boyfriend until college."

"No shit."

"I'm serious." I frowned. "You don't believe me?"

"I believe you, but it's just—damn. Why not?"

"Because I had four older brothers and they enjoyed scaring away the high school boys."

"Ah. And you didn't do anything wrong? You didn't sneak out? Stay out past curfew?"

"It didn't seem like that much fun—lying to my parents. Excessive drinking, puking in bushes, the shame so many of my friends had the next day after being told how they behaved in public. I didn't even do that much in college. I focused on my studies. I graduated early."

I felt like I was saying too much, but Smoke was easy to talk to.

"What about you?" I asked him, wanting the spotlight off of me.

"What about me?"

"What were you like when you were my age?"

"Way to make me sound old," he said with a laugh.

"I think we've established that you're young…for a dad," I teased.

"When I was your age, Tavy's mom and I had already split. I was in the Tarnished Angels and knee deep in some bad shit."

"What kind of bad shit?" I pressed.

He snorted. "Nice try."

"It was worth a shot," I grumbled. "So…you were the complete opposite of me."

"Pretty much."

"And the complete opposite of the country club boy you used to be, huh?"

"Yep. I figured if I was going to piss off my old man, I needed to *really* piss him off. He always took it personally. Made it all about him. Like I changed my entire life so I wouldn't be anything like him."

"Was he right?"

"Maybe." He shrugged. "My life wasn't bad. But it didn't fit, you know? Dad wanted me to join the family business and I didn't really have any interest in that."

"What was the family business?"

"Finance." He grimaced. "He wanted Crawford to become Crawford and Son. I'm a junior."

"No," I said in feigned shock.

"It's true. Clinton Crawford, Junior."

"I can feel the weight of your father's aspirations on you."

"Heavy, huh?"

"Sounds like it." I tied my hair up into a messy ponytail and fixed it with the tie around my wrist. "So, you're really not going to tell me a thing about this bad shit…"

"No use talking about it. I'm not involved in it anymore. The club isn't, either. We're legit now. That's all I can tell you—so no more questions about it." He pinned me with a stare.

"Ah, there it is."

"There what is?"

I chuckled. "The *dad* voice."

"Ha." He shook his head. "It's why I asked Tavy if she'd consider coming out to Waco for a while. I wasn't in her life when she was a kid because of the club shit. Now there's no more shit. I don't have to worry about her getting hurt."

"I see. The invitation did seem to come out of nowhere. I didn't like you when she told me that she was moving to Waco to be near you," I said in a playful tone.

"I'm surprised she agreed to come," he admitted. "I thought for sure she still held a grudge against me for not being there for most of her life."

"Well, I guess it's going to work out okay."

"For all of us."

I nodded. "For all of us."

Chapter 9

We were an hour outside of Amarillo when the rainstorm hit. It was just past dusk as dark thunder clouds tore through the sky before opening up into a torrential downpour.

The windshield wipers were on their fastest speed, but it barely did enough to keep the glass clear. I couldn't see more than a few feet in front of us.

Smoke gripped the steering wheel as he drove, and all of a sudden, we began to hydroplane. Tavy's hitched up car fishtailed behind us.

I braced against the door and my heart leapt into my throat.

Smoke took his foot off the gas and regained control of the vehicle by steering gently back into the lane. "Fuck," he growled. "We gotta get off the road."

An exit sign appeared through the murky rainstorm a moment later.

"There's a motel at this next exit," I remarked.

"Good."

He flipped on the blinker and slowly coasted onto the

exit ramp. Smoke pulled into the full parking lot of the small motel and looped around back to the oversized parking area.

"I'll run inside," Smoke said. "See if they have any rooms."

"If not, it looks like we'll be sleeping in this truck," I said. "The road isn't safe right now."

"Hang tight." He unlatched his seatbelt, opened the door, and jogged to the lobby. I pulled my cell phone out of my bag and shot off a text to Tavy that we'd stopped early due to an unexpected downpour.

Smoke returned not ten minutes later and climbed into the truck. His dark hair was wet, and he hastily shoved it off his forehead. His skin glistened with moisture and his black T-shirt stuck to his muscular arms.

"So, I have good news and bad news," he began.

"Good news?"

"They have one room left."

"Bad news?"

"There's only one bed."

He stared at me.

I stared at him.

"We're both adults," I said. "And it's just for the night, right?"

"Right." He paused. "There's more bad news."

"What's that?"

"Internet and cable is out. Storm did something and they can't get it back up. So basically, it's cell service only."

"Oh. Well, that's fine."

A small motel room in close proximity with a man I found extremely attractive who was also easy to talk to...

What could possibly go wrong?

"I guess we better grab our suitcases and get inside," I

said, looking out the window. "The sky is getting even darker."

"Wind has picked up too. The rain is coming down in sheets now. When we get out, I'll get our stuff. Head right to the lobby and I'll meet you there."

"On three?" I suggested, grabbing my shoulder bag and slinging it across my chest.

He nodded. "One, two, three!"

We thrust the doors open and jumped out of the truck. In only a few seconds, my hair was stuck to my forehead and neck. Smoke rushed to the hitched-up car and quickly unlocked the driver's side door and opened it to pull out my suitcase and his duffel. A flash of lightning appeared in the darkening sky and thunder boomed in the distance.

He met me in the lobby where we stood dripping wet, a puddle forming around us on the tile floor.

I marched up to the check-in desk and asked for two towels. The check-in agent disappeared from the desk into a back room of sorts. A moment later he returned with two white towels and handed them to me.

I gave one to Smoke and then used the other on myself immediately, focusing on my hair.

Smoke had water streaming down the sides of his face and across his brow. He hastily swiped the towel across his cheeks.

"I suggest taking the stairs," the desk attendant called. "Power keeps going in and out. You're liable to get stuck if you take the elevator."

My shoes squished across the tile floor as we made our way toward the stairwell and I nearly lost my footing. Thankfully, Smoke was close enough that he was able to grab my elbow and steady me before I face-planted.

"Thanks." I was breathless from the adrenaline rush, but also from Smoke touching me. My skin was clammy and a bit numb from the cold rain, but I still felt the heat of Smoke's fingers on me.

He nodded and then released me.

I pushed open the door and held it for Smoke who carted our bags up three flights of stairs. Our room was right off the stairwell which was also the fire exit.

Smoke pulled out the keycard from his back pocket, and naturally, my eyes gravitated to his ass.

It was a crime not to ogle, if you asked me.

And ogle I did.

The lock clicked and Smoke pushed on the door. He held it open and gestured for me to go in first.

I slid past him, wondering how a man who'd gotten caught in the rain was still emanating heat.

He flipped on the light switch next to the door. "How bad is it?"

I took my suitcase to the farthest end of the room—which wasn't far at all. "I've seen worse," I admitted.

There were two small nightstands with tiny lamps, an ancient air conditioner that was barely keeping up with the humidity, and a full-sized bed.

Not a king. Not a queen. A full.

And no couch.

"You shower first," Smoke said as he came farther into the room and let the door swing shut.

"You sure?" I asked.

"Yep. I'll scrounge up some dinner."

"Where?" I asked. "Even if there was a diner or a restaurant close by, I wouldn't recommend venturing out in this storm. Did you see that lightning?"

As if on cue, there was a flash of light behind the window curtain and a crash of thunder echoed through the sky.

I jumped in surprise, causing Smoke to laugh. "I think I just proved my point," I said.

"I wasn't going to go out there," he assured me. "I'm heading to lobby to see what I can do."

He trekked to the door and opened it. "I'll find us food, and hopefully a drink. I think we both earned it today." Smoke looked at me over his shoulder and winked before disappearing.

The wink.

The fucking wink.

I wrestled my shoes off and tossed them into the corner, hoping they'd be dry by morning. I unzipped my suitcase and searched through it for a pair of clean underwear and an old T-shirt and sweats that weren't at all flattering. Maybe that would stem this flow of attraction that was brewing between me and Smoke.

After I finished my shower, I opened the bathroom door to let the steam out. I wiped a section of the mirror so I could see and went about my nighttime skin routine.

I heard the click of the lock quickly followed by the door opening. Smoke stepped inside and shut the door.

"You're done showering?" he asked in surprise. "That was fast."

I rubbed the last of the lotion onto my skin. "You expected me to take a two-hour shower while you're suffering in cold, wet clothes?"

"Not exactly." He moved past the doorway. "I found us some stuff."

I came out of the bathroom and followed him to the bed where he'd set the plastic bag down.

"It's not great, but at least we won't starve. I've got boxes of cereal, fruit, and yogurt. There is a vending machine in the lobby, so if we get desperate, we can always hit it up. But I saved the best for last." He reached into the bag and pulled out a few mini bottles of liquor.

I took the bottles. "Where did you get these?"

"I'm magic," he quipped.

I peered at him. "You bribed the desk agent, didn't you?"

"Told you. Magic."

I laughed. "Shower's all yours."

He stripped out of his leather vest and hung it up in the closet. Next came his thick boots.

"Wet socks are the worst," he said. "I can handle anything else, but wet socks are the devil's work."

I barely heard what he was saying because I was too busy staring at his muscular chest. The wet T-shirt suddenly looked two sizes too small on him, and I wanted to peel it off him and explore his damp skin with my fingers.

"Logan?"

"Huh?"

"I asked if you needed to get back into the bathroom before I shower?"

He's going to be naked...

"Nope," I squeaked. "Enjoy your shower..."

He met my gaze and stared at me for a long moment, a slight smile curving his lips. "Oh, I will."

He walked toward the bathroom and turned and winked at me before he closed the door. A moment later, I heard the shower turn on and then the sound of him undoing his belt buckle.

You can hear everything through the walls.

While Smoke was in the shower—and while I was trying not to think about him naked and wet—I put the liquor bottles and the plastic cups that he'd gotten on the nightstand.

I sat on the far side of the bed, the one closest to the air conditioner, and waited for Smoke to finish his shower.

He was taking longer than I expected and I was getting hungry. I reached for a banana, but a sound coming from the bathroom made me pause.

I froze when I realized what I was hearing.

My cheeks flamed with heat and a throb settled between my thighs.

Smoke was wet, naked…and pleasuring himself.

With me in the next room.

Surely, he knew I could hear him…

Did he *want* me to hear him?

Was I brave enough to ask him?

There was something between us. Something I'd been trying to ignore.

My ego had been raked over the coals. And now there was a sexy, funny, easy to talk to man masturbating in the shower within ear shot.

If I had any courage, any bravado, I would've gotten up off the bed and entered the bathroom and asked if he wanted some help.

I heard the shower turn off and I hastily grabbed the remote and flicked on the TV. The screen was fuzzy and then I remembered the cable was out.

The door to the bathroom opened and a cloud of steam billowed out and then Smoke appeared.

With a towel around his waist.

With a towel around his waist and nothing else.

I turned off the TV and leveled him with a glare.

"What?" he asked.

"What?" I repeated. "*What?*"

"Yeah, what?" His brows rose and he hastily swiped his dark hair off his forehead.

"You're doing this on purpose," I said accusation.

"Doing what on purpose?"

"You're walking around in a towel."

"So?"

"So why didn't you grab your clothes to change in the bathroom?"

"Because that bathroom is microscopic," he pointed out.

The blood had long since rushed from my head and begun to pulse between my legs. That was the excuse I gave myself even as I asked, "Did you know the walls are paper thin?"

"Are they?" he asked, his voice pitching lower so it came out a husky purr.

Shivers erupted all along my spine. "Yeah. They are."

"So, you heard me?" he asked.

"Why aren't you embarrassed?" I demanded.

"Why *are* you embarrassed?" he shot back.

I paused. "You wanted me to hear, didn't you?" When he didn't reply, I repeated, "Smoke? Did you want me to hear you?"

Chapter 10

"Yeah, Logan," he rasped. "I wanted you to hear me."

My eyes widened. "Why?"

"Why? You're seriously asking me *why*?"

"Yes, I'm asking you why."

"Because I saw the way you were looking at me before I got in the shower. I want to fuck you, and I know you want to fuck me too."

"*What?*" I gasped in shock.

He groaned. "You're not that naive, are you? Please tell me you aren't."

"No, I'm not naive," I spat. "But we can't. *I* can't. And *you* can't. And you shouldn't be masturbating where I can hear you. And dear Lord, I just said the word *masturbate* to a man I hardly know."

"Why can't we?" he asked.

"You're Tavy's father."

"So what?"

"Um, *hello*. I'm Tavy's best friend," I said.

"Forget that. Forget how we met. I know you want me."

"I—please, can we talk about something else?"

"You brought this up. So, let's finish it."

"You brought this up when you masturbated in the shower, *loudly*."

"You want to know what I was thinking about?"

"No," I lied.

"I was thinking about you touching yourself out here. I hoped you heard me. I wanted you to get so turned on that you slid your fingers into your panties and made yourself come. I was hoping you were out here biting on your lip to stifle your cries of pleasure, and when I thought of that I came so hard my balls still ache…"

"Stop," I said halfheartedly. "I don't want to hear any more."

"Your eyes are dilated. Your cheeks are flushed. And I bet if I touched you between your legs, I'd find you wet."

"Why are you doing this to me?"

"Doing what to you?"

"Making me want something I can't have."

"And why can't you have me? Just for tonight. Just while we're stuck in this hotel room. One night to let this run its course. It's been killing me trying to play it cool. Not to reach across the truck and set my hand on your leg."

"I just ended an engagement," I protested weakly.

"So the fuck what? I've seen your rage. Take it out on me tonight, in this bed. Use me. I promise you I won't complain." He flashed a grin. "But if you don't want this, fine. I'll leave it alone. I'll go sit in the lobby until we can get out of here."

Silence fell between us, but it was tangled with emotion, with want.

"One night?" I asked finally.

"One night."

"And no one finds out? Especially not Tavy?"

"No one finds out. Definitely not Tavy. She won't get hurt if she doesn't know."

"And we never mention it again?"

"We never mention it again." He pinned me with a stare.

My throat was dry and my body was on fire. The picture he'd painted had my nerves kindled. I was so turned on, so tired of fighting my attraction to this man.

I could handle one night. One night of revenge sex. One night to feel like a woman who didn't need to settle for a cheating ex who'd always focused on his own pleasure more than mine.

The way Smoke was looking at me, like he wanted to devour me whole, made me think I wouldn't have to worry about my pleasure while I was with him.

He sat on the edge of the bed but made no move to touch me.

"We'll go at your speed, Logan," he said quietly. "However fast or however slow. You want to stop. You say stop. No hard feelings. Tell me what you need and I'll give it to you, yeah?"

I opened my mouth to say yes but the word was lodged in my throat.

He watched me carefully and then reached over to the mini bottles of liquor. "Which one do you want?"

"The vodka."

He unscrewed the lid and handed it to me and then he took the bourbon for himself. "You've never done this before, have you?"

"Done what? Have sex with a man I hardly know? I don't have a lot of experience with that," I blurted out.

"Okay."

"I don't know how to ask for what I want."

He leaned in so our faces were close to one another,

close enough that I could feel his warm breath on my skin. "I'll teach you."

Smoke's free hand reached up to gently tuck a strand of hair behind my ear. His thumb grazed my chin. His touch was light, hardly there at all, but it caused me to shiver.

"Has anyone ever truly taken care of you, Logan?" he whispered.

I closed my eyes and shook my head.

His lips flitted across the apple of my cheek.

"Lie back, baby. Let me take care of you."

My heart pounded in my ears and I kept my eyes closed. I felt Smoke take the mini bottle of vodka from my hand and heard the small clank as he set it on the nightstand.

I fell back against the pillows, nerves and excitement swirling in my belly.

I cracked my eyelids open as the mattress shifted. Smoke moved next to me and propped his head up on his elbow while staring down at me. With his other hand, he traced my hairline, the shell of my ear, the column of my throat.

He seemed in no hurry, as if he had all the time in the world to memorize my face, to caress my jawline, to play with the sensitive skin behind my ear.

Smoke leaned over and gently placed his lips on mine. When he didn't immediately demand entrance into my mouth, my shoulders loosened, and I melted into the mattress.

His lips never left mine. He kissed me over and over until I was feverish and restless. I finally opened my mouth, and he took full advantage.

Smoke's tongue stroked mine and my hands moved of their own volition. My fingers sank into his hair and I pulled him closer, wanting him on top of me, wanting the feel of his weight.

My hands slid down his back. He was muscular, but also sleek and lean.

I lost time to Smoke's lips. He was a warm, virile man—and his scent swirled around me, bathing me.

Suddenly, I wanted more. *Needed* more.

"Smoke," I whispered against his mouth, desperate to peel off my clothes so I could feel more of him against me.

He kissed me deeper, pushing me farther into the bed. He slid a hand beneath my shirt and let his palm rest on my lower belly. When he made no indication that he was planning to move it, I growled in annoyance.

He lifted his lips from mine and stared down at me, a smile curving across his mouth. "Impatient?"

I glared up at him.

"What do you want, Logan?" he rasped.

"For you to touch me," I nearly begged.

"Where?" His voice was low and gravelly.

Shivers erupted along my skin until I was nearly shaking beneath him.

"What do you mean *where*?" I asked.

"Tell me where you want me to touch you." His eyes implored me to speak the words—words I'd never felt comfortable saying.

"Can't you just…figure it out?" My cheeks felt like they were on fire, and I suddenly didn't want to look at him anymore.

But when I attempted to turn away, he removed his hand from beneath my shirt and grasped my chin.

"Hey," he said quietly, gently caressing my jaw and forcing me to look at him.

"What?" I grumbled. My ardor was quickly cooling with the direction of our interlude. I wanted nothing more than to push Smoke down, roll on top of him, and silence him with my mouth.

"You don't have to be embarrassed," he said. "About anything. Whatever you want, you tell me."

"I'm not good at that."

"You know how you get good at that?"

"How?"

He flashed a sensuous grin. "Practice." Smoke brushed his lips lightly across mine, but then he pulled back so he could stare down at me again.

I swallowed. I wasn't sure I was brazen enough to outright ask for what I wanted, but maybe I could show him.

I pressed a hand to his chest, tacitly asking him to move, just a bit.

He gave me space immediately.

I sat up. With a moment of hesitation and a deep breath, I grasped the bottom of my T-shirt and then lifted it over my head.

His gaze dropped from mine and then drifted lower to stare at my tight nipples, which hardened more as I got turned on at him watching me.

"Beautiful," he whispered.

I took his hand and placed it on my breast, my eyes imploring.

He swiped a thumb across my nipple.

I threw my head back and let out a low moan.

He did it again.

"You're sensitive."

I nodded. Blood rushed to my cheeks, but I boldly met his gaze.

He cradled both my breasts in his large hands, holding the weight of them while he continued to stroke my nipples.

Smoke was in no hurry. It was such a contrast to Knox, who only used foreplay as a means to an end.

I tried to shut down my brain and prevent it from ruining my moment with Smoke, but the thought of my cheating ex-fiancé had taken root and I was pulled from my enjoyment.

Smoke's thumbs ceased their tender ministrations. "Hey."

I looked at Smoke.

His forehead was creased. "Where'd you go?"

"Nowhere," I lied. "I'm here."

"Don't do that," he commanded.

"Do what?"

"Lie to me when we're in bed. One moment you were enjoying yourself, and the next it was a like a curtain came down across your face."

I bit my lip. I was half naked with a man whose hands were holding my breasts. I suddenly wanted to cover myself and flee from embarrassment.

"I was thinking about something I shouldn't have been thinking about."

"And now you're all in your head," he guessed.

I nodded.

He let go of my breasts and slid his hands down the curves of my hips. Smoke grasped the waist band of my pajama pants. "Lift up."

I did as he demanded.

He peeled off my pants and underwear and tossed them both aside. He glided his hands between my legs to my upper thighs. Smoke urged them open, so I was bare before him, like a silent offering.

"I know just the thing to get you out of your head." His eyes flashed with wickedness.

I swallowed. "You sure?"

He raised his brows. "Hell yes. Now keep these gorgeous thighs open while I taste you."

"Oh my." My heart fluttered in my chest.

Smoke scooted off the bed and dropped to his knees. He then grasped my ass and hauled me toward him until I was almost hanging off the mattress.

"I'm not stopping until you come, Logan," he said, his eyes glinting with hunger. "I'm not stopping until you're crying out, writhing on this bed, and demanding more. This is all for you, cupcake. I want you to enjoy it."

And then to prove his sensual monologue, he leaned forward and gave me one slow lick.

I gasped at the pleasure.

Smoke took my vocal enjoyment as inspiration.

He did it again, only this time, he used his tongue to slide between my folds.

My back bowed off the bed.

"Just like that," he whispered, his hands on my ass tightening. "God, you taste incredible."

He licked and sucked, teasing me until I was a wet, writhing mess.

There were no thoughts in my head. It was blissfully empty. The pleasure between my legs commanded all of my attention.

His breath was warm, his tongue magic.

I thought nothing could feel as good as Smoke's tongue and then he gently slid a finger into my body.

My skin was on fire as rapture swirled in my belly. My hands gripped the comforter as I shook from delight.

Smoke kept me pinned in place.

I couldn't escape.

He lifted his mouth from my clit, his lips wet from pleasuring me. Smoke stared at me as he added another finger.

He curled them up and brushed them against the sensitive pad inside my walls.

"Oh, God," I moaned. "I'm going to—"

My eyes rolled, my back arched, and a scream tore from my lips.

I crested the wave of my orgasm, but as soon as I thought it was over, another one came. Ripple after ripple rushed through my body.

Finally, I stilled, my legs flopping open.

He slowly removed his fingers from inside me.

The ancient air conditioner cranked on, blowing cold air across my damp, heated skin.

My throat was drier than the desert on a hot summer day.

I kept my eyes closed, unsure if I wanted to face Smoke. But finally, I took a deep breath and looked at him. He was still crouched on the floor. His eyes were hooded and his lips were wet from my desire.

Suddenly, I was very aware that I was naked. I hastily closed my legs and reached for my shirt.

"Hey," he said quietly.

"Hey." I kept my gaze away from his. I was mortified. Utterly mortified.

"Logan."

The way he said my name, gently, quietly, had tears prickling behind my eyes.

"I'm fine," I muttered.

"Fine," he repeated.

"Yep. All good. Thank you…for…that."

"For what?"

"For…you know. Going down on me."

When I tried to get up off the bed, Smoke moved quickly, and before I knew it, I was pinned beneath him.

The towel was still around his waist, and I felt the evidence of his desire against my leg.

"Oh," I said immediately. "It's your turn. Right, let me just—"

"What the fuck do you mean *it's my turn?*"

A scowl drifted across his face; all traces of his usual good humor were completely gone.

"You did that for me, it's my turn to do it for you," I said.

His mouth gaped open. "Please don't tell me you think it works that way."

"What way?"

"I went down on you so I could pleasure *you*. If you *want* to go down on me, then fuck yeah, I won't say no. But this obligation shit…is this the kind of crap your ex pulled with you?"

"I don't want to talk about him."

"We most certainly *are* going to talk about him. He's the reason you were in your head earlier, isn't he? He's the reason you think you owe me something."

"Then how does this work?" I blurted out. The tears I'd been holding back suddenly filled my eyes, marring my vision. "I'm starting to think I don't know anything about anything!"

I burst into tears and buried my head against Smoke's chest, as if that would prevent him from seeing or hearing my meltdown.

He didn't reply, he just hugged me tighter, and stroked my head as I cried all over him.

When my cries turned into hiccoughs, I finally attempted to move away. I wanted to roll over and pretend none of this had happened. Not the intimacy with Smoke, and definitely not my crying on him after.

Smoke's arms didn't budge.

"I'm fine," I muttered.

"You're not fine," he insisted. "A few minutes ago you were trying to burrow into me. If you were fine, you'd look me in the eye."

I forced my head back.

"Nice try," he said lightly. "You're looking at my chin."

I sighed. "You caught me. I don't want to look at you. Can we just forget about all this?"

"Which part?"

"All the parts. The orgasm, the tears, you seeing my tears."

"Hmm. No. Afraid I can't do that."

His tone was easy and it pulled a watery smile from me.

"I'll make you a deal," he said.

"What deal?"

"I'll let you go and you can even put your clothes back on if it makes you feel less vulnerable, but we're still going to talk."

"Talk," I repeated. "No way out of talking?"

"Nope."

I sighed again. "Fine. Have you seen my pants?"

Chapter 11

I rolled out of Smoke's arms and sat up, giving him my back. This entire situation was far more intimate than I thought it was going to be.

Smoke had been a thorough and attentive lover. I'd been prepared for that. But I certainly hadn't expected him to want to talk about my feelings and what was going on in my head.

Knox has really done a number on you, kid.

"Logan?"

"Yeah?" I asked, my back still to him as I leaned over and found my pajamas.

"Logan, stand up," he commanded.

"Let me just put my clothes on—"

"No."

My head whipped around to glare at him. "You just said I could—"

Smoke rose from the bed and marched around toward me, a dangerous glint in his eye.

"What—"

"Bruises," he clipped.

I frowned. "Where?"

He reached out and gently clasped my elbow, urging me to rise. And when I stood, completely naked in front of him, I expected a blush of embarrassment to stain my cheeks.

It never came.

Because Smoke wasn't looking at me with desire.

He was perusing my body with murderous rage in his eyes.

"Here." He stroked my side where my hip flared and then disappeared into my lower back. His hands skated up and down my body as he continued to examine me.

"And here." His fingers ghosted over my upper arm. "They've faded, but I can see them. These marks were left by a man's hands." His eyes met mine. "Did Knox do this to you?"

I blinked at the ferocity emanating from him. He was practically vibrating with fury. Up until this moment, I'd only seen the good-natured Smoke. The sensually attentive Smoke.

I'd never seen the protective Smoke. The I'm-about-to-go-feral-at-the-idea-of-someone-hurting-you Smoke.

"Yes," I said softly, so softly it was barely more than a whisper of truth escaping my lips.

"That motherfucker put his hands on you." His nostrils flared and he clenched and unclenched his fists.

"Smoke?"

"I never should've touched you."

My eyes widened. "What? Why?"

"Why? *Why?* Christ, Logan. You're vulnerable, and I…"

"You what?" I hastily reached for the coverlet and pulled it around my body, no longer wanting to stand in front of him without a shield.

"Took advantage."

"You didn't. You absolutely didn't. Please, Smoke. I don't want you to worry about this. You didn't know about that. It's done now. He can't hurt me anymore."

He raked a hand through his hair in a show of frustration. "I should've been gentler with you. I should've—"

I took a step toward him and placed my hand on his warm chest. "You were perfect."

He covered my hand with his. "Are you really okay?"

I nodded.

"I still think we should stop. This shouldn't go any further. I don't want to fuck with your head."

"You'll fuck with my head now if you *don't* touch me." I swallowed. "You didn't take advantage of me. You're protective and I feel safe with you. I want you, Smoke."

"You sure?"

"Yes."

His hand dropped from mine, but only so he could reach up and cradle my cheeks. "We'll go slow. You tell me to stop, I stop. I want you Logan, but I don't want you to have any regrets, okay?"

"Okay," I whispered.

He gently lowered his lips to mine. The kiss was soft, tender.

When he pulled back, I loosened my hold on the coverlet and then spread it out on top of the bed before climbing underneath the covers.

Smoke slowly removed the towel from around his waist.

My breath caught in my throat.

Smoke was virile and looked cut in his clothes. Out of them, he looked like a marble statue of a Greek god. Muscular thighs, lean upper body.

Well-endowed.

He slid into bed next to me and lifted his arm. "Come here."

I rolled into his embrace until I was settled against his side.

Smoke reached over my body and grasped my leg, urging me to lift it and set it across his waist.

"Is this comfortable for you?" I asked.

"Yeah."

I pressed my cheek to his chest and took a few deep breaths. My heart was drumming a mile a minute.

"Didn't take you for a cuddler," I said finally.

He ran his fingers through my damp hair. "Anything goes with you."

"So, you're not normally a cuddler?" I asked.

"I'm not normally around long enough to know."

"Shocking." I giggled.

His fingers left my hair and inched down my body. "The women I've been with are the type that want the same thing from me as I want from them. No-strings attached fun."

"We're no-strings attached fun," I pointed out. I placed my hand on his chest and gently began tracing circles across his skin.

"True."

"Then why are you cuddling *me*?"

"Because cuddling you calms the homicidal rage inside me that wants to kill your ex-fiancé."

I pressed my palm flat against his heart. "I don't have to worry about Knox anymore."

"How long did you have to worry about him laying his hands on you?"

"Only recently."

"So, that kind of shit wasn't going on the whole time?"

"No." I sighed. "Please, Smoke. Please don't ask me

about it anymore. I don't want to think about him when I'm in bed with you."

"Fine. I'll drop it." He adjusted his position and then placed his hand on the small of my back, urging me even closer. "Why did you cry earlier?"

"Because it was intense, and I was overwhelmed. And I've never…"

"Never what?" he prodded.

"Come that hard."

I wanted to bury my head in his shoulder, but I refused to cower. Something about Smoke made me brave.

His arms tightened around me.

"Sleep, Logan. We've got all night."

Chapter 12

"You lying sack of shit!" I yelled.

My elbow shot back and hit a very solid, very warm stomach. A masculine grunt sounded from behind me. Arms fell away from me and I scrambled from the bed in a rage.

I fumbled with the lamp on the bedside table and a moment later, an amber glow illuminated the motel room.

Motel room.

"Damn it," I muttered as the last traces of heavy sleep cleared from my brain.

The fear in the pit of my stomach wasn't so quick to leave.

Smoke rubbed his belly where I'd hit him. "At least it wasn't my balls."

I closed my eyes and sighed. "I forgot where I was. I thought you were Knox."

"Yeah, I got that."

The air conditioner kicked on and blasted cold air across my skin, causing me to shiver. I'd fallen asleep completely naked. I never slept naked.

"Oh."

Smoke's gaze heated when he looked at me.

Desire swirled in my belly as I settled back down next to him.

How could I have forgotten I was in bed with Smoke?

I leaned over and cut the light. It was dark and quiet, my heart thumping like a terrified rabbit.

Smoke pulled me into his arms and tangled his legs with mine. "Bet you've got one hell of a right hook."

I smiled even though he couldn't see me. "I do. Four older brothers, remember?"

"I remember."

"How's your stomach?"

"I'll live."

I paused and then I asked, "Want me to kiss it and make it better?"

"Yeah, cupcake. Kiss it and make it better."

I rolled over and felt for him in the dark, and when I did my heart jumped in my chest for an entirely different reason.

I ran my hands across his body and over his flat stomach. I placed my lips on his skin and peppered him with kisses, moving downward.

He was already half-mast when I took him into my mouth. I sucked gently, my cheeks hollowing.

"God, you're fucking good at that," he groaned.

I smiled around him and continued.

"Logan..."

I hummed around his shaft.

"Logan. I'm gonna come if you keep doing that."

I released him from my mouth but grasped him in my hand and gave him a squeeze. "So?"

"So? I need to be inside you."

A tingle sparked between my legs. "Oh."

I slowly let go. The lamp came on and he got up. He padded naked to his duffel bag and pulled out a box of condoms.

Smoke sauntered back toward the bed. He pulled out a condom and set the box onto the nightstand. He took himself in hand and gave a few slow pumps. Smoke ripped the wrapper with his teeth and rolled the condom onto his length.

He lowered the covers to reveal me and then straddled my body. Smoke clasped the back of my neck and pulled me toward his mouth. His lips covered mine while his free hand roamed my body and slipped between my thighs.

"So wet," he murmured. "Let me in, cupcake."

I opened my legs just enough so that he could slide a finger into me.

With a moan, I gripped his bicep and held on while he pleasured me.

He kissed his way down my breasts and stomach. Smoke's mouth was hot and I shivered. He licked my clit, his tongue swirling at the heat of my body.

"Smoke," I whispered. "Please."

"Please what?"

When I didn't reply, he gently eased his finger out of me so he could slide his hands beneath me to grip my ass. "Please what?"

"Please—I want you inside me."

His dark eyes seemed to glow with desire. He gave me one last lick and then he rose in bed and got to his knees, palming his massive erection.

Because of the lamplight I could see everything. The ripple of Smoke's muscles, the clenching of his jaw.

I swallowed.

Smoke leaned over and brushed his lips across mine and then his tongue was in my mouth. All thoughts and worries suddenly evaporated. There was nothing but this moment, the here and now. My feverish body craving his. The need to have him inside me, wringing pleasure out of me.

He gently grasped my leg and swirled the crown of his shaft against me.

I was wet. So wet.

And when he guided himself inside me, my body took him easily.

"Oh, fuck," Smoke groaned.

I arched my back and he slid all the way to the hilt.

He was so big and I was so full. My eyes rolled into the back of my head as pleasure filled every part of me.

"Open your eyes," he growled.

My eyes flipped open and I met his gaze.

Smoke began to thrust, slowly pulling out of me and then driving back in. His hand slid down my outer thigh and then underneath my ass.

I wrapped my leg around his waist, meeting him stroke for stroke, demand for demand.

My nails scored his back as he relentlessly pleasured me.

Every time my eyes began to close, Smoke commanded me to open them again and focus on him. So, I stared at him, his angular clenched jaw, the dark hair falling across his brow, his broad shoulders above me while he drilled into me.

My body was a slave to his.

He was dominating and commanding, and it short-circuited my brain so I couldn't think—only feel.

Smoke stretched me wide.

The scent of us was in my nose, a heady perfume of lust that only our bodies could create. Something about it made me feral.

I clamped around him.

"Yeah, baby. Just like that," he growled.

Our gazes were locked as I felt the spark of my orgasm blooming low in my belly.

I wanted to close my eyes. I wanted to lose myself in the moment, but I was compelled to look at Smoke.

My gaze widened as he shifted his angle, driving deeper, hitting that spot inside of me that he'd found once already.

"Oh," I gasped.

He repeated the movement, again and again, until I was clutching his ass and writhing against him. My orgasm swept through me and obliterated everything I thought I was. It scrambled my brain, it set fire to my nerves, it brought the cries of pleasure from deep within me.

And while I was in the throes of passion, Smoke slammed into me one final time, his grip on me tight as he came.

My leg fell from his waist and I collapsed against the mattress.

Smoke was still inside of me and made no move to leave my body. He lifted himself up and peered down at me.

We locked eyes and it felt like something snapped into place between us.

I planted a hand on his chest and gently urged him to move.

He took the hint and slid out of me.

I quickly escaped toward the bathroom, my eyes landing on the alarm clock. It was just past two in the morning.

As I did my business, I hissed in discomfort. My body had been thoroughly worshipped, played like a well-loved instrument by someone who knew the intricacies of it.

The afterglow of my release slipped away and in its place was a knot of anxiety and worry.

I wasn't ready to face Smoke. My engagement had just ended, and I was already in bed with a man who knew my body better than Knox ever had.

I turned on the shower and made it scalding hot.

There was a knock on the bathroom door. "Logan?"

"I'm just gonna shower real quick," I called out, and then stepped into the steam.

"Can I come in?" His voice was muffled, but I heard him clearly enough.

"Yeah, sure."

The door opened and then closed. When I heard no sound of movement, I ventured out, "You still here?"

"Yeah."

"Why?"

"I wanted to make sure you were okay."

"Make sure I was okay," I said slowly as I grabbed the bar of cheap motel soap. "Why wouldn't I be okay?"

"You tell me."

"I'm fine, Smoke."

"Well, it's official. Now I know you're not okay because you said you were *fine*."

"You think I'm lying?"

"Yes."

I glared at the shower curtain. "You're not the first man I've had sex with. You get that, right?"

"But I am the first man you've had sex with since you found out your ex cheated on you."

"So?"

"So, I imagine you're feeling pretty raw. Exposed."

"What are you, a shrink?"

"You wouldn't be getting defensive if I was wrong."

I gritted my teeth. "I just need a moment to myself."

"Okay."

When I didn't hear the sound of the door open, I poked my head out from behind the shower curtain. "That means you can go."

He was leaning against the sink counter. He'd put on his boxers, but he was otherwise bare.

Bare, with his beautiful tattoos and muscles on display.

My nipples immediately stood at attention.

Traitors.

"You can talk to me," he said quietly. "About what's going on in your head."

"Maybe I don't want to talk about it." I shut the curtain and dowsed myself under the spray.

"What if *I* want to talk about it?"

"Smoke," I pled. "Please, just drop it. We had sex. It was great. Now I'd like to shower in peace."

He fell silent and I hoped that meant he was going to leave. But I was wrong because he said, "I'm going to take a shot in the dark and say you regret what happened between us."

If I truly wanted to put Knox behind me, to no longer give him power over me, I had to face the truth.

"No," I said quietly. "I don't regret what we just did. I just…it's a lot, okay?"

"That's all I needed to know." I heard his heavy footsteps as he trekked toward the door.

"Wait."

His retreat stopped.

"I changed my mind."

"About?"

"Will you shower with me?"

He paused for only a moment before he said, "Yeah. I'll shower with you."

Chapter 13

Smoke stepped into the shower behind me. I rinsed the soap from my body and then gave him use of the shower spray.

He turned his back to me and I gasped.

"What?" he asked as his face was under the water.

"I made you bleed!"

Smoke looked at me over his shoulder and grinned. "Yeah?"

"Yeah. God, I'm sorry."

"I'll live, you saucy little minx."

"You didn't just call me a minx."

"I did. Because you are."

"I guess I was out of my mind with pleasure," I murmured.

"Unhinged." He turned and gave his back to the water, and when he did, he grimaced in pain. He reached out to cradle my face in his hands. "I like you unhinged."

You bring out the beast in me.

I gently eased away from him and grabbed the soap. "Let me clean your battle wounds."

"Battle? If that was the battle, what will the war be like?"

"Should we find out?"

He grinned. "Definitely."

I snorted. "Will you survive?"

"I'm willing to chance it."

"Turn," I commanded.

He showed me his back and I softly washed his skin. "We still have an entire box of condoms," I pointed out. "It would be a shame not to make use of them."

"Glad you agree."

"Do you always travel with a box of condoms?"

"No. But I usually travel with a few."

"Then where did you get the box of condoms?"

"The front desk."

"Seriously?" I demanded.

"Yup."

"My, weren't you optimistic."

"Hopeful. That's for damn sure."

"Such a Boy Scout. I bet you can start a fire with nothing more than a bit of kindling and twigs."

I removed my hands from his back. He turned and let the water wash over him.

"Speaking of fire," he murmured. His dark eyes peered at me as drops of water ran down his cheeks.

I leaned forward and tilted my head up.

And then he brought his lips to mine and devoured them.

~

Soft morning light filtered through the blinds. I cracked my eyelids open which were heavy with exhaustion.

Smoke's arm was thrown across my hip and his solid thigh pinned me to the bed.

I wiggled against him.

He tightened his arm around me and pulled me back to his chest. Smoke's morning erection nudged my ass.

I smiled and bumped against him.

"Morning, cupcake," he rasped.

"Hmm. Morning."

His hands wandered across my stomach and down between my legs. "How are you feeling?"

I adjusted my leg so his fingers could find my slippery heat.

"Really?" he asked, brushing his lips across my shoulder. "You're not sore?"

"I'm sore, but I want more."

"I'll be gentle."

His fingers circled my clit and then dipped inside me. I gasped at the pleasure.

"Always so fucking wet," he growled. "Fucking love that."

I reached up and lifted my arm to wrap around his neck and turned my head, my mouth searching for his.

Our lips met and his tongue greeted mine. Smoke played with my body as I gyrated against him.

He pumped his fingers inside me until I came all over them. And while I was recovering my breath, Smoke slid them out and then rolled over to grab a condom from the nightstand.

Smoke quickly sheathed himself and then he positioned me so I was still on my side. He eased into me from behind and let out a low groan.

He grasped my thigh and gently rocked his hips forward. This position was new for me and I felt him deep. My hand traveled between my legs.

"Fuck, Logan," he whispered.

His warm breath, the stubble on his jaw rubbing against the skin of my neck, his shaft stretching me, my hand between my thighs…

Our skin heated and became slick with sweat.

I orgasmed again.

Smoke gathered me close, a low moan hitting my ears as he came.

He didn't pull out immediately. We stayed like that for a few minutes until finally I said, "Bathroom."

He slid out and I hissed.

"Fuck, I hurt you," he said, contrite.

"No, I'm just sore. Deliciously sore." I sat up and before I jumped out of bed, I leaned over and kissed him.

He grabbed the back of my head and deepened the kiss.

When I pulled back, his eyes were languid and he looked in danger of falling asleep.

"Give me a few, then come join me in the shower." I pecked his lips and then rose from the bed.

I glanced at the box of condoms on my way to the bathroom. "I think we put a pretty good dent in that box."

He smirked. "Yeah. We did okay."

I was still smiling to myself as I was getting the shower ready. My smile slipped though, when I realized it wouldn't continue. The night was over. We had to get back on the road.

Which meant everything we'd done had to be packed away, never to be repeated or discussed again.

Regret blasted through my heart.

With a frown, I climbed into the shower.

Sex with Smoke had done a lot for my wounded ego. My body sure as hell didn't mind the attention either.

The door to the bathroom opened and then closed. He pulled the shower curtain back and stepped in with me.

I gave him the spray and then offered him the bar of soap.

He looked at it and then at me. Smoke frowned. "You're not going to wash me?"

"I don't think that's a good idea," I said slowly. "Considering it's morning."

"Morning."

"And we're leaving today. In fact, I probably shouldn't have invited you into the shower in the first place."

His frown deepened and he took the soap. Smoke scrubbed his body, almost violently.

"Why are you angry?" I demanded.

"Because I'm not ready to leave this motel room."

My eyes widened and I sucked in a breath of air.

"Are you really going to tell me you're ready to leave?" he asked.

I opened my mouth to reply when the faint sound of the phone ringing distracted me. I hastily got out of the shower, wrapped a towel around me, and went to answer it.

I quickly walked to the nightstand and picked up the phone. "Hello?"

"Hi, this is Vernon at the front desk. I was just calling to let you know the phones are working now."

"I see."

"No internet or cable yet, though. Hope you found something to occupy your time during your stay."

Heat stained my cheeks. "Yeah, we found something to occupy us. Thanks."

"You like biscuits and gravy?"

His change in conversation topics momentarily threw me for a loop. "Uh—Yes."

"Then get down to the cafeteria. We're going to be

cooking up a storm. Ha, get it? Storm? You need a hearty breakfast before you get back on the road."

The door to the bathroom opened and a cloud of steam escaped, followed by Smoke who came out in nothing but a towel.

His skin was damp and glistening and all I could think about was kissing my way down his body.

Our eyes met.

Vernon finished his monologue about breakfast and almost hung up when I blurted out, "Can we book the room for another night?"

"Let me check the bookings." I held Smoke's gaze while Vernon clacked on the computer. "Yeah, the room is free. I'll book you for another night."

"Thank you," I said. "We'll see you for breakfast in a few."

I set the phone back in its cradle but didn't move.

"So, you want us to spend another night together," he murmured.

"Yes." I swallowed. "We haven't used all the condoms in the box. It would be a shame if they didn't get to fulfill their purpose."

His lips twitched. "You're worried about condoms not fulfilling their purpose?"

"Will you let me have this one?" I demanded with a glower.

"Yeah, cupcake. I'll let you have this one." His mouth curved into a wicked smile.

"You sure you haven't had your fill of me yet?"

"Oh, I'll be filling something…"

A laugh escaped my lips and the tension in my chest eased. "Yeah, before any of that can happen again, I need food. Real food. Not dry cereal and yogurt. Vernon promised biscuits and gravy."

"Hearty shit." Smoke nodded and dropped the towel. "We burned a few calories."

"Hmm." My gaze wandered over him. His ink, his muscles, his Titan legs.

How did women get anything done with a man like Smoke walking around in the wild?

"Don't look at me like that," Smoke growled. "Or we won't get out of this room."

I slowly removed the towel from around me and then sauntered over to my suitcase. I bent over to hunt through it and found a thong, giving him a view of my ass. Then I stood up and looked at him over my shoulder. I winked.

He grasped his erection in his hand, and gave it a few slow pumps. "You may have won the battle, Logan. But you'll lose this fucking war."

"I can't wait." I grinned. "Breakfast, first though."

Chapter 14

I thought stepping out of the motel room, out of our sexual bubble, would immediately make the intimacy between me and Smoke disappear.

But when Smoke pulled me into his side and walked with me, hand settled on my hip, I realized I had nothing to worry about.

We walked into the main lobby of the motel, past the vacant front desk toward the cafeteria that had been closed down last night.

Guests of all different ages were grabbing plates and filling them with buffet food. My stomach moaned in delight.

"Well, this is a pleasant surprise," I stated, dragging Smoke to the waffle makers. "I didn't think a place like this was going to have a good breakfast. Just mostly cold stuff. Cereal. Hardboiled eggs. Things like that."

"I've never seen anyone get this excited over a breakfast buffet," he said with a smile.

"Breakfast buffets are the best. Especially in Vegas." I placed my hand on his chest. "Here's what we're going to do. Divide and conquer. You get the biscuits and gravy, the sausage, the bacon. Forget the scrambled eggs. We don't need them. I'll get the waffle and pancakes and maybe some oatmeal. Are you ready?"

Smoke was smiling down at me, his eyes lit with amusement.

"What?" I asked.

"I feel like you would've made a great NFL coach."

"NFL. That's soccer, right?"

He let out a laugh. "All right." Smoke pressed a kiss to my forehead. "Divide and conquer."

Several minutes later, we were taking our plates of food to a vacant table. We'd missed the utensils and napkins, so I went to grab them and then realized we needed juice.

When I came back to the table, Smoke was setting down two mugs of hot coffee.

"Coffee," he explained.

"Juice." I set down the plastic cups and then took the chair next to his. I handed him a fork and then dove into a waffle.

"Got enough syrup on there?" he asked. "Need me to tap a tree?"

"You'd tap a tree for me?"

He tucked a strand of damp blonde hair behind my ear. "To see your face light up when you take a bite of a waffle? Yeah, I'd tap a tree."

We stared at each other; our food momentarily forgotten.

"Just ask them," a man grumbled.

"I can't ask them," a woman replied. "They're lost in each other right now."

"Then I'll ask them," the man stated.

I finally ripped my gaze away from Smoke to see an

elderly couple standing at the table, plates of food in their hands.

"You mind if we join you?" the man with white hair asked.

"Not at all," Smoke replied.

"Sorry to interrupt you lovebirds." The woman dimpled. "But all the other tables are full."

"We have more than enough room," I assured her.

"You both are darling," the woman crooned. "Just darling. Aren't they, Harry?"

Harry mumbled around the fork shoved in his mouth, his head bent over his plate.

"How long have you been married?" the woman asked as she took a napkin and placed it in her lap.

"Oh, we aren't—"

"Two days," Smoke interjected, shooting me a smile.

"I knew it," the woman beamed. "I knew you were newlyweds. You have that love glow about you."

"Edith, leave them be," Harry said. "Let them enjoy their breakfast."

I didn't have the heart to tell Edith it wasn't a love glow, but a sex glow.

"But I have to know the story of how you two met." Edith blinked blue eyes that looked huge behind her thick, coke bottle lenses. "Harry and I were high school sweethearts."

"I love that," I said.

"Tell them how we met, cupcake." Smoke picked up his fork and cut a bite of his biscuit and gravy.

Edith looked at me in expectation. Something told me it would break her heart if I told her the truth about how we met.

"We were both at a casino in Las Vegas," I said.

"Which one?" Edith inquired.

"The Rex," Smoke supplied.

"Oh, The Rex! That's so fancy," Edith said.

I nodded. "Very fancy. He was at a blackjack table when I walked up. He was losing. Losing bad. Almost all his chips were gone. But when he saw me, he said, *I think my luck is about to change.* He doubled down on his bets and won twice in a row. When he stood up from the table, he said, *I know I'm still on a hot streak. Have a drink with me.*"

I shrugged and tossed Smoke a wicked smile. "What could I do but have a drink with him?"

"That's not even the whole story," Smoke said.

Harry set his fork down. "Well, now I'm invested. Go on, son, tell the rest of it."

"Yeah, love muffin. Tell the rest of it." I placed my hand on his thigh and slid it up.

Smoke's hand reached under the table to cover my hand with his. I thought he was going to stop my movement, but he surprised me when he glided his hand up toward his fly.

I palmed him through his jeans, wondering if I could make him lose his train of thought.

"I was supposed to go home the next day," Smoke said. "But I'd fallen head over heels for her. So I stayed in Vegas, trying to convince her to do the craziest thing in the world and marry me."

I squeezed his hardening shaft that felt like he'd stuck a roll of silver dollars in his pants.

"And you married him," Edith said with a dreamy sigh.

"I did," I replied because Smoke was too busy clenching his jaw, trying not to let his eyes roll into the back of his head. "We eloped a few days ago. That moving truck in the parking lot? That's all my stuff. We were on our way to Waco when the storm happened." I shot her a wink. "Not that I'm complaining."

"No, I wouldn't be complaining either." Edith giggled like we were both still in high school. She reached out and touched Harry's cheek. "He makes me feel young still. After all these years."

Harry harrumphed, but he also turned his head into her palm and kissed it.

"The secret to a good long marriage," Harry announced. "You want the secret?"

"Please," I said, my eyes trained on Harry as I rubbed Smoke harder and faster.

"Respect, communication, laughter—and tons of hanky panky."

"*Harry*," Edith admonished, her cheeks heating in embarrassment.

"Relax, honey," Harry drawled. "We're all adults here. Just giving these two lovebirds words of wisdom from our fifty years together."

"Fifty years," I repeated. "Wow!"

"Wow," Smoke huffed.

"We should be so lucky. Right, darling?" I looked at Smoke right as I felt him tense for a moment and then suddenly relax.

He leaned back in his seat, a lazy, sated smile drifting across his face. "Right, cupcake."

Chapter 15

"It was nice meeting you both," Edith said as she and Harry stood up from the table. "We need to get on the road. Hopefully our daughter doesn't have our grandbaby before we get there."

"Safe drive to Waco," Harry said.

Smoke made a move to stand up, but Harry shook his head. "No need to get up, son. Enjoy your honeymoon." The elderly man winked and then he and his wife ambled away.

"I'm pretty sure Harry knew what was going on beneath the table," Smoke drawled.

"What? No, he didn't."

"He told me to stay seated and then shot me a wink. That old lothario definitely knew."

My cheeks heated. "Oh. Well, that's…" I cleared my throat and straightened my spine. "They just told us the secret to a long and happy marriage is a ton of hanky panky. And I just hankied your panky."

He chuckled. "You hear me complaining?"

"No."

"Exactly. But don't think I won't be doing the exact same thing to you. I could barely hold a coherent conversation."

"That was the entire point." I grinned. "You didn't have to tell them we were newlyweds."

"No, I didn't," he agreed. "But Edith is crazy for Harry's ornery ass. She wants the entire world to be in love. I obliged. Plus, it was easier than explaining what we're actually doing."

"A couple of nights of crazy, raunchy get-over-my-ex sex? Yeah, doesn't have the same ring to it as being newlyweds."

"How'd you come up with that fake story so fast?"

"The night we met—skip past the bailing me out of jail." I grabbed the last piece of bacon off his plate and took a bite. I swallowed it before going on. "You went back down to the casino because you said you were on a hot streak."

"But the blackjack table story? Inspired."

"That comes from reading many romance novels over the years."

"Romance novels, huh?"

"We call it the meet-cute. When the main characters meet for the first time."

"I see." He leaned in close and kissed my lips. "How do you feel about having a naked meet-cute?"

"I just ate enough food to feed an army. I need a few minutes."

"You ever play strip blackjack?" He raised his brows.

My gaze dropped to his lap. "Do you have a deck of cards in your pants or are you just happy to see me?"

"He's always happy to see you."

"He's a good little soldier, always standing at attention."

"Little?" He mock glared. "You don't want to give him a complex, do you?"

"Huge. Gargantuan. You nearly broke me in half."

"Honey, the kids!" He gestured his head to the other side of the room where two children below the age of ten were squabbling and their aggrieved parents were trying to minimize the damage.

"That looks exhausting," I muttered.

Smoke looked over his shoulder. The children were in a ceasefire, and then the boy threw cereal at his sister. The screaming began immediately.

"Exhausting," Smoke said quietly. "Yeah, it does."

Something about his tone made my smile drop.

"What is it?" I asked.

"Nothing."

"Not *nothing*. You get in my face when you want me to admit something," I pointed out. "So now I'm doing the same to you."

"By getting in my shit?" Smoke asked, a ghost of a smile flitting across his lips.

"Yep." I dunked my fork into the leftover gravy and licked it clean.

His gaze dropped to my action. "You don't fight fair."

"Come on," I said gently. "Tell me what's resting on those broad shoulders of yours."

"I never got to be exhausted," Smoke admitted.

It took a moment for me to understand his words, but when they penetrated, I nodded. "Because you weren't around to watch Tavy grow up."

"We split when she was so young. I missed out on a lot."

I didn't know what to say, so I said nothing. Whatever I said wasn't going to turn back the clock. It wasn't going to change the choices he'd made.

"You want kids?" Smoke asked me suddenly.

"Oh. Well, eventually, yeah. I know I said that looked exhausting—and it does. But eventually I want a family."

"Big family?"

"I don't know. Yeah, I guess."

"You *guess*? Didn't you talk about this with your ex?"

"Not really. Talk of the future and family was always a passing comment. Like, maybe one day. But not one day soon."

"That's a big thing not to discuss before you get married. Were you going to change your name?"

"What does that have to do with anything?" I demanded.

"Curiosity."

"Yes, I was going to change my name." I wasn't going to admit that I'd spent hours testing out my new signature.

"Was that because *he* wanted you to change your name, or because you wanted to?"

"Both."

"Interesting."

"You've said that a lot. About several things I've said."

"You say a lot of interesting things."

"I think you're digging for information."

"Digging implies there's shit to be uncovered. The stuff I'm finding is all on the surface."

I was in the middle of glowering at him when Edith suddenly appeared at our table, her cell phone stretched out toward us, completely oblivious to our turn in conversation.

"My daughter had a daughter!" Edith said, her blue eyes bright.

I pulled my attention away from Smoke and looked at the screen of the mom and new baby who was wrapped in a pink blanket.

"She's beautiful," I said, meaning it.

"I wish we could've been there, but the baby wanted to come. So, she came," Edith said with an elated smile.

"Edith," Harry called from the doorway of the cafeteria.

Edith waved Harry over. "I was just showing Smoke and Logan the picture of Annalise."

"You've showed them," Harry said. "Let them get back to their fight."

Edith frowned. "Fight? You're having a fight?"

"It's not a fight," Smoke said. "It's a discussion. How did you know, Harry?"

"Body language. Logan is clearly trying to get away from you right now," Harry said as he trekked across the room.

Smoke grabbed the back of my chair and scooted me even closer to him and then placed his hand on my thigh.

"Maybe you can give us some advice," Smoke said.

"I'm sure they don't want to hear about our squabble, darling," I said through gritted teeth.

"Oh yeah, she's mad at you." Harry nodded. "The way she said *darling* makes me think she's envisioning strangling you."

"What happened?" Edith asked as she took a seat across from us. Harry sat next to his wife. "When we left earlier, you were as happy as two little magpies."

"Our conversation was about starting our family," Smoke said.

I grabbed my cup of coffee and took a swallow. There was a special place in hell for people who lied to cute old married couples.

"Is the problem about *when* you want to start your family?" Edith asked.

"I'm not ready," I said. "I want it to be just the two of us for a little while."

"And you don't agree?" Edith looked at Smoke.

"Oh, I agreed," Smoke lied easily. "The discussion is more about how many we want."

Harry nodded. "I see. We have two. Two is a good number."

I took another sip of my coffee.

"Two is a great number," Smoke said. "But I like the idea of six."

I choked on my drink and nearly spit it all over the table. Smoke pounded me on the back and I shot him a glare. He had the nerve to grin.

"Six is a lot," Edith said. "How many do you want, Logan?"

"I hadn't thought much about it," I lied.

"I want a big family," Smoke said, picking up the lie of the story. "I think it would be fun. Plus, Logan comes from a big family. It makes sense."

"You're not the one who has to be pregnant," I snapped.

"So what do we do, Harry? Edith?"

"You compromise," Edith said. "You settle on a number you're both happy with."

"What if one ends up being all I want?" I asked.

"Then we'll have one." Smoke shrugged. "Problem solved."

"Glad we could help." Edith beamed.

"You'll make the right choice for you. Don't listen to your parents or anyone else's thoughts on the matter. It's you two against the world," Harry said.

Smoke caressed my cheek and stroked a thumb across the apple of it. "That's exactly how I feel."

"Kiss and make up," Edith said with a grin.

Smoke leaned in and kissed me before pulling back, a happy smile across his face.

"You'll be fine," Harry said. "Okay, we're seriously going to leave you two be."

"Let's exchange numbers," Edith suggested. "I want to know when you start your family so I can knit you baby things."

I am going to kill Smoke.

"That would be so sweet," I said, completely defeated.

We exchanged numbers and they left the cafeteria. When they were gone, I inched my chair away from Smoke.

"We kissed and made up," Smoke said. "Why are you moving your chair away?"

"I don't want to get struck by lightning when God smites you for your lies."

"You lied too," he pointed out.

"We're terrible. Baby clothes, Smoke? The woman wants to give us baby clothes."

"It's sweet. I don't have any grandparents still alive. Edith and Harry can be my surrogate grandparents."

"And when they find out we're not even together, let alone married and starting a family?" I shook my head. "It started out as a fun inside joke. Now I just feel awful."

"Because we lied."

"Because we lied. And because we were fighting about something completely made up. This is ridiculous. I'm going for a walk."

"Where? There's nowhere to go."

"I'll walk around the motel." I shrugged. "I just need to be alone for a few minutes."

I peeked out the front doors of the cafeteria, hoping Edith and Harry were gone so I didn't have to face them again.

The air after the storm was a little muggy, but tolerable. As I walked around the motel, I thought about what had just happened. Smoke and I joking around and enjoying the intimate warmth of being together had quickly morphed into something else. Though it was playful and fun to pretend that we were newlyweds, we weren't. We weren't even dating.

And strangers had assumed we were together.

Why?

Smoke and I hadn't even been overtly handsy. It was something else. Something in the way we spoke to each other, interacted with each other.

We just *were*.

There was an ease between us, something that had never existed between me and Knox. I hadn't even realized Knox and I didn't have it until I met Smoke.

Smoke, who was not even my boyfriend.

A chime sounded in my back pocket. With a frown, I pulled it out and unlocked the screen. The text I'd tried to send to Tavy last night finally went through.

My phone rang and Tavy's name flashed across the screen.

"Hey," I said as I put the phone to my ear.

"Oh my God! I've been calling and calling but your phone goes to voicemail. I thought you were dead!"

Not dead. Just having a bunch of "little deaths" with your stupid-hot father.

"Sorry about that," I said. "We got caught in a really bad rainstorm and stayed at a motel. The storm was so bad there was no cable or internet. I guess cell service went out sometime last night, too. I'm sorry you were worried."

"Yeah, I know. I talked to Dad a few minutes ago. He said the road got washed away and so you're stuck in the motel for another day until they can fix it."

"Right," I said, glad Smoke had already thought of a lie.

"Jeez, that's annoying. You must be so bored."

"Yeah, so bored."

"Dad isn't giving you any grief, is he?"

"Grief over what?"

"I dunno. You guys were in the truck together for hours. No doubt he's been bugging you into talking about Knox and all that stuff."

"You think your dad is the bugging type?"

"I think he has the potential to be the bugging type." She paused. "I kind of like that idea, actually. He'll feel like a real dad."

"Your stepdad is a real dad."

"Oh, he totally is," she agreed. "And he's wonderful and I love him like my dad. But it's different with Smoke. You know?"

"Yeah."

"So, it's not weird that you two are hanging out on this road trip?"

"Oh, no, it's definitely weird." I laughed, but my amusement was genuine this time. "You all but shoved us together."

"I didn't want you to be alone," she said quietly. "And I couldn't be there for you the way a best friend is supposed to be there for you."

My heart melted.

My guilt raged.

"You're the best, you know that?" I asked.

"You!"

"How's the job?"

"I'll tell you when you get to town."

"Tomorrow."

I wanted to see Tavy. But I wasn't ready for this door to close with Smoke. Even though it had to.

"Talk to you later," I said.

I hung up with her and stared down at the screen.

There was no real purpose to being outside and walking around. The only thing I had a view of was the highway and the parking lot.

I ambled in the direction of the hotel room, prepared to face Smoke.

I never should've slept with him. It would've been easier not to know what I was missing.

Because I was definitely going to miss him.

Transference.

Of course!

My feelings weren't for Smoke. I was only on day two of my post-Knox recovery period. Smoke and I were just sex. It wasn't complicated at all. It was fun. *He* was fun.

I immediately felt lighter, and my heart bounced in my chest. Everything I thought I was feeling toward Smoke was an illusion.

He was making the hotel bed when I entered.

"Hey," he greeted.

"Hi. Clean sheets?"

"I picked them up at the front desk. Clean towels too."

"Clean sheets," I repeated, threading the chain into the lock. "What do you say we dirty them up?"

"I thought you were pissed."

"Nope. I'm okay."

He raised his brows. "Yeah?"

"Yeah."

"If you were pissed, would you really tell me?"

"I'd tell you."

"Damn." He shook his head.

"What? You wanted me to be pissed off at you?"

He cracked a grin. "I wanted to see how good we are at angry sex."

I stripped off my shirt. "You've heard of role playing, right?"

His eyes heated. "Right."

I tossed my shirt aside and then sauntered toward him. "What are you waiting for?"

Chapter 16

I watched the alarm clock turn to 5:00 AM. Smoke was asleep and he was curled around me.

My body was spent and sore, and I didn't want to move even though I had to.

"You're awake," Smoke said.

I startled and then quickly melted into him. "Yeah."

"Didn't I tire you out earlier?"

"You did."

"Then why are you awake?"

"I just am."

He paused for a moment. "I don't want to get out of this bed."

"Neither do I. If I do, that's the end of it. The end of *this*."

"We said it was only going to be for one night," he reminded me. "And it wound up being two."

"But now it's really over," I murmured.

Smoke pulled me tighter, so my back was pressed against his warm chest. And then he brushed his lips against my shoulder before gently releasing me.

Disappointment cascaded through me.

I wanted just one more moment with him. One more feel of his fingers or tongue between my legs.

But it was better this way. Better to end it before I was totally addicted.

I eased out of bed and found my discarded clothes. I hastily pulled them on. With each piece, I donned my armor. I shoved away the memories of the last two days.

"I can be ready to go in a few," I said without looking at Smoke.

Smoke threw the covers off and climbed out of bed. He faced away from me and stretched his arms over his head.

His naked backside had my stomach fluttering.

I quickly pivoted and got to packing.

Thirty minutes later, our suitcases were in the car, and I was sitting in the passenger side of the truck while Smoke checked the tires out and made sure we were road-worthy.

I sipped on the weak coffee from the motel, wondering how I was going to maintain my cool during the last leg of the trip. It was nearly eight hours to Waco and the idea of sitting in awkward silence or trying to talk about mundane things after he knew how I looked when I came had nerves skating through me.

My phone rang just as the driver's side door opened.

Nerves turned to dread when I saw *Mom* flash across the screen. It was two hours earlier in Idaho, but my mom was an early riser. We were close and the fact that I hadn't called and told her about Knox…

But now was not the time to talk to her. Not with Smoke next me.

I silenced the call and set the phone in the middle seat between us.

Smoke looked down at it. "Your mom calls early."

"Really early," I agreed. "We kind of have a ritual."

"What kind of ritual?"

"It started when I was in college. I had a couple of 8:00 AM classes. Pure torture, really. On those days, Mom would be my alarm clock—my literal wake-up call. She'd water her plants while I watered myself with coffee." I shot him a grin.

He smiled back. "Sounds like a nice ritual."

"It was—*is*. We still do it sometimes. Not as much after I moved in with Knox. He likes *quiet* mornings." I shook my head. "Man, every time I think about something in relation to him, I realize how wrong he was for me."

The man sitting next to me wasn't the right man for me either, but it did make me wonder. Would Smoke be annoyed at my mother's early morning calls? Would he get jealous of the family conference chats I had once a month just to catch up?

"Why didn't you answer?" he asked.

"Because she would know something was wrong. She *always* knows. Just by my tone. I can't bullshit her. And I'm not ready to tell her about Knox or my zip code change."

Smoke buckled his seatbelt. "Fair enough." He put the truck in gear and then slowly drove around the parking lot to the exit.

"I should tell them sooner rather than later. I mean, they'll know soon enough when they get the deposit back from the wedding venue. I called yesterday to cancel and left a message."

"Face them head on," he said. "Don't hide from the news. You broke up with your fiancé. You moved to a different city. It's done, and you made the decision. End of discussion."

I shot him a grin. "End of discussion?"

"Yeah."

"Not how that works in my family. *Everything* is up for discussion."

"Why?"

"Why what?"

"Why is everything up for discussion? It's your life. It was your relationship. It was your choice. Furthermore, you're an adult."

I looked at him. "You don't discuss anything with anyone? You keep your own council all the time?"

"When it comes to personal shit? Yeah, pretty much. Club stuff is a different story."

"And not one of your biker brothers would dare weigh in on any of your personal life decisions?"

"Let me ask you something," he said. "And I'm not trying to be a dick here. Okay?"

"Okay."

"When you got with Knox, what did your parents say when they met him?"

"They were polite."

"Your brothers met him at some point?"

"Christmas that first year. They were…" I thought back to the holiday. "They teased him. But not in the way they tease me. They tease me because they love me and I'm their sister. They teased him differently. It's hard to explain."

"It's not hard to explain—I get it. They teased him because they were making fun of him. They didn't like him."

"No, they definitely didn't like him. And neither did my dad."

"Sounds like an uncomfortable holiday."

"It was. What were we talking about again?"

"Your family, and how they discuss your life. Okay, so

clearly they didn't like him from the beginning. Did that affect your decision to be with him?"

"What do you mean?"

"Come on. You know what I mean. You stayed with him even though you knew how your entire family felt about him. You stayed with him because you felt like you had something to prove. That you could make your own choices. Choose your own career. Follow your own path. Pick your future husband."

"You make it sound like a rebellion."

"Wasn't it?" he prodded.

"I'm the baby of the family. And the only girl. They're naturally overprotective. They didn't like that I chose to go to the University of Las Vegas instead of staying close by."

"Why did you?"

"Because I was never going to be able to figure out who I was if I stayed around them." I sighed. "I'm not painting them in the best light, am I?"

"I think you're painting a picture of a family who loves you and wants what's best for you—even if you have different ideas on what that is."

"How do you do it?" I asked softly.

"Do what?"

"Get it. You just *get* it, Smoke."

He flipped on the turn signal and slowly changed lanes. He glanced at me. "Maybe I just get *you*."

Chapter 17

By the next hour, my phone was blowing up. Calls and texts blasted my cell.

"What the hell is going on?" Smoke asked.

"I imagine my family found out about my engagement ending."

"How? Did Knox call them?"

"Doubtful," I replied. "Knox doesn't like anyone knowing about his dirty laundry."

My phone buzzed with another incoming text from my middle brother Chase.

> **CHASE**
>
> The wedding hall called Dad to confirm the refund and cancellation of your wedding.

"Shit," I muttered. "Cat's out of the bag."

"That was fast," Smoke said.

"The wedding hall called my father. Since he was the one paying for the wedding."

"You mean your father—who doesn't like your ex—was still going to pay for your wedding?"

"Yeah."

He clamped his mouth shut.

"What?" I demanded. "What are you not saying?"

"That's unconditional love right there," he said.

"Yeah, I know that! Why do you think I feel so guilty not telling them right away?"

Smoke put on the turn signal and slid into the exit lane.

"Where are we going?" I asked. "We don't need gas."

"You need to talk to your family," he said. "You'll feel better. They'll feel better."

"It'll make it real," I blurted out. "Telling my family my engagement is over means it's *really* over."

"Cupcake, your engagement was really over the moment you were in my bed."

My cheeks blazed. "You weren't ever supposed to bring that up again."

"I don't remember that being one of the rules."

"One night, one night only, remember?"

"It was two nights—and we never said anything about not talking about it."

"I think we're remembering the past differently."

Smoke pulled into a gas station parking lot and parked the truck. He left the engine running and unbuckled his seatbelt. "I'm getting a breakfast sandwich. You want anything?"

I shook my head.

"Hey," he said, reaching across the seat and touching my thigh. "It'll be okay. You did the hard part already. Your family loves you. They just want to make sure you're okay."

He squeezed my thigh before letting go. Then he climbed out of the truck, giving me privacy.

It wasn't going to get any easier. Dodging their calls and texts would only make it worse.

Time to face it head on.

I dialed Chase.

"Rug Rat," Chase said in greeting.

"Can you not call me that?" I demanded.

"Okay. How are you, LoLo?"

I could hear the smile in his voice and my annoyance vanished. "I'm okay."

"Okay? Really?"

I thought about it for a second. My eyes drifted across the lot to Smoke. He was holding the door to the gas station open for a little old lady.

"Logan?"

"Sorry, yeah. I'm here. I'm okay, Chase."

"The family is going nuts, you get that, right? Dad's looking at plane tickets to Vegas."

"Are you with them?"

"I'm with all of them. Mom's in the kitchen punching the hell out of the bread dough."

"Put me on speaker." I sighed. "Hello?"

"What's going on?" my dad groused. "I got a call from the wedding hall not half an hour ago."

"Yeah, Chase told me."

"This is the part where you explain," Grady, my eldest brother, commanded.

"Don't take that tone with me," I snapped. "It doesn't work on me."

"Honey, are you all right?" Mom asked.

"I'm fine," I assured her. "Look, the short of it is this: I ended things with Knox. I gave him back his ring."

"We got that much. The question is *why* did you end things with Knox?" Killian asked. My second oldest brother was not the type to let something go.

"Because he's a lying, cheating bastard," I replied.

Silence reigned on the other end of the line.

"I'll book six tickets to Vegas," my dad said. "We'll help you pack your things and get you moved back home."

"I'll go round for round with that fucker," Harlan said. "Been waiting for a reason to crack his skull."

Harlan was my youngest brother. He was still six years older than me and was the hothead of the bunch. Always wanting to fight, and able to back it up, too.

"There's no need to come to Vegas," I said.

"Where's my wallet?" my dad asked.

"Laundry room," Mom replied. "I almost washed it."

"Where are we going to stay?" Grady asked.

"I vote MGM," Chase said. "I want to walk the yellow brick road."

"Guys—"

"This isn't a vacation," Killian groused. "We're going to get Logan and her stuff and get her home."

"It'll be nice to have her home," Mom said. "Honey, make a list of the meals you want me to cook while you're here."

"HEY!" I yelled. "EVERYONE STOP. I'm not moving home. I'm moving to Waco. I'm already in a moving truck, and I'm about six hours away."

"You can't move to Waco," Chase said. "What about your job?"

"I'm working remote. My boss went through a nasty divorce a few years ago. I called expecting to quit, but she understood my situation so it's all good."

"How will that even work?" Killian demanded.

I took a deep breath. "Look, I appreciate that you're trying to help, but I've got this. Really, I've got this sorted."

"You're driving to Waco yourself? I don't want you staying in those cheap motels by the highway alone," Mom said.

"I'm fine," I said. "Tavy's father came to help her pack up her apartment. She had to fly to Waco last minute because her job needed her to start sooner, so I'm riding shotgun. Everything's fine. When I get to Waco, I'll be crashing with Tavy while I figure out some stuff. Okay?"

The line was silent.

"Okay?" I pressed.

"Okay," Grady replied.

"Can I still fly to Vegas and punch Knox in the face?" Harlan inquired.

"I'd prefer if you didn't," I said. "Anyway, I took care of it."

"Took care of what?" Killian asked.

"Never mind," I said quickly.

"Logan, what did you do?" Chase asked.

"I might've poured concrete down his pipes, and it's possible that I keyed his sports car."

Harlan let out a howl of laughter. "'Atta girl! I taught you well."

"Good going, Rug Rat," Grady said, a chuckle escaping his lips.

"I picked up a few tricks." A smile bloomed across my face. "I love you guys. I really do."

"You'll keep in touch," Mom said. "Check in more."

"I will," I promised.

My brothers all said goodbye, but my dad still hadn't spoken.

"Dad?" I pressed.

"You really okay, LoLo?"

Something in his tone made tears prick my eyes. Smoke was walking out of the gas station, holding a plastic bag.

I remembered how we had fallen asleep together, his

body cradling mine. I remembered him holding my hand when I told Knox never to call me again.

"Yeah, Dad. I'm okay."

Chapter 18

"So?" Smoke asked as he set the plastic bag in the center seat between us. "How did it go?"

"It went," I said. "A little crazy at first, but it's all okay now. Though, I'm worried about Harlan. He might jump on a plane to Vegas and have some words with Knox. And by words, I mean fists."

"Where is Harlan in the lineup of siblings?" Smoke asked. He pulled out an energy drink and set it in the drink holder and then ripped into a chocolate bar. He held it out to me first and I shook my head.

"Harlan is the second youngest," I explained. "Grady is the oldest. He's 37 and the architect of the family. Killian is next. He's 35 and is the family engineer. Then there's Chase who's 33. He's the numbers guy. Harlan's 30 and the family hothead."

"You didn't say what Harlan does for the business."

"He's the General Contractor. Electric, plumbing, drywall, demolition. He knows about it all. Supervises the crews. He's the trade guy."

Smoke crushed the chocolate bar and then reached for the energy drink.

"You eat like a twenty-year-old college kid on a finals deadline," I said with a laugh.

He grinned. "I don't normally eat this way. But I need the sugar and caffeine. I didn't get a lot of sleep the last few nights."

My cheeks heated and I cleared my throat. "Yeah. So, that's my family."

"Any of your brothers married? Have families?"

"Nope. They're not even dating anyone seriously. I was going to be the first." I snorted. "My mom is hungry for grandbabies."

"Sounds about right," he said with a chuckle. He polished off the rest of the drink. "You need to use the bathroom?"

I shook my head.

"You sure? I want to get a few more hours under our belt before we have to stop again."

"I'm good," I assured him.

An hour later, I was squirming in my seat. Smoke saw, and without a word, he turned off the highway to a gas station.

An hour after that pit stop Smoke wanted to stretch his legs, so we stopped at a rest area. We dragged our feet getting back into the truck.

Neither of us admitted it, but we weren't ready for our road trip to come to an end. When it ended, there would be no reason for us to talk, to laugh, to share stories about our families.

So long as we were on the road, we were in a bubble, a little pocket that was just the two of us.

I thought it would've been uncomfortable, us driving together after the intimacy we had shared. But the physical intimacy seemed to bleed into our conversations and made them more personal and easy.

The sun set and when we were thirty minutes from Waco, Smoke pulled into an abandoned lot.

"Everything okay?" I asked, facing him.

He squeezed the steering wheel, his knuckles turning white. And then he looked at me with wanting eyes.

"Smoke," I said quietly. "We can't. We agreed."

"I know. But why can't we?"

"Because Tavy is my best friend and the idea of doing anything that would hurt her, hurts me. And I'm not willing to risk our friendship for—" I gestured back and forth between us "—a few rolls in the hay with her really hot dad."

I mashed down the desire that hummed beneath the surface of my skin. I clenched my hands and sat on them so I wouldn't reach for him. So I wouldn't unzip my jeans and ask him to make me feel the way I wanted to feel.

With an aggrieved sigh, he put the truck into drive.

The rest of the ride to Waco was silent, charged with words we didn't have to say, punctuated by sexual desire that showed no signs of abating.

Smoke turned off the main road onto a gravel one.

"Clubhouse is just down this road."

The truck bounced and jostled, and I grabbed the door to brace myself as we rode.

Two men wearing leather vests stood at a gate, which they opened after seeing Smoke. They waved as we drove through. Smoke parked along the far edge of the gravel lot where a bunch of motorcycles were currently parked.

"Home sweet home," Smoke said as he cut the engine. "Welcome to the clubhouse, cupcake."

Lights illuminated the porch, and I could see shadowy

figures currently perched in chairs. One of the shadows jumped up and ran down the steps.

"Incoming," I said with a laugh as I quickly unbuckled my seatbelt and wrenched open the door.

"You're here!" Tavy screamed.

I hopped down from the truck bed, and she launched herself at me. She was close enough that I could smell tequila on her breath.

"Margs?" I asked in amusement, pulling back.

"Raze makes a mean margarita," she said with a wide grin. "Want one?"

"I'm good for now."

The driver's side door slammed shut and Smoke came around the hood of the truck. "Should I be offended that you're happier to see your best friend than you are your own father?"

"Hi, Daddy," she greeted as she embraced him. "Thanks for taking care of my friend."

Smoke's eyes met mine. "My pleasure."

My cheeks blazed with heat.

Oh yeah, he took really good care of me…

"You guys hungry?" Tavy asked as she pulled back from hugging Smoke. "We ordered a ton of Mexican food."

"I could eat," I admitted.

Tavy linked her arm with mine and all but dragged me up the porch steps. "We can get your luggage later."

Three leather-clad figures stepped into the light of the porch. They appeared to be in their late thirties or early forties, but it was hard to tell because they were muscular and good looking.

Tavy pointed to a man with dark hair and blue eyes. "Bones." Then she gestured to the other two. "And that's Kelp and Raze."

"I'm Logan," I introduced.

"Logan?" Raze repeated. "*You're* Logan?"

I looked at Tavy. "You told them about me, didn't you?"

"I told them my best friend was coming to live with me," Tavy said with a devious grin.

"Seriously? You're Logan?" Bones asked.

"You want to see her fucking ID?" Smoke snapped.

Kelp raised his brows. "Tavy didn't tell us you were hot."

"Uh, sorry?" I looked at Tavy in confusion.

"Oh, honey, don't be sorry," Kelp drawled.

"She's off limits," Tavy said, placing her hands on her hips.

"Stand down, Tav." I smirked.

My pugnacious friend relaxed from her fighting stance.

It was amusing to think that Tavy could warn off three virile, testosterone-riddled bikers. And maybe if I hadn't just had a two-night stand with Smoke, I would've been interested in sowing my wild revenge oats with one of them.

But as it was, none of them did anything for me. There was no belly flip. No crackle of desire, no tingle of excitement.

We all headed inside the clubhouse. It was clean and well organized, but it was clear men spent a good deal of time there. The furniture and decor was masculine, and there were several framed pictures on the wall. Oddly enough, I'd been expecting posters of half-naked women on motorcycles, not black and white prints of famous musicians and vinyl album sleeves.

"Can I make you a margarita?" Raze asked me.

"Just water for me," I said.

"Smoke?" Raze looked to his biker brother who hadn't fully come into the room.

"Nah. I'm gonna get the suitcases."

"I'll help," I said.

"I don't need help," Smoke said. His tone sounded off, but he suddenly grinned. "I got it. Relax."

He disappeared through the door.

"Enchilada, taco, or burrito?" Tavy asked as she went into the connected kitchen.

"Yes, please," I said with a smile.

Tavy grinned back as she fixed me a plate and brought it to me.

"So," Bones said. "Tavy told us your ex cheated on you."

"*Tavy*," I snapped.

"What?" She took a seat in one of the chairs and reached for her glass, which looked more ice than cocktail. "It's not like I told them we got arrested." She gave me a cheeky grin.

"Wait, wait, wait," Kelp said. "You guys got arrested? When?"

"On my last night in town," Tavy announced. "We had to call Dad to bail us out of jail."

I had taken a bite of the carnitas taco, and it took me a moment to put in my two cents. "It's not an exciting story."

"You don't have to be embarrassed," Bones said. "Most of us have been behind bars at one time or another. Probably for a lot worse than what you two did."

I raised my brows.

Has Smoke been in jail?

Then I remembered what he'd said about his sordid past. These men, no doubt, had the same kind of skeletons in their closets.

"So come on, let's trade war stories," Raze said. He picked up the bottle of tequila and came over to the couch where he took a seat. Kelp was at the other end and Bones leaned against the kitchen peninsula counter.

"We spent the night in jail for public urination combined with yelling at a cop," Tavy bragged. "And then Logan puked on his shoes."

"Amateurs," Kelp joked.

"Well, what did you guys do?" Tavy demanded.

"You're not to tell her anything," Smoke interjected from the doorway. He carted in both my suitcases and set them down out of the walkway so no one would bump into them.

"Oh, come on," Tavy whined. "I want to know. I told them what Logan and I did."

"Rule number one," Smoke said. "*You don't talk about Fight Club.*"

"You mean we're not supposed to talk about why we were in the pokey?" Tavy asked.

"You were hardly in the pokey." Smoke smirked. "A few hours, max."

"I'm gonna start telling people I shot a man in Reno," Tavy grumbled.

"Please don't," I said after I polished off the last of the taco. "I'd like to leave my life of crime behind. Okay?"

"You three come help me unhitch Tavy's car," Smoke commanded.

"Sure, boss. Right away, boss." Bones rose, looked at me and winked before following Smoke out the door.

Raze and Kelp trailed after them.

When they were far enough away that I thought they were out of ear shot, I said to Tavy, "Okay. Which one?"

"Which one what?" Tavy asked, widening her eyes.

"Which one do you want to sleep with?"

"How did you know?" she grumbled. "I thought I was being discreet."

"You were—by flirting with all of them." I grinned.

"Gotta keep 'em on their toes."

"So that means…"

"They're all in the running." She shrugged. "But I doubt any of them will touch me."

"Why not?"

"Raze told me about the rules."

"What rules?"

"Club rules. Brothers can't put the moves on other brothers' family. No daughters, no sisters. That kind of thing. It's about respect. But I'd *love* to be disrespected by any of those three. They're *hot*."

"They are all pretty attractive," I agreed. "You're really not leaning toward any one of them?"

"Too soon to tell yet." She flashed a grin. "This is gonna be fun."

I laughed. "You have more hormones than sense."

"I'm young. I'm single. I'm itchy."

I blinked. "You should see a doctor about that."

"I mean, I have an itch that needs scratching. Like *bad*."

"I still think steering clear of them is a good idea."

She leaned forward and dropped her voice. "But I just *know* they'd be good in bed."

"How do you know?"

"Well, they're at least a decade older than me. Experience. I need an experienced man in my life."

"Then why were you warning them about flirting with me?" I demanded. "Shouldn't you be sharing the wealth?"

"You're going to need to rebound with someone sooner or later," she said. "I don't want it to be with one of them. It would also make things very complicated for you."

"Complicated for me how?"

"You need someone you'll never see again. Not one of my dad's biker brothers who you'll be forced to see again out of general proximity to me and the club. Make sense?"

"I guess." I frowned.

The clomp of heavy boots up the porch stairs alerted us that we were no longer alone. Smoke came in with his duffel and dropped it on the ground.

"Have they been treating you well, Tav?" Smoke asked, setting his hand on his daughter's shoulder and giving it a squeeze.

"Yep." She nodded. "Bones has been giving me rides in the morning to work. And Kelp has been giving me rides home."

"Good. And the job?"

"Job is good." She shrugged. "I'm ready to crash though. I've been up since five."

Smoke dropped his hand and Tavy stood up and came to me. "I wanted to stay up until you got here. Now you're here, so I'm going to bed. Dad'll take you to your room."

I made a move to get up from my chair, but Tavy waved me down and looped an arm around my shoulders. "I don't know if I'll see you tomorrow before I go to work. I have to leave at six."

"Yeah, maybe I'll catch you in the afternoon when you're done," I said with a grin.

"And then we can drive over and check out our new apartment."

"Have you seen it yet?"

"Nope. I was waiting for you." She kissed her hand and then touched the top of my head. "Sleep well, everyone."

"Night, Tav," Kelp called out.

She gave a little finger wave to him and then headed down the hallway toward the stairs.

Smoke took Tavy's vacant seat, his eyes on me while I bit into the burrito. My brow furrowed.

"What's wrong?" Smoke asked. He held his hand out to Raze who passed him the bottle of tequila.

"I don't know. The burrito tastes funny." I set it down and picked up my fork and dove into a cheese enchilada. When I'd had my fill, I got up from my chair and went into the kitchen. As I dumped my scraps into the trash, I saw Smoke kick Bones' booted foot.

Bones looked at Smoke and grinned.

Smoke took a long draught of the tequila bottle and then stood up. "You wanna see your room?"

"Sure," I said, wondering what the hell was going on in the living room. There was tension in the air and I didn't understand why.

I went to grab my suitcases, but Smoke said, "I got them."

He handed the bottle of tequila to Bones before picking up my bags.

"Night, Logan," Kelp said.

"Good night," I replied.

"Hey, if you get scared in the middle of the night— what with sleeping in a new place, come and knock on my door," Bones said with a wide grin. "I'll protect you."

"I'm guessing it's a better idea to run *from* you than *to* you," I said.

"You're a smart woman."

"Hmm. Debatable. I did choose my ex." I shrugged and then moved out of the way so I could let Smoke lead.

We were out of sight, heading up the stairs when I heard, "Damn, she's fucking hot."

"Fuck yeah, she is."

I didn't know which two of them had spoken, but it didn't matter. The ego boost was much appreciated.

Smoke's shoulders tensed and the back of his neck turned pink.

We went to the second floor to the end of the hallway. He set one of my bags down so he could open the door, and then he walked through with my luggage.

The room smelled like lemon cleaner and the sheets were fresh. A folded bath towel rested on the blue coverlet. It was small room with a chest of drawers, a nightstand, lamp, and no bathroom.

"Bathroom is shared. It's down the hall. I hope that's okay," Smoke said.

"Oh, that's fine. It's just for tonight," I said.

Smoke stood in the center of the room. It wasn't big to begin with, but he engulfed the space and it was charged with sexual tension.

"If you need anything, I'm—"

"I'll text Tavy," I said quickly. And then I swallowed. "Please don't tell me where your room is. I don't need the temptation."

He closed his eyes and took a breath, like he was steeling himself. Finally, he opened his eyes.

I thought he was going to say something, but instead he just turned and left.

Chapter 19

"I didn't think anyone was awake," I said as I came into the kitchen the following morning. I blinked tired eyes at Smoke.

The man looked as exhausted as I felt.

But still delicious.

He was dressed in a pair of worn jeans and a black tee. His leather vest was missing, but he wore the same boots he'd had on when I met him. His dark hair was askew, like he'd run his fingers through it and hadn't bothered with a brush.

"I wanted to get up and have a few minutes with Tavy before she went to work. Coffee?"

"Sure," I said.

He turned back to the cupboard over the coffee maker and grabbed a mug. "Why are you awake?"

"Didn't sleep much," I admitted.

He set the coffee mug down in front of me and then pushed the carton of cream in my direction.

"I didn't sleep much either," he admitted.

"No?"

"Not until I fisted my cock and came to thoughts of you in my bed."

The carton of cream slipped from my fingers and fell onto the counter, spilling everywhere.

I cursed and hastily reached for it, but Smoke's hand on mine stopped me.

"Logan—" His voice was low, raspy.

"*Don't*," I snapped.

His tone was the same one he'd used when he'd been inside of me, speaking dirty words into my ear.

With a sigh, he pulled away and grabbed the dish towel hanging on the refrigerator door handle.

The clomp of heavy boots announced someone's presence, and a moment later Raze appeared.

His gaze darted from me to Smoke, and then back to me and the container of creamer all over the counter. "Looks like someone creamed themselves…"

"*Shut the fuck up*," Smoke gritted.

Raze grinned.

My cheeks flamed in embarrassment. "I've got some work to do. See you later."

I grabbed my coffee and quickly escaped back to my room. I wasn't sure if Raze knew that Smoke and I had slept together, but I was sure he sensed the heat between us.

Shit.

Did that mean the others could feel it?

Could Tavy?

In that moment I made a new rule for myself. I would not be in the same space as Smoke alone. I'd excuse myself, avoid him at all costs; lie or do whatever I had to do to make sure this thing was dead and buried.

I closed the door to my room and then set my mug of coffee onto the nightstand. I grabbed my laptop from my bag and then attempted to lose myself in work.

I glanced at my phone. It was a little before three and I'd left the room once to go to the bathroom.

A soft knock sounded at the door.

I took a deep breath. "Come in."

The door opened and Tavy entered.

Disappointment curled through my chest when I saw it wasn't Smoke.

Wrong emotion.

I forced a smile. "Hey."

"Hey." She bounded over to the bed and plunked her bottom down. She wore blue scrubs and her dark hair was in a high ponytail. "Didn't want to interrupt you, but I wanted to interrupt you."

I laughed. "Please, interrupt. I've been going over some CAD drawings and I could use a break."

"Well, my shift is over and I was wondering if you were ready to go look at the apartment."

I clam shelled my laptop and tossed it aside. "I'm ready."

"Cool. Let me tell Dad we're ready to go. He'll follow us in the truck with a few prospects. With their help we'll have all the big stuff settled by tonight. We can crash at our new place and start the next chapter of our lives."

"That sounds incredible."

I quickly packed up my toiletries bag and threw it into the suitcase.

I was wrestling my luggage down the stairs as Bones was coming up.

"Need help, sweetheart?" he asked.

"Please," I begged.

Chuckling, he grabbed both suitcases with his muscly arms and carted them down for me.

"Thanks," I said when we got to the first floor.

"No sweat." He winked. "So, you're new in town."

"Yep."

"I'd love to show you around on the back of my bike," he said.

"Oh—"

"*Bones!*"

I jumped at the bite in Smoke's voice. I hadn't even realized he was in the living room. His glare was directed at me.

What did I do?

"Hey, brother," Bones said with a grin. "Just helping Logan with her baggage."

"She's got enough baggage," Smoke clipped. "She doesn't need you adding to it."

"Whatever you say." Bones took my suitcases and walked past Smoke out of the clubhouse.

"What the hell is going on with you and Bones?" Smoke demanded.

My brow furrowed. It was on the tip of my tongue to say *nothing*, but I didn't actually owe Smoke an explanation.

So I threw my hair over my shoulder and said, "None of your business."

I attempted to march past him but he clasped my wrist with his muscular hand. It wasn't hard; just enough to get me to stop moving. "He's not a good guy."

I raised my brows. "He's your club brother."

"Yeah, how do you think I know? Don't get involved with him."

"I thought the club was done with the bad stuff."

"It is. Still doesn't mean he's a good guy."

He released me before I could tell him to let me go.

Smoke turned and marched out of the clubhouse. I followed at a slower pace.

Clearly, sleeping with Smoke had been a mistake. Now he thought he had a right to tell me who I could and couldn't hang out with?

I had no interest in Bones, but I'd had enough of men strong-arming me and I wasn't in the mood to be bossed around.

New chapter, indeed.

Smoke climbed into the moving truck and shut the door. I walked over to Bones, who was straddling his bike and said, "I'd love to take you up on your offer sometime."

"Would you now?" he asked slowly.

"Yup. Soon."

His lips quirked into a smile. "All right then."

I sauntered to Tavy's car and climbed into the front seat.

She turned down the radio.

"Hey," she greeted. "Ready?"

"Ready. How bummed would you be if I took Bones up on his offer to show me around town?"

"Not bummed at all," she assured me. "He's hot, but he doesn't give me the quiverings."

"Just last night you were talking about being unable to choose between Raze, Kelp, and Bones," I pointed out.

"Hmm."

"You have one in mind, don't you?"

"I have two of them in mind…"

I blinked. "You're not saying what I think you're saying…"

"Oh, I think you know *exactly* what I'm saying. I'm dying for a sandwich."

My mouth dropped open.

She grinned wickedly. "Shall we get going?"

Chapter 20

"It's cute," I said.

"Very cute." Tavy twirled in the living room. "But tiny."

"So tiny," I agreed. "Not enough room for two people."

"Don't say that. It's big enough," she assured me.

"Even a fold-out couch would have me sleeping in the living room slash kitchen." I smiled. "It's okay, Tav. I'll get my own place."

"Well, at least it has a good number of windows and high ceilings," she said. "That bathroom, though. Yikes."

"Not even a tub," I remarked.

"Make sure your new place has a tub that I can come over and use when I need a soak after a long day." Her face fell. "I'm really sad. I wanted to live together. You understand my new job set this up, right? I didn't pick this place…"

"It's all good. Honestly, it's probably for the best that we don't live together," I assured her. "I don't want to keep you up in the middle of night with my ranting and crying over Knox."

She peered at me. "Have you cried over Knox?"

"Not since the night we got drunk and went to jail," I admitted.

"Hmm."

"Thoughts on that?"

"Not sure yet. Though you seem oddly calm about the whole thing."

"My family knows," I said. "That was a fun conversation. It was a group project. All my brothers on speaker phone with my parents. You know, the works."

"Do they know why you left Knox?"

"I told them he cheated on me. Dad got the call from the wedding hall about the deposit refund. That's what started the avalanche of texts and phone calls."

"And Harlan's whereabouts?" she asked with a knowing grin about my hot-headed brother. "Is he still in Idaho, or is he hunting the streets of Las Vegas for your ex?"

"I hope he doesn't go to Vegas. But it's Harlan, so who knows." I snorted. "They were all going to fly down and pack up my stuff and move me home. Mom was making up my old room. They were kind of shocked when I told them I was already on my way to Waco."

The front door popped open and Smoke appeared with a box in his arms. He set the box on the ground and then looked around. "Awful small."

"Yep," Tavy agreed.

"Not big enough for the both of you," he stated.

"We could get bunk beds," Tavy suggested.

"Pass," I remarked. "I'll find my own place. It'll be fine."

"She can stay in the clubhouse for a few days. Can't she?" Tavy asked, looking at Smoke.

"Sure. Are you going to come down and help us unload the truck?"

"Hmm, I think I'm better suited to going grocery shopping so I can fill my fridge."

He shook his head and smiled. "It's okay. I brought young brawn to unload the truck anyway. You can trust them."

"Perfect. That means I don't have to do manual labor. I'll give you two a ride to the clubhouse before I hit the grocery store," Tavy said.

My phone vibrated in my purse and I quickly fished it out. I opened the screen to check the text.

It was sent from Knox's email address.

> **KNOX**
>
> Baby, please come home. I miss you. We can work this out.

With a sneer, I punched a few buttons and blocked his email address. The snake was going to contact me using any means necessary.

"Everything okay?" Tavy asked.

Smoke's attention was locked on me, his gaze intense.

I forced a smile and shoved my phone back into my purse. "Everything's fine."

We left the prospects to unload the truck and Tavy drove Smoke and me to the clubhouse.

She dropped us off and then immediately turned around to leave. My stomach rumbled as I tromped up the porch steps.

I'd only had a cup of coffee and was ready to eat.

The clubhouse wasn't empty. Bones and Raze were in

the kitchen standing around while Kelp was staring into the fridge.

"Hey kids," Bones greeted. "How's the apartment?"

"Cute, but small," I stated. "Not enough room for us both to live there."

"Logan will be crashing here for the time being," Smoke stated. "Until she can find a place."

"Cool," Bones said.

"There's nothing in this fridge," Kelp grumbled as he shut the door. "And I'm fucking starving."

"Me too," I admitted just as my stomach rumbled again.

Bones cracked a grin. "I can hear your belly from here."

"Rude," I said, but I laughed.

"There's a wing place close and it's pretty solid food," Raze said.

"I'm in." My tastebuds were tingling and I began salivating at the idea.

"You can ride with me," Bones said.

"*No.* She rides with me," Smoke gritted out.

Bones and Smoke stared at each other until Bones smiled suddenly. "Sure, brother."

Even I wasn't oblivious to the proverbial pissing contest between them. Ever the people pleaser, I jumped in and said, "Let me change real fast. I'll be ready to go in a minute."

"Meet you guys out front," Raze said.

Kelp followed him, but Bones stopped near me before he went to the door and said, "Tight jeans, babe. Wear tight jeans."

I swore I heard Smoke growl as Bones moved past him.

When it was just the two of us, Smoke looked at me and asked, "You ever been on the back of a motorcycle?"

"No."

"You got boots?"

"Yes."

"Good. Wear them."

Without another word, Smoke strolled outside.

I knew Bones was winding him up, but I wasn't a fan of grumpy Smoke. I missed easy, smiling Smoke.

But I definitely appreciated jealous Smoke.

I quickly changed out of my skirt and flats and threw on a pair of dark jeans that hugged my ass. I had a well-loved black racer tank top that I paired with a white camisole underneath. Chunky ankle boots completed my outfit. I quickly threw up my hair into a messy ponytail, grabbed my purse, and headed out to meet the guys.

They were already on their bikes. I walked up to Smoke who was straddling his motorcycle, looking far too sexy in his leather vest and sunglasses.

Danger and virility rolled off him.

My nipples hardened.

Smoke handed me a helmet and I set it on my head. I clipped the buckle and made sure it was tight.

And then I climbed on the back of Smoke's motorcycle.

I pressed my front to his back and wrapped my arms around him.

It took all of my willpower not to rub my cheek against his leather vest and purr like a kitten.

"Hang on, cupcake." The engine growled to life and before I knew it, we were zooming through the gates of the clubhouse.

My fingernails dug into Smoke's belly as adrenaline coursed through me.

Fear and excitement warred in equal measure.

I took a deep breath and felt it all the way to my stomach. When I exhaled, I released something. Something I'd been carrying with me for a long time.

Smoke pulled into the parking lot of the restaurant and cut the engine. I got off the bike with a bright smile on my face.

"Thank you," I said, unlatching the helmet. "That was...I can't even begin to...I *needed* that."

Smoke took the helmet, our eyes meeting. Something moved between us and the planes of his face relaxed.

My gaze dipped to his mouth.

"How'd you like the ride, sweetheart?" Bones asked from behind Smoke.

Smoke turned and scowled at him but said nothing.

I faced Bones. "It was incredible."

Bones wrapped a friendly arm around my shoulder and pulled me into his muscular side and all but dragged me toward the restaurant, away from Smoke. "Thanks."

"For what?" I demanded.

"Wearing tight jeans."

I elbowed him hard enough to make him grunt and he let me go.

"Man's got a death wish," Raze said to Kelp.

"Right?" Kelp said with a laugh.

The restaurant was fairly empty and the air conditioning was earning its keep. I wished I'd thought to bring a sweater. Goosebumps scuttled up and down my arms.

A female bartender pulling pints called out, "Anywhere's fine."

"Lady's choice," Bones said.

I headed toward the booth against the far window, the men all trailing behind me. I slid into the booth and Bones took the seat next to me. Kelp and Raze sat on the opposite side, and Smoke pulled up a chair at the end of the table, shooting Bones another glare.

The cute bartender approached our table with a wide smile. "Hey. What can I get everyone to drink?"

We put in our orders.

"You know what you want to eat?" she asked.

Bones looked at me. "You like spicy?"

I nodded.

His smile was slow.

I rolled my eyes and elbowed him again.

After we ordered, the bartender glanced at me with a grin and said, "Loving this for you, by the way."

"Loving what for me?" I asked in confusion.

She raised her brows. "Really?" Her gaze bounced between all the bikers. "How does it feel to be living my dream?"

Before I could reply, she walked back to the bar.

"Loving what for you?" Raze asked.

"And living her dream?" Kelp inquired. "I'm so fucking lost."

My cheeks flamed. "It's not important."

"Oh, honey, you're blushing," Bones teased. "Now I gotta know what this is about."

"She thinks I'm dating you," I replied, my gaze landing on the table. "All of you...like at the same time."

"At the same time?" Kelp asked. "Like you're playing the field?"

I shook my head. "No, like *at the same time.* You know. As a unit. All of us together..."

The men fell silent.

"Is that even a real thing?" Raze asked in confusion.

"It is in romance novels," I muttered.

"Romance novels?" Kelp asked, pulling out his phone. "Color me curious."

"I'll give you five dollars to put your phone away," I begged.

Kelp shrugged and stuck his phone back in his pocket.

Bones touched my cheek. "You're bright as a tomato, babe."

"Don't call her babe," Smoke growled.

Before a brawl occurred, I announced, "So I need a place to live. And a car. I think a car first."

"You don't have a car?" Kelp asked. "What were you driving in Vegas?"

I pursed my lips. "My ex-fiancé's car."

"What kind of car are you looking for?" Bones asked.

"I don't know. Something reliable. Affordable."

"Sounds fun," Bones drawled.

"Would I love a fun car? Yes. Would that be practical? No."

"I'll take you car shopping," Bones offered.

"Thanks," I said. "But Smoke already volunteered."

The words tumbled out of my mouth before I had a chance to stop them. What was I doing? Accepting Bones' offer would have only put more distance between me and Smoke, which was exactly the way it was supposed to be.

Only, my mouth and brain couldn't quite agree.

The table fell silent and all eyes turned to Smoke who stared at me with a penetrating gaze. "That's right. I offered to help Logan."

My insides unfurled.

The bartender returned to drop off our drinks. When she left, the table was quiet. I didn't like the silence so I said, "Tavy told me a few of you guys joined the Waco chapter recently."

"Yeah," Bones said.

Silence again.

"So, you're also from South Dakota?" I pressed.

"Yep." Kelp lifted his beer to his lips.

Smoke apparently took pity on me because he said,

"The four of us—and Viper, who you haven't met yet—joined the Waco chapter a couple of months ago."

"Why?" I asked. "Why did you leave your chapter?"

"There wasn't much of a chapter left," Raze explained. "Our president got into some shit, the club fell apart. Colt needed more brothers down here. So here we are."

"Colt," I repeated.

"Prez," Smoke clarified.

Though they'd explained their move, I got the feeling they were being tight-lipped about things and didn't want to discuss the real reason they'd made the switch. Something to do with their less than lawful past.

The idea was only reinforced when Kelp said, "So you and Tavy were college roommates?"

"Yep."

When I didn't expound, Kelp grinned. "I get it."

I smiled back and then I gently nudged Bones.

He didn't budge.

"I need to use the restroom," I said.

Finally, he climbed out of the booth. I wandered toward the back down the hallway and found the restroom. I did my business and washed up.

As I returned to the table, the bartender was bringing out our food. She placed the basket of fries in the center of the table and distributed the wings.

"Anything else I can get you?" she asked.

"We're good, babe. Thanks," Raze said, flashing her a megawatt grin.

She returned the smile. "Holler if you need anything."

Bones had seen me approach and got out of his seat. When I scooted into the booth, my phone buzzed, the screen flashing.

"That's the third time your phone's gone off," Bones said as he retook his seat next to me.

"Really?" I asked in surprise.

My boss preferred to communicate via email or regular phone calls. A pit of anxiety formed in my belly.

I reached for my cell like it was a loaded pistol. I had a pretty good idea who was trying to contact me. The number read UNKNOWN, but the texts were from Knox.

> **KNOX**
>
> You fucking cunt you ruined my car I'm going to find out where you are we're not over. You're not leaving me not ever.

Swallowing, I turned my phone off and shoved it into my bag. My gaze caught Smoke's. His eyes were blistering with concern. I minutely shook my head even though fear clawed up my throat and settled there.

The bikers dug into their food with voracious appetites. Mine had suddenly disappeared.

"What's wrong?" Kelp asked. "Don't like your food?"

"Food's fine," I said even though I hadn't yet touched it. I reached for a carrot stick and opened a mini plastic container of bleu cheese dressing.

"Then what's wrong?" Raze asked.

I didn't want to admit that Knox's texts had me shaking. Even though I'd blocked his regular number, email, and social accounts, he still had access to me. Access in a way that was invasive. And terrifying. I never should've let my temper get the better of me. I should've just walked out on him and let it go.

It was easy to put him out of my mind when I was no longer in Las Vegas. But he was infecting my present with his persistence and his inability to accept our broken engagement. Not to mention his threatening texts…

"Can we just eat?" I asked.

Raze looked at Smoke and then back to me and shrugged. "Sure."

The bleu cheese whet my appetite. I took my first bite of the spicy wing and my hunger roared to life.

It wasn't until I was licking the last bone clean that I realized the table had gone eerily silent. Four pairs of eyes were watching me. Smoke's mouth flickered with a smile.

"What?" I asked, dropping the chicken wing.

Smoke reached for a wet nap packet and opened it before handing it to me. "You got a little..." He pointed to his mouth.

I hastily put the wet nap to my face and scrubbed. "Did I get it all?"

"Yeah." Smoke's grin didn't disappear. "You're good."

I cleaned my fingers and then bunched up the wet nap. "Anyone going to eat the rest of those fries?"

Raze pushed the basket toward me. "Have at it."

"Did Smoke not feed you on the road trip?" Kelp demanded.

"He fed me," I replied.

Boy, did he feed me.

Raze gestured to the bartender for the check and the guys threw in cash before I even had a chance to reach for my wallet.

"Thanks for lunch," I said to them as I polished off the last of the fries.

"No sweat," Kelp said.

They got out of the booth and headed to the front door. I gathered my belongings and ambled my way toward the bar.

"They tipped okay, right?" I asked the bartender.

"Forty percent," she said with a grin. "Nice guys."

I looked at the exit where Smoke was patiently waiting for me.

"Yeah, nice," I agreed.

"I'm dying to know… Are you dating any of them? All of them?"

I snorted out a laugh. "Let me guess. You read romance novels?"

She grinned. "Is it that obvious?"

"Kinda. I'm not dating any of them."

"You sure? The one at the door looks like he wants to be dating you."

Her words shot a quiver through me—a thrill I quickly squashed. "It's complicated."

She sighed. "Isn't it always?"

With a wave goodbye, I went to meet Smoke. He held the door open for me.

"Thanks," I said, genuinely appreciating the gesture.

"It was Knox, wasn't it? Who was blowing up your phone."

"Yes," I said quietly as we headed to his motorcycle. The other guys were already straddling their bikes.

"See you back at the clubhouse," Smoke said to them as he handed me a helmet. "I'm taking Logan car shopping."

They revved their engines and then drove out of the parking lot.

"You don't have anything else you need to do today?" I asked as I placed the helmet on my head.

"Several things," he said. "Including getting you a new phone."

"A new phone? I don't need a new phone."

"You need a new number."

"I can't—if I change my number, I'll have to tell my parents why…"

"Logan," he stepped closer and grasped my hips. "I

saw your face when you read those texts. You went pale and you looked terrified."

"I did?" I asked quietly.

"Yeah, you did. We all saw. Don't let Knox fuck with you. Get a new phone. A new number. You'll feel better. Trust me."

Chapter 21

"Aside from an affordable reliable car, do you know what brand?" Smoke asked as we walked across the used car lot.

"Nope."

When I'd started dating Knox, he'd made it clear he didn't like my car. It was old, and he didn't think it was reliable. Six months into our relationship, he'd bought me a car. He'd picked out the make, model, and color.

At the time I thought it had been a thoughtful gesture. Looking back now, I saw it for what it truly was. A manipulation tactic. He'd been slowly giving me things, nice things, so that I'd grow accustomed to the luxury and wouldn't want to leave when I inevitably found out he was a cheater.

And every time I accepted something he'd chosen for me, I'd helped outfit my gilded prison by accepting his gifts.

"Logan?"

"Sorry," I murmured. "I was thinking about stuff. Cars, right."

He grabbed my hand and linked his fingers through mine. I didn't pull away. We were alone, and for the time being I could pretend our two-night stand could turn into something more.

A salesman wearing a black polo and khaki slacks strode across the lot to greet us. "You've come to the right place," he said with a wide smile. "What are we looking for? A safe family car, eh? For the little ones?"

I shot Smoke an amused look.

Here we go again.

"She's here to buy a car," Smoke said, not responding to the salesman's assumptive comment.

"Sure," the salesman said easily. "What are you thinking, Ma'am?"

"I want an SUV. Something with four-wheel drive," I said. "And pearl white. I want a pearl white car."

"I have something in mind. Follow me."

We trekked to the other end of the parking lot and stopped at a gently used Toyota 4Runner in pearl white. I needed the four-wheel drive if I ever wanted to take the car to Idaho to visit my family, and I wanted something that would be fun to drive.

"This one won't last long on the lot. I know, I know, we all say that right? But seriously these sell like hot cakes. She's only got fifteen thousand miles on her and the warranty will transfer to the new owner. Toyota calls this color Blizzard Pearl, and since it's a higher end TRD model it's got all the bells and whistles. Take it for a test drive," the salesman suggested. "Let me know how you feel about it and we'll talk when you get back. I just need to see a state issued ID from each of you and once I make a copy, you're good to go."

I looked at Smoke. "You up for a little spin?"

"I'll ride shotgun. But first…" He moved to the front

of the car and popped the hood. A few minutes later, he closed the hood and nodded. "You're good. Thing is basically brand new."

My heart did a little pitter patter. He was making sure I was safe before I got behind the wheel. I loved his attentiveness. And his protective instinct.

I must've been giving him a dopey look because he met my gaze and smiled. Wide. Wide enough that I was sure he knew what I was thinking.

Smoke opened the driver's side door for me and I climbed in. I adjusted the seat and mirrors, getting a feel for the car. The salesman returned with our IDs.

"You two are good to go. See you when you get back and we'll get that paperwork started." He winked like it was a done deal and shut the driver's side door for me.

"You ready?" Smoke asked as he buckled himself in.

"Yeah," I said. I put the keys into the ignition and started the car but made no move to reverse out of the spot.

"What's wrong?"

I swallowed. "Why don't you want Bones showing me Waco on the back of his bike?"

"Why did you say I was going to go car shopping with you?" he fired back.

"Yeah." I sighed. "Okay."

"Okay."

This thing between us hadn't run its course. And by giving into it, even for a few nights, it was a can of worms that could no longer be contained.

But there was nothing I could do about it at the moment. So, I put the car in gear, backed out of the spot, and took the car for a test drive.

"Well?" the salesman asked as I stepped out of the car. "What did you think?"

"I think I'd like to talk to you about making a deal," I said bluntly.

The salesman blinked, momentarily stunned by my directness even though it was exactly what he'd wanted. But he quickly pulled it together and smiled. "Wonderful. Why don't you two step inside my office while we draw up the paperwork?"

"I'm not involved," Smoke said as he came around the car. He had his sunglasses on, shielding his eyes. "She can handle it."

I bit my lip to stop my grin.

Damn this man. He makes it so easy to want him.

"Of course," the salesman said. "Sir, you're welcome to sit in our air-conditioned lobby." He addressed me. "Shall we?"

An hour later, I walked out of the salesman's office, shaking his hand and holding the keys to my new car.

Smoke looked up from his cell phone and stood as I approached him.

"Thank you for your business. You're gonna love your new car," the salesman said. He looked at Smoke and jested, "Your girlfriend drives a hard bargain."

"Does she?" Smoke looked at me.

"Apparently," I said, my lips twitching in humor.

"Are you going to tell me what happened in there?" Smoke asked as he walked me to the parking lot.

"I told him that I didn't need financing, and that I would take the car today and cut him a Cashier's check from the bank once I had the total amount. They hate that. Every dealership in the country makes money when they sell you a loan. The car is just how they get to sell you a loan. So then he said if I went with financing, he'd knock off a few grand. I said no thanks, and after he realized I was serious he said if I financed today, he'd waive all the fees and markups." I shrugged and grinned. "So, I financed it and saved like five grand. And by the way, why didn't you offer to help wrangle me a deal?"

"I figured if you needed help, you'd ask. Clearly, you didn't need it."

Before I could think too much of it, I leaned forward and brushed my lips across his. "Thanks. Knox would've... well, he would've handled it differently."

"I'm not Knox."

"No," I agreed. "You're not Knox."

He slid his hand to my hip to pin me down and prevent me from moving away from him. "Tell me something."

"What?"

"Where'd you learn how to negotiate such a good deal?"

"My dad. And my brothers," I said with a wry grin. "Family business, remember?"

"They taught you a valuable skill set."

"Yep."

He let out a subtle laugh. "Do you really have that kind of cash squirreled away?"

"Nope."

"So, you were bluffing?"

"Damn right I was."

Smoke threw his head back and laughed. "We need go back to Vegas. I need to see you in action at the poker table."

My good humor faded and so did my smile when I realized we'd never go to Vegas together.

Smoke's hand slipped from my waist. "I'll follow you back to the clubhouse."

Fire & Frenzy

~

"Come over for dinner," Tavy said on the other end of the line.

"You just moved in," I said with a laugh. "What would you make?"

"Nothing. We'd order take-out and sit on the couch and eat," she said.

"Pass," I said. "I just got back to the clubhouse and I'm going to spend the rest of the night looking at apartments for rent."

"Ick."

"Hey, not all of us have a job that will give us a place to live."

"I'm bummed we're not living together," she said.

"Same," I admitted. "I bought a car today."

"You did? Wow, that was fast."

"Yeah, well, I need my own set of wheels so I can look at apartments. Otherwise, I'd have to rely on Bones to take me around town, and I have a feeling that's not a good idea."

"Why not? You seemed curious about him. What happened?"

"Bones and I—he' a flirt. And I definitely wouldn't know how to handle a man like him. You were right. He's not the man to sow some oats with."

"Hmm. I'm glad you came to that conclusion. So did he take you car shopping?"

"No. Your dad did."

I instantly winced.

Dangerous game I'm playing.

"Oh, good. I'm glad he took you. Is it weird that you're seeing him more than I am? I feel bad because he *just* got back into town, and I feel like I haven't made any time for him."

"Why don't you invite him over for take-out instead of me?" I suggested.

She fell silent for a moment. "Yeah, you know what, that's a great idea."

"Yeah, just don't tell him he was your second choice…"

"I definitely won't. Thanks, Logan."

"I'll see you soon enough. Hopefully I'll find an apartment pretty fast and then you can go furniture shopping with me. I don't own anything," I said with forlorn melancholy.

"Hey, don't feel sad about that. That just means you get to start from scratch, paint the walls whatever color you want, get that couch that might be just a bit too expensive but that makes you feel like you're napping on a cloud. You deserve nice things."

Unbidden emotion lodged in my throat. "Thanks, Tav. You always know what to say so to cheer me up."

"You'll be okay, Logan. One day, you'll look in the rearview mirror and wonder if any of this ever actually happened. Memories fade. If you let them."

Chapter 22

"I'm never going to find a place," I groaned two nights later. "I'm going to have to live in the clubhouse until the end of time, eating leftover pizza for breakfast and salt and vinegar chips for dinner."

"Meals of champions," Bones said as he passed me the container of take-out fries.

With a sigh, I leaned across the couch and grabbed a handful. "This is no better."

"Is this that thing that you're complaining about but you're not *really* complaining about?" Bones asked. "It could be worse. You haven't even seen people having sex in the common room yet."

I blinked. "Does that happen often?"

He shrugged.

"Lovely." I wrinkled my nose.

"Don't worry, babe. I'd never have sex with you where someone could walk in and see us."

"You're such a gentleman." I batted my eyelashes, which caused Bones to grin.

There was nothing sexual between us. He knew it and I

knew it. Still, he was a flirt, turning it on high when Smoke was around, which hadn't been often the past two days.

No doubt he was avoiding me like I was avoiding him.

"Who's a gentleman?" a younger biker asked as he walked in the front door.

He was tall, blond, and had twinkling blue eyes.

"Me," Bones said.

"Yeah," the biker said. "Such a gentleman. Didn't Angela call you a crass bast—"

"Shut up, Savage," Bones said.

Savage grinned and waved to me. "Hi. I'm Savage. Who are you, darlin'?"

I raised my brows. Between the testosterone and the flirts, I wondered how women ever kept their clothes on around these men.

Oh. Right...

"I'm Logan," I said. "Tavy's friend."

"Ah, Tavy." He nodded. "Right. Smoke's kid. Wait, *you're* Logan?"

"Uh huh."

"But you're a girl."

"You should be a detective," I said dryly.

Bones' crack of laughter echoed through the room.

Savage smiled. "No, it's just that Tavy never gave me any indication that her best friend was female."

"It's kind of our party trick," I said in amusement.

Savage wandered over to the fridge and pulled out a beer. "Speaking of parties. There's a barbecue happening tomorrow."

"No one told me," Bones said.

"I just saw Mia at the new space," Savage explained. "I'm sure you'll get the text soon."

"Mia?" I asked.

"Colt's wife," Bones said. "The club president's wife."

"Ah." I was familiar with Smoke and his South Dakota boys, and I'd met a few of the prospects, but I didn't know the other club members or their wives and girlfriends.

My phone buzzed from a number I didn't recognize. I hesitated, worried it might be Knox. But I quickly shook off the thought when I remembered I'd changed my number. I'd been emailing property management companies and I didn't want to miss out on a potential apartment.

I answered the phone and got off the couch and headed to the exit for a measure of privacy. Five minutes later, I ended the call. I had an appointment in the morning to see the place.

A text came through with the address.

Hopefully this apartment would be the one.

∾

The gates to the clubhouse opened and I drove through. Several cars were already there, parked on one side while the bikers were parked on the other. I didn't see Tavy's vehicle and I knew she wouldn't get off work until later that afternoon.

I cut the engine and climbed out of the car, my spirits low.

A few younger bikers were hanging out on the porch, laughing, drinking bottles of soda.

"Hey, Logan!" Savage called.

"Hey," I greeted.

"You don't sound happy," he said.

"I saw an apartment today. Actually, that's a lie. I saw the neighborhood and then refused to even look at the apartment," I said.

"Damn," Savage said. He wrapped his arm around me

and gave me a friendly hug. "Well, there's nothing like a bottle of moonshine and a few hotdogs to cheer you up."

"Moonshine?" I inquired.

"You've got to taste Boxer's moonshine," Savage said. "Just don't drink too much."

"Yeah, you wouldn't want to wake up in the backyard of the clubhouse snuggling a raccoon." A biker with dark hair grinned, his cheek dimples popping.

"Dude, that only happened once," Savage quipped. "Logan, this is Duke. He was once my best friend."

"You'd be dead without me," Duke said to Savage.

"That's the fucking truth," another biker piped up. "I'm Acid."

The door to the front porch opened and a tall blonde who looked about my age popped her head out. "You guys coming in?"

"Yeah." Duke walked over to the woman and dragged her into his arms. "Come meet Logan."

"Logan. Oh! Tavy's friend," the woman said with a bright smile at me. "I've heard a lot about you."

"Already? My reputation precedes me?" I joked.

"I met Tavy briefly a few days ago when I came to the clubhouse," the woman explained. "She mentioned her best friend was moving to town. I'm Willa, by the way."

"Nice to meet you."

The group of us headed into the clubhouse. Two dogs were running through the living room. Kids were yelling and chasing after them.

"Silas!" a petite brunette called from behind the kitchen counter.

A gangly teenager with a mop of dark hair looked at her. "Yeah?"

"Take this platter of patties outside and then get your

sister from her playpen," the woman commanded with the authority of a drill sergeant.

"I'll take the patties," Acid offered.

"Thanks," the woman replied. "Silas?"

"Yeah, I'll get Scarlett," Silas said as he turned and headed down the hallway.

"Take the dogs with you!" the woman called out.

"Monk! Captain!" Silas barked. "Let's go outside!"

The two dogs bounded after Silas.

"Whew," the woman said as she went to the kitchen sink to wash her hands. "The chaos started early today."

"What else can we take out back," Duke asked.

"Condiments, the chips, the salads in the fridge," the woman said.

Savage saluted. "Sir, yes, sir!"

"Corral him, would you?" the brunette said to Willa.

"Oh, I wish I could. Believe me." Willa grinned.

The brunette looked at me. "You're Logan."

"Yep," I said with a nod.

"Hi, I'm Mia."

"The club president's wife, right?" I asked.

She nodded. "There's soda and beer in the coolers out back. Help yourself to anything you want. If we don't have it, ask and I'll get a prospect to run out and get it for you."

"Ah, thank you." I blinked in surprise.

"How do I get that kind of treatment?" Savage demanded.

"You *do* get that kind of treatment," Willa said with a laugh.

"You guys go, I'll be out in a minute," Mia said.

Acid led the brigade and I brought up the rear.

"Hey, Logan, wait a second," Mia said.

I hung back for a moment and looked at the woman who couldn't be more than a few years older than me.

"I know this is overwhelming," she began. "There's a lot of us. We're all going to be new to you. But seriously, if you need anything, please let us know. Let *me* know."

"Are you always this kind to relative strangers?" I asked with a smile.

She chuckled. "You're Tavy's best friend. Tavy is Smoke's kid. We take care of people close to the club."

"Ah, well I find that very comforting."

"Good." She grinned. "Now go on back there and meet everyone."

When I got outside, I was completely overwhelmed. Though I recognized several of the bikers, there were still a handful who were unfamiliar. And that was nothing compared to seeing the group of women gathered in a circle of chairs, many of whom held babies or were pregnant.

As I looked around, I caught Smoke's eye. He stood with a few of the South Dakota boys and I almost took a step in his direction. He was clearly the person I was most comfortable with aside from Tavy, but I quickly changed course. If I sought him out, everyone would know something was going on between us.

I also had to be extra careful when Tavy showed up. She'd spot it before anyone.

"Logan!" Willa called out, gesturing to me. "Let me introduce you to everyone."

I turned my back on Smoke and approached her.

"Everyone, this is Logan, Tavy's friend," Willa announced.

My mind whirled as the ladies introduced themselves.

"Where is Tavy, by the way?" Brooklyn asked. The brunette rested a hand on her baby bump.

"Still working," I explained. "She'll be here this afternoon."

"How are you liking Waco so far?" Allison asked. The bottle-blonde bounced her toddler on her knee as she peered at me with curious eyes.

"Not sure yet," I admitted as I took a vacant chair. "I haven't really explored much. I'm on an apartment hunt right now. It's not going very well."

The back door opened and Mia came out, carrying a platter of humus and veggies. She set it down on the table in the middle of the circle and then sat down. "What are we talking about?"

"Logan's inability to find an apartment," Sutton said.

"If only you and Viper would stop the baby making fever long enough to go house hunting, Logan could move into The Hostel," Joni joked. The infant in her arms made a cooing noise, momentarily pulling her attention.

"Viper's got a one track mind," Sutton said. "He's *very* determined. I'd hate to try and stop him, you know?"

I glanced in the direction she was looking to see her staring at a hulk of a man who stood with Smoke and the other South Dakota boys.

"The Hostel?" I asked in confusion.

"It's a running joke," Mia said. "I own a house that I turned into a rental. Brooklyn and Slash have lived there. Willa and her sister have lived there. And currently Sutton and Viper live there."

"No one ends up staying for very long," Willa expounded. "It's like a landing pad. Hence the nickname The Hostel."

"I could use a landing pad," I admitted. "The clubhouse is fine for now, but I could really use my own space."

My own space away from Smoke, so I don't accidentally-on-purpose knock on his door and ask him to—

"Wait," Brooklyn said. "I have a solution."

"Your apartment," Willa said.

Brooklyn nodded. "I own a bakery and there's an apartment over it. It's vacant and it's already furnished. There's even a new intercom."

"Are you my fairy godmother?" I asked with a laugh. "I'll take it!"

"We get deliveries really early in the morning, though. Big trucks that make a lot of noise," Brooklyn said.

"I sleep like the dead," I assured her. "When can I move in?"

"I'll be at the bakery tomorrow if that works for you. I can give you keys then."

"That's perfect." I let out a sigh of relief.

"Her bakery makes the best coffee," Willa said. "You're going to get spoiled."

"Coffee?" Joni shook her head. "Brooklyn makes the best pastries."

"You guys, stop," Brooklyn said, her cheeks flaming with embarrassment.

Without a word, Darcy abruptly stood up from the group and went inside. She had only introduced herself, but she hadn't said anything else.

The mood of the women suddenly shifted and a few of them made eye contact, seemingly to have a conversation I wasn't privy to.

"What is it you do?" Willa asked me, breaking the momentary silence.

It was a clear attempt to change the conversation, so I went with it willingly. "I'm a virtual interior designer. Clients send me photos of a room or a house they want to redesign and give me ideas about their desired aesthetic. I three-dimensionally model the space and include product listings for them to purchase and put them in touch with contractors for paint or other modifications. If they like what they see, they just make a few phone calls and buy a few things and soon they have the exact space I've designed for them."

"I could use that kind of thing for our kitchen remodel," Joni said. "I'm struggling hard with the space."

"I'll help you," I offered.

"Really?" Joni asked, her face lighting up. "That would be incredible."

I smiled. "Yeah, absolutely. It can be daunting when you know what you like when you see it, but you're not really sure how to bring it all together. That's where I come into play."

"Exactly." Joni nodded. "We bought a fixer-upper and it's been a cool experience bringing the house back to life. I feel like I had a pretty good grasp on the rest of the house, but the kitchen…"

"The kitchen is also the hearth of the home," Brooklyn said. "When that space is wrong or incongruent, you never want to spend any time in there."

"Not all of us want a state-of-the-art kitchen," Mia joked with Brooklyn.

Brooklyn snorted. "My work follows me home. I'm contemplating redoing one of the counters to be a massive butcher's block."

"I don't think Slash would mind," Sutton said as she pulled her brown hair up into a messy ponytail. "That man is crazy about you."

Brooklyn grinned. "He is, isn't he?"

"When are we firing up the grill?" Willa asked. "I'm starving."

"How's the morning sickness, Willa?" Brooklyn asked.

"Gone. Now I'm just hungry all the time," Willa said.

I raised my brows at Willa. "I had no idea you were pregnant."

Willa grinned. "Well, I'm not going to go up to

strangers and say, *Hi, I'm Willa. I'm growing a fetus.* Kind of a weird introduction, don't you think?"

I chuckled. "Little bit."

Willa looked at Duke with a dreamy expression flitting across her face. I'd noticed most of the women looking at their biker spouses with the same kind of facial expressions.

I couldn't stop my gaze from seeking out Smoke's.

His eyes were already on me.

The back door slamming shut pulled my attention. Two women strode across the lawn toward us. One was a blonde sporting an adorable pixie cut and the other was…

"*Rachel?*" I yelled in surprise.

"Logan?"

Before I knew it, the two of us were running toward each other.

"Oh my God," I breathed. "What are you doing here?"

"*Me?*" Rachel asked with a laugh as we began to walk back toward the group. "What about you?"

"Wait, they know each other?" Mia said to Joni. "This is wild."

"So wild," Joni agreed.

"Rachel used to date my brother Chase," I explained.

"Eons and eons ago," Rachel said with a laugh. "How's Chase? Still in Idaho?"

I nodded. "Runs the books for Dad's business."

"I'm so confused about how you two know each other," Brooklyn said.

"They just explained it," Sutton said.

Brooklyn rolled her eyes. "I know that. But Rach is from Wyoming."

"Not quite. My mom recently moved there, but that

was only a few years ago. I'm actually from Sandpoint in northern Idaho."

"That's where I'm from, too," I added.

"Small world," Mia said.

"Super small world," Rachel said, hugging me again.

"What's with all the squealing?" Savage demanded as he strode toward us. The other bikers were naturally curious too, so they followed suit and came over.

"Rachel and I know each other from like, another lifetime ago," I said.

"Yeah." Rachel nodded. "Another lifetime ago."

I looked at her closely. Her eyes dimmed ever so slightly.

"I'm Linden," the blonde with pixie cut introduced, momentarily stealing focus. "Everyone calls me Doc."

"Nice to meet you."

A yellow lab ran up to Doc and almost knocked her over. "And this beast belongs to me. Speaking of beasts, anyone see my biker beast?"

"Boxer's handling the moonshine," Mia said.

"Of course he is," Doc said with a grin.

"What can I get you to drink, Doc?" Bones asked her.

"Sparkling water, please. Thanks." She smiled at him.

"Logan? Rach?" Bones asked. "Drink?"

"Same for me," I said.

Rach nodded in agreement.

Everyone began breaking off into smaller conversations so Rach used the opportunity to pull me away from everyone toward the picnic tables.

We each took a seat on opposite sides and faced each other.

She shook her head. "I can't believe you're here."

"I can't believe *you're* here," I fired back. "How did you get involved with a biker club?"

"I married one of them," she said wryly.

"Yeah?" I looked around. "Which one is yours?"

"None of them. My husband died."

"Oh, Rach, I'm so sorry. When?"

"Over a year ago." Her brown eyes saddened. She reached into her back pocket and pulled out her cell phone and showed it to me. "We have a son. His name is Cash."

I took her phone and looked at the background photo of her cell. "He's beautiful."

"Yeah." Her smile wobbled. "He is."

I handed the phone back to her. "I'm sorry, Rach."

She shrugged. "*C'est la vie.*"

I didn't want to pry any further—we'd only just reconnected. It didn't feel right.

"Where's Cash now?" I asked.

"With my mom. After my husband died, I moved back to Wyoming for a bit. But I never did like harsh winters. I was able to convince my mom to leave again and come back to Waco with me. She watches him when I want to come and hang out for a bit. It's nice having some free time."

"Nice." I nodded. "Yeah. A support system is good."

"So, what the hell are you doing here?" Rach demanded. Her grin was tempered but authentic.

"What the hell am I doing here," I repeated. "Jeez, it's a story."

Rach drummed her fingers on the table. "Good thing I've got time."

Chapter 23

"What a shit bag," Rach said after I told her about Knox.

"Major shit bag," I agreed. "Thank God for Tavy. She kind of gave me a way out. Have you met her yet?"

Rach shook her head. "Where are you staying? You need a place? I've got a spare room."

"You're so sweet," I said. "But no. I was staying here for the time being. Brooklyn just offered me the apartment over her bakery."

"You mean you'd rather live in your own apartment and sleep the night through instead of having a roommate with a baby that screams randomly in the middle of the night to wake you up?" she quipped.

"Pass." I laughed. "But I would love to meet your son. If that's okay, I mean."

"Of course it's okay." She reached across the table to squeeze my hand. "It's so weird. The last time I saw you, you were what? Twelve?"

I nodded. "We've both lived so much life between then and now, haven't we?"

"Seriously."

We fell silent for a moment and she pulled her hand away. She reached for her glass of sparkling water and ventured to ask, "How is Chase?"

"You already asked me that," I said with a slow grin.

She cleared her throat and her cheeks bloomed. "Damn, I was hoping that would slide under the radar."

"Still single, if that's what you were getting at."

"It wasn't," she protested. "But I'm surprised he's still single. He was such a good—"

"Please don't say lover. He *is* my brother."

She snorted. "No. I was going to say he's such a nice guy. Like, genuinely nice. Solid."

"That's why his last three girlfriends broke up with him. Apparently, they want men with a little more *edge*."

"I married a man with edge. I buried him too." Her tone was sharp, but then her expression softened. "I like to think that if Chase and I had met when we were a little older, my life would've taken a different turn."

"Is he the one who got away?" I asked.

"Hey, guys!" Savage called out. "Grub is ready!"

"Thank goodness. I'm hungry. I didn't eat breakfast," Rach said. "Come on, I've all but kidnapped you from the party. Let's get some food and you can get to know the Old Ladies."

"What are Old Ladies?"

"Biker lingo for wives and serious girlfriends of club members."

A little girl with blonde ringlets was throwing a temper tantrum and Darcy grabbed a plate of food and then the little girl's hand, and all but dragged her into the clubhouse.

"Crap," Rach muttered. "I'll be back."

She followed after Darcy and I wondered what was

going on, but my attention was diverted when Savage handed me a plate with a cheeseburger.

"Thanks," I said.

"Lemme know if it's cooked the way you want it," Savage said.

"It's perfect."

"You haven't tried it yet."

I picked it up and took a bite. "Delicious," I muttered around the beef.

Savage grinned.

I loaded up my plate with sides and then headed back toward the group of ladies. The conversation was put on hiatus as we all chowed down. I was halfway finished with my burger when Tavy came outside.

She hadn't stopped off at home to change and she was wearing a pair of lavender scrubs.

My best friend immediately beelined to me. I had a fork with some potato salad on it, and without a word or greeting Tavy reached over and picked up my cheeseburger and took a huge bite.

"If you'd waited two minutes, Savage would've had a fresh burger ready for you," I said.

"Can't." She chewed and swallowed. "Low blood sugar."

"I like you already," Sutton said to her.

"Thanks, I like you too. Whoever you are."

Sutton grinned. "I'm Sutton."

It was another round robin of introductions. Even though Tavy had been in town a few days longer than me, she'd been working most of the time and the Old Ladies, aside from Willa, hadn't come by the clubhouse.

"How's the apartment hunting? Wanna gouge your eyes out yet?" she asked.

"Actually, that's settled. Brooklyn is my savior," I said,

shooting the pregnant woman a look of gratitude. "She's got a vacant apartment over her bakery and she's offered to rent it to me."

"Bakery?" Tavy asked. "I need a bakery."

Brooklyn squinted in confusion. "I don't understand."

"Sorry. What I meant to say was I have a patient on bed rest post-op, and she *loves* scones. Like loves loves loves them. So, I thought if I could find a stellar scone it might make her not so crotchety. And I really need for her not to be crotchety."

"If I was laid up in bed post-op, I'd be crotchety too," Mia said.

Tavy nodded. "Yeah, but apparently she was crotchety before she had the surgery, so she's like doubled her dose of crabby. Plus, I'm hoping if I bring her a scone, she won't throw any more vases at me."

"You should get a new job," Allison said.

"It pays too well to quit." Tavy shrugged. "And I've got fast reflexes."

"If you're going to eat the rest of my burger, you have to bring me more chips," I said.

"Fair trade," Tavy said as she took another gargantuan bite.

"Chew," Doc said to her with a laugh. "I don't want to perform the Heimlich today."

After Tavy swallowed, she said, "It's okay, I've got like zero gag reflex."

Savage had just approached with his plate of food when he clearly heard Tavy's announcement.

She looked at him.

He grinned. "Hello, future wife."

Willa sniggered. "Smoke will kill you if you touch his daughter."

Smoke was several feet away talking to Viper and Kelp,

but when he heard his name, he sauntered over to us. "What will I do if what?" Smoke asked as he took a sip from his beer bottle.

"Nothing," Savage said quickly. "Oh, look. A tree. *Bye.*"

"My best friend has no sense of self preservation," Willa said wryly. To me, she said, "I've known Savage since we were kids. It feels like all I do is try to save him from himself."

"Hey, kid," Smoke said to Tavy, wrapping his arm around her. "I didn't say hi to you."

"Hi," she mumbled around a full mouth.

"Do you not eat regular meals?" Smoke inquired with a smile.

"Granola bars and energy drinks," Tavy said. She eyed his beer. "Can I have that?"

Smoke gave her his beer.

"You promised to refill the chips," I said to her.

"Right." Tavy nodded and then all but galloped off to the folding table laden with food.

Smoke and I looked at each other and then I hastily glanced away and met Brooklyn's gaze. Her eyes bounced to Smoke and then to me. A smirk appeared on her lips and she quickly covered her mouth with her hand.

Fuck.

I stood up from my chair. "Restroom," I announced awkwardly and then I dashed toward the house.

The screen door opened just as I was about to reach for the handle.

Rach had the little girl with blonde ringlets by the hand. "Logan," Rach said. "Have you met Lily?"

I looked down at the girl and smiled. "No. Hi, Lily."

"Hi," she said. "You have pretty hair."

"Thanks. So do you." I couldn't contain my grin.

"Why don't you ask Uncle Boxer for a cookie," Rach said to her.

"Okay!" Lily dropped Rach's hand and then dashed toward the playful biker who stood with Doc. I watched him scoop Lily up into his arms, and cart her over to the dessert section.

"Where's Darcy?" Mia called to Rach.

"Headache," Rach said. "She's laying down for a bit."

"I'm just going inside to use the restroom," I said. "I'll be back."

I didn't actually have to use the restroom; I just needed a moment to settle my nerves. Brooklyn had made it clear she could tell there was something between me and Smoke.

How was it that I'd been actively ignoring him, and yet in the few moments we spent together in the presence of others, we were completely obvious?

I wanted a glass of water and headed down the hallway as my phone buzzed in my back pocket.

My mother's name flashed across the screen.

"Hi, Mom," I answered, pivoting my direction and going out to the front porch instead.

"Hey. Just calling to check up on you."

I smiled even though she couldn't see me. "I thought you might."

"So. How're things? Any word from Knox?"

"Not since I changed my number," I said. "And things are good. I found an apartment."

"I thought you were going to live with Tavy."

"Her place is too small for both of us."

"Is the apartment in a safe neighborhood?"

"Yes." I rolled my eyes.

"Don't strain your eyeballs too hard when you roll them."

I chuckled. "How did you know?"

"Because I know you." She paused.

"What's up?" I pressed.

"Nothing. I just—how *are* you?"

"I'm fine, Mom," I said quietly. "Seriously. I'm okay."

"Huh."

"Huh what?"

"You're not as devastated as I thought you'd be. I don't know if that's a good thing or a bad thing."

I frowned. "Not sure I follow."

"If you'd really been head over heels in love with Knox, his betrayal would've cut you a lot deeper."

"Oh. I see."

"Yeah."

"Mama?"

"Yeah, baby?"

"Can I ask you something?"

"You can always ask me something."

I bit my lip, knowing when I asked the question, it was going to blast me open and put me under the parental microscope. But I forged ahead anyway. "When you were marrying Dad, did you have cold feet?"

"No."

"That was a fast answer," I said with a laugh.

She didn't chuckle. "I didn't have cold feet. In fact, I didn't have any doubts at all. I knew he was the one for me."

"So many people told me they had cold feet before they got married," I said.

"Like who?"

"Co-workers mostly."

"You gotta lead with your gut. I don't think a lot of people do that. It's easier for most people to let their brain lead. But if you let your brain lead, you start doing those pros and cons lists, and your brain can mess that up.

You might decide to be with someone who's good on paper, but wrong for you in all the ways that actually matter."

I pondered her words. "And if the guy on paper is completely wrong for you? What then?"

She paused. "You've met someone, haven't you?"

"What? No!" I protested, albeit a little too loudly. "Just a hypothetical."

"Well if it's hypothetical, I'd ask you how he makes you feel…"

Safe.

Seen.

Adored.

"Can I ask you something? And you'll be one hundred percent honest about it?" I asked.

"Sure."

"You promise?"

"Promise."

"You never liked Knox, did you?" When she didn't reply, I went on, "You promised to tell me the truth."

"You already know the truth. Otherwise, you wouldn't have asked me."

"Ouch," I joked.

"I never thought he was right for you," she said. "But it wasn't my place to tell you. When you have children you gotta let them make their own mistakes."

I shuddered at the thought of marrying Knox and finding out he was cheating on me after we had been legally bound to one another.

"I wonder if part of me stayed with Knox to prove to Dad that I wasn't wrong about him," I said quietly. "Only I *was* wrong about him. So wrong."

"That's a lot to unpack," she said with a laugh.

"I need a good long tea therapy session with you," I

said, suddenly so homesick for my family it made it hard to breathe.

"You can fly home any time you want," she said. "I'll make up your old bed and cook you all your favorite meals. Laundry, though… That's all on you."

"I know how this works. I come home and then you refuse to let me leave."

"You know I hate having you so far away."

My throat tightened. "Thanks. For always being there when I need you."

"Ah, LoLo," she crooned. "Thanks for still confiding in me. I know you have Tavy to turn to."

"Tavy's Tavy, and she's my best friend and she gets me. But you're my mom. No one loves me like you do."

"Stop that, or I'm going to cry."

I laughed softly. "Tea and FaceTime? Sometime this week? Just you and me?"

"I'd love that. I really would."

"I love you, Mom."

"I love you, too. Oh, and Logan?"

"Yeah?"

"Your new guy? Let it breathe. It might turn into something you don't expect."

My mom hung up before I could have the last word.

"How does everyone know?" I muttered.

My tail bone was numb from sitting on the porch steps, so I got up and went back inside.

Darcy was in the kitchen, in the middle of pouring a hefty amount of vodka into a red Solo cup.

When she saw me, she froze. And then a strained smile appeared across her lips. Her face was tense and her spine snapped straight.

"Logan. Hey."

"Hi." I gestured to the front porch. "I was just talking

to my mom on the phone. She was checking in. Doing what moms do."

"You must miss her."

"I do," I said. "Are you feeling better?"

"Hmm?"

"Your headache?"

"Oh. Right. Yeah. I'm fine now. Can I make you a drink?" she asked.

"No. I'm good. Thanks. I better get back out there before Tavy eats all the potato salad." With a smile and wave, I headed toward the hallway.

Something about Darcy was nagging at me, but I wasn't sure what. I didn't know her well enough to even have an idea of what was going on, but my antennae were up.

As I ventured out into the backyard, my eyes landed on Smoke.

"Logan!" Mia called. "Come here a second."

My attention immediately went to the petite brunette who was holding her daughter while she stood next to a man who loomed over them.

I walked to them, my gaze bouncing from Mia to the man.

"This is my husband, Colt," she introduced.

"Nice to meet you," I said.

"Same." A smile drifted across his face, softening the ruggedness of his features. "Mia was telling me you're an interior designer?"

I nodded.

"The club just bought an apartment building," he clarified. "The lobby needs an update. None of us know shit about design. Would you take a look? Maybe help us put together a plan?"

I shot Mia a glance.

"What?" she asked, widening her eyes.

To Colt, I said, "Sure. I'd be happy to take a look."

"Great." Colt smiled. "Smoke can show you the building."

Mia kissed Colt's cheek and then gestured with her chin at me to follow her.

"What are you doing?" I asked.

"Wondering if I should feed Scarlett the mashed peas or the sweet potatoes."

"Sweet potatoes," I said immediately. "And that's not what I meant."

"I'm not sure I follow."

"Joni asking my help with her kitchen? And now your husband asking my help with the lobby of an apartment building?"

"You have the skills and the know-how. It's nothing more than that. I swear. You're helping us out."

"Okay, if you say so."

"I do say so." She nodded. "But I am curious about something."

"Shoot."

"Have you ever thought about running your own design business?"

I paused. "No. Not really."

"Maybe you should." She shrugged. "Just a thought. Dare to dream. Reach for the stars, or whatever."

"Dare to dream." I snuck a quick look at Smoke. "Dare to dream."

Chapter 24

"Oh my God," I said to Brooklyn. "This is perfect."

Brooklyn grinned. "Yeah? You like it?"

"It's so freakin' cozy. And it smells like cake batter in here."

"One of the many perks of living over a bakery." Brooklyn dropped the keys into my palm. "Change whatever you want. I'm not married to any of the furniture or even the colors."

"No, it's seriously exactly as it should be."

The apartment over the bakery was what I needed. Over time, I could add personal touches, but for now, it was like walking into a warm hug. It was bright, cheerful, and homey.

Completely unlike the home I had shared with Knox.

"Come downstairs for a cup of coffee and a biscotti," Brooklyn suggested.

I locked up the apartment and followed her downstairs into the kitchen in the back of the bakery. A finished wedding cake rested on one of the large tables and it was truly a work of art.

I inhaled deeply and nearly shuddered.

"I know that look," a young woman with dark hair said as she came into the kitchen from the front of the bakery.

"What look?" I inquired.

"You just became a sugar junky." She grinned.

I laughed.

"Jazz, this is Logan," Brooklyn said. "She's going to be renting the apartment upstairs. Logan, this is Jazz. One of my best friends and business partners."

"Nice to meet you," I said.

"Likewise." To Brooklyn, she said, "Brielle just called. She's at the venue and the bride is having a meltdown about the cake. Apparently it doesn't look the way it was promised."

Brooklyn sighed. "The not-so-fun part of running your own business."

"You could delegate," Jazz said.

"We're in a growth phase," Brooklyn said. "I have to handle stuff like this myself."

"You refuse to slow down even though you need to."

"Now you sound like Slash," Brooklyn said. "I'm getting better about delegating other things."

Jazz snorted. "No, you're not."

A cell phone rang and Brooklyn reached into her apron pocket and pulled it out. She answered the phone. "Hi, love. Hold on a second."

Brooklyn angled the phone away from her mouth and said to me, "Sit and enjoy a cup of coffee. I might be awhile."

She headed in the direction of the back office and a moment later I heard the door shut.

"Come on," Jazz said. "I'll make you a coffee."

There was a lull of customers, but a few patrons sat with their laptops and half empty mugs at tables in the café. I took a seat at the counter in the corner, which had a direct line of sight to the fancy espresso machine.

"What would you like to drink?" Jazz asked.

"Surprise me."

She nodded and crouched down to the fridge and pulled out a gallon of milk. "So…"

"So," I said.

"You hung out at the clubhouse yesterday—barbecue, right?"

My brow furrowed. "Right. How did—"

"Brooklyn told me," she said with a smile. "And I'm assuming you got the third degree from all the Old Ladies."

"Third degree," I agreed. "Are they all so…"

"So *what?*"

"Welcoming."

"Hmm. They are to those they deem close to the club."

"Do you know them well?"

"Fairly well," she said. "Brielle and I get invited to a lot of club barbecues because of Brooklyn."

A few minutes later, Jazz placed a mug with a mountain of whipped cream on top in front of me. "This is called Witches Brew. It's got enough sugar to launch you to the moon and enough caffeine to make your teeth vibrate."

"Sign me up," I said with a laugh.

Jazz went to the bakery display and used the tongs to grab a few biscotti and put them on a plate.

The bell chimed, announcing the arrival of customers.

While Jazz tended to them, I dunked my biscotti and looked around the space. It was a perfect blend of industrial and homey. Very much like the apartment upstairs. There was exposed brick, and the walls behind the counter had been painted pastel pink.

Brooklyn came out of the office and shoved her phone

into her apron pocket. She easily moved behind the counter and worked with Jazz to tend to all the customers that had seemed to come out of nowhere.

"Whew," Brooklyn said when the rush had finally died down. "That was fun."

"We're like a well-oiled machine at this point," Jazz said to her. "We've worked long enough together that it's second nature."

"Is it always this busy?" I asked.

"Yeah," Jazz said with a grin.

Brooklyn's gaze dropped to the empty plate in front of me. "So, you liked the biscotti?"

"I did." I nodded.

"And the coffee?" Jazz prodded. "How did you like that?"

"I feel like I could push a train with my bare hands," I joked.

"Then my job here is done." She looked at Brooklyn. "You good if I take my ten?"

Brooklyn nodded.

"Did you call Brielle?" Jazz asked as she maneuvered around Brooklyn to get to the espresso machine.

"I did. I talked to the bride. I got it sorted. Her meltdown wasn't about the cake."

"What was it about?" I asked.

Brooklyn's lips twitched. "Commitment."

Jazz raised brows and pulled an espresso shot. "Cold feet right before she walks down the aisle? Shocker."

My mother's words floated back to me.

"I'll be back in a few," Jazz said as she picked up her espresso. "Call if you need help, though. I'll be out back."

"I love this space," I said to Brooklyn.

"Thanks." She beamed. "This part of the bakery used to be my dad's leather workshop. When he died, I converted it to a bakery and the upstairs office into a living space. We only recently bought the building next door and expanded." She paused. "You didn't ask for any of that information."

"No, but I appreciate the story all the same." I laughed. "When are you due?"

"Couple more months to go." She patted her belly. Brooklyn's face glowed with joy and contentment. Her wedding ring caught the sunlight shining through the big front window, reminding me that I'd worn an engagement ring not long ago.

How fast your life can change in the blink of an eye.

I quickly hopped off my stool. "Thanks for the coffee and biscotti. I think I'll get my suitcases up to the apartment."

"Oh. Yeah. Good idea." Brooklyn nodded. "Need help?"

I raised my brows. "Aren't you the pregnant one?"

She chuckled and gestured with her head in the direction that Jazz had disappeared. "Jazz can help."

"Nah. I'm okay. It's not a lot," I murmured. "I didn't bring much."

I took a deep breath when I got outside. It wasn't that Brooklyn's happiness made me uncomfortable. It just reminded me that I'd never been as happy with Knox as she was with Slash.

Why had I been willing to tie myself to a man who didn't bring unbridled joy into my life?

I popped the hatch of my car and then dragged out my first suitcase. An hour later I was pretty well unpacked, but I had no food in the fridge.

I hadn't ever lived alone. I'd gone from my parents' house directly to college where I shared a room and a suite with roommates, and then I'd moved in with Knox.

My phone rang, jarring me out of my pondering.

"I'm coming over tonight," Tavy said.

"Damn right you are," I said with a laugh.

"What are we doing for dinner?" she asked.

"You bring the pizza. I'll handle dessert."

∽

"I might've gone overboard," I said the moment Tavy stepped into the apartment.

She was holding a pizza box and looked around for a moment, her gaze landing on the coffee table that was covered with a plethora of pastries.

"I was going to say you didn't go far enough." She grinned. "Where can I set this?"

"Counter."

She set the pizza box down. "Well, give me the grand tour."

I chuckled. "This is pretty much it. But it's all mine."

"It's cute," she said. "And it came furnished?"

"Yep."

"Are you going to change anything about it?" she inquired, kicking off her slip-ons, showing off painted blue toenails.

"I don't know. Should I?"

"Well, don't you want to make it more *your* home than Brooklyn's? Not that she doesn't have a cute design aesthetic, but you're the interior designer. Don't you want to make it yours?"

"Eventually," I said. "But for now, I think we should eat."

"Plates?"

I grabbed the dishes from the cabinet and tore off two paper towels. "Beer is in the fridge."

"Great," she said. "You want one?"

"Sure. Thanks."

We ended up sitting on the floor and eating at the coffee table.

"How are you liking your place?" I asked Tavy.

She shrugged. "It's fine. I don't see myself being there a lot. So for now it's okay."

"I'm glad to hear that. You know what's weird? I feel more at home here in this tiny place than I ever did at Knox's massive house."

"Key word—Knox. That was never *your* house. You never changed anything about his space."

"He wouldn't let me," I protested.

She paused. "Seriously?"

I sighed and set my pizza aside. "I asked him a few times if we could change the color palate. Get a new couch. A new bed set. He brushed it off. He didn't want to change anything about it. So, yeah, it was definitely *his* house."

"Oh," she said quietly.

"Am I a total idiot?" I blurted out. "I mean, shit, Tavy…who stays with a man who won't even entertain the idea of changing the living space to make it their home instead of *his* home?"

"I don't think you're an idiot," she said softly. "But I don't know why you stayed with him as long as you did."

"I think I wanted to prove everyone wrong." I shook my head. "Stupid. It shouldn't matter what anyone thinks about the man I choose to marry. I should've been making that decision because I loved him and he was the right one. Not because I had something to prove."

"Want another beer? I mean, if we're unpacking the Knox stuff, I feel like it's a multi-beer conversation."

I shook my head. "No thanks, I'm good."

"I think I know what you need," Tavy said.

"Shots?" I teased.

She grinned. "No. A new guy."

"I don't need a new guy."

"Not to keep," she said. "But like a revenge fuck. Clean out all the pipes. Help you get your ego back."

"Not my style," I averred, even though I'd done just that only a few days ago.

"You don't have a style," she protested. "Jeez, Logan. There weren't many men before Knox, you know? Live a little. Now's the time to try new things. Like new dick."

"I'm not ready to date."

"Who said anything about dating?" Tavy asked. "I said new *dick*. Take a ride on the dick-mobile, have a bunch of orgasms. No commitment."

"I'm good, Tav." I smiled. "Let me heal in my own way, okay?"

She sighed. "Okay. I just don't want you to think that all men are bastards just because Knox cheated."

"I don't think all men are bastards," I assured her.

"Glad to hear it. When you're ready to get back on the horse, tell me. I'll be your wingwoman."

"I'll let you know," I said with a laugh. "This is good pizza."

"Very good," she said. "It's gonna take a while to find all our new spots."

"Something to look forward to."

"Yep."

"Now you," I said.

"Now me what?" she asked as she got up from her seat and walked into the kitchen.

"Any men on the horizon? Or are you still lusting over bikers you can't have?"

"Can't have? I can have anything I want—except soy. Makes my lips itch."

"Tavy."

"I know, I know," she groaned. She opened the pizza box. "Pursuing one of my dad's biker brothers isn't a good idea."

"Definitely not a good idea," I agreed.

"I just want one night with Raze," she said as she plopped two pieces onto her plate.

"Not Raze *and* Kelp?" I teased.

She grinned. "You know, I'm a big talker. I never would've gone through with it—even if both of them had been on the table—which I know they're not. Raze won't touch me anyway, I know he won't."

"Did you ask?"

Tavy snorted and brought her plate back to the living room and sat down. She put a piece of pizza onto my plate before replying, "Did I ask? No. I know what he'd say, and I'm not really in the mood for rejection. It would just make it weird. So I flirt and make sure to wear really tight jeans around him—and I *definitely* make sure my dad isn't anywhere in the vicinity so he can't see what's going on."

"You're a sneak," I said with a laugh.

"If my dad had a girlfriend, I think that would do a lot for my chances with Raze. If he wasn't always paying attention to me when I was around, I could go in for the kill."

"You're a seductress and a huntress."

"Damn right. I think I'm going to set Dad up with one of my nurse co-workers."

The pepperoni in my stomach suddenly felt like a ball of grease.

"Does he want to date?" I asked, hoping I sounded curious instead of jealous.

"I don't know if he does," she said.

"Then maybe you shouldn't butt into his social life."

She frowned. "I'm not butting in."

"You're talking about fixing your father up with someone you work with and you're not even sure that he's open to dating someone…"

"He hasn't dated someone seriously since my mom," she said. "I want him to be happy."

"I know you do." My spine unbent. "Just like you want me to be happy. Right?"

She blinked. "Oh, I see. You're calling me Captain Butt-inski. Aren't you?"

"If the captain's hat fits…"

"Okay, okay, I'll back off."

"Tell me more about what it is about Raze that does it for you," I said with a grin. "I'm really curious."

"I think he's hot." She shrugged. "And I'm pretty sure it's even more delicious because he's forbidden. I want what I can't have. I want the damn apple."

"What apple?"

"You know, the apple. Garden of Eden. Temptation. Just knowing Raze is there, reminding me of a juicy, delicious apple…that looks good in a pair of jeans."

"The age thing doesn't bother you?" I asked. "Isn't he like, the same age as your dad?"

"I don't think of my dad as old," she said. "And Raze is a few years younger than my dad."

"How do you know?"

"I asked him."

"Sly." I chuckled.

"Right?"

"I admire you, Tavy."

"You do? Why?"

"Because you're fearless," I said.

"Fearless? No. I'm not fearless. If I was fearless, I would go after Raze in spite of my dad standing in the way."

"Okay. There is that. But for the most part? You're fearless. How do you do it? How do you live your life that way?"

She paused a moment as she pondered, and then she said, "I guess I'm more afraid of living with regrets than the fear of not going after what I want. And it's not being fearless. I think it's about doing it in spite of the fear. Overcoming the fear. You know?"

"No, Tav." I met her eyes. "I don't."

Chapter 25

When I told Brooklyn I was a heavy sleeper and the early morning delivery trucks wouldn't bother me, I ended up cursing myself.

For the first time in forever, I actually heard the street traffic.

With a cracked eyelid, I looked at my cell phone. Just shy of 5:30 AM.

I kicked off the covers and sat up. I went to the bathroom and washed my face, threw my hair into a messy bun, and went down to the bakery.

The bakery smelled like fresh bread and sugar and there was already a short line of customers. Women in pencil skirts and men dressed in suits. They would be taking their coffees and pastries to go.

I got up to the counter.

Jazz raised a brow. "Someone's an early riser."

"Not normally," I commented with a grin. "I'll have a vanilla latte please."

"You got it," she said. "Was it the delivery truck that woke you?"

"Yep." I dropped a few bucks into the tip jar. "Do you work every morning?"

"Not every morning. Four days a week," she said as she stood at the espresso machine. "I like it actually. Usually done by three and I have the rest of the day to myself."

"Sounds okay, if you're a morning person, that is."

"Yeah, I am. What's on tap for you today?"

"Not much," I admitted. "I have some work to do, but other than that, I'm free."

"Brielle's off today. And I'm done at two. You want to hang out?"

"I'd love to," I said.

Jazz handed me my drink.

"See ya later." I took my coffee and headed back upstairs.

I answered emails and made a few product lists for clients. It wasn't even 8:00 AM by the time I was finished. As I polished off the last of my lukewarm latte, I began thinking about working for myself.

Mia had planted a seed. I wondered if she—and the club—would help with word-of-mouth advertising. Organic, word-of-mouth advertising was still the most powerful force on Earth for a business. I'd learned that from my dad, who still got most of his customers that way.

I couldn't sit around waiting for Jazz to get off work, so I looked up the nearest gym.

It was within walking distance.

Maybe I could work out my plan on the treadmill.

∼

My phone rang as I exited the gym and I pressed the screen to answer.

"Hello?"

A woman with a stroller approached the gym and I held the door open for her.

"Logan." Smoke's voice teased my ear, instantly causing shivers to work their way up my spine.

The grateful mother smiled as she wheeled the stroller inside.

"Uh, hi," I said to Smoke.

"You busy?"

"I just got done at the gym."

"You work out?" he asked.

"Sometimes…"

Silence reigned on the other end of the phone.

"Can I help you with something?" I demanded.

He sucked in a breath. "I was going to ask if you wanted to check out the club's investment property this afternoon."

"I've got plans this afternoon."

"With who? Bones?"

As I walked toward the bakery, I couldn't stop the slow grin appearing across my lips. "You jealous?"

"If I said yes, would that make you happy?"

Dangerous territory.

"I don't have plans with Bones," I said, not answering his questions. "Jazz gets off work at two and I'm going to hang out with her and Brielle."

"Ah."

"I can see the property tomorrow, though."

"Four o'clock okay?"

"Yeah, that's works."

"I'll come to you. Then we'll take your car."

"Sounds good."

"Okay."

"Okay."

There was a slight pause.

"Well, I'll see you tomorrow then," he said finally.

"Tomorrow," I agreed. "Smoke?"

"Yeah?"

I took a deep breath. "I like that you're jealous."

I hung up before he could reply.

Still grinning, I walked into the bakery. Willa and Mia were sitting with Jazz at a table in the corner, along with a beautiful redhead I didn't recognize.

"Logan," Jazz called out, waving me over.

"Did you just work out?" Willa asked. "You're flushed."

"Yep."

"Hi, I'm Brielle," the redhead introduced.

"Oh, hey!" I looked at Jazz. "You told me two, and that Brielle wasn't working today."

"I did," Jazz said. "But the four of us are planning Brooklyn's surprise baby shower, so Brielle came early to discuss the menu, the cake. Stuff like that."

"Fun," I said.

"You and Tavy are invited," Willa said.

"Oh," I said, feeling warm inside. "That's nice. Is there a registry?"

"Sure is," Brielle said.

Mia smiled and picked up her phone. "I'll text you the link."

"Thanks."

"Go shower," Jazz said. "We'll be finished with all of this by the time you're done, then Brielle and I will show you around."

"Take her to Leather and Ink," Willa said. "If she's gonna run with a biker club, she needs to dress the part."

"I'm not running with a biker club," I protested.

"No?" Mia asked, raising her brows. "Then why is Bones telling everyone who will listen that he's pursuing you?"

I blinked and slowly collapsed into a vacant chair. "Why would he do that? Bones and I—there's nothing there. Sure, he's flirted with me since I got here and offered to show me around, but that's just flirting. It isn't even a thing."

"Clearly he has other ideas on the matter," Willa said.

"But *why*?" I demanded.

"Uh, maybe because you're hot?" Jazz suggested.

"And you've got freckles right across the bridge of your nose," Brielle pointed out.

My hand hastily went to my nose. "What's that got to do with anything?"

"It makes you look innocent. And corruptible," Brielle said.

"And you've got this vulnerable thing going on," Mia added. "Like you need to be protected."

Willa nodded. "That's like, biker bait."

"Totally," Mia added.

"My head is spinning," I murmured.

"You really aren't interested in Bones?" Mia asked.

I shook my head.

"What about one of the other guys?" Mia pressed.

"Don't tell her anything," Jazz warned with a teasing smile. "You never tell one of the Old Ladies if you have a crush on someone. They talk amongst each other, and then before you know it everyone knows your business."

"They're also like busy-body matchmakers," Brielle added.

"We're not busy-bodies," Mia protested. "And we don't gossip."

Jazz pinned her with a stare.

"Okay, so we gossip. But not maliciously. And only so we can get people together so they make cute little biker babies. It's for the common good," Mia said.

Willa snorted. "You guys were relentless when Duke and I were getting together."

"It worked though, didn't it?" Mia flashed a grin. "You got married. You took his last name. And now you're pregnant. See? Job well done."

"I don't know why you're opening up another bar," Brielle said. "You should offer match-making services instead. I'd hire you. My dating life is shit."

"You've got three protective older brothers. Of course your love life is shit," Jazz said.

"Oh, I hear that," I said to Brielle in commiseration. "I'm the youngest of five and the only girl."

"How did you ever get a date?" Brielle asked.

"I went to college in another state," I said with a grim smile. "And then fell in love with a cheating bastard. Protective older brothers aren't always a bad thing."

"I need to pick your brain," Brielle said. "I need to know how to escape the older brother problem. My brothers scare off any man I bring home."

"Maybe you're bringing home the wrong men," Jazz said.

I rose from the table and looked between Jazz and Brielle. "Give me an hour to shower and get ready?"

"Sure thing," Jazz said.

"Mia, will you give me Bones' number before I go?"

I wasn't even halfway up the stairs when I had my phone out and I was dialing Bones.

"Well, hey there, babe. I was wondering when I was going to hear from you."

"Did you or did you not tell everyone in the club that you're pursuing me?"

"I did." His tone was pleasant, downright amused.

"Bones, you and I both know there's nothing sexual between us."

"*We* don't know that. In fact, I think we owe it to ourselves to find out. Besides, I offered to show you around town and you took me up on the offer."

"I just broke up with my fiancé."

"I'll help you get over him."

"I don't want you," I seethed.

"I know that. You want Smoke."

My eyes widened even though he couldn't see me. "I don't want Smoke."

"Sure you do." He laughed. "And my boy totally wants you back."

"Even if I did—and he did—which we don't—we can't be together."

"Why not?"

"Tavy."

"She's an adult. She'll get over it. Babe, both of you are shit liars. You get that, right? Like, every time you're both in the same space, you can't stop staring at each other. It's only a matter of time before Tavy finds out you guys hooked up on the way to Waco."

I gasped. "How did you know that?"

"I didn't. But you just confirmed what I thought."

I groaned. "Bones, *please*. Please don't tell anyone..."

"Your secret is safe with me."

"You swear?"

"On my life," he said, suddenly temperate. "I keep my promises. And if you want me to keep your confidence, I will."

"Thank you," I murmured. "Why are you doing this?"

"Doing what?"

"This big show of pursuing me. Is it just to piss off Smoke?"

"Let me ask you something," he said instead of answering.

"Okay…"

"You never actually wanted me to show you around town, did you?"

"No."

"Then why did you say yes?"

I sighed. "Because Smoke warned me away from you…"

"So, to piss him off, you said yes to my offer?"

"Yeah."

He let out a laugh. "My boy wants you. I'm just helping move things along."

"Can you just do me a favor?" I asked.

"What?"

"Don't feed into this anymore," I said. "I'm not ready to jump into another relationship. And even if I was, playing around with my best friend's father would not be the way to do it. A lot of people could get hurt here. So just drop it."

He was silent for long enough that I worried the call had cut out, but then he said, "A lot of people could get hurt? Or *you* could get hurt?"

It was the second time that day that I hung up on a man.

Chapter 26

"I can't wear these," I announced from the privacy of the dressing room at Leather and Ink.

"Why not? What's wrong with them?" Brielle asked. "Are they uncomfortable?"

"Are they too tight?" Jazz inquired.

With a sigh, I pulled back the curtain to show them. "I look like Olivia Newton John in *Grease*. They had to sew her into her leather pants, you know."

"Really?" Jazz asked. "I had no idea."

"Fun little movie trivia fact for ya," I said.

"Turn," Brielle commanded.

I dutifully twirled.

"Well, it's official," Brielle said with a sigh. "I've got to get uglier friends."

I snorted out a laugh.

"You've got a nice ass, Logan. I know we just met, but I feel honor bound to tell you that," Jazz said with a grin.

"Thanks." I shook my head. "But these are going back on the rack."

"No!" Brielle protested. "You can't put them back. They look *so* good on you."

"I'm on display. I don't like it."

"That is *exactly* why you need to buy them," Jazz said.

"They'll just sit at home in my closet. I'll never wear them. And every time I look at them, I'll feel guilty for spending money knowing I'd never wear them."

"It's just a pair of leather pants," Jazz said with a frown. "What's the big deal?"

"The big deal is that I don't wear stuff like this."

"Stuff like what?" Brielle asked.

"Stuff that shows off my…"

"Junk in the trunk?" Jazz supplied.

Brielle exchanged another look with Jazz before focusing on me. "What's this really about?"

"I hear his voice in my head," I blurted out.

Jazz's brow furrowed. "Whose?"

"My ex." I sighed.

"Let me guess. He didn't want you to *display* yourself," Brielle said gently.

I absently rubbed my wrist as if I could still feel his biting grip on my skin. "We fought about it one night over some stupid party for his work. He said one of his colleagues was flirting with me because I looked like a slut."

I flinched at the memory of his ugly tone.

"Please don't look at me with pity," I said, my gazing bouncing between them.

"Never pity," Jazz said.

"Nope," Brielle agreed.

"But hearing all that only makes me want to encourage you to buy them. To prove a point," Jazz said.

"I'm with Jazz on this one. Plus, it just makes sense since you'll be on the back of a motorcycle soon."

"When will I be on the back of a motorcycle?" I demanded.

"Bones?" Brielle asked.

"Back to that, are we?" I shook my head. "I'm not into Bones."

"Why not? He's hot," Jazz teased.

"He's not my type," I said.

"He's a super-hot biker in the prime of life who clearly wants to pursue you like a wild animal, and he looks great in leather. That's not your type?" Brielle asked.

"*Down girl*," Jazz said with a laugh.

"I need to get laid," she mumbled.

"Yeah, you do," Jazz agreed.

"Tell you what," I said. "I'll buy the pants, but only if we stop talking about me, and find Brielle a way to get laid."

"Can we do it over margaritas?" Brielle asked.

"And nachos," Jazz added.

My phone chimed in my purse. "I'll be out in a second." I stepped back into the dressing room and pulled the curtain closed. Before I changed out of the leather pants, I checked my cell.

Edith had sent a photo with her new granddaughter decked out in a pair of booties she'd knitted. I fired off a quick response. Her reply was just as fast.

EDITH

When do I get to knit booties for you and Smoke?

"Fuck."

"Everything okay?" Jazz called.

"Oh, yeah, fine."

I shoved my phone back into my purse and quickly changed. I held up the leather pants. I was no longer in a relationship with Knox. I didn't have to let him dictate what I wore.

But how was I going to stop hearing him in my head?

I'll drown him out with new friends, a new apartment, and a new life.

And hopefully, in time, his voice—and all the pain he'd caused me—would fade.

～

"Okay, the hostess knows you by name," I said once we were seated in the booth.

"We come here at least once a week," Jazz explained. "Twice if it's been a rough week."

"And it's been a rough week," Brielle explained. "Pitcher of margs?"

"Yep." Jazz nodded.

I shook my head and reached for a menu. "None for me, thanks."

"You're not like, on a cleanse, are you?" Jazz asked.

"Because that would be totally okay," Brielle voiced.

"No." I laughed. "No cleanse. Just…the last time I drank hard liquor, Tavy and I got arrested and her dad had to bail us out of jail. Besides, I don't feel like another hangover."

"Arrested?" Jazz raised her brows. "For what?"

I told them the story.

"We need to meet this Tavy character," Jazz said.

"She *is* a character," I assured them. "And my best friend since college. She's my *I know your every secret and I can predict your next move* kind of best friend."

Not all my secrets…

"We're that way," Jazz said, gesturing to Brielle.

"Friends since high school. I'm like part of their family. Guac?"

I nodded.

"And queso," Brielle added.

The server came by and we ordered drinks and appetizers.

"So, if you're not going to date Bones," Brielle said. "Does that mean you have another biker in mind?"

I rolled my eyes. "I'm not going to date a biker."

"Excellent!" Brielle straightened her spine, leaned over to the chair next to her, and began rummaging through her purse. She pulled out her cell phone. "You should date one of my brothers. I have three of them to pick from—"

"She's fresh out of a relationship," Jazz said. "I doubt she's ready to date anyone."

"Jazz is right," I agreed. "But I'm still curious."

Brielle scrolled through her phone and then showed me the screen. "That's Roman. He's the oldest."

I nodded. "Handsome."

"He does nothing for you physically. Got it." Brielle grinned and swiped. "This is my brother Virgil. He's the playful one."

"Totally Tavy's type," I suggested.

"Oh, good to know." Brielle swiped again. "And this is Homer."

"The grumpy, surly, pain-in-the-dick one," Jazz supplied, reaching for her margarita.

"*Hey*, I'm trying to sell it here," Brielle snapped.

Jazz shrugged. "She'll learn soon enough when she meets him. Homer's an ass."

"He's not an ass." Brielle glared at her best friend. "He's just…"

"An ass?" Jazz supplied.

Brielle's phone rang. "Speak of the devil." She pressed

a button and put the phone to her ear as she shoved back from the table. "Hello?"

She strode away to take the call, leaving me with Jazz, who was staring into her glass.

"So, you're in love with Homer, huh?" I asked gently.

Jazz's head shot up. "*What?* No. I'm not in love with Homer."

I raised my brows.

"Please don't say anything to her," she said, pitching her voice lower. "Not that it matters. Homer won't date me. Much to my dissatisfaction. Pining for someone who doesn't want you sucks."

She swallowed a few gulps of her margarita.

Without a word, I took her hand and gave it a squeeze.

Brielle returned to the table, her phone clutched in her hand. "They're joining us. As soon as Virgil finishes with his last customer for the day." To me she said, "They own Three Kings Tattoo Parlor. They ink all the Tarnished Angels."

"Ah," I said. "That's the connection. I was wondering."

"You should call your friend," Jazz said to me. "Might as well make this a party."

I grinned. "Parties are good."

Two hours, three pitchers and four rounds of nachos later, Tavy looked at me and said, "I think moving here was the best decision either of us could've made."

I grinned and reached for my glass of water. Everyone else at the table—including Brielle's brothers were drinking margaritas. Spirits were high along with a healthy dose of good-natured sibling bickering.

Brielle threw an errant chip at Virgil, causing Roman to laugh. Homer sat by and glowered, sneaking glances at Jazz when he thought she wasn't looking.

But I was looking.

And their dynamic was fascinating.

Even more fascinating, Brielle seemed completely oblivious to her best friend's feelings about her brother.

"Stop!" Virgil said, holding up his hands to fend off the onslaught of Brielle's chip attack. "I never would've told you if I thought you were going to react like this."

"Plus, we kind of assumed you already knew," Roman added.

"*Already knew?*" Brielle demanded, her cheeks pink with rage. "You're telling me I didn't have a date to my senior prom because you threatened all the boys in my class?" She looked at Jazz. "Did you know?"

Jazz's eyes widened and she opened her mouth to answer, but Homer spoke up. "No, she didn't know. If she knew, then she would've helped you find a date for the prom."

Brielle rose from her chair. Her porcelain skin was flushed with anger. "You guys are out of control. Any man I bring home, you scare away."

"No one is good enough for you." Roman's brow furrowed. "And if a man can't take the heat from us, then he's *really* not good enough for you."

Our table was drawing attention, but Brielle didn't care. She was on a roll. Twenty-five years of pent-up anger at not being able to live her life on her terms was coming to a head.

"I've got to get out of here." She yanked her bag off the corner of her chair with such force that she knocked the chair over onto the floor.

"You didn't drive," Roman reminded her.

"And Jazz is too buzzed to take you home," Virgil said.

Brielle looked helplessly at Jazz who shot her a look of apology.

"I'll drive you," I offered. "I'm sober."

Brielle gratefully nodded. "Thank you. Don't bother with the bill. These goons can pay."

I looked at Tavy and mouthed *sorry*.

"It's fine," she whispered back.

Brielle marched out of the restaurant and I followed at a slower pace. I looked over my shoulder at the table, noting that Homer had leaned closer to Jazz and he was staring at her with an intense expression—which she was purposefully attempting to ignore.

It was late afternoon, and the fall breeze tugged at my hair.

Once we were in the car, I asked, "Where am I taking you?"

"To a different planet," she muttered. "I guess you can drive me home. Jazz and I actually live together."

"That sounds like fun." I handed her my phone to plug in the address.

"Very fun," she said. "I love my brothers, but they drive me crazy sometimes."

"I get it. Believe me, I get it."

She sighed. "I hate to admit this, but they have a valid point. If a guy can't handle the heat, then he's not strong enough to be in my family."

"Maybe you're not really mad at them."

"Oh, I'm mad at them," she said lightly.

"Yeah, but maybe you're also mad because you haven't found a man who can go toe-to-toe with them; who can stick it out."

"I know who could stick it out—a biker." She rubbed her third eye and thought for a moment. "Actually, I talk a big game but I don't really want to get involved with a Tarnished Angel."

"No?"

"No. They don't really scream *bring me home to your*

parents, you know? Even though they're cleaning up their image, they aren't what I'd call shining beacons of morality. And it doesn't matter how many clinics they fund or charities they start, they'll always be on the other side of the law."

Brielle was clearly intoxicated and running her mouth, so she had no idea how her words were affecting me.

"I thought the club wasn't involved in shady shit anymore," I said.

She shrugged. "I don't know if they are or not. I'm not part of the club—pun intended. I've heard my brothers talk though, when they thought I wasn't around."

I frowned. "What did you overhear?"

Brielle's phone buzzed in her bag, effectively derailing our line of conversation. She fished out her cell and her fingers flew over the screen. It wasn't until I was pulling up to her apartment complex that I finally had her attention again.

She unlatched her seatbelt. "I'm off tomorrow. So is Jazz. Come over for breakfast."

"Breakfast sounds great." I smiled. "Sleep off the hangover if you can."

"I'll try."

She climbed out of the car and waved as she headed inside.

I drove back to my new apartment, turning down the wrong streets because I was thinking about what Brielle had said. What ties did the club have? Why did I want to know? Staying away from Smoke—and the club—seemed like a good idea. A safe idea. I didn't know what they were involved in, but if Brielle's words had any merit, I needed to steer clear.

The next morning, I knocked on Jazz and Brielle's apartment door. A moment later, Jazz answered. Her hair was in a lopsided ponytail, and she was dressed in pair of loose pants and a tank top.

"You're not wearing pajamas," Jazz said in way of greeting as she took the bakery box from my hands.

"I didn't know I was supposed to," I said. "Besides, I've already been to the gym, so I'm showered and dressed for the day."

She stepped back and let me in. They lived in a loft-style apartment built into an old warehouse. It was one large, open room with high ceilings and big windows.

"You've already gone to the gym? Man, you've had a day already and I just woke up." She held up the box of baked goods. "Thanks for this."

"Least I could do," I said with a smile as I set my purse down by the door. "Perks of living above a bakery. Where's Brielle?"

"Brielle isn't home yet."

I blinked. "She's not *home* yet? But I drove her here yesterday."

"Yeah." Jazz rubbed her third eye. "By the way, your friend Tavy is awesome."

"I think so too. So, Brielle?"

"Juice? I've got grapefruit and orange."

"Can you mix them?" I asked.

"Weird, but sure."

I sat down on a kitchen stool while Jazz moved around the space. "So, after you guys left, the five of us went to a bar. I got a text from Brielle sometime around nine saying she'd gone out and would be back late. I got home around midnight and she wasn't here. I sent a text to check on her and thankfully she replied. She said she'd see me in the morning. Only now it's morning and she's still not home."

Jazz placed my drink in front of me.

"And you have no idea where she went?"

"Nope."

"Or who she was with?"

"Nope."

"You worried about her?" I asked.

"Yes. She wasn't in a good headspace and I—I just hope she hasn't done anything she's going to regret."

As if on cue, the front door opened and Brielle strode inside. She wore a teeny black dress that left little to the imagination. Her red hair must've been curled at some point but it was flat now, and she had raccoon eyes.

Jazz's mouth dropped open. "You got laid!"

"I don't kiss and tell," Brielle said, but a triumphant grin split her face.

"Oh my God!" Jazz jumped up and down. "I want to hear everything!"

"I missed all the fun last night," I said lightly. "I was asleep by eight thirty."

"Grandma, what are we going to do with you?" Jazz demanded.

"Though, to be fair, I did have several missed texts from you," I pointed out. "But my phone was on silent so I didn't get them until this morning."

"Tavy warned me that texting you to come out was a lost cause. She said when you were home, *you were home*, and that there was no getting you out of the house after that."

"Yep."

While Jazz and I had been talking, Brielle opened the pastry box and dove into it.

"Don't eat the cardboard," I joked.

She shot me a grin.

"Okay, seriously. I need details. Where did you go? Who did you do?" Jazz asked.

"Not telling," Brielle said after she swallowed a bite.

"*Why not?*" Jazz demanded. "I'm your best friend."

"You also get drunk with my brothers and get incredibly loose-lipped. I know that about you. I accept that about you. But you'll spill, and I want to keep my personal life personal."

Jazz pouted. "Damn me and my big mouth. I want to know!"

"Is it going to happen again?" I inquired, curious beyond measure.

"Nope. One and done. He gave me exactly what I was looking for." Brielle walked over to the fridge and pulled out the milk carton. She opened it and drank right from it.

"Brielle," Jazz moaned.

"What? There's barely any left." Brielle polished off the last of the milk and then tossed the carton into the garbage.

"Did you go home with him?" Jazz asked.

Brielle paused. "I did not."

"Please, please, please tell me you didn't have sex in a club bathroom," Jazz said.

"I did not have sex in a club bathroom," Brielle said.

The apartment door opened and Homer strode inside, carrying a small white dog.

"Um, excuse me. You don't live here," Brielle said. "You might want to learn how to knock."

Jazz walked over to Homer and took the ragamuffin dog and cuddled it close. "Homer time-shares a dog with us since he lives in the building," Jazz said. "This is Fluffernutter. He was a stray we rescued. For some reason he really enjoys snuggling Homer."

The dog licked Jazz's face in greeting.

"Where have you been all night?" Homer's gaze landed on his sister.

"Out," she said.

"Out where?"

"Out *none of your beeswax*," Brielle said. "We're having a girls' breakfast. You can go home now."

Jazz opened her mouth to say something and Brielle looked at her. "Before you say something, don't."

Jazz immediately closed her mouth.

"Bye, Homer," Brielle said pointedly.

Homer glowered, but seemed to realize he wasn't going to get the information he wanted, so he left. The door thudded as it shut behind him.

"Say nothing," Brielle stated. "He isn't gone. I can't hear any footsteps."

"I'll cook while you shower," Jazz said to Brielle.

"You're a peach." Brielle reached for the dog in Jazz's arms. The dog jumped toward Brielle who gave him a quick snuggle.

"Nothing is ever chill with you guys, is it?" I asked.

"Drama keeps the blood flowing," Jazz said. "You like hollandaise?"

Chapter 27

SMOKE
> I'm downstairs.

SMOKE'S TEXT came through as I was putting the finishing touches on my eyelashes.

Though I knew I shouldn't have taken as long as I had with my appearance, I'd done it anyway. With one final look in the mirror, I turned away. I didn't care if it looked like I tried. I wanted Smoke to see me at my best. I wanted Smoke to know that I'd taken the time, because I needed to see his eyes flash with heat when he looked at me.

Smoke was standing at the bakery counter having a conversation with Brooklyn. He said something that made her laugh and nod her head eagerly.

Smoke's gaze drifted to mine and suddenly we locked eyes.

"Hey," I greeted as I strode toward them.

"Hi," he said.

I turned to Brooklyn. "I didn't know you were coming in today."

"I wasn't supposed to," she said. "But I can't seem to stay away. Slash is blowing up my phone telling me not to stay too long."

"I was telling Brooklyn that we'll find a way to keep Slash busy so he's not ragging on her all the time about keeping off her feet," Smoke said.

"I think it's sweet," I said with a small smile.

"I do too," Brooklyn agreed. "But don't tell Slash. You give that man an inch and he'll take a mile. You guys are checking out the new property today, yeah?"

"Apparently," I said. "Can I get a vanilla latte to go?"

"Sure thing," Brooklyn said as she turned her bulk toward the espresso machine. "Anything for you, Smoke?"

He pulled out his wallet. "Just a black coffee for me. Thanks."

While Brooklyn made us our coffees, Smoke said to me, "How are you liking your new place?"

"I like it a lot," I said.

"You don't have to lie," Brooklyn said over her shoulder. "You can be honest even though I'm standing right here."

I chuckled. "I am being honest. I love the apartment. It needs some of my own touches added to it, but I'll get there in time."

"So, you like it better than the clubhouse?" Smoke asked with a slow grin.

"I like it better than the clubhouse. Not that you guys aren't fun, but I have my own bathroom. That goes a long way."

Brooklyn set the coffees down in front of us. "Put your money away."

"If you insist." Smoke put his wallet back into his pocket. To me he said, "You ready?"

I nodded and grabbed my vanilla latte. "Thanks for the coffee. Bye, Brooklyn."

Smoke followed me out of the bakery. When we were in the sunshine, he pulled his glasses off of his white T-shirt and put them on.

"I'm down this way." I gestured with my coffee and we headed toward my car.

"You look good," he said.

A thrill of pleasure shot through me.

"Do I?" I feigned casually.

"You know you do," he said with a laugh.

I bit my lip to stifle a grin and glanced at him. "Still nice to hear."

"Don't get me wrong, you do look good. I meant what I said, but there's something else about you…"

"What do you mean?"

"I don't know. A lightness. An ease."

"Oh." My pleasure deepened. "I think it's being here."

"Here? Waco?"

"Yeah. But mostly, I think I'm finding a rhythm. And people. Tavy and I hung out with Brielle and Jazz and Brielle's brothers last night and it was—"

"You hung out with the Jacksons?"

"Yeah. They remind me of my brothers so much. I miss my family," I said wistfully. "You don't think you need them and then your life falls apart and suddenly you just want your mom to hug you and your brothers to threaten to track down your ex and do him bodily harm."

"I thought you didn't want that," Smoke said as he came around the driver's side of my car.

"What are you doing?" I asked.

He opened the door. "Having manners."

I blinked. "Oh. Right." I climbed into my car and threw my purse into the back seat. I set my coffee into one of the cup holders and buckled my seatbelt. Smoke came around to the passenger side and climbed in.

"I don't *actually* want my brothers to go after Knox, but it's nice that they offered," I said, picking up the thread of conversation.

"Fair enough. So you had fun last night, huh?"

"Jazz and Brielle are great. I think because we're the same age—we're all in the same chapter of life. Tavy too."

"Christ," he muttered.

"What?"

"I'd forgotten how young you are. And then you say something that reminds me that you're my daughter's age."

"Don't start that again," I said lightly.

"Nah, I don't mean it the way it sounded. I guess, you seem older. More mature. And when it's just the two of us, I forget your age."

"I forget your age," I taunted. "Old man."

He snorted. "I'm coming into my prime."

"Yeah, you're prime silver-fox material."

He bent his head. "You wanna run your fingers through my hair and check for grays?"

It took all of my effort not to plow my fingers through his thick head of hair.

Smoke raised his head and inched closer to me—close enough that if we both leaned ever so slightly forward, our mouths would touch, our lips would connect, our tongues would meet.

"You have little lines," I said quietly.

"Yeah?"

I nodded. "At the corners of your eyes." I reached up and gently ran my thumb along his skin.

He froze.

"I like them. They make it seem like you've really

lived." My hand dropped into my lap and then I faced the front windshield. "Where are we going?"

He cleared his throat before he spoke. "I'll put the address into your phone."

"My phone is in my purse," I said. "In the back seat. Will you get it? I can't reach at this angle."

Smoke grabbed my purse and dug around for my phone. He found it and pulled it out. "You got a text."

"Thanks," I said, taking the phone from him. I glanced at the screen and sighed.

"Bad?" he asked.

"No. It's Edith." I unlocked my phone and glanced at her message.

"Then why are you sighing?" he asked.

"She point-blank asked when we were having a baby so she could start knitting baby booties."

Smoke let out a chuckle. "That's sweet."

"Sweet... I feel like a shit for not being honest with her and Harry. But I don't really have the heart to tell her the truth. I feel like it would crush her spirit."

I handed the phone back to Smoke so he could plug in the address.

"So, what have you been telling her?" Smoke asked.

"I've tried maneuvering around the conversation. I don't think it's working." I put the car into gear. "I think she just wants everyone to be happy and in love."

The maps program chirped a direction.

"There are worse things," Smoke said as he looked out the window. "There are definitely worse things."

∽

I snapped another photo of the empty apartment and then walked to the window to get a different view of the space.

"What's going to be done with this building? I mean, I know the club wants to keep it as an apartment complex, but for who? And why?"

Smoke leaned against the open doorway; his thumbs hooked into his jeans pocket. "It was Doc's idea, actually."

"Yeah?"

He nodded and pushed away from the frame. "The club's been wanting to get into pro bono work. Charity type stuff, you know? Help out the community. Doc runs the Wellness Clinic and it's been good for the town."

"Oh?"

"Yeah. Well, she mentioned to Colt that she keeps seeing patients who need a clean, safe place to land to help them transition out of their situations. Single mothers, women getting out of abusive relationships, that sort of stuff. They just need a place where they don't have to worry about money for a while or anyone showing up to hurt them. This vision is gonna be something like a halfway house—help women in bad positions get on their feet again and start a new life."

I looked at the space with a new perspective. "What a great idea."

"Yeah. It was unanimous when the club voted on it. And the Old Ladies loved the idea too."

"Did they get to vote on the idea also?" I asked.

"No. Just the brothers. It's club business."

"Which means?"

"We don't involve our women in business."

"But you told them about it…"

"*After* we voted."

"So…is this the new direction of the club? The non-shady stuff?"

He rubbed the back of his neck. "I shouldn't have said anything about what the club was involved in."

"Why not? It sounds like it'll help the community."

"Look, we're not good men, okay? Just because we helped get Doc's clinic set up and we're doing this half-way house doesn't mean we can make up for the things we've done. We're the *Tarnished* Angels, get it?"

"I get it," I murmured, my mood souring. It was the reality check I needed. I cleared my throat. "So do all the apartments have the same layout?"

Smoke stared at me for a moment before nodding. "Either just like this or mirrored. You want to see one that's mirrored so you can get some photos?"

"Yeah. That'll help, for sure."

I moved past him into the hallway. He closed the door and then gestured to the apartment across the hall. It only took a few minutes to snap photos, and then we took the stairs down to the lobby floor. The entire building smelled musty and damp, like the air conditioning couldn't keep up with the Texas humidity. The paint was peeling, and the front desk looked like mold had set in years ago along the base of the wood.

"So, cupcake," Smoke drawled. "What do you think of the building?"

"It has potential."

He arched a brow. "What's that really mean?"

"Truth?"

"Truth."

"The truth is the club is going to have to spend a small fortune updating all the systems and fixing the damage I can see, and I've barely done a walk through, let alone a full inspection."

"We're prepared for that."

"Yeah?" I asked. "Because it looks to me like it would've been cheaper to buy a plot of land and build from scratch versus having to fix all the problems in a building that wasn't taken care of in the first place."

"Aside from the HVAC, what other problems are you seeing?"

"The walls and ceilings have water stains. I'm guessing it's either a leaky pipe that was never fixed properly or the roof has been patched and the patch failed during one of the many infamous Texas rainstorms. Water has nowhere to go except down and the path of least resistance. And the mold. There's definitely a lot of mold."

"The inspection came back clean of any mold."

"Look at the wood around the base of the desk," I announced. "Now look up near the water marks from the leak. This building has mold."

"Fuck," Smoke muttered.

"Whoever did your inspection hosed you," I said. "Sorry to be the bearer of bad news."

His jaw clenched. "*Motherfucker*."

"Real estate is a wild business," I said. "A lot of people cut corners and the so-called experts aren't even doing their due diligence."

"I'll talk to Prez," Smoke gritted out. "See how he wants to handle it."

The way he said *handle* made me think Smoke meant violence. I didn't like the anger rolling off him in waves, and I instantly took a step back.

His expression immediately cleared, and his mouth softened. "Hey."

"Hey," I croaked.

"I'm sorry."

I shook my head. "You have nothing to be sorry about."

"Did I scare you?"

"Yes."

"Then I have a reason to be sorry."

My shoulders slumped. "You went from zero to fist-clenching in just a few seconds, and I…"

"You don't have to explain." He exhaled in frustration. "We're out of our league here. With real estate, I mean."

"We all make mistakes."

"Yeah, but some mistakes are easier to rectify than others. And this mistake will cost a lot of money." He paused. "I shouldn't be telling you about our business."

"My lips are sealed. I won't say a word."

"I appreciate it."

"We should probably—"

"You hungry?" he asked suddenly.

I blinked. "Yeah."

"Let's grab dinner."

We walked to my car in silence. He opened the driver's side door for me and closed it once I'd gotten in.

I started the vehicle, but Smoke hadn't come around to the passenger side yet. He pulled out his cell, pressed a button, and then put the phone to his ear. Smoke began walking down the sidewalk away from the car so I couldn't hear the conversation. His expression said enough. I assumed he was talking to Colt.

After a few minutes, Smoke hung up and came back to the car.

"Everything okay?" I asked hesitantly.

Smoke nodded.

"What do you want to eat?" I asked.

"Your choice."

My phone buzzed and because it was connected to Bluetooth, the computerized voice chanted, "Call from Bones."

I silenced the call and hastily looked at Smoke.

"Why is Bones calling you?" Smoke demanded.

"Because he still wants to show me around town."

"I thought you were going to stay away from him."

"What gave you that idea?"

"Because I told you he wasn't a good guy."

"*You're* not a good guy," I pointed out. "And I didn't stay away from you, did I?"

"That's different."

"Why do you care if I spend time with Bones?" I pressed. "I'm an adult and I can make my own decisions."

He was silent for a long a moment and then he said, "You're right. Spend time with whoever you want."

"Fine, I will."

We drove back to the bakery in silence, and parted ways without so much as a goodbye.

Chapter 28

I set my dirty dinner plate into the sink and washed my hands. As I was drying them on a dishrag, the buzzer for the back door downstairs went off.

With a frown I went to see who'd shown up randomly without calling. I hadn't been expecting anyone, so I couldn't even imagine who it was.

I pressed the intercom button. "Hello?"

"It's me."

Smoke.

My heart suddenly tripped in my chest. "I'll be right down."

I threw on a pair of flip flops, grabbed my keys, and then went downstairs to let him in.

He stood in the doorway, illuminated by the overhead light. His dark eyes were never-ending pools of yearning.

"What are you doing here?" I asked quietly.

He grasped the back of my neck with one hand and with the other he clasped my hip and pulled me toward him until I was flush with his body.

"Fuck it," he growled, right before his lips covered mine.

His tongue thrust into my mouth, branding me with possession and heat.

I strained closer, wanting to press into him, wanting to wrap my legs around his hips while he dominated me.

"This is a bad idea," he said against my mouth.

"Terrible idea," I agreed.

He went back to kissing me, kissing me so deep I felt it all the way to my toes. My eyes rolled into the back of my head and my knees were in danger of giving out.

Smoke pushed me against the wall and suddenly his fingers were delving into my lounge pants. He slid his fingers into my panties and stroked my sex.

"Fuck. You're wet."

I peppered his jaw with small kisses and nodded, words stuck in my throat.

He sank his fingers into my body, pumping in and out until I was whimpering with need. The ache of pleasure bloomed between my thighs.

His thumb grazed my clit and my fingernails dug into his shirt as I rode out my orgasm.

My eyes flung open and I stared at the man I craved.

Smoke gently eased his hand from my pants and lowered his forehead to press against mine. "So, am I coming up, or what?"

I leaned closer and brushed his lips with mine. "Yeah, you're coming up."

He pulled away and shut the door behind us. We said nothing as we climbed the stairs. When we got into the apartment, Smoke closed the door and locked it. And then he strode toward me and took me into his arms.

"I haven't been able to stop thinking about how you taste," he growled, lowering his mouth to mine.

I opened to him immediately and sank into his touch. He scooped me up and carried me toward the bedroom. Smoke laid me down on the bed and then slowly stripped out of his clothes.

He pumped his erection slowly, his thumb teasing the crown of his shaft that glistened with pre-cum.

I was suddenly ravenous.

"Me first," I commanded, somehow feeling bold and brave.

I got up on all fours and crawled across the bed toward him and opened my mouth.

"Fuck," he moaned when he slid between my lips. He gently thrust into my mouth and gripped my hair.

I skated my fingers up and down his thighs while I pleasured him.

"God, your fucking mouth," Smoke growled. "I've missed your mouth."

I sucked harder and my hands cupped his testicles gently. I played with them, stroking, teasing while I took him deeper into my mouth. I lost sense of time while I made him moan.

"I'm gonna come," he rasped as his hands clenched my hair.

He was warm and salty and I swallowed every last drop of him.

Smoke released me and then eased out of my mouth. He collapsed onto the bed, his breathing rapid.

"Give me a few minutes to catch my breath and then I'll return the favor."

I chuckled and settled down next to him. "You're so giving."

"So are you."

I trailed my finger up and down his chest. "I couldn't help myself. I was overcome with lust."

"I've been driven insane by it the last week. Every time I thought about you, I got hard. I nearly rubbed myself raw thinking about you. Wishing you were in my bed."

I leaned over and kissed his stomach. "Poor baby. Guess I have to make it up to you."

"Guess you do." His hand grasped my thigh and he urged me closer. "Seems like we've got a problem here."

"Problem?"

"We can't stay away from each other."

"Ah." I smiled slowly. "The sex is just too good to say no to."

His hand slithered up my leg. "Two nights wasn't enough, clearly."

"Clearly."

"So, what if we do more of this?"

"More of what?" I asked.

Smoke sat up and grasped my elbows. Suddenly I was flipped onto my back and he was over me, a wicked grin on his face.

"More of this." His hand rested on the heat of my cleft.

I opened my legs to give him better access.

Smoke worked my pants off, baring me to his warm gaze. He leaned over and licked me until I shuddered. "More of *this*," he whispered.

His head went back between my legs and I closed my eyes until I was bucking beneath him, riding out my pleasure on his tongue.

When the tremors faded, I opened my eyes to find Smoke staring at me, his face still between my legs. He slowly licked my release from his lips and another shiver went through me.

"Why did you come back? Does this have anything to do with Bones?"

"If I said yes?"

I smiled. "I shouldn't like you jealous…"

"But you do."

"I should say no," I said.

"Why should you say no? Because of Tavy?"

"She's just one reason why I should say no. Hooking up with you in secret is playing with fire."

"And if you're not careful you'll get burned?" he asked with a wry grin. "What else is making you hesitate?"

"You're seventeen years older than I am."

"It just means you'll be able to take advantage of all my experience."

I raised a brow. "Did you just inadvertently mention your sexual history and put it in the *plus* column?"

"Yep."

"Ballsy move. This has *mess* written all over it. We both know it."

"Doesn't have to be messy. If we hash out what this is going to look like, there's no reason we can't have some fun."

"We need a few ground rules," I said.

"Class is in session and the teacher is *hot*."

I quirked a brow.

"Sorry." He shot me a devastating grin. "I'm listening."

"You have to leave before the bakery deliveries arrive. Jazz, Brielle, Brooklyn—none of them can know what we're doing."

He sighed. "Agreed."

"Nothing in public. No heated looks that scream *we've seen each other naked*. No one can find out that we're doing this. Especially not Tavy."

"All right."

"What about Bones?" I asked.

"What about him?"

"He's made his interest known."

"So, tell him it's not gonna happen."

"You make it sound so easy."

"It *is* easy. You want me, I want you. We hashed it out. Are we done talking?" he asked.

"I guess so."

"Are you ready for me to fuck you?"

My breath caught in my throat and I nodded.

"Then get on all fours and stick your ass in the air like a good girl."

∽

"This bed is too small," Smoke mumbled into the pillow.

"The room doesn't really allow for a bigger bed," I pointed out. I grazed my lips across his shoulder blade and then got up.

"Where are you going?" he demanded.

"Water. I'm not usually involved in such athletic activities this time of night."

I reached down and grabbed his T-shirt and threw it on over my head but didn't bother with underwear.

My body was tender and my legs felt like jelly. But I was happy, and at the moment there was a big, brawny biker in my bed.

Life does not suck.

"Nice place," Smoke said as he followed me to the kitchen, pulling up his boxers. "I didn't get to see much of it before, but it's nice."

"I like it," I said. I went to the cabinet and pulled out a glass. I filled it from the tap and then drank half of it before handing it to Smoke.

He downed the rest of it and then his stomach rumbled.

I grinned. "Hungry?"

"I got a lot to eat, but I didn't get dinner."

My cheeks heated. I glanced at the clock. Just past nine.

"I can make you something, if you want."

"I want."

I nodded and went over to the fridge. I opened the door and pulled out a block of cheese, a loaf of bread, butter, and mayo.

"Grilled cheese okay?" I asked.

"Grilled cheese is perfect."

"Want a beer?" I asked.

"What've you got?"

"Amber ale."

"That'll do." He walked over to the fridge and pulled out a bottle. I opened a drawer and found the bottle opener and handed it to him.

"You look cute in my shirt," he said after he took a sip.

"Do I?" I asked as I spread the butter on the slices of bread.

"You do."

"You look cute sitting in my apartment," I said, leaning over and kissing him.

He grasped the back of my head and kissed me deep, and with tongue.

"You're insatiable," I said as I pulled back with a grin.

"For you? Definitely." He nodded his head at the bread. "What's with the mayo?"

"You put mayonnaise on the outside of the bread so when you sear it in the pan it gets nice and crispy. I'm about to make you the best grilled cheese you've ever had."

I took out a pan and turned on the burner. I moved around the kitchen as the pan heated.

Smoke stood by and watched me, sipping on his beer every now and again.

"Here you go," I said, placing the plate with a grilled cheese in front of him.

"Looks good," he said, setting his beer aside.

"You want to sit on the couch to eat?" I inquired.

"Nope. Here's good." He picked up the sandwich and took a bite. Smoke closed his eyes and momentarily ceased chewing.

When he opened his eyes and looked at me, I smirked. "Told ya."

He didn't say anything until he polished off the last of his grilled cheese. "I'm gonna need one of those every night I'm here. It's just become my new obsession."

I grinned. "Will make grilled cheese for orgasms."

"Sign me up." He polished off the rest of the beer and threw the bottle away. Then he began to tackle the dishes.

"You don't have to clean up," I said.

He looked at me and frowned. "You cooked. I clean. Those are the rules."

"Okay," I agreed. "But I need a baby grilled cheese. Watching you eat yours kinda whet my appetite."

He arched a brow.

I rolled my eyes. "Not everything has to be dirty."

"But it's more fun that way."

I ate my sandwich as I watched him stand at the sink and do the dishes. When he was finished, he grabbed the dishrag and dried his hands.

"What?" he asked, raising a brow.

"Nothing." I finished the last of my sandwich. I was fully satiated and relaxed.

"Nah, come on, what is it?"

"Where did you learn to wash dishes?" I asked.

"You mean, since I was a little rich boy with a butler; where did I learn such a skill?"

"You had a *butler*?" I asked in surprise.

"Yeah."

"Oh. Wow. Okay."

"I worked as a dishwasher in a restaurant as a second job to keep the lights on when Tavy was little."

He tossed the dishrag aside and leaned against the counter.

"Does she know?"

"Know that I used to work two jobs to keep her and her mom safe and warm? I don't know. Maybe."

I shook my head. "I meant, did she know what you gave up?"

He paused for a moment and ran a hand along his scruffy jaw. "She knows about how I grew up. But it's one thing to know it and it's another thing to *know* it. See it, I mean. She never saw it since I wasn't close with my parents."

"Because of her, right? You chose to be her father over being their son. You gave up their money and a life of obligation because she was born."

"Money isn't everything."

"It's definitely not," I agreed.

"Makes life easier though."

"It definitely does." I smiled. "Money gives you choices. Freedom. Time."

"Was it Knox's money that turned your head?"

"Yes, but no…but yes?"

"What the hell does that mean?"

I laughed at his confusion. "I didn't grow up wealthy, but I also didn't want for anything. I had new clothes for school. We took family vacations. Knox…he threw his money around like it was a tool to be used. He didn't hold tight to it, and if he saw that I wanted something, he'd get it for me. What I didn't realize until much later was that he was using money as a form of control. Not that he wouldn't give it to me, but it was like a power stance. I could've had anything I wanted, but I had to be with him. I'm not explaining it well, am I?"

"I see what you mean."

"He bought me a car. And it *was* my car. He never drove it. He never rescinded my use of it when he was pissed. But there were these moments…when we'd fight. All of a sudden it was *his* house. *His* money had bought it. *His* career had allowed him the money to buy the cars. You know? Like he was generous with his money, but there were strings. He was never the type of man to be generous for the sake of generosity or love."

"Strings." He nodded.

"Strings. I was tangled up in them. I didn't see it right away. And then suddenly I was living this life, wearing these clothes, going to the salon every four weeks just to look the way *he* wanted me to look. I woke up one day and I wasn't me."

"The bastard preferred it straight, didn't he?"

I nodded.

"God, I love your hair," Smoke said, his voice lowering. "The first time I saw it, all wild and wavy…fuck, Logan, I couldn't even think."

I smiled shyly. "It's been so long since I've been able to decide what *I* want. From my clothes to my hair, to my decor. The car I drive. Everything." I shook my head, my eyes staring off into the past. "I lost myself for a long time. Now I get to find myself again."

The conversation was straying too far into the deep end and I wanted nothing more than to wade back to shallow water.

I walked to Smoke and placed my hand on his bare chest, feeling his muscles jump beneath my touch.

He settled his hand over mine and slowly backed me up to the bedroom. I flopped onto the bed and Smoke covered me with his body.

And when his lips met mine, I ceased to think at all.

Chapter 29

"Logan," Smoke whispered.

"Hmm?"

"I gotta go."

I snuggled closer. "Mkay."

He laughed softly. "It's three in the morning."

"Five more minutes." I lifted my leg and angled it across his thigh so he couldn't move.

"If you do that, I'm gonna fall back asleep, and then there's a chance I'll miss my window to leave."

Yawning, I reluctantly rolled off him and made a move to climb out of bed.

"Don't get up," he said, brushing his lips against my shoulder. "Go back to sleep."

"Hmm. Okay."

"See you tonight."

"Tonight." I sighed and fell back to sleep.

The next time I awoke, I was alone and my phone was buzzing.

"Hello?" I croaked into the phone.

"Jeez, you sleep like the dead," Tavy said.

I yawned so hard my jaw popped. "What time is it?"

"Seven."

"Why are you calling me at this ungodly hour?" I asked, glancing at the alarm clock on my bedside.

"Because I'm downstairs."

"You're downstairs?" I asked, my spine suddenly snapping straight.

"Yeah." She laughed. "I thought about getting us coffee and pastries and bringing them up to your apartment, but I know you're an ogress in the mornings. So, I'm giving you five minutes to splash some water on your face and then you come meet me before I have to zip off to work."

"Order me a—"

"Vanilla latte. I know."

I paused. "Make it a cinnamon latte, instead."

"Get out."

"What?"

"You never change your order. What's up?"

"I'm trying new things."

"I like this adventurous side of you. Hurry up and get down here. I can't be late."

I jumped out of bed and quickly brushed my teeth and splashed some water on my face. I looked like I'd been on a bender. Puffy eyes, wan skin, whisker burn against my lips and neck.

Whisker burn?

"Shit, shit, shit." I hastily doctored my face, hoping like hell Tavy would be too distracted to notice that I looked like I'd been thoroughly and exquisitely fucked.

I brushed my hair and left it down.

Smoke needed to shave. Otherwise, our secret wouldn't remain a secret for long.

I grabbed my keys and headed down into the bakery.

Jazz and Brielle weren't working that morning, but I waved to the girl behind the counter who I'd met briefly.

Tavy was sitting at table in the corner by the window of the café. She sipped on her coffee and then tore a piece of her cinnamon roll that was globbed with frosting.

"Morning, sunshine," she said with a smile.

I glared at her.

"What's with the look? Is that any way to treat your best friend who came to see you first thing in the morning before her busy day?"

I peered at her. "What do you want?"

"I want for nothing." She leaned back in her chair. "Can't I just come and see you? You look like hell, by the way."

"Tavy, I love you. You know I love you. You also know I'm not a morning person and I haven't had caffeine yet. So, either get to it, or let me go back to bed."

"No seriously, are you sick or something? You look like you haven't even slept."

"Getting used to a new place. New mattress," I lied. "And the delivery trucks are loud…"

"Ah." Her expression softened. "Sorry. Can I do anything? Get you something? Like a white noise machine? Maybe that'll help."

"Maybe." I lifted my coffee mug to my lips and took a tentative sip.

"How is it? The cinnamon?"

"Good. Not as good as vanilla, but good."

She nodded. "Okay, so here's the thing."

"You slept with one of Brielle's brothers," I guessed.

She frowned. "What? No!"

"Really? Huh. I thought for sure something happened with you and one of them. You stayed out with Jazz that night, so I assumed something transpired."

"You think you know me so well."

"Don't I?"

"Well, yeah. But no. Roman wasn't my type. Virgil and I are buddies. And Homer's in love with Jazz, so that definitely isn't going to happen."

I raised my brows.

She rolled her eyes. "Oh, please. Everyone with two eyes can see they have the hots for each other."

"Not Brielle," I said. "And Jazz would really like to keep it that way."

"My lips are sealed. But I like them. Brielle, Jazz, the entire lot of them. They're fun and playful. I think we could have a good friend group here."

"Agreed." I nodded and filched a piece of her cinnamon roll. "So, what's up? Really?"

"My grandfather called me yesterday."

"Your mom's dad?"

"No. My dad's dad."

"Smoke's father called you? Did you talk to him?"

She shook her head. "He left a message saying he wants to talk to me and I wasn't sure what to do with it. So, I came to you. What do I do?"

"What do you want to do?" I asked carefully.

"I don't know. My grandparents were jerks. Cutting Dad off because he got my mom pregnant. And then they didn't want to have a relationship with me. Why now? Why's he calling now?"

"I don't know. You'd have to ask him that." I paused. "Are you curious about them?"

"Yes. But talking to them feels like I'd be betraying Dad, you know?"

"People get really weird in old age. Things that they thought were important at one time just aren't anymore. I think it starts to happen when people face mortality."

"Totally. Makes sense."

"You could call him. Hear what he has to say. Maybe he's calling to apologize. Maybe he wants to know you."

"Maybe he's dying," Tavy mused. "And he wants to make shit right with Dad but he doesn't know how to do that."

"Would Smoke even take his father's call?" I asked.

"I doubt it. Dad doesn't talk about his parents often, and when he does, he seems indifferent about the whole thing." She glanced at her phone. "Crap. I gotta go. Finish the cinnamon roll for me."

"Okay."

"Thanks, Logan. I just needed to talk about it with someone."

"Any time. Keep me posted, yeah?"

"I will." She got up and hugged me while I was still sitting. "Thanks. And you don't look that shitty."

I chuckled. "You with the compliments. You'll make me blush."

"Dinner this week?"

"Yes. Drive safe. Don't let anyone throw another vase at you."

"But my day would be so boring otherwise."

She turned and headed for the door, and soon the bell of the cafe chimed and she was gone.

I took my time devouring the last of her cinnamon roll. While I ate, I pulled my phone out to text Smoke.

> ME
> I have a request.

A moment later, my phone buzzed with his reply.

> SMOKE
> Sexual? I'd love to hear it.

Smiling, I typed out an answer.

> **ME**
> Not sexual. Will you shave? I have whisker burn on my cheeks and neck. Probably some other places, but I haven't looked.

> **SMOKE**
> I'll look for you tonight. After I shave.

I set my phone aside, but it buzzed immediately with a text from an unknown number.

My heart tripped in fear, and I reached for it with cold fingers. But when I took a deep breath, I remembered that I'd changed my number and Knox didn't know it.

> **UNKNOWN NUMBER**
> Hey, Logan. It's Joni. Hope you don't mind but I got your number from Mia. Are you still cool to come check out my disaster of a kitchen and help me do some planning? I'm desperate!

A smile bloomed across my face and I fired back a quick response.

I'd gone to sleep with a hot man in my bed, I'd tried a new coffee, and I was suddenly feeling like I was exactly where I was meant to be.

∽

"Say it," Joni said.

"Say what?" I asked as I pulled my eyes away from the garish kitchen that needed a gut renovation.

"Say how awful this kitchen is," Joni said. "Don't even try to be diplomatic. It's awful."

I sighed. "It's awful."

"It needs a gut renovation, doesn't it?"

"Yep."

"It's gonna cost a lot."

"Ah, yep."

"Yeah, I knew you were going to say that. You want something to drink?"

"Sure. Thanks."

Joni had given me the grand tour of the house Zip had bought as a surprise for her. It was a Queen Anne style home and they'd gone from room to room renovating and preserving the charm and craftsmanship.

All that was left was the kitchen. The biggest project. The most expensive project. The most time-consuming project.

"I've wanted to redo the kitchen for months," Joni said as she opened a cabinet. "But between the club taking most of Zip's time and Everett taking the rest, it hasn't been a priority."

She grabbed a cup and went to the fridge. "We brought Everett home from the hospital with light sockets still unprotected."

"The house is a work in progress," Zip said as he came into the kitchen, carrying his infant son. "You wanted the backyard done so we could entertain, and I made that happen."

"Yes you did, you big strong man," Joni teased.

Zip flashed her a grin. "We used the help of several young prospects and their brawn."

"We did."

"Speaking of young brawn, your son has been bathed and he's in a fresh diaper. But he's definitely hungry and I can't take care of that." Zip looked at me. "Hi Logan."

I grinned. "Hi Zip."

"So, what's the verdict?" Zip asked.

Joni handed me a glass of water and then took her son from his arms.

"Do you want me to lie, or do you want the truth?" I asked.

"What's going to hurt the wallet less?"

"You promised me when you proposed that I would want for nothing—that money was no object," Joni said.

"I remember."

"Well, I'm just reminding *you*."

Zip sighed. "Just send me the bill. I'll sign on the dotted line."

"Good man," I teased.

"The bigger question," Joni said. "Do you have a vision for how to turn this kitchen into the kitchen of my dreams?"

"How do you feel about knocking down walls?" I inquired.

"I feel good about it," Joni said.

"I don't feel good about it," Zip muttered.

Joni glared at her husband.

"You're the love of my life, the mother of my son, you get whatever you want," he intoned like an automaton.

"Damn right," Joni said with a grin. "So what walls were you thinking of knocking down?"

"The wall that separates the kitchen and the dining room," I said. "If it's not load-bearing, it shouldn't be that challenging. It'll open up the space and give you more to work with."

"How can you tell if a wall is load-bearing?" Joni asked.

"Is there an attic?"

"Yeah."

"Will you show me? Once I'm up there I'll be able to tell," I said.

"Sure."

"I've got to get out of here," Zip said. "Colt's waiting on me."

Joni nodded. Zip walked toward her, placed his hand on her hip, and kissed her. Kissed her deep enough that her eyes closed and she looked like she forgot they had an audience.

He gently brushed his hand over his son's head. "Later, babe," Zip said to Joni as he pulled back. "Bye, Logan."

"Bye."

"What about dinner tonight?" Joni called after him.

"Call Waverly," he said. "I'm taking you out to dinner."

The front door shut and he was gone.

"Who's Waverly?" I asked.

"Willa's younger sister. She didn't come to the barbecue, so you didn't get to meet her. She babysits for all of us."

"Ah, nice."

"So, the attic?" she asked.

"Yes, please."

I tromped up the stairs behind her, stopping when we got to the landing. She opened the door to the attic and stepped in first. Joni was tall so she had to be mindful of her head not hitting the rafters. I was a bit shorter so I didn't have to duck. The attic had the usual boxes labeled Christmas and seasonal clothes. But I found the wall in question and grinned.

"Yep. See the way the joists are laid out and the wall is parallel to them just below?"

"Yeah." Joni nodded.

"The wall isn't load-bearing. Your contractor should have no trouble removing it."

Joni rubbed the back of Everett's back as he slept pressed against her. "Can I say that I love that you know about this sort of stuff?"

"Goes with the territory," I replied as I followed her out of the attic and down the stairs. "My dad was relentless in showing me his job sites. Taught me a little bit of everything."

"He teach you anything about electrical work?"

"A little. Not a lot. I can put in dimmer switches, and that's all I really feel comfortable with."

"Plumbing?"

"I can replace a toilet. Though I'd prefer never to do it."

She chuckled. "I don't blame you. So, what do you say? Will you help me come up with a vision for this kitchen and turn it into place I love instead of loathe?"

"I'd be happy to."

"Now I have to find a contractor who won't hose me."

"Before you sign off on the project, show me the quote. I can tell you if he's hosing you or not."

"You're the greatest."

"I haven't even shown you my real skills yet. Wait until I give you a mockup of how this kitchen is going to look when it's done. Then you'll really think I'm the greatest."

I left Joni's house and got into my car. Joy bubbled to the surface and I couldn't stop the smile from spreading across my face. My old life was slipping away. With each smile, each laugh, each step forward, I felt like I was shedding the old me. The me that primped and polished her hair and face. The old, fearful me was disappearing in the rearview mirror and I was building a new life for myself.

And Smoke.

Whatever he was to me…

No.

He couldn't be anything to me. Even if he wasn't Tavy's father, it was too soon to jump into a new relationship. I needed time by myself. Time to figure out what I wanted. Time that I didn't owe to anyone except myself.

But Smoke had never done anything to demand my time. He'd come to me because he wanted to spend time with me. Not because he expected it. And he'd even attempted to stay away.

We both had.

Something kept drawing us back together.

The sex was out of this world. Maybe that was all this was. But if that was the case, then why did we laugh together? Why did I have so much fun with him, watching him do the dishes after sharing grilled cheese?

I was not built for casual sex.

My phone rang, jarring me out of my thoughts.

Thank goodness for that.

I pressed a button on my steering wheel. "Hello?"

"Hey!" Rach greeted. "I've got a bone to pick with you."

"What did I do?" I asked as I stopped at a red light.

"You haven't come over for dinner yet. And you haven't met Cash."

I let out a laugh. "I'm sorry. It's been sort of crazy."

"Uh huh. Well, I heard you went out with Brielle, Jazz and the Jackson boys for dinner. And then you went over to Brielle and Jazz's for breakfast. That's two meals already, so…"

"How the heck did you know all that about my life?" I demanded.

"Jazz and Brielle told Brooklyn. Brooklyn told me and the Old Ladies. It's kind of how the grapevine works."

"Like a game of telephone?"

"Pretty much."

"Well, you didn't get the entire story. I went out to dinner with Brielle and Jazz and then Brielle's brothers joined us. But then Brielle lost her shit on her brothers and needed a ride home. So, I obliged. Technically I didn't even hang out with them."

"Are you coming over for dinner or not?"

I laughed. "Give me the time, address, and what I can bring."

"I'll text you everything. And just bring yourself. I've got the food handled."

Chapter 30

After what was supposed to be a quick cat nap that turned into passing out all afternoon, I stood on Rachel's front doorstep holding a blueberry pie.

Rach opened the front door, a sleepy boy on the curve of her hip.

She smiled. "Come on in."

"Thanks," I said, stepping inside the foyer. It was a two-story red brick home with blue shutters. Everything about the place screamed modern white-picket-fence. I couldn't imagine a biker living here.

"What did you bring? I told you not to bring anything," Rach said. She shut the door and then kicked the pairs of shoes that rested by the door out of the walkway.

"But I live above a bakery. Seems ridiculous not to bring anything. And it's blueberry pie." I grinned. "It's not huckleberry, but it'll have to do."

"Huckleberry." Rach moaned. "I miss huckleberry everything. Oh, Idaho, I love you, except for your winters…"

"Same." I peered at the baby on her hip. "Is this your son? Or a loaner?"

"This is Cash. He's six months old." She patted the baby's back and in a moment of pure bashfulness, he tucked his blond head into the crook of Rach's neck.

"He just woke up from his nap," Rach explained. "He's normally very friendly."

"Well, I won't take it personally."

"Sorry, I'm blabbing. Come into the kitchen," she said. "What can I get you to drink? Soda? Wine?"

"Soda's great for me." I followed her into the kitchen. "Love the space. Joni must be jealous."

Rachel sniggered as she set Cash in his highchair and buckled him in. "You saw her kitchen, didn't you?"

"I was there this morning," I admitted. "Beautiful house, though. The kitchen…not so much. We're working on a plan."

"Love that."

Rach walked to the double-door fridge and pulled out a can of soda and handed it to me. "Ice?"

"Nah, I'm good, thanks. Is your mom here?"

"No. She's at the community center with some new friends. They're having dinner and seeing a movie tonight. My mother has a more active social life than I do," Rach joked.

She grabbed a banana from the counter and cut a few small pieces and placed them on Cash's highchair tabletop. He greedily grabbed them with his pudgy fingers and shoved them into his mouth.

"And you want your social life to be more active?" I asked.

"Hmm. I don't know," she said. "I've only been back in town for a little while. After Reap…"

She glanced at her son and smiled at him. Cash had his

mouth hanging open like a baby bird and he was pounding on the highchair tabletop demanding more food.

"I couldn't stay here. I was pregnant and I went home to live with my mom for a while. But the girls—the Old Ladies—kept bugging me to come back."

"Why *did* you come back? Weren't the memories too much for you?"

"Here you go, Pudge-a-muff." She sliced a couple more pieces of banana and put them in front of Cash. "I wanted my son to grow up around his father's friends. They're good men. Brave. Loyal. I knew they'd do anything for Reap. For me. For our family."

"They're not really *good* though, are they?" I asked. "I mean, your husband died because of the club and what they were involved in…"

Rach's eyes widened. "You know about the cartel?"

"*What?*"

"What do you mean *what?*" Rach demanded. "You just said you knew what they were involved in."

"Um, that's not what I said. I said I knew they were involved in something, but Smoke only vaguely mentioned it on our drive from Vegas. He never said anything about the cartel. *Holy fuck*—"

"Oh." Rach looked at her son and fell silent.

"Um, hello? You can't just mention the cartel *oh so casually* and then not elaborate."

"I shouldn't have said anything."

"Well, you did. So, out with it."

"I can't."

"But you just—"

"You're not involved, Logan. You're not an Old Lady. You're not family."

"Ouch."

"I'm not saying that to be mean. I'm saying that to protect

you. You don't want to know about this. I'm not supposed to discuss *any* of this with you. All I'm going to say is that the club isn't involved in that shit anymore, hence why they're getting into real estate and going in a different direction."

"Wow." My mind whirled. "And you came back to town knowing about the cartel? Wouldn't it have been safer to stay away?"

"Maybe. But the club is family and the world is a dangerous place. You can't run from that."

I was suddenly sick to my stomach.

Smoke had asked Tavy to move to Waco. The timing of it made sense now.

"Dinner's going to be weird, isn't it?" Rach asked.

"Well, yeah. Probably. I'm trying to wrap my head around this. Why did you marry a biker if you knew what kind of stuff he was involved in?"

"I didn't know at the time, but it wouldn't have mattered. I was in love. They keep the Old Ladies out of club business for a reason. Only, with the cartel, it was going to affect all of us, so we were on a need-to-know basis."

"You know that's crazy, right?" I asked.

She shrugged. "I don't expect you to understand."

"Why not? Why can't I understand?"

"Look, some of us don't want to live within the boxes society demands we put ourselves in."

"They're *criminals!*"

"Like I said, you don't understand."

"Yeah, I guess I don't. There are some things that are right and wrong. Clear as day."

"Knox is an attorney."

I frowned. "Yeah. What does that have to do with anything?"

"He's an attorney. He wears a suit to work. He pays his taxes. By societal standards, he's a good guy, right?"

"Yes…"

"He's also a cheater. So, he clearly has his own moral system in place, even though he's part of polite society."

My expression softened. "I think I see where you're going with this."

"I hoped you would. It's not so black and white. Life's not that way."

I sighed. "It would be easier if it was."

"Look, I get it. I do. I know what you're thinking. But imagine the wildest, most passionate, most protective-do anything for you-kind of love. I couldn't walk away from that. Could you?"

"I don't know," I admitted. "It's not like I've felt that way about anyone."

"Not even the man you were going to marry?"

"Not even him. Maybe that was the problem all along. Well, that and his inability to keep it in his pants."

"Are we okay?" she asked.

"What? Oh, Rach, of course we're okay." I shook my head. "You don't owe me an explanation. Your life is your life. Your choices are your own. I won't judge you for them."

"I know. But we're friends. And friends are allowed to have opinions that differ from one another. Like I said, I know not everyone understands. And I don't really care if they do. But out of respect for our history, I'm happy to share my story."

"Does that mean when you're ready to date, it'll be with another biker?"

"I don't think I'm ready to date," she said slowly. "But can I admit something to you?"

"Always," I said, lifting the can of soda to my lips and taking a sip.

"I miss sex."

I spit the soda out all over the island counter and hastily covered my mouth.

Rach's peal of laughter echoed throughout the kitchen. She grabbed a dish rag and hastily mopped up the mess I'd made.

"Sorry, I don't know why that caught me off guard," I said with a wry grin. "So, you miss sex, huh?"

"A lot," she admitted. "It was like my entire body shut down for a while. It was all I could do to remember to eat after he died. But I don't know…about a month ago, it was like I woke up and realized how much I missed it. But I don't want to date. I just want something physical. I'm not interested in a relationship. I've got Cash and my job and my friends. I had my husband. I don't want another one. But sex? I need that like, *pronto*. Scratch that itch."

As someone who was currently scratching an itch myself, I understood. "Any thoughts about who you'd like to scratch the itch with?"

"A few men have made their interests known," she said slowly.

"Bikers?" I supplied.

She nodded. "But I don't feel right about it. It's too close to home, you know? At the same time, vetting a stranger? It's wild out there. From what I've heard anyway."

"It was wild even being in a committed relationship. I use the term *committed* in quotation marks because, obviously that didn't work out…" I shook my head. "Thank God we were using condoms."

"You were together three years?" she asked.

"Yeah."

"And you were still using condoms?" she asked.

"Yep." I nodded. "Of all the shit Knox wanted to control, for some reason, he gave me that one. I told him when we were married, it would be different. But not until then. Looking back, I realize I never really trusted him."

"You said he gave you that one…did he control a lot?" she asked softly.

"Yeah." I sighed. "Young and dumb. I won't make that mistake again."

"Well, at least you found out he was cheating before you got married. It made it a hell of a lot easier to leave. You hungry?"

"I could eat something," I admitted.

"How do you feel about mushroom risotto?"

I blinked. "That sounds fancy and involved."

"Yep." She grinned. "Cash and I had to find a way to occupy our nights. So, I'm working my way through the cookbook."

"Tell me what to prep," I said as I went to the kitchen sink.

"Nothing. You sit and keep me company and every now and again, feed Cash some more banana."

"You sure?"

"Positive."

I took a chair at the kitchen table and when Cash began banging on his tabletop, I gave him a few pieces of fruit.

"What about you?" Rach asked.

"What about me, what?"

"How are you feeling about Knox?"

I sat for a moment and pondered her words. "I don't know. It's weird."

"Weird how?"

"Weird like, everything happened so fast. I found out

he was cheating and then I left Las Vegas—left him—and was already on my way to Waco when he figured out I was gone. I don't know if I've processed or mourned the relationship yet."

"Did you cry? Scream?"

"I got drunk and went to jail for a few hours," I mocked, causing us both to laugh. "But I don't know. I had a few days in a moving truck with a man who I basically held hostage with my emotions, but I think it helped. We talked a lot."

"Right, you and Smoke spent a few days together. Was that weird? You guys were strangers."

"It was weird, in the beginning. But I got over my embarrassment about the entire situation pretty quickly. Smoke bailed me and Tavy out of jail. There wasn't much I could do to be even *more* embarrassed after that point. I mean, he'd seen me at the lowest of the low."

"So, you felt comfortable enough around him to talk about what happened with Knox?"

"I was comfortable enough around him to let him watch me pour Quikrete down Knox's pipes. My brothers were proud of that one."

"I bet they were."

I watched her dice, sauté, prep and stir, all the while remaining tuned into her son.

Dinner was wonderful and conversation flowed easily. It was like no time had passed since the last time I'd seen her, even though it had been years. She was only eighteen then, and I hadn't even been a teenager. But six years when you were both adults didn't seem that big of an age difference.

"I don't mean this to sound condescending," Rach said as she picked up her glass of white wine. "But I really like who you've turned into."

"I always thought you were cool," I said with a wry grin. "Six years older than me and the way you dressed… the way my brother would follow after you like a lost little puppy."

She shook her head and glanced at her son. "It's weird when you think about what your life could've been like if you'd made different choices. But timing, you know?"

"Timing," I repeated.

My phone chimed in my purse, but I ignored it. Several more chimes occurred in rapid succession.

"Maybe you should get that," Rach said.

"Nah, it's fine." I stood up and grabbed my plate. "You done?"

"Yep."

I took our plates to the sink and rinsed them off.

"It's not Knox blowing up your phone, is it?" Rach asked.

I opened the dishwasher and loaded the plates. "Nope. I changed my number. It's probably Grady, just checking in."

"You got a new number?" She frowned. "Were you worried about Knox being able to contact you?"

I nodded. "He didn't take the news that I left him well. He went from cajoling to angry, scary texts. So I blocked him on all social and changed my number."

"Scary texts?"

"He's got a short fuse," I admitted. "I should never have let my rage get the better of me when I destroyed his car—even if he did deserve it."

"Are you scared of him?"

"Knox doesn't know where I am."

"That's not what I asked…"

Cash started to fuss so Rach removed his bib and took him out of his highchair. "Can you stay a little while longer? I just want to clean him up and put him to bed. Shouldn't take long. Maybe about twenty minutes?"

"Sure, I can hang out a bit longer."

Rach smiled. "Great."

While Rach was upstairs putting her son to bed, I checked my phone. A huge smile crossed my face when I saw it was Smoke who'd text-bombed me.

> **SMOKE**
>
> Where are you?
>
> I'm at your place and you're not answering the intercom.
>
> Is this you playing hard to get?
>
> Please tell me you didn't fall asleep.

I took my phone and went out onto the front porch to call him back.

"Hey," he said after the first ring. "Where are you?"

"Out," I said.

"Out?"

"We didn't make concrete plans."

"So, we should've talked about what time I was coming over?"

"Yep."

"I don't usually make plans that are set in stone. Club business gets in the way of shit sometimes."

"Smoke," I said quietly. "We don't owe each other anything. Not really. I want to see you, but I'm having dinner with a friend and I'm not ready to leave."

"I wasn't asking you to," he said.

"What we're doing, this thing…I'm just now getting my own time back. My freedom back. I won't get myself into a position like I did with Knox…"

"Hold on just a second," he interrupted. "I'm nothing

like Knox. I will never ever treat you the way he treated you. I'm blowing up your phone because I'm excited to see you, not control you."

I softened immediately. "I appreciate what you just said. And I know you're nothing like Knox. I'm sorry, I didn't mean it to come out that way."

"Guess we should've laid a few more ground rules last night, but I was a bit distracted."

"Same." I laughed. "What other ground rules?"

"Let's talk when we're in the same room."

"Okay."

"And when might that be?"

"Give me an hour to have dessert. Okay?"

"Yeah, okay."

"And Smoke?"

"Yeah, cupcake?"

"I'm over at Rach's for dinner."

He fell silent for a moment and then he said, "Thanks for that."

"You're welcome."

"I'll see you in an hour?"

"An hour."

Chapter 31

Rach was sitting at the table, sipping on her glass of wine when I came in.

"Everything good?" she asked.

"Yep."

"I love this house," Rach said, her brown eyes meeting mine. "But there's one thing I'm not a fan of."

"What's that?"

"The windows. They're single pane and you can hear the street noise…" She pinned me with a stare.

I took a deep breath. "You heard my conversation."

"I heard your conversation." A slow grin spread across her face. "Logan, you shady lady."

I groaned. "*Don't*. I already feel like shit."

"Sit. We'll discuss this over pie. Now, why do you feel like shit?" she asked.

"Because I'm not supposed to be sleeping with my best friend's father. And you know what's even worse? I'm doing it in secret, so I *know* it's wrong."

She handed me a fork and then opened the pie box that rested between us. "I see the complication, but I'm not sure I agree with you. But before we get into all that, I have to know how this happened, because *oh my God, this is juicy*."

I dug into the pie. "There was a spark from the very beginning." I told her about our interactions, our looks, the talking in the moving truck, the one bed in the motel room.

"It wasn't supposed to happen again," I said. "We agreed, just those nights so I could get some of my ego back and we could get it out of our system. But then I don't know what happened."

"You got here and realized you weren't able to put that cat back in the bag after all."

"We tried," I said. "We really tried. And then Bones had to stick his nose into our business."

"Oh, right. The Bones thing. I think I heard about that, but I sort of forgot." She flashed me a grin. "Mom brain. You actually like Smoke, don't you?"

"Yes. Which is *so* not good for me."

"Why not?"

"Why not? I just ended a three-year relationship. An engagement. I'm still healing. I don't trust my own judgement right now."

"Hmm." She took another bite of pie.

"Hmm? What does that mean?"

"I think we talk ourselves out of things because we worry about how it's going to look."

"Explain."

"Everyone would tell you not to jump into something new after what you've been through. Take your time. Heal. Feel through it. Get your head on straight. But life doesn't always work that way. Sometimes the right person comes along at the worst time."

"Hold on, though. Smoke isn't the right person for me."

"How do you know?"

"We're just having fun. Keeping things casual."

"Yeah...the conversation out there? That didn't sound *casual*."

I suddenly felt lightheaded. "No?" I gripped the table.

"When you guys spend time together, is it only naked time? Do you have sex and then kick him out?"

"Well, it only happened last night. So, there's no pattern yet."

"Did you kick him out last night after sex?"

"No."

"Did he sleep over?"

"Yes."

"Did you guys talk? Do anything besides have sex?"

"I made him grilled cheese and then he did the dishes."

"Uh huh. Thought so. He spent last night in your bed and he came back tonight to see you."

"I also asked him to shave because of the whisker burn he gave me, which feels like the equivalent of wearing a scarlet letter in public. Everyone will know I'm hooking up with someone."

"And did he tell you he wasn't going to shave just because you asked?"

"No. He said he'd shave."

"Interesting. So, you talk, have sex, eat food together, and he's willing to give up facial hair. Sounds like a relationship to me. A pretty healthy one, at that."

"Don't say that," I pleaded. "I was trying to be strong and not give into temptation, but *son of a bitch*! He's *so* hot..."

"Yeah, agreed. He's very good looking."

"But that's not even why I like being with him. He's just..."

"What?"

"He makes me feel safe. Like I can tell him anything and he just gets it."

"Would dating him in the open really be that bad?"

"Tavy will kill me," I said. "She moved here so she could get to know him better. And then what? I come along and start to monopolize his time. Now I'm the one taking his attention? And I'm supposed to jeopardize my relationship with my best friend for a situationship with her dad? It's mental."

"Okay, please don't call it a situationship. I just can't with the lingo."

I sniggered.

"And second of all—what if this is the real deal?"

"What if it's not?" I set my fork down. "You're not going to tell anyone, are you?"

"Who would I tell?"

"The Old Ladies."

"Give me a little credit. I'm not going to blab about your relationship."

I stood. "This thing with Smoke is just a *thing*. Not a relationship."

"Where are you going?" she asked with a smirk.

"I promised him I'd see him in an hour."

"Yeah, definitely a relationship."

~

Smoke was leaning against his bike when I pulled into a parking spot next to him. He looked sexy and masculine. The streetlights illuminated his smile and it made my heart cartwheel in my chest.

He grabbed the driver's side door handle and opened the door for me, and then held out a hand to help me out of the car.

I placed my palm in his.

"You didn't shave," I said in way of greeting.

"Not yet," he agreed. He continued to hold my hand and closed the car door with his other. "But I brought all the stuff."

"Where is it?"

He reached over to his bike and grabbed a plastic bag off the seat. "Got something in there for you, too."

"Is it chocolate?"

"No."

"Hmm."

We walked to the back of the bakery and he leaned against the brick wall while he waited for me to rummage in my purse for my keys. I found them and unlocked the door.

He followed me up the stairs to the second floor. The moment we were inside the apartment, Smoke had me pressed against the door, his body pinning me in place.

"Hi," I said breathlessly.

He grinned. "Hey. Do I get a hello kiss?"

I ran my hands up his chest. "Depends on how good the present you brought me is."

Chuckling, he pulled back and gave me room to breathe. I suddenly wished he hadn't.

He reached into the plastic bag and pulled out a can of shaving cream, a razor, aftershave, and a toothbrush and set them on the counter. And then he dug back into the bag to remove a flat object wrapped in white tissue paper.

He handed it to me.

I gently unwrapped a stained-glass pink cactus bloom.

"I thought you might miss the desert, and your place doesn't have any plants. So, consider it a housewarming gift."

I looked at the stained-glass piece that was the size of my hand and then I stared at him.

"Logan?" His expression was quizzical.

"This is really sweet," I said.

"Then what's wrong?"

"I know the club was involved with the cartel," I blurted out.

"How did—"

I winced.

He sighed. "Rach."

I nodded.

"Fuck."

"She didn't know that I didn't know."

"Huh?"

"I was telling her about our drive to Waco and how you'd mentioned the club being involved in shady stuff. She thought that meant you'd told me about the cartel. It was an honest mistake."

"An honest mistake," he repeated. Shaking his head, he grasped my hand and led me to the couch.

I moved away from him and sat down on the opposite end, as far away from him as I could get.

He raised his eyes. "You scared of me?"

"I—" I cleared my throat. "I don't want to get distracted by you and forget we need to have this conversation."

He laced his fingers together and leaned over so his forearms rested on his thighs. "You're not supposed to know about that kind of shit."

"Yeah, I know. Rach made that very clear." I blinked. "Oh my God…Tavy doesn't know, does she?"

"No, she doesn't," he said.

"If she'd known, she would've told me," I said, thinking aloud.

"Which is why she doesn't know. Among other reasons."

"What other reasons?"

"It's in the past. We're not involved with the cartel anymore."

"How far in the past?" I asked warily. "Were you guys doing business with the cartel?"

"Fuck," he said again.

"Fuck like *this is going to be hard to explain* or *fuck, I can't explain?*"

"I *can't* explain, because it's club business, but I also know you won't let this go."

I waited patiently, my heartbeat thudding in my ears like a drum.

"First thing's first—whatever I say, you cannot repeat it. Not to Tavy, not even to another Old Lady. You're not supposed to know shit. Okay?"

"Okay," I whispered.

"Waco's been a hotbed of kidnappings. Human trafficking. Women…children…the club was attempting to shut it down. That's why Raze, Bones, Viper, Kelp and I joined the chapter down here. Colt needed more manpower after it went sideways."

He scrutinized me for a moment, gauging how I was taking the news.

Nausea swam in my belly and the back of my neck felt hot. "Did you win?"

"No. We didn't win. You don't win with the cartel. You just live long enough to keep them at bay, and if you're really lucky, protect the people you love. Anyway, we've been told to stay out of it. To walk away. So we did, and now we're not involved."

My brain turned over the cruel reality of what he'd said as silence loomed between us.

Smoke broke the tension, determination in his voice. "Logan, you've heard enough now. Just know that we aren't involved anymore. I need you to trust me on that."

I rubbed my third eye. "And you were trying to stop it…the human trafficking?"

"We were," he clipped. "We lost good men trying. But like I said, it's out of the club's hands and now we're trying to clean up Waco in other ways."

"By opening a clinic and a half-way house," I said in realization.

"We've done a lot of bad shit to make money and provide for our families. Helping the community won't wipe our souls clean."

I smiled slightly. "I get it now. You're the *Tarnished* Angels."

He clenched his jaw and nodded. "Do you think differently of me now?"

"Hard not to," I said quietly. "I just…what do I do with all this, Smoke?"

Smoke stood up. "I'm gonna go."

"What? Why?"

"Because I'm not going to try and convince you to let me stay."

"Hold on a second," I said, rising and facing him. "You can't just drop that bomb on me and expect me to work it all out and come to terms with it immediately. Give me a minute, here."

"Logan," he said, his voice raspy. "You don't owe me anything. You're not my Old Lady. You're not obligated to stand by my side. So, I'm gonna do the thing I should've done all along. I'm gonna let you go and let you get on with your life. Now you don't have to worry about being involved with a criminal."

Was Smoke a criminal? Yes. But he was so much more than that.

And when he walked toward the door, my heart lurched in my chest.

"*Don't go,*" I croaked.

He stopped with his hand on the door and looked at me over his shoulder. "Why not?"

"Because I need you," I said simply.

Rach's words came roaring back as I spoke to him. Smoke and I weren't forever, but the idea of never having him in my bed again, never feeling his strong arms wrapped around me while we slept, or never having him brush tears from my cheeks saddened me to the depths of my soul.

"Please stay, Smoke. Your past is your past. Let's leave it there."

His hand dropped from the knob and then suddenly he was marching across the room toward me. Smoke took me into his arms and slanted his mouth across mine.

"Blueberries," he said against my lips.

"Hmm?"

"You taste like blueberries."

"I had pie."

"Do I have to shave right this minute? Or can I put my scruff to use one last time?"

I pulled back and opened my eyes. "What did you have in mind?"

∽

My head rested on Smoke's bicep and I reached my hand up to grasp his fingers. It was the middle of the night and my heartbeat had slowed from its rapid rhythm to a melodic series of thuds.

"I didn't tire you out?" Smoke asked.

"Oh, you did. I'm just enjoying the moment."

He fell silent for a while and then he said, "This is gonna be hell on my sleep routine."

"Mine too."

"Guess it would've been easier if I didn't live at the clubhouse."

"How so?"

"If I had my own place, you could spend the night. The whole night."

I smiled. "And you wouldn't kick me out the moment we were finished?"

"Nah." He scooted closer, wormed his free hand underneath the coverlet, and rested it on my belly.

"Did you ever kick women out of the clubhouse? The ones you've slept with?"

"I'm not gonna talk about other women I've been with. And I'm definitely not gonna talk about them while I'm in bed with you."

"So thoughtful," I murmured.

His scent and warmth were luring me to sleep. It was amazing what good sex could do to relax a person.

"Talked with Prez today," Smoke said.

"Hmm. What about?"

"The apartment complex. Colt wants to hire you. He's going to call you to discuss it."

"He hasn't even seen the mockups for the space," I said. "Why would he want to hire me before he knows the kind of job I can do?"

"Apparently he trusts you—what with being such a straight shooter about the state the apartment building's in."

"On a scale of one to angry, how bad was it?"

"Livid."

"Yeah, I don't blame him."

"Zip also told Prez you were at his house yesterday morning talking to Joni about joists and stuff. So he gets that you know what you're talking about."

"For their kitchen renovation. We were discussing load-bearing walls."

"Looks like you've got work coming out your ears."

"It would seem that way. I wonder how much longer I can pretend that I don't have a viable business waiting for me to take the plunge."

"I think you'd be great at it."

I laughed. "You say that with such authority."

"Well, let's look at the facts. Your brothers work with your father in a family-owned business."

"Check."

"You clearly have enough projects under your belt to handle anything from a home kitchen renovation to a hotel lobby."

"How do you know I worked on a hotel lobby?"

"Mia might've looked you up online and saw your portfolio."

"Ah. Well, I didn't handle the hotel lobby on my own. I was part of a team."

"Splitting hairs."

"No, I'm just not taking credit that's not mine."

"I'm ignoring that part. You're looking for a fresh start. This could be part of that fresh start."

"Why are you so adamant that I do this for myself?"

"And that's the question you need to be asking. Why *wouldn't* you do this for yourself? Are you saying you're not worth betting on?"

"Oh, I see what you're doing."

"What am I doing?"

"Lighting a fire under my ass so I have something to prove."

"You don't have to prove anything to anyone. If you're happy with your career and the company you work for, fine. But if you want to go out on your own, I think you'd be great at it."

"Okay, can you not be so perfect?" I demanded.

He laughed. "How am I perfect?"

"You're just—you're so supportive. And kind. And good in bed."

"I am all those things. Plus, I've got great hair."

"Modest, too." I snorted. "Thanks, Smoke. Thank you for the stained glass, it was thoughtful. Thank you for shaving because I asked. Thank you for talking to me when you don't have to."

He roped his arm around me and tugged me tightly against him. "You should ask for more in life. You deserve it."

I fell asleep nestled in the crook of his arm, wondering if I deserved him.

Chapter 32

Tavy and I sat down at a hole-in-the-wall Italian restaurant for one of our impromptu catch-ups. It had been a crazy few days for me. Between juggling illicit meetings with Smoke and pondering my next career move, I'd finally found a window of time that coincided with Tavy's schedule.

"I think my dad is dating someone," Tavy announced.

"What makes you say that?" I asked lightly even though my heart was pounding in fear.

Yelling from the kitchen interrupted her reply and a moment later the kitchen door swung open and a woman who looked like she could be cast as an Italian grandmother in a film came out carrying several plates. She dropped them off at tables as she spoke in rapid-fire Italian.

I watched in fascination as she moved about the room, conversing with people who clearly didn't speak Italian, yet they were nodding along and smiling.

Finally, the woman came to our table.

"Hello," Tavy greeted with a smile.

The woman looked at Tavy, glanced at me, said a few sentences I couldn't understand and then dashed away, disappearing into the kitchen.

"What just happened?" Tavy asked.

"No clue," I said.

"No one's brought us any menus," she said.

The front door opened and my eyes widened when I recognized the couple strolling through.

"Logan!" Willa called.

Willa and Duke strode to our table. Her blonde hair was piled into a messy top bun and her skin glowed in the candlelight of the intimate restaurant.

"Hi," I said in surprise. "What are you guys doing here?"

"This is our spot," Willa explained. "Hi, Tavy."

"Hey." Tavy bobbed her head.

"I took her here on one of our very first dates, back when I was trying to get her to fall in love with me," Duke said.

"I was already in love with you. The meatballs just solidified my feelings," Willa teased, placing a hand on her husband's chest. "We come here or do take out at least once a week. It's our ritual."

"I love that," I said with a smile.

"How do you get a menu?" Tavy inquired.

"You don't," Duke replied. "Mama Leonardi will bring you food and wine."

"What if I don't like what she brings me?" Tavy asked.

"Won't happen," Duke assured her.

"She's like a food savant," Willa said. "Her husband is the one cooking in the kitchen. Just sit back and enjoy the magic."

The kitchen door swung open and Mama Leonardi came out carting a platter of antipasti, which she set down in front of us. She turned to Willa and Duke, her expression morphing into utter joy.

She kissed their cheeks, patted Willa's belly, and then whisked away to the bar. She poured two glasses of white wine and returned to our table. Mama Leonardi gestured to our food.

"Mangiare."

"That means *eat*," Duke said.

Tavy chuckled. "Got that. Thanks." She picked up an olive and popped it into her mouth. I watched as her expression completely changed into one of pure delight.

"That's the best olive I've ever had," Tavy commented.

"Try the roasted red peppers," Willa suggested. "You'll never be the same again."

Mama Leonardi looked at me and arched a brow, as if tacitly saying *Why haven't you tried my amazing food?*

I took Willa's suggestion and reached for a roasted red pepper. I nodded as I chewed. "Yep. Total convert." I beamed at Mama Leonardi.

She spoke again in Italian and then turned to address Duke and Willa. Duke nodded. Mama Leonardi floated away to the kitchen.

"Do you understand Italian?" I asked Duke.

"Yep," Duke replied.

"He's learning Italian with my sister," Willa explained.

"What did she say to you?" Tavy wondered.

"She said our food was almost ready but to sit at the bar and have a drink. Well, I'm supposed to have a drink. Willa will have something non-alcoholic."

"We'll let you guys get back to your dinner," Willa said.

The two of them went to the intimate L-shaped bar and sat down.

"Try the wine," Tavy said to me. "It's diabolical. And I have no idea what it is."

I took a small sip and nodded. "Bright and crisp. Cuts the heaviness of the food."

She rolled her eyes but smiled. "You sound like you know what you're talking about."

"Hmm, all those expensive Michelin-star restaurants Knox took me to taught me a lot about food and wine."

"You said his name without tripping over it."

I thought for a moment and nodded. "I did, didn't I?"

"How are you feeling about the whole thing?" she asked.

"Each day I feel better, but mostly because I refuse to think about it."

"Then I'll stop asking about it," she said with a smile.

We polished off the antipasti in record time. Mama Leonardi swept away our empty plates after she'd gotten Duke and Willa a round of drinks.

"I wonder what the next course will be," Tavy said.

"I wonder how many courses there *will* be," I said with a laugh.

The salad course came next and Mama Leonardi brought us four plates. She didn't bother explaining what any of them were, but Tavy and I figured them out.

"The fig and endive is my favorite," Tavy said.

"No way. The prosciutto and melon."

Mama Leonardi came out with several to-go bags for Duke and Willa. Duke handed over cash and then they hugged the grandmotherly woman goodbye. They waved to us on their way out.

"Okay, now I can talk about my dad again," Tavy said. "I didn't want to say anything while Duke was here. Small restaurant, you know?"

"Oh. Right. Your dad…"

I'd hoped Tavy had forgotten about our line of conversation, but apparently, she needed to talk about it.

"So why do you think your dad is dating someone?" I inquired.

"He's smiling. Like, a lot."

"And he's not a smiley kind of guy?"

"From what I've seen he is, but this is different. Like—*I'm getting a steady supply of ass* kind of smiley. And *ew*. Look, I can't believe I just mentioned my dad and sex in the same sentence, but I'm telling you, he's dating someone. Plus, he was singing Sweet Emotion under his breath."

I had to force myself not to smile. "If that is the case, would that bother you?"

"No, of course not. I want him to be happy, and I was even going to set him up with a coworker of mine, remember? My mom remarried, but Dad has never had a long-term relationship as far as I know. Not after Mom, anyway."

"No, he hasn't." I realized what I'd said and mentally cursed myself for my loose lips.

Tavy raised her brows. "And how would you know *that*?"

"We talked about it," I said. "On our drive to Waco."

"You did?"

I nodded and shrugged, feigning nonchalance. "I was talking about Knox, kind of purging everything, you know? Naturally your dad's past came up."

"Naturally," Tavy repeated, but her expression told me she didn't buy the explanation.

"Anyway. I think it's good you want him to be happy."

"I hope she's not a twit," Tavy said.

"You think your dad would date a twit?" I asked in wry amusement.

"I don't know the kind of woman my dad would date," she admitted. "He got with my mom when they were so young that I don't think she's a good indicator of what he'd want now. Did you know he shaved?"

"What does that have to do with anything?"

"Nothing. But I just find it weird and noteworthy considering what we're talking about."

"Maybe it's time for *you* to get a love life."

"I'm trying, babe." She shook her head. "Anyway, what's up with you?"

"I quit my job," I said.

"You *what*? When?"

"A few days ago."

"But why? You love your job!"

"I know." I smiled. "But I've decided to go into business for myself."

"Seriously?"

"Seriously." I nodded. "Colt wants to hire me to help with the apartment building. Joni is hiring me to mock up her kitchen for renovation. Seemed foolish not to dive in."

"What apartment building?"

"The one the club bought to help women who need a safe, affordable place to land after getting out of bad relationships, that sort of thing. It was Doc's idea," I said.

"Hmm. I'm all for community outreach and charity, but let's face it. You're not into real estate unless you want to make a buck. I wonder what the story is there, you know?"

"Yeah, me too." I frowned. I knew what the story was, but I wasn't at liberty to share it with Tavy.

Another secret between us.

"How's your crush on Raze?" I asked.

She sighed. "I dreamed about him the other night."

"Oh?"

"Yeah." She shook her head. "There's something about Raze that is just so…"

"Taboo?"

She nodded. "Yeah. Maybe I need to see a shrink and work out why I want a man who doesn't want me."

"You know he doesn't want you? You've asked?"

"Doesn't really matter, he won't touch me. I'm Smoke's daughter. They have rules, you know?"

"Apparently."

"I guess I should be grateful Raze doesn't want anything to do with me. Like I need to get tied up with a biker anyway." She paused. "Hmm…tied up…"

I sniggered.

"Don't laugh at me," she pleaded with a roguish smile. "You don't know what it's like."

"I don't?"

"No. You've dated every guy you've ever wanted."

"Hmm. Not really true. I wasn't sure I was into Knox. It was more like Knox told me I was into him and I let myself get swept away by his attention."

"Too bad a controlling narcissist lurked beneath the facade of his good looks."

"Well, it was a shit lesson," I admitted. "But I got out. And thankfully, he never gave me anything that required antibiotics."

She raised her glass. "I'll toast to that."

∼

"I'm so full I can hardly move," Tavy said. "And yet I still want to take an extra tiramisu to go."

"I won't say no."

"I'm not ready to go home, but I don't want to go to a bar," Tavy said. "Wanna hang out?"

"Sure," I said with a smile. "My place or yours?"

"Yours. I have neighbors who fight and then have loud makeup sex."

Mrs. Leonardi swept by our table, clearing the last of our dishes. I couldn't remember the last time I'd eaten so well. Middle of the night grilled cheeses with Smoke crossed my mind, but that was different.

"What's got you grinning?" Tavy asked.

"Hmm? Oh, nothing," I lied. "Let's get some dessert to go and head to my place."

"I need to use the restroom real fast."

While I was alone at the table, I shot off a quick text to Smoke.

ME

> Tavy's coming over to my apartment for a bit. I'll text you when she goes home.

He didn't reply right away and I shoved my phone into my purse as Tavy came back to the table.

"Everything good?" she asked.

"Yep."

Mama Leonardi brought us desserts to-go and our check. We paid and exited the restaurant.

"I think she said to come back," Tavy said. "But I'm not entirely sure."

"I'll be back. The food was unbelievable. See you at my place," I said.

Tavy made it there before I did, and by the time I was climbing out of my car in the parking lot of the bakery Tavy was bouncing up and down.

"I have to pee," she said.

"You just went," I said with a laugh.

"I broke the seal. Doesn't matter that I only had one glass of wine. My bladder is full."

"Okay, okay, let's go."

We hurried to the back door of the building and I quickly unlocked it. I gave her my keys and then turned off the alarm. I would set it again after Smoke came over. I'd given him the code so he could arm it when he left in the morning, which I appreciated because it meant I got to remain asleep. He really did have the short end of the stick, having to get up when it was still dark and ride his motorcycle back to the clubhouse just so no one would find out about us.

I entered the apartment and heard the toilet flush. A few minutes later, Tavy came out of the bathroom and pinned me with a stare.

"What?" I asked in confusion.

"You're keeping a secret from me."

"I am?"

My heart immediately began to run a marathon. Had she found the shaving cream and aftershave?

"There's a second toothbrush in your bathroom. You're having sleepovers with a guy!"

"What?" I let out a laugh, hoping it didn't sound as fake and maniacal to her as it did to me.

"Admit it! You're getting some!"

"I'm not getting any," I protested. "It's my new toothbrush. I'm throwing the old one away."

"Really?" Tavy asked.

"Really. Sorry to disappoint you."

"Damn, here I thought you were hooking up with Bones and getting, well, *boned*."

"Nope."

"Looks like we're both in a dry spell," she said. "It's probably better that you're not sleeping with anyone."

"Why is that?" I took the desserts out of the paper bag and put them in the fridge.

"Because you just broke up with someone."

"I thought you wanted me to have sex with someone new to get over Knox."

"The more I've thought about it, the more I think you're not wired that way, and pushing you to hook up with a random stranger isn't being a good friend."

"Can we please move along from my non-existent love life?" I begged.

"Sure. Just promise me one thing."

"What's that?"

"When you're ready to start dating, you'll tell me. I want to make sure he's worthy of you."

I smiled. "You're a good egg, Tavy."

"A really good egg," she agreed. "Don't judge me, but I'm ready to dive into the dessert."

"Have at it. I'm too full."

Tavy went to the fridge and pulled out her tiramisu. "So, about this interior design business you're starting…"

"Yeah?"

"Have you thought of a name?"

"Not yet."

"What kind of clients do you want?" She brought back the dessert with a fork and took a seat on the couch. "Like, do you want to do the kind of work you did with your firm in Las Vegas? Or do you want to do something else?"

I'd worked with several higher end clients, including billionaires and hoteliers. Those projects had been large scale, and very impersonal. The vision for a hotel lobby was different than what the club was doing with the apartment complex.

"Do I have to choose?" I asked.

"I guess not. But when you work for a firm, there's a team involved, you know? Not having a huge staff to work with will limit what you can do—in the beginning, I mean."

"Point taken," I agreed. "Budgets will be different too." I pondered for a moment. "But I like the idea of helping people turn a house into a home. You know?"

"Yeah. Just whatever you do, give yourself room to grow. The nice thing about working for yourself is that you can take your business in any direction that you want."

"Huh. You mean I get to choose what *I* want? That's new."

She laughed. "It's nice to have you back, Logan."

"It's nice to be back."

"Thought I lost you there, for a while," she said softly.

I leaned over and grabbed her hand. "Thanks for never abandoning me. Even though you probably wanted to shake some sense into me."

"I just saw you slowly slipping away. And I didn't know how to do anything to help you."

"You were perfect." Tears gathered in my eyes. "You could've lost your patience and left. Why didn't you?"

"I guess I always held out hope that you'd see the light before it was too late. I'm sorry it took you getting hurt to walk away."

I swallowed. "I—I haven't been completely honest with you. About Knox."

"Oh no…you're not talking to him again, are you?"

"*No*," I said quickly. "I'm done with him. Forever."

"Good. Then what is it?"

"He was starting to get…physical."

"Physical." Her eyes widened. "You mean, abusive?"

I nodded, my eyes meeting hers. "He never *hit* me. But last year after his firm's Christmas party, he thought I was flirting with one of his colleagues. When we got home, he grabbed my wrist hard enough to leave a mark."

"Logan," she whispered.

"And a few weeks ago, before I even knew he was

cheating, he got jealous and when we were intimate, he—he—"

"What did he do?" she demanded.

"He branded me," I blurted out. "He left bruises on my hips and back. Just from gripping me so hard. And it wasn't like, in the throes of passion he got carried away. He did it on purpose. To prove a point. So that every time I put on clothes, I winced in pain."

"*That God damn motherfucker, son of a bitch.* I'll castrate him! I'll—"

"Tavy," I interrupted.

"What?"

"There's more."

"More? Seriously?"

I bit my lip. "I didn't just change my number to avoid hearing from him. I did it because his texts were starting to become…terrifying."

"Terrifying how?"

"He was furious when he found out what I did to his car…and he was livid that I'd left him. He said he's going to find me, Tavy…" I met her gaze.

"Shit."

I nodded. "He doesn't know where I am, thank God. My life is here and I'm trying to move on." A flicker of a smile appeared on my lips, more for show than anything else. "I don't want to talk about it ever again. I just thought you should know."

"Okay." She nodded slowly. "You're my favorite person in the world. If you ever need help disposing of a body, I hope like hell I'm your first call."

I grinned. "You're number one in my Favorites on my phone for a reason."

Chapter 33

Tavy stayed far later than either of us expected. We had a deep dive about life, and what the future was going to look like. She left just shy of midnight despite the fact that she had to be up in a few hours.

I was tired and emotionally wrung out. And when I thought about calling Smoke to tell him to come over, guilt swamped me.

Though I'd been honest with Tavy about Knox's darker nature, I'd purposefully lied to her about my love life.

What was I doing? Jeopardizing my relationship with my best friend because I was hooking up with her dad?

God, I'm a soap opera character.

I picked up my cell phone and called Smoke.

"Cupcake," he said in greeting.

I hated the warmth curling through me at his endearment, and how much I enjoyed the raspy growl of his voice.

He'd answered on the first ring. Had he been sitting by the phone, waiting for me to call?

"Logan?"

"Hi. Yes, sorry."

"Tavy leave?"

"Yes."

"I'm leaving the clubhouse now."

"No. Wait. Hold on." I fell silent.

"What's up?"

"I don't think you should come over tonight," I said.

"Why not?"

"I'm tired."

Not a lie, but not the entire truth either.

"So I'll come over and we'll sleep."

"That's ridiculous. Why would you ride your motorcycle at this hour just to come over and sleep?"

"What's this really about?"

"We shouldn't be doing this," I blurted out. "It's wrong."

"Hmm. I disagree."

"We're lying to everyone. We're lying to Tavy. *I'm* lying to Tavy."

"What happened tonight?"

"She saw your toothbrush in my bathroom and she asked me if I was dating someone. I said no." I rubbed my forehead. "What are we doing, Smoke?"

"Having a good time."

"Right. A good time. I'm lying to my best friend about who I'm sleeping with. And for what? This isn't a serious relationship."

"If it was serious, would you tell her then?"

"That's not what I meant."

"What did you mean then?"

"I mean it doesn't matter if it's serious or casual. The fact is, we shouldn't be doing what we're doing."

"Because of Tavy."

"Yes."

"You're choosing your friendship instead of whatever this is between us."

"Whatever this is? Come on, Smoke. We're just fooling around."

"Are we?"

My lungs seized and suddenly I couldn't breathe easily.

"Yes," I wheezed out. "We're just fooling around."

"I miss you when I'm not with you," he said. "And I know you miss me too."

"Smoke, don't."

"Don't what? Don't tell you what we both know is true? If this was just fucking, would we talk the way we do? Laugh the way we do?"

"I just got out of a serious relationship."

"So?"

"So, I'm not emotionally ready to fall for someone else."

"Doesn't mean it's gonna stop you, cupcake." His voice was gentle, like he was talking to a spooked horse. "I've been around long enough, dated my fair share of women. I've never felt this way about anyone except you."

"I'm not ready for this."

My legs gave out and I collapsed onto the bed. I hadn't bothered turning on the light, so I sat in darkness.

"I think you're using Tavy as a convenient excuse not to admit how you really feel."

"And I think you don't care enough about her feelings."

"You don't think I care about her feelings?" he demanded. "Because I won't tell my adult daughter what I'm doing in my private life?"

"But your private life includes me, and me being Tavy's best friend means we're both lying to her and sneaking around and I don't like it."

"Then we should tell her, because you and I both know this is turning into something real." When I didn't reply, he said, "Good night, Logan."

The line went dead.

I tossed my phone aside and then fell back onto the bed, my legs still hanging off the mattress.

My mind was a whirl.

Is Smoke right?

I was fresh off a breakup. An intense breakup with a man who'd fucked with my head for longer than I cared to admit. A man who had a temper, a man who made me walk on eggshells for fear of upsetting him.

Smoke was the opposite of Knox in every way.

Good humored, easy to be with, in tune with my body.

I knew it wasn't just sex.

I'd realized that after we'd gotten stuck in the motel and were finally able to get back on the road.

We'd shared things with each other; personal things that you didn't go around telling strangers. And even though Smoke and I hadn't known each other long, there was something about him that made me feel safe enough to discuss private thoughts that I usually guarded.

"Fuck," I whispered.

I liked him. I liked him in and out of bed.

The person I'd usually talk to about this sort of thing was Tavy—and once again my brain looped around in an attempt to dissuade me.

I knew enough about psychology to know that my mind was designed to keep me feeling safe and in a pattern I recognized.

But what was my heart saying?

And was it loud enough to drown out the noise?

I finally rolled out of bed at 6:00 AM after not having fallen into a deep enough sleep. Not only had I tossed and turned, but I couldn't get comfortable. I was hot, then cold. Just as I'd fall asleep, adrenaline would spike and wake me up.

So I went to the gym and pushed myself hard on the treadmill. Unfortunately, it did nothing to quiet my brain.

I looked at my phone far more often than was healthy, hoping I had a text from Smoke even though I knew it was better if we broke off all contact.

Distance was necessary. This thing with Smoke needed to die. Not just to preserve my relationship with Tavy, but also to safeguard my heart.

He was easy to fall in love with.

I wiped down the machine, grabbed my stuff, and left.

The café was busy when I got there and I didn't want to wait for coffee. The lack of sleep made my head throb. What I really needed was a shower and a nap, not caffeine.

I showered and threw on a tank top before settling back into bed. My eyes closed and I passed out.

My ringing phone woke me.

With a groan and a crack of my eyelids, I looked at the alarm clock. I'd slept two hours, but it wasn't enough.

I grabbed my phone and saw it was Tavy. "Hello?"

"Were you asleep?"

"Yes."

"Perks of working for yourself. You get to sleep in."

"Ha, ha. I've already been to the gym."

"And you went back to bed?"

"Indigestion," I lied. "From the food last night."

"Really? That sucks."

"Yeah."

What's another lie to my best friend?

"So, what's up?" I asked her, throwing the covers off me and heading to the kitchen.

"I called my grandfather back."

"You did? When?"

"This morning," she said. "I paced and paced around my apartment, trying to think of a reason why I should ignore him, but my curiosity was too great, so I called."

"And?"

"He apologized for not being around when I was growing up," she said. "I guess I appreciate the sentiment, but really, I don't know what I missed, you know? I told him he was apologizing to the wrong person."

"Whoa."

"Yeah. I kind of didn't hold back just because he's in his eighties. I kind of let him have it."

"Of course you did."

"Oddly enough, my grandfather, Clinton Crawford the First, appreciated that I was a straight shooter."

"He knows your worth."

"Yep. Anyway, he asked me if I'd be willing to talk to my dad and see if I could convince him to speak to his father."

"Your grandfather wants you to be the liaison?"

"Yep. Except, I don't know how that'll go."

"Yeah, that's a lot to put on you."

"It is." She paused. "Will you be there?"

"There? There where?"

"When I talk to Dad?"

"Are you serious? You can't be serious."

"I am serious," she said. "Please, Logan. I don't know how to navigate this. I'm not—I'm not the most delicate when it comes to these things, and I just think you'd be a calming presence."

"Tavy…"

"For me, Logan. Do it for me?"

I closed my eyes. "For you."

~

"I'm buying your dinner," Tavy said the next night as she sat across the table from me.

"Damn right you are." I reached for my glass of water, nausea swimming in my belly at the thought of facing Smoke after our conversation.

Tavy and I sat in a corner booth of the bar and grill while we waited for Smoke.

"Does he know I'm here? Or did you pretend this was just one of your father daughter dinners?" I asked.

"Um…"

"Tavy, no. We're ambushing him!"

"The conversation was going to be an ambush no matter what," she protested. "So might as well do it with you here."

"Well, at least you warned *me*."

"Ouch. That hurts a little. You don't think I should do this?"

"What? Tell your dad about your grandfather in a public place with me here? Definitely not."

"But you do think I should tell him."

"I think your family is your family."

"That's diplomatic of you," she muttered. "Crap. There's Dad."

Smoke strode across the restaurant and my heart jumped into my throat. He wore his leather cut and jeans, his muscular, tattooed arms on display. His clean-shaven jaw made him look younger, almost boyish, as did the smile appearing on his lips when he saw Tavy.

When he realized I was there, his grin dissipated and he frowned.

Tavy slid out of the booth and embraced him.

"Hope you don't mind that Logan's here," Tavy said, her voice pitched unusually high.

Smoke pulled back from his daughter. "Not at all."

"We waited to order drinks," Tavy said, sitting back down and sliding all the way over so Smoke could take the spot next to her.

I had a direct line of site to the man who I didn't know if I was still sleeping with.

The server arrived at our booth and took our drink orders.

"Haven't seen you for a few days," Smoke said to Tavy. "How are things?"

"Things are good," she said.

"The job?"

"Good."

I played with the straw in my soda.

"How are you, Logan?" Smoke asked.

My gaze whipped to his. "Fine. Thanks."

"You're liking your living situation?"

I nodded.

"Dating anyone?"

Tavy shot her dad a frown. "Why would you ask her that?"

He shrugged. "Just making polite conversation."

"I'm thinking about joining a dating app," I lied.

Tavy looked shocked. "Wait, what? Just last night you said you weren't ready to date."

I glanced at her and smiled. "I changed my mind."

The server returned and asked if we were ready to order.

"We haven't even looked at the menus yet," Tavy said with an apology.

"I know what I want," Smoke said, not taking his eyes off me.

Tavy reached for her menu. "Go ahead."

"Burger medium rare, bleu cheese, side of fries."

"Great," the server said. He looked at me. "Do you know what you'd like?"

"She can't choose between a burger or a salad," Smoke said before I could talk. "She thinks she should have the salad because it's a healthier choice, even though she really wants a burger."

Tavy looked at him in confusion. "That's a strange thing to say."

"He's right," I said to Tavy. My smile had a little more teeth than usual. "He knows *exactly* what's going on in my head. I'm impressed, Smoke. So why don't you order for me."

"Nah, I'd never take away your choice," he said. He took a long pull of his beer. "You order."

I wasn't hungry and my stomach was in knots, but I looked at the server and smiled. "Do you have any *smoked* meat?"

"No. Sorry."

"Hmm. Okay. Guess I'll settle for a bowl of the soup of the day. I'm not really that hungry."

Smoke arched a brow.

"Ma'am?" The server looked at Tavy.

"I'll have the same thing as him. Thanks."

We handed off our menus and the server flitted away.

"I need to use the restroom," Tavy announced.

Smoke stood up to let her out.

When she disappeared down the hallway, I looked at Smoke and glared. "You're a jack ass."

"Am I?" he asked quietly. "What are you really doing here, Logan? I thought I was having dinner with my daughter. I had no idea you were tagging along."

"Tagging along? She asked me to be here."

"Why?"

"That's for her to explain." I glanced in the direction of the bathroom. "Can we not do this right now? This dinner isn't about us."

"Oh, so there's still an *us*?" he asked.

I was spared from having to answer because Tavy returned to the table.

"That was fast," he said as he got out of the booth.

"I just needed to wash my hands." She settled back into her seat and then grabbed her cocktail and took a few healthy swallows.

"Easy there, kiddo," Smoke teased. "Pace yourself."

Tavy looked at me, her eyes wide. I nodded.

She took a deep breath and faced her father. "Grandpa called me."

"Grandpa? Grandpa who? Leslie's father?"

"*Your* dad," she clarified.

Smoke brows went toward his hairline. "Seriously?"

She nodded. "He wants to—ah—make amends."

"Wow." He sat back in the booth. "And you were worried how I'd feel about it? You talking to your grandfather."

"No." She swallowed. "He wants to make amends with *you*. He thought you wouldn't listen to him, so he called me and asked…asked if I'd be the bridge."

Smoke didn't say anything and Tavy went on, "I think he's actually really sorry about how everything happened all those years ago."

"Is he dying?" Smoke asked.

She paused. "Not that I know of."

"Hmm. Okay." Smoke lifted his half-finished pint and downed the rest. He slammed it on the table, got up, and left without saying another word.

Tavy looked at the exit and then to me. "That kind of went the way I expected it to."

～

"You going to be okay?" I asked her as I pulled into a parking spot near her apartment building.

"Yeah. I'll be fine." She unlatched her seatbelt. "Thanks for coming with me."

"Well, I did get a free meal out of it," I said with a smile.

"And I have breakfast for tomorrow." She lifted Smoke's meal that the server boxed up.

"Bleu cheese in the morning? Yuck."

She laughed, but quickly sobered. "How long do you think he's going to be mad at me?"

"I don't think he's mad at you," I said quietly. "I think he doesn't like the idea of his father using you to get to him. He doesn't want you to get hurt, you know?"

"Yeah. Makes sense. I mean, my grandparents didn't just write me off, they wrote off their own son because he made a choice they didn't agree with."

"Would you do that?" I asked.

"Write off my kid because they knocked someone up?"

"No, I mean. If someone made a mistake, would you forgive them?"

"I guess it depends on what the mistake is, but yeah, it would have to be pretty bad for me not to forgive someone."

Now. Now is the time to tell her.

"Tavy, I—"

Her phone rang, stopping my admittance in its tracks.

"Hold on." She dug her cell out of her bag. "It's my boss. I have to take this."

She answered the call and I planned on telling her the truth as soon as she hung up the phone.

"Sure, no problem at all. Okay, bye." She dropped her cell in her lap. "Sorry about that. There's a patient that needs a live-in nurse for about a week. The patient lives an hour away. I leave tomorrow."

"Oh. Okay."

"Probably for the best. Give my dad some time to cool down."

"Yeah. Probably."

"Better get in there and pack," she said.

I reached across the car and hugged her. "Safe drive tomorrow."

"Thanks. And thanks for coming with me tonight."

I pulled back. "What are friends for?"

She reached for the door handle. "He was being weird tonight."

"Was he?"

"Yeah. Before I told him about his father, I mean. What the hell was the deal about you wanting a salad versus a burger?"

"I couldn't even begin to guess," I said.

Tavy got out of the car and closed the door. She waved before heading into her apartment building. I waited until I knew she was safely inside and then I drove home.

I parked underneath a streetlamp, grabbed my purse, and then locked the car. I turned the corner into the back alley of the bakery, my heart tripping in a fear.

A man leaned against the wall, his body cast in shadow.

I grappled with my purse, wondering why the hell I hadn't thought to walk with my pepper spray in hand.

The shadow came toward me and I opened my mouth to scream when a patch of moonlight suddenly revealed his identity.

Chapter 34

Smoke came into the light.

The scream died on my lips, but I snapped at him anyway. "*What the hell?* You scared the shit out of me!"

"I'm sorry," he said. "That wasn't my intention."

"Why are you here?" I demanded.

"Several reasons. Can I come upstairs?"

"I don't think that's a good idea," I said.

"Why?"

"You know why."

"I promise I'll sit on one side of the couch and you can sit on the other and I'll keep my hands to myself."

I sighed. "It's probably stupid of me to concede, but okay. Come upstairs."

When we got into my apartment, I closed the door after him. "Something to drink?"

"No. I'm fine." He stared at me from several strides away.

"Where do you want to start?" I asked.

"How about we sit."

I nodded. "Yeah. Sitting. Sitting is good."

Neither of us made a move.

He raked a hand through his hair. "I shouldn't have left the restaurant."

"Maybe not. I get why you did, though."

"No, you don't." He shook his head. "I left as much from Tavy's news as I did because you were sitting across from me. I can't be in public with you and not want to touch you, hold you, look at you. God damn it, Logan. It's all I can do not to stare at you like a fucking schoolboy with his first crush."

"I don't know what to do with that."

"I'm just telling you. My cards are on the table, okay? I know you just got out of a shit situation. I know you uprooted your life and you're just getting your bearings. I know I'm seventeen years older than you. I know I'm your best friend's father. I know all that. But it doesn't change the fact that I want this. I want *you*."

"Smoke," I whispered.

"I don't want to hide this. I get why you do. But the longer we hide, the more pissed she's going to be. Because you and I both know this isn't casual. This isn't just two people hooking up and going our separate ways."

"How can you know that?" I asked, my voice cracking. "I was with Knox for three years and I was never sure about him. How can you know after, what, a couple of rolls in the hay? A couple of late-night conversations?"

Smoke marched toward me and gently cradled my face in his palms. "I know because I *know*. Are you scared because you feel things with me you never felt with him? Or are you scared that I'm going to break your heart?"

"I'm scared that you know exactly what I'm feeling without me even having to vocalize it," I admitted.

Tears leaked from the corners of my eyes. Smoke bent down to brush them away with his lips.

"I'm worried it's too soon," I said.

His lips grazed the apple of my cheek.

"I'm worried I don't know how to be by myself so I'm falling in love with the first man who's good to me."

His mouth covered mine.

Gentle.

Understanding.

Without any sort of agenda.

Smoke lifted his lips from mine and then pulled me into his arms. I snuggled against his chest.

"If there's a chance of this working—" he said quietly, "—then we have to tell Tavy. Sooner rather than later."

"She just got a week-long job caring for a patient out of town. I guess we should tell her when she gets back."

It terrified me. Not only because it meant being honest with her and letting her have her feelings, but because it meant Smoke and I were out in the open. It was the right thing to do, yet I dreaded it.

Smoke pulled me toward the couch. He sat down and then patted the spot next to him. I sat and he grasped my legs and dragged them across his lap.

"I'm fucking pissed that my father went through Tavy to try and get to me," he said.

"Are you surprised?"

"No. I can still be pissed about it though. He should've called me."

"Would you have taken his call?"

He looked at me. "Yeah, okay. Fair point."

I smiled.

"I don't want him to hurt her," Smoke said quietly.

"You mean, you don't want him to reject her the way he rejected you all those years ago."

"Now whose turn is it to be astute?"

"Smoke, he already rejected her. I mean when her

mother was pregnant, your parents said they didn't want anything to do with her. So, she grew up without them. That's their loss, not hers. What's this really about? Are you worried your father hasn't changed? Are you worried that he's just trying to pull you back into a life you're no longer part of?"

"People don't change."

"They don't?"

He looked at me. "You really believe people can change?"

I thought about his question for a moment and then I nodded slowly. "Yeah. I do. I believe they have to *want* to change, but yeah."

"You stand behind that?"

"I do."

"I hope you never become jaded," he said. "Fuck."

"You're going to call him, aren't you?"

"Yeah."

"It'll be okay," I said. "You want me to sit with you and hold your hand the way you did when I spoke to Knox?"

"Maybe," he joked and then smiled. He blew out a puff of air. "It would be easier not to call. It's been so long already. I could just let this go. Move on with my life. Wait for news of his death."

"If you don't call, you might regret it later. You don't have to open the door all the way, but maybe leave it cracked and see what happens. Yeah?"

"Yeah."

I leaned forward and kissed him. "You want to stay the night? The whole night?"

"The whole night? No alarm?"

"Nope."

"We get to wake up together?"

"Yep."

"So, I can go downstairs in the morning and grab us coffee and pastries and bring them up so we can have them in bed while you're wearing my shirt?"

"Or you can stay in bed and I'll get the pastries and coffee."

"Not ready for Brooklyn to find out about us yet, huh?"

"Something tells me that news would spread like wildfire. Let's just decide which direction the fire burns first, okay?"

"Okay. I'll let you get the pastries and the coffees, but you still have to promise to get back in bed and wear my shirt. I like you in my clothes."

He reached up and cupped my face, grazing his thumb across my cheekbone. "You look tired."

"I didn't sleep well last night," I admitted.

"No?"

I shook my head.

"Neither did I."

I swung my legs off his lap and stood up. "Let's get an early night."

We brushed our teeth side by side in the tiny bathroom. I kept looking over at him, wondering how this was real.

I'd gone from thinking Smoke and I *had* to end, to the realization that our relationship was allowed to breathe. I had a week to figure out what I was going to say to Tavy—and a week to find a present to give her so that she was in a good mood when I told her I was sleeping with her father.

I let out a giggle.

Smoke spit toothpaste into the sink. "What's funny?"

I spoke around the toothbrush in my cheek. "My life. I feel like I belong on one of those talk shows where they drop some truth bomb on their friends and family and then chairs get thrown across the stage."

"You didn't accidentally sleep with my twin brother and are now pregnant, are you?"

"No, but that sounds like a pretty good set up for a romance novel."

"Speaking of romance novels…I finally did some research about reverse harems…"

"Research? What kind of research?" I asked.

"I might've started reading one of them. You little bookworms are *filthy*." He grinned. "I like it."

I laughed and bumped my hip against his. I leaned over the sink and spit out the toothpaste. "Give me a minute. I need some privacy."

He rinsed his toothbrush and set it in the holder and then left me alone and went into the bedroom. I closed the door and finished up my bedtime routine.

When I came out of the bathroom, Smoke was already supine in bed and his eyes were closed. By the rise and fall of his breath, I deduced he was asleep.

I turned off the light and gingerly climbed into bed next to him. With a sigh, I curled into him and closed my eyes.

His arm came around me and urged me closer.

"I thought you'd fallen asleep," I said.

"No. Just thinking."

"About?"

"After I left the restaurant, I drove around for hours. I kept thinking about what Tavy said about my father. I was halfway to the clubhouse a dozen times, thinking I'd find Raze or Kelp to talk to about everything. But I didn't want to tell them."

"No?"

"No. You were the only one I wanted to see. The only one I felt comfortable enough to talk to about it all with. Good night, Logan."

Lips brushed my bare neck, drifting down across my collar bone.

"Mmm," I moaned as Smoke's fingers dipped into the seam of my body.

I writhed against him as he teased and stroked. I was just on the brink of coming when he removed his fingers.

A noise of objection escaped my lips.

Smoke chuckled as he gently tugged my shirt off. My panties quickly followed.

"*Smoke*," I murmured.

His lips captured mine in a drugging kiss.

I yearned for more. I wanted him inside me.

"I have to see you," he said, his mouth still pressed against mine.

A moment later he reached over and turned the lamp on, bathing us both in a warm, amber glow.

He knelt on the bed, looming over me, blissfully and beautifully naked. He took himself in hand and began to glide up and down his shaft.

I reached for him.

He shook his head. "Touch yourself, Logan."

My eyes met his as my hand drifted down my body. I was already wet and aching, and Smoke's focused gaze on what I was doing quickly lit a fire within me.

I slid my fingers between my folds, dancing and skating around my clit.

He pumped harder and faster, his ink morphing in the light across his rippling muscles.

"I want to come like this," he rasped.

I nodded. We pleasured ourselves to the sight of one another. We didn't touch, but we were linked through our eyes.

I was captivated and couldn't look away.

My back arched as my orgasm ripped through me. And while I was riding out my release, Smoke threw his head back, gritted his teeth and came.

His warm seed painted my breasts and belly.

I felt possessed and wanted, and I silently crowed with feminine power.

He collapsed onto the bed next to me, his breathing labored. Smoke propped himself up on one elbow as he began to calm. He swirled his essence onto my skin.

"Taste," he whispered, lifting his fingers to my lips.

I sucked his fingers deep into my mouth, licking them clean.

"Fuck," he growled. "That's hot."

I slowly sat up and then I made my way into the bathroom to turn on the shower. I slid the curtain aside and climbed into the steamy water and let out a sigh of pleasure.

There was light rap on the door followed by the sound of it opening. The curtain pulled back just enough for Smoke to step in behind me. My face was turned up to the spray and Smoke pressed himself to my back.

"This is beginning to feel familiar," I said.

He soaped my back and then reached around to wash my breasts and belly. His hands lingered and I leaned against him and enjoyed his touch.

It was a quick shower, and before I knew it we were back in bed, cuddling.

I didn't want to say it out loud, but I couldn't stop the thought.

I feel safe in his arms.

Sunlight streamed through the blinds, gently easing me awake. I yawned so hard my jaw popped. I glanced at the clock.

Just past nine.

Smoke was still asleep. He was on his back and I had a perfect view of his chiseled jaw and the five o'clock shadow that had grown since he'd shaved.

Smiling, I crept from the bed and hastily threw on some clothes. I slid into my flip flops and quietly left the apartment and closed the front door.

I was beaming, lost deep in thoughts of the sexy man upstairs in my bed when I entered the bakery. Thankfully, there were only a few people in line, and neither Jazz nor Brielle were on the floor.

When it was my turn, I gave the barista my order.

"I'll put it on your tab," she said.

"Thanks." I grinned and dropped a few bucks into the tip jar and then moved off to the side to wait for my coffees and pastries.

"Logan!"

I turned at the sound of my name.

Willa, Mia, and Sutton were sitting at corner table with pads of paper, pens, mugs and plates in front of them.

I couldn't avoid them now that they'd seen me, and immediately began to wonder if there were no other place in the city to have breakfast.

"Good morning," I said as I came over. "What are you guys up to?"

"We're having a meeting about Mia's new bar," Willa said. "We're talking website design."

"My bar with Boxer," Mia corrected. "We're opening a jazz bar with a speakeasy feel."

Sutton grinned. "It's really exciting."

"Sutton's going to be the GM," Mia explained.

"Oh, wow. Cool," I said.

"We'll need people to taste test the cocktails," Mia said. "You and Tavy in?"

"I'm sure Tavy and I can help you out," I said with a smile.

"Logan, your drinks are ready," the barista called.

"Drinks?" Willa asked. "As in plural?"

"You double fisting the caffeine?" Mia teased.

"Um. Yeah, double fisting."

"Sounds kinky," Sutton joked.

"Oh." Willa blinked, her stare zoning in over my shoulder.

With a sigh, I turned even though I knew exactly who I was going to see.

Smoke.

He saw me and smiled and then his gaze landed on the three Old Ladies.

"And the plot thickens," Sutton said.

Smoke ambled over to us as we froze in awkward silence.

And without a word, he wrapped his arm around me and rested his hand on my hip.

Mia lifted her mug to her lips, but it didn't hide her smile.

Sutton doodled a little heart on her pad of paper and Willa just continued to stare.

"I've got to go," Smoke said to me, pressing a kiss to my forehead. "I'll call you later."

I nodded.

He released me and addressed the trio. "Ladies. Always a pleasure."

The doorbell jangled as he passed through the exit, and Smoke was gone.

"So," Mia said.

Fire & Frenzy

I sighed. "Yeah…"

"Get your coffees, pull up a chair, and give us the dirt," Sutton said.

"Do I have to?" I asked.

"Yep," Willa said.

"You guys don't seem that surprised," I said.

"Oh, we're not," Mia said. "We already knew you guys were going to get together."

"Wait, we *who*?" I demanded.

"Me," Mia said. She pointed to Willa and Sutton. "Them. The rest of the Old Ladies. Pretty much everyone, actually."

"And the club," Sutton added. "Viper and I have already talked about you guys in great detail."

"Yeah, okay, I definitely need those coffees." I walked back to the counter, grabbed the drinks and pastries and brought them over to the table.

"Aww, so cute," Sutton drawled. "Were you bringing him pastries and coffee in bed?"

"Maybe." I sighed.

Willa got up and grabbed a vacant chair from the table nearby. I plunked my bottom into it and clutched one of the coffees in my hands.

"How did everyone know?" I asked. "We were being so careful."

"*Careful.*" Mia snorted. "Everyone knew at the freakin' barbecue that something happened between you guys on the drive to Waco."

I groaned. "Do you think Tavy noticed?"

Willa shook her head. "No. She definitely didn't notice."

"I don't know how though," Sutton said. "It was like, *obvious* obvious."

"Why do you think Bones told everyone he was

pursuing you?" Mia asked. "He was trying to get Smoke to admit he wanted you."

"Yeah, he wanted me—in his bed," I said.

Sutton looked between Willa and Mia and then back to me.

"What's that look mean?" I demanded.

"Who's gonna tell her?" Willa asked.

"I'll do it," Mia volunteered. "Look. It's not as simple as saying Smoke just wanted you in his bed. These men don't date. They either sleep with a woman and never see her again, or make them an Old Lady."

"The concept of dating is lost on them," Willa said.

"Wait a second." I held up my hand. "Smoke and I just agreed to tell Tavy. And now you're telling me it's got to be more than that? I'm not ready for more than that."

"You don't know how the club operates," Mia said slowly. "You don't know these men. They don't fuck around when they want a woman. And I really doubt Smoke is the kind of guy to fuck his relationship up with his estranged daughter by screwing her best friend. He could screw anyone and they wouldn't have a connection to Tavy. But he's risking being with you. That has to mean something."

"I just ended an engagement," I said.

"Yeah," Willa said with a nod.

"With a really bad guy who fucked with my head a lot," I added.

"I noticed you didn't say *heart*," Mia said.

I scoffed. "Not you too. It seems like everyone but me realized I was more pissed than hurt that Knox cheated on me."

"Well, if your heart really wasn't on the line," Sutton said. "Then why does it matter if you're falling for Smoke?"

"Who said I'm falling for Smoke?"

The three of them looked at each other.

"You guys have to stop doing that," I stated.

"Sorry. It kind of happens when you become an Old Lady," Willa explained. "We can say a lot without having to *say* anything."

"Okay, here's the thing about secrets, too," Sutton added. "They're not secrets if even one person knows your business. And judging by your business, the entire world knows what's going on between you and Smoke."

"Telling Tavy is the right call," Mia said.

"And what am I supposed to tell her?" I asked in desperation.

"The truth," Willa said. "That you're totally falling for her father."

Chapter 35

I DIDN'T HAVE time to internalize Willa's words because Sutton's phone chimed. She looked at the screen. Her cheeks instantly flamed. "Gotta go," she said quickly. "We're done here, right?"

"Yeah, go on." Mia laughed.

Sutton gathered her stuff, shoved the pad of paper and pen into her shoulder bag, and scurried out of the bakery without a backward glance.

"What was that about?" I asked in confusion.

"Viper and Sutton are trying to make a baby," Mia said. "They're both very committed to the cause."

"I see," I said with a laugh. "She ran out of here like her pants were on fire."

"Burnin' loins," Willa joked. She rested a hand on her lower abdomen.

"Does everyone have baby fever?" I asked. "You're pregnant. Brooklyn's pregnant. Sutton's trying to get pregnant. And Mia, Allison, Rach, and Joni all already have babies."

"Biker baby fever," Mia explained. "It hits different."

"Hmm, I'll have to take your word for it." I didn't even want to think about little biker babies. But of course, my brain was my brain, and I instantly wondered if Smoke wanted more kids. I doubted it. He was in his early forties. He had his life settled.

"So, the new bar, huh?" I asked Mia.

Mia nodded. "I sold my old bar. I want to do something different this go round. Something a little…what's the word I'm looking for? Classier. Less bar brawls, for starters."

"To be fair, our boys didn't start most of those brawls," Willa pointed out.

"True. Listen, I'd love to stay and keep talking, but I have a meeting with Silas's teacher." Mia stood up. "We all need to hang out again."

"Why don't we do another club barbecue?" Willa suggested.

"We could," Mia said. "But the clubhouse land is such a mess, what with all the construction going on right now. I'll be glad when it's finished. Anyway. We'll figure something out. Bye guys."

Mia waved and then left.

"What about you?" Willa asked. "Do you have to get going?"

I shook my head. "No. Not right away. Now that I quit my job, my schedule is open."

"You quit your job?"

"That was a bit dramatic. I didn't quit because I hated it or anything, I quit because I'm starting my own design business."

Willa smiled. "You are?"

"Yep. Between Joni's kitchen remodel and the club's apartment complex, I'd be a fool not to capitalize on the momentum."

"You'll need a website."

"That I will," I agreed.

Willa's phone rang, and she sent me an apologetic smile before answering it. "Hey, no I haven't forgotten. I'll be right there. Okay, bye."

She hung up. "Sorry. I have a standing pedicure appointment with my sister. She's waiting for me, so I need to get going. I'm free this afternoon, though. You want to come to my house and we can sit and discuss what you're looking for as far as branding goes?"

"I'd love that," I said, rising from the table. "It's clearly none of my business, but isn't it a school day?"

"Waverly's homeschooled." She smiled. "My home life is kinda out of the ordinary. I'll tell you about it when you come over. I'll text you the address. Three o'clock okay?"

I nodded. "Three sounds good."

∼

"I've arrived safely," Tavy said. "And I'm currently having tea and a Danish in the study."

"Why does it sound like you're playing a board game? Did you kill the professor with the knife in the kitchen?" I leaned against the side of my car and hit the clicker to lock it.

She laughed. "It did sound like that, didn't it?"

"How's the patient?" I asked.

"Um, I actually can't talk about it. I had to sign an NDA. Can't even use generalities on this one."

"Whoa, so he must be a pretty big deal, whoever he is," I said.

"Can't even tell you if it's a *he*."

A horse whinnied, momentarily pulling my attention. I

looked into the pasture and saw two beautiful horses standing at the fence.

"Was that a horse?" Tavy asked.

"Yep."

"Are you at the rodeo?"

"Nope. I'm at Willa and Duke's. They live out in horse country."

"Was that *their* horse neighing?"

"I don't think so," I said. "I think it was their *neigh*bor's."

"You didn't."

"Oh, I did."

"Dad joke alert," she quipped.

"Of the highest order," I agreed.

"So why are you at Willa and Duke's?"

"I'm here to talk to Willa about my website," I said.

"Oh, cool! I can't wait to hear all about it when I get back."

"Yeah, about when you get back," I said. "Can we have dinner the night you get back in town?"

"I'd love to, but I already made plans with my dad. He called almost as soon as I got on the road. He's not upset with me about my grandfather making contact."

"That's good."

"Yeah, I think so. I don't know if he'll call his dad, but that's not really up to me to decide. You know?"

"Yeah. Hard decisions all the way around."

"But he said he wants to talk to me about something important. Ten bucks says he finally comes clean about having a girlfriend. Maybe I'll get a new mommy."

I forced a laugh even though I felt sick inside.

"But the night after," she promised.

"Sounds good."

I doubted she'd be talking to me when she found out the truth, but all I could do was hope for the best.

"Talk to you later," she said.

"Enjoy your Danish."

I hung up with her. An autumn breeze wafted toward me, bringing with it the scent of horses and manure.

The front door of Willa's home opened and two teenagers stepped outside. "Willa," the redhead called. "There's a strange woman lurking outside our home."

Willa appeared, wrapped her arm around the redhead and jostled her. "Why are you the way that you are?"

The redhead grinned. "You're responsible for my behavior, therefore you should look in a mirror."

"Don't mind my sister," Willa called to me. "She's a heathen."

I laughed as I walked toward the front steps. "I have four older brothers. I get it. You must be Waverly."

"Guilty," she said.

"And this non-heathen is Sailor," Willa introduced.

The blonde smiled. "Nice to meet you."

Willa released Waverly.

"We'll be back for dinner," Waverly said.

"Dylan too?"

"Dylan too." Waverly looked at me. "It was nice meeting you."

"You too," I said.

The teenagers climbed into an old green pickup truck and reversed out of the driveway and disappeared down the street.

"Come on in," Willa said.

"Thanks." I stepped into the foyer. I glanced at Willa's bare feet and red toenails. "Want me to take off my shoes?"

"If you want," she said.

I kicked off my shoes and followed her through the hallway to the kitchen. "Your sister is a pistol."

"That she is. But I'd take pistol any day over the alternative. She knows her own mind, and at fifteen that doesn't seem to be the norm."

"Wow, she's fifteen?" I shook my head. "And her friend? Sailor?"

"Sailor's sixteen. She lives with us, too. Drink?"

"Oh, water's fine. Thanks. So your fifteen-year-old sister lives with you and Duke, and so does Sailor?"

"Yep." Willa grinned. "And Savage has a room here too."

"You're like a regular youth hostel. Is Sailor homeschooled also?"

Willa shook her head and went to the cabinet to grab a cup. "No. We're not legally her guardians, so she has to attend school. But her home life was a shit situation. Her dad doesn't even care where she is."

"Wow," I said quietly. "That's sad. But also, that's incredible that you and Duke took her in."

Willa handed me the glass of water. "We definitely have a full house. But we like it that way. Plus, Waverly's boyfriend Dylan is over all the time, so he feels like part of the family too."

"I love the chaos of a big family," I said. "I miss mine."

"And does Smoke like the chaos of a big family?" She blinked blue eyes at me.

"You couldn't look less innocent," I said with a laugh. "But I didn't come here to discuss me and Smoke."

Motorcycles rumbled in the distance.

"I bet your neighbors love that," I said.

"I don't complain about the livestock that get out or the smell of manure, and they don't complain about the motorcycles."

"Is livestock getting out a regular thing around here?"

"Yep. Last week it was the goats. The week before that it was the pigs."

The front door opened and a few moments later, Duke strode into the kitchen, followed by Savage and Acid.

Duke kissed his wife and slung an arm around her waist. "Sorry to interrupt girl time. Hi, Logan."

"You're not interrupting girl time," she said with a smile. "You're interrupting a business meeting."

"Business meeting?" Savage immediately went to the fridge and pulled out a can of soda and tossed one to Acid, and then took another for himself.

"I'm opening my own interior design business and Willa and I are talking websites," I explained.

"Interior design, huh?" Savage cracked the can of soda. "So, I could hire you to design my sex dungeon?"

"When you have your own house and no longer crash regularly in our spare bedroom, you can have a sex dungeon," Willa said. "Until then, no dice."

"Sex dungeon design isn't really part of my domain," I quipped.

"Where's Squirt one and Squirt two?" Savage inquired.

"They went to meet up with Dylan," Willa explained. "They'll be back for dinner. Are you guys staying for dinner?"

"Nope. Acid and I have dates," Savage said.

"Dates?" Willa asked.

"Okay, not so much dates as women who will suck our—"

Duke reached out and clapped the back of Savage's head.

Savage grinned. "Congrats, by the way."

I frowned. "You're saying that to me?"

"Yeah. You're with Smoke, aren't you?" Savage pressed.

"We're not allowed to talk about it," Willa announced. "Sorry, Logan. This meeting has kind of gotten away from us."

"No kidding." I chuckled. "And how the hell did you know about me and Smoke? I thought it was a secret."

"Dude." Acid shook his head. "Cat's out of the bag."

"I think it's great. What you're doing," Savage said.

"Doing?" I asked in confusion.

"Yeah, you're caring for the elderly. It's noble work." His eyes twinkled with humor.

"You're a dick," Acid said to Savage.

"That he is," Duke agreed. "We'll get out of your hair and let you two have your business meeting."

He grasped the back of Willa's head and kissed her passionately, clearly not caring that they had an audience.

I quickly looked away and caught Savage's gaze. He winked.

Duke pulled away from Willa and let her go.

"It's a good thing you can't get pregnant from a kiss," Savage said as he slapped Duke on the back.

"Get out of here," Willa said in exasperation. "Acid, keep him on a leash tonight. He's liable to scare off his date."

"I would if I could," Acid said. "But Savage is... *Savage*."

"That I am."

The three bikers left the kitchen. Only when the front door closed did Willa look at me and say, "Sorry about that. Let's talk."

An hour later, I felt more confident about the direction of my business. And as with all things, it became clear it would evolve over time. Just as we were finishing up, there was a chorus of voices and heavy footsteps echoing throughout the house.

"Ah, the kids are home," Willa joked.

I got up from the comfortable chair in her home office and followed her into the hallway.

"Why do we keep having this fight?" Waverly demanded, directing her attention to the tall, dark-haired young man who towered over her.

"Because you want to keep having this fight and I don't," he said. His tone was calm, but his hands were clenched at his sides.

"You're being an idiot," Waverly stated. "And I won't let you do it."

"You don't have control over this. I do."

Sailor stood by the staircase, looking like she wanted to be anywhere else.

"Hey," Willa said. "What's going on?"

"My boyfriend is throwing his future away," Waverly said. "Maybe you can talk some sense into him."

Waverly blew past me and Willa, marching down the hallway toward the kitchen. The back door slammed shut.

Sailor hurried after her.

"Dylan?" Willa prodded. "Are you okay?"

Dylan raked a hand through his dark hair. "You should talk to Waverly."

Boy code for I'm not going to talk about this with you.

Willa looked at me. "I'll call you."

I gave her a brief hug, grabbed my stuff, and quickly headed outside. Willa had her hands full with two teenage girls in the house. I didn't envy her—but I was insanely curious about the situation brewing between Dylan and Waverly.

There was something so angsty about watching them fight.

My phone rang and I stood on the sidewalk to search through my bag for my cell.

"I don't know if I'm mad at you," I said as I put the phone to my ear.

"Let me take you to dinner and convince you why you're not mad at me," Smoke said.

"You came down to the bakery this morning and the Old Ladies might as well have walked in on us in the middle of coitus."

"I came down to the bakery because you didn't have your phone on you and I had to leave. I didn't want to slip out the back without a word. Plus, it wasn't like I knew the Old Ladies were going to be there."

"Okay, fair. But I've been dodging questions left and right and now everyone knows what's going on between us. Everyone except Tavy."

"I'm talking to Tavy the night she gets back into town."

"Yeah, I know that. I called and asked her to have dinner and you had already nabbed the spot. Now I'm supposed to meet up with her the day after. That is if she'll even still talk to me after what you tell her. I should come to dinner with you the night you tell her. Yes, that's—"

"No."

"What? Why not?"

"Because if she gets pissed—"

"When. *When* she gets pissed," I said.

"Right. When she gets pissed, I don't want you to have to deal with the blowback."

Part of me wanted to let him handle it. The other part me of realized I had to be brave. Face this head on. Even if I didn't like the fallout that happened.

"I appreciate that," I said softly. "I do. But you can't do this alone."

"Logan—"

"Are we in this together or not?"

He sighed. "Yeah, okay. But if she yells at you—"

"You let her. You let her, Smoke. Because if there's any chance that Tavy will accept that I'm dating her father, then she needs to be able to let out her feelings and say whatever it is she needs to say. Even if it's really bad."

"You know her better than I do," he said quietly. "I kind of hate that."

"I know. You'll get to know her. That's why she moved here."

"Let me take you to dinner tonight."

I smiled. "All right. You pick a place. I still don't know the town."

"I'll text you."

We hung up and I shoved my phone into my purse.

"So, you're dating your friend's dad?"

I whirled, my hand flying to my chest. Waverly stood behind me, her hands shoved into the back pockets of her jeans.

"It's impolite to eavesdrop," I said.

"Yeah. Sorry about that. I was gonna go for a walk, blow off some steam. But then I heard you talking and I…"

"Got enthralled in my drama?" I asked with a raise of my brows.

A hint of a smile painted her lips. "Maybe."

"Okay, tit for tat," I said.

"What do you mean?"

"I mean, I'm dying to know why you were fighting with your boyfriend. Your really cute boyfriend, who looks at you like the sun rises and sets on you."

"I thought you had to go to dinner," she said. "With your friend's dad."

"*Hey*," I mock-warned. "I grew up with four older brothers. I'm not above older brother tactics."

"I grew up with Duke and Savage. I could take you," she teased.

"Come on." I gestured with my chin. "I've been wanting to meet your neighbor's horse. Is she friendly?"

"Hmm. Sure?"

I raised a brow.

Waverly relented. "She's usually friendly. But she can be temperamental. If we had an apple, we'd forever be in her good graces. Willa has apples inside, but Dylan is in there, so…"

"No worries."

My phone chimed, but I ignored it thinking it was just Smoke giving me details on the restaurant for the evening.

We approached a brown mare slowly, but she was friendly when we started to pet her and didn't attempt to take off my fingers. I stroked her glossy nose and waited for Waverly to speak.

"Dylan's a senior," she began. "His plan all along was to apply to Harvard. His SATs are off the charts. He's got the grades, recommendations, everything. He's an ideal candidate. And there's a good chance he'd get a full ride."

"Wow," I said. "Smart guy."

"Very smart." She nodded. "But he's also so, so stupid. He's actually considering going to a local college instead, just to be near me."

Waverly leaned against the fence, looking dejected. "He's willing to sacrifice his future for me. Which I so don't understand. Assuming he gets into Harvard—and he totally will—I told him that he needs to go, and when I turn eighteen, I'll be right behind him. I'll follow him wherever he goes because I can do what I do from anywhere. But that's not for at least two years."

I frowned. "What is it you do?"

"Willa didn't tell you?"

"She told me you're homeschooled and that Sailor isn't. That's all I know."

Waverly nodded. "I live in the guest house out back. It's attached to a shop. A big shop because Sailor, Dylan, and my best friend Jess—we run a business together. We flip furniture and resell it. You know the desk in Willa's office?"

"Yeah. Beautiful piece."

"I gave that to her." She sighed. "Eventually I want to get into woodworking and learn how to make my own stuff from the raw materials. I think that would be really cool."

"And here I thought you were just a smart-ass teenager," I said with a laugh.

She laughed with me. "I'm that too. For sure."

"Have you talked to Willa about any of this yet? She's your sister," I said. "I'd feel bad if I dragged the story out of you before you even got a chance to tell her."

"You didn't," she assured me. "And she'll talk to Dylan. I think Dylan needs to talk to her more than I did, actually."

"So, Dylan must really love you. If he's considering giving up the chance at Harvard."

She arched a brow. "I know what you're thinking."

"What am I thinking?"

"You're thinking it's stupid. That teenagers can't possibly know what it's like to be really in love. But Dylan and I are different. He's *it* for me. And I'm it for him. Which is why I don't understand why he'd do this."

"You just said you're *it* for him," I reminded her. "And you can't understand why he doesn't want to be separated from you?"

She swallowed. "I'm never going to college. I don't *want* to go to college. But Dylan does. And he shouldn't lose out on the experience just because he has a girlfriend he doesn't want to leave."

"Sometimes we don't want things to change," I said. "Sometimes we don't have a choice. Change comes anyway."

"Yeah. Change can suck it."

I let out a laugh.

The mare tossed her head and pulled away from the fence to prance toward another horse in the middle of the pasture.

"And you're wrong, you know," I said.

"About what?"

"I think teenagers know better than anyone else what real love feels like."

She sighed. "It's all encompassing. Like, sometimes I actually hurt when we're not together." She looked at me. "Is that how you feel about your friend's dad?"

"Smoke," I said. "It's Smoke."

Her eyes widened. "Really?"

"Really."

"Well done. He's hot. For an older guy, I mean."

"Compromise," I said.

"Huh?"

"Talk to Dylan and lay out your non-negotiables. Find out what his are. And you meet somewhere in the middle. Two people who love each other as much as you two do can surely work this all out."

"Wow."

"What?"

"You're like, a real grown up."

"Trying to be," I admitted. "I'm just taking it one day at a time."

Chapter 36

"Sorry I'm late," I said as I approached the table.

Smoke rose and without a word, grasped the back of my neck and pulled me to him. His mouth covered mine in greeting.

I settled my hands against his chest and my lids fluttered closed.

He kissed me deeper, his tongue sweeping between my lips, obliterating any thoughts about the public setting.

Finally, he lifted his mouth from mine, but he didn't release me. Smoke's eyes glittered with desire and he smiled. "Hi."

"Hi." My voice was breathless and my cheeks heated. I hastily looked around to see if we'd made a scene, but everyone else was paying attention to their own food and conversation.

I took a seat opposite Smoke and set my purse down in the corner.

"You're not that late," he said with a wink. "You get caught up with something?"

A server walked by our table with a fresh, steaming

pizza. The scent of pepperoni and mozzarella hit my nose and my stomach rumbled.

Smoke laughed. "Order first, then we talk."

"That," I said, pointing to the pizza. "I want one of those."

"Done."

After we'd ordered and Smoke was sipping on a pint of beer, I said, "I was at Willa's, discussing my website design."

"Your website?"

"Didn't I tell you? I've officially decided to go into business for myself."

"Hey, congratulations." He lifted his beer and I raised my plastic cup of soda and we clinked.

"Yeah, I'm excited. Anyway. I was on my way out and got to talking to Waverly."

"Willa's younger sister?"

"Yeah. You know her?"

"Met her a few times," he said. "She comes to the club barbecues with her friends and boyfriend."

"Ah." I nodded. "Anyway, we got to talking. She's cool. Really cool."

"Her boyfriend's a good kid. According to Duke and Savage, at least. I can't vouch for him."

"He's the kind of guy you'd hope your teenage daughter got involved with," I said with a smile. "He's crazy about Waverly."

"Teen love," Smoke said. "Nothing like it."

"Nope."

"So, am I forgiven?" He took my hand that rested on the table and linked his fingers through mine. "For this morning?"

"Yeah." I snorted. "They weren't even that surprised.

Apparently, everyone knew there was something going on between us."

"Someone's always watching," he joked.

I hastily looked around. "Then maybe we shouldn't be out together in public. What if it gets back to Tavy before we get a chance to tell her?"

"Nobody except the club and their Old Ladies know we're together. And Tavy's work friends don't run with the club. It's fine. We're off the hook. I can take you to dinner every night this week and she'll be none the wiser."

"Every night this week?" I asked. "We could just cook at my place."

"We could do that too." His eyes raked over me in hunger.

"Hmm, maybe dating outside the house is a good idea. Otherwise we might turn into sex fiends who don't want to do anything else."

He raised his brows.

"Okay, clearly you wouldn't be opposed to that."

"Speaking of opposed, what are you opposed to? In the bedroom?"

"That conversation, we shelve for when we're alone," I said primly.

His smile was slow and then it grew into a wide grin.

"What?" I demanded.

Smoke took a sip of his beer before setting it down and releasing my hand. "Go to the bathroom."

"What?"

He leaned forward and dropped his voice. "Go to the bathroom. I'll meet you there in a minute."

"But—" My eyes widened. "Everyone will know!"

"No, they won't. It's down the hall all the way in back and I'm dying to taste you. Now be a good girl and go to the bathroom."

I blinked and then I was moving on autopilot, Smoke's heated gaze watching me. I all but skipped to the bathroom. My breathing was already erratic when I shut the bathroom door. A few moments later, Smoke entered.

He locked the door and leaned against it.

"Lift your skirt," he commanded.

I hiked up my skirt to reveal a black lace thong.

Smoke pushed away from the door, guiding me until my back hit the wall, and then lowered himself to his knees. He grasped one of my legs and lifted it to his shoulder.

And then his mouth was between my thighs, licking me through my damp panties.

I bit my lip to stifle a moan.

He grabbed my ass and kept me open so he could pleasure me. The friction of the wet lace against my skin had me writhing and bucking in demand of more.

With one of his fingers, he teased my panties aside and then his tongue was sliding into my core.

"Oh God," I whispered, my throat tight.

The gliding of his tongue, the warmth of his breath, the potential of being discovered…and the fact that Smoke was devouring me like it was his God-given mission, had me spasming and coming.

He gently kissed my inner thigh before lowering my leg to the floor.

"You look fucking gorgeous," he growled as he rose. He leaned forward and kissed me, thrusting his tongue into my mouth.

I tasted myself on his lips and I greedily wanted more.

He pressed his forehead to mine, both of us breathing hard. Smoke pulled back and helped me straighten my skirt.

"You go out first," he said. "And walk with your head high."

"But I—everyone will *definitely* know."

"Yeah, and they'll be jealous as fuck." He skimmed his thumb along my cheek. "Your skin is flushed, your eyes are bright, and you look alive, Logan."

I let out another quivery sigh. Nodding, I glanced in the mirror, made sure my appearance was decent and then I unlocked the bathroom door.

I kept my head up. I slid into the booth and reached for Smoke's beer and took a sip.

A man in a button-down shirt and slacks sitting at a table across the restaurant caught my eye and winked.

Oh God, does he know what Smoke and I just did?

My cheeks bloomed and I downed the rest of Smoke's beer.

Smoke returned to the table and sat down across from me. He didn't say a word, he just glided his finger across his lips.

My stomach flipped.

I reached for my purse and pulled out my cell. I unlocked the screen, found my text conversation with Smoke, and typed out:

ME

Next time it'll be me on my knees.

His phone chirped and he reached into his leather cut interior pocket to pull it out. He read the text on the screen, and without looking at me, he replied:

SMOKE

You'll be on your knees, my dick in your mouth, your fingers buried in your pussy. I don't come unless you do.

"Here we go," the server announced.

My phone slipped out my hands and clattered to the table. I hastily swept it off into my bag and smiled up at the server.

"Great," I croaked. "I'm starving."

I glanced at Smoke whose mouth was curved into a wicked grin.

Yeah, starving.

⁓

Smoke's head rested on my inner thigh as my fingers plowed through his hair. The bed sheets were tangled and my foot was falling asleep, but I was so comfortable, so happy, so sated, I refused to move.

My hand glided down to his shoulder blade to trace one of his tattoos. "Will you tell me what your ink means?"

He lifted his head to look at me. "Sure."

Smoke sat up and pointed to the symbol above his heart. "The infinity sign. If you turn it right side up, it's an eight. Eight for Octavia."

I smiled. "For Tavy."

"Yeah. Ran out and got it the day she was born. My love for her is infinite." He grinned and then guided me down his left sleeve to a tattoo of a motorcycle appearing through fire and smoke. His shoulder blade had the club logo—a skull with angel wings.

"No tattoo of your ex's name, huh?" I asked with a wry grin.

"Nope. Guess I should've realized we weren't going to last when I didn't want to get her name on me." He flopped down onto the bed next to me and showed me the inked canvas of his back. It was an image of the back of a man in a tuxedo and top hat looking into a large, ornate oval mirror with intricate scroll work. The reflection of the man was a skeleton wearing that same top hat with wisps of smoke rising from around the coattails of the tuxedo, engulfing the entire skeleton.

"This must've taken forever to finish," I said, tracing down his shoulder blade.

"Yeah. I love how it came out, though."

"What's it mean?"

He paused for a moment. "It's a tattoo that explains my road name. It's the name my club brothers gave me."

I nodded and waited for him to continue.

"The man in the top hat and tuxedo is a tongue in cheek reference to the life I grew up in. Tuxes, cotilions, society shit. But then I took a path that was the complete opposite of the life I was born into—I became a biker. The old me is gone. The skeleton is a biker's symbol for the grim reaper—and that's who I really am."

"I get it. Smoke and mirrors. You're not what you seem. It's beautiful work."

"Thank you. You don't have any ink."

"That is true."

"Any interest in getting any?"

"Not really. I don't think I'm the tattoo type."

"Why not?"

"Ink is permanent. And until I find out what I'm willing to have branded on my skin until the end of time even when it's faded and disappearing into wrinkly old skin," I grinned, "I'll leave my canvas untouched."

"Fair enough."

Smoke's hand inched up my T-shirt to rest underneath the curve of my breast. "So, what we did at the restaurant was fun…"

"Hmm. Yeah."

His thumb grazed my nipple, making it bead. "It was adventurous," he said.

"I guess so."

"Care to have a few more adventures?"

"What did you have in mind?" I let out a low moan as he pinched my nipple, sending shockwaves straight to my core.

"I want to fuck your ass."

My pleasure evaporated and was quickly replaced by anxiety. "Oh…"

His hand underneath my shirt stilled as he peered at me. "You don't like that idea."

"I—uh—would prefer *not* to explore that."

"Okay. Can I ask why?"

"Does it matter why?" I demanded. "I don't want to do it."

I wrenched away from his touch and scrambled from the bed.

"Logan." His tone was soft and he didn't move. "We don't have to do anything you're not comfortable with. I'll never push you into trying something you don't want."

I went to my dresser and yanked open a drawer to pull out a pair of sweats, but I made no move to put them on. I continued to face away from him.

"Knox was really vocal about wanting to try it. He brought it up *a lot*." I paused for a moment and took a deep breath. "I was going to try it on our honeymoon. Not because I wanted it, but because *he* was so vocal about wanting it. Actually, it's not that I didn't want it, that's not really true. It's just that he was so demanding about it, it turned me off to the idea…"

I heard Smoke's feet hit the floor and then his hands gently settled onto my shoulders before pulling me back into his embrace. He wrapped his arms around me as he said, "Hey, it's okay. It's your body. I'll never disrespect you. You want to try something, you let me know. But I won't pressure you into trying something if you're not comfortable with it."

"I never thought you would." I turned in his arms and stared up at him. "It was a knee-jerk reaction, saying no. That was about Knox, not you. But the truth is I don't really know what I want to try because I've never been in a relationship where I've felt safe enough to explore."

I looked up at him, imploring him to understand. "Smoke, I—I want you to take charge as our relationship progresses. I want you to lead me where I might want to go with *you*."

"Only if you promise me that you'll tell me if something makes you uncomfortable, okay?"

I nodded. "I promise."

"Cupcake." He hugged me to him. "Whatever you need, I'll give it to you."

I squeezed my arms around him and closed my eyes.

Whatever I need...is he talking about more than just sex?

∽

"Son of a bitch!"

Smoke's curse roused me from my sleep. I rolled over and opened my eyes. The sun was streaming through the blinds and I sat up just as Smoke nudged the bedroom door open.

He was carrying a tray and it was laden with goodies from the bakery downstairs.

"I didn't even hear you get up," I said with a smile.

"I planned it that way." He grinned back and came over to the bed and gently set the tray down. There were two plates of pastries and to-go cups of coffee.

"What made you curse?" I asked.

"I almost dropped the tray."

He hadn't bothered putting on his leather cut, but he'd donned his heavy motorcycle boots. Smoke gently sat on the edge of the bed so as not to disturb the coffee while he took off his shoes.

"I thought I was supposed to be the one to get up and get the coffee and pastries. That was the deal."

"I changed the deal." He turned and grasped one of the to-go cups and offered it to me. "Vanilla latte."

"Thank you." I leaned forward and he met me halfway. His lips brushed mine, his minty breath wafting to my nose.

"It was only fair," he said when he pulled back. He picked up the Danish. "You made grilled cheeses the other night. The least I could do was bring you pastries and coffee in bed."

"Ah, a food exchange situation. Got it," I teased.

We ate our pastries and sipped our coffees and when the food was finished, Smoke moved the tray into the kitchen.

"Brooklyn says hi, by the way," he said as he came back into the bedroom.

"She was down there?"

"Yeah. She and Brielle were discussing some wedding cake decorating."

"Oh. Was Jazz down there, too?"

"Yep."

I ran a hand across my face. "So there's no way to quietly escape out the back without seeing them?"

"They've already seen me."

"I was talking about me."

"Why don't you want them to see you?"

"Because I'll get the third degree," I said. "Now that

we're…you know."

"Having sleepovers?"

I snorted. "What a fourth-grade way of putting it."

"I didn't think you wanted me to say *fucking*. Besides, you're the one who just alluded to it instead of coming out and saying it."

"Valid." I raised my nearly empty cup to my lips. "What's your day looking like?"

"I'm meeting Bones and Raze at The Ring."

"What's The Ring?"

"The club's training gym," he explained.

I set my empty cup aside on the nightstand. "Training? For what?"

"Boxing, MMA, fighting sports in general."

I flinched as it momentarily reminded me of Knox. "Huh."

"What?"

"I didn't take you for a fighting sport kind of guy."

"I'm not. We're just going to take care of some club business."

"Club business," I repeated. "And that means what, exactly?"

"It means you don't need to worry about it."

"Are you always going to use *club business* when you want to be cryptic and not explain something to me?"

"Yep," he said.

He got up and stripped off his shirt. Smoke tossed it on the bed and then his jeans and boxers followed. As he strode naked to the bathroom, he looked at me over his shoulder and with a wicked grin, he asked, "You joining me? I'll make it worth your while."

Chapter 37

An hour later, freshly showered and with a few orgasms under my belt, I was ready to face the day. I stood at the kitchen counter while Smoke pulled on his leather cut and made sure he had his cell and keys.

"I'll see you tonight," he said, resting his hands on my hips and pulling me close. "What are we doing for dinner?"

"We're going to cook," I explained.

"I don't cook."

I grinned. "But *I* cook."

He leaned down to take my lips in a kiss. "I'll bring the dessert."

"Hmm. Yeah, I think I know what kind of dessert you have in mind," I teased.

Smoke chuckled, kissed me one last time, then forced himself to let me go. "All right, cupcake. I better get out of here before I say *fuck it* and take you back to bed."

"That wouldn't be such a bad thing." I stared imploringly at him.

He groaned. "Stop. You're making it impossible to leave."

My phone buzzed on the counter, momentarily pulling my attention.

"Saved by the phone." He kissed me on the forehead and stepped back.

Another vibration sounded, followed quickly by another few.

"What's going on?" I wondered aloud, grabbing my cell and opening it. "Oh. That's fun."

"What?"

I looked at Smoke. "Mia invited me to lunch with the Old Ladies."

"You going to go?"

"I don't know. Maybe." I smirked. "If I can promise them not to pepper me with questions about you and me."

"Yeah, good luck with that." He laughed. "Anyway, I better get going before you maul me again."

"Sir, you mauled me!"

"Damn right, and I'll do it again later tonight." He pecked my lips.

"Looking forward to it."

∼

"Easy, Doc," Mia said with a laugh. "The food's already dead, it's not going anywhere."

"No time," Doc said around a mouthful of beef burrito. "I have to get back to the clinic."

Darcy lifted her hand and caught the attention of the server. She pointed to her empty margarita glass, silently asking for another.

The group of us was a spectacle of chaos. Old Ladies

were trying to wrangle their babies with one hand while attempting to eat their food with the other.

Cash grabbed a handful of rice off Rach's plate and threw it to the floor. "*Cash*," she moaned.

"Here," I said from the seat next to her. "Give him to me."

She gladly handed him over. "I'd love just one meal that was still hot by the time I got to eat it."

"I don't even remember the last time I ate a hot meal," Allison remarked as she moved her son to her other leg.

"We need a biker baby daycare," Mia joked. "For days like today where we just need a few hours to ourselves."

"Where we can use both our hands to eat," Joni added. She looked down at a sleeping Everett who was in his sling, strapped to her chest.

Doc swallowed her bite. "You're a freakin' *genius*."

"I know," Mia said with a smile. "But perhaps you could tell me why you think I'm a genius."

"The clinic could use a daycare," Doc said. "For the staff, I mean. I can't believe I didn't think of it sooner."

"How can I get in on that?" Rach asked. "I'd pay extra to be able to leave Cash with qualified people—and with doctors nearby? Sign me up."

"Seriously," Allison added.

The server brought another margarita to Darcy and took away the empty glass, along with the baskets of chips that we'd depleted.

Willa and Brooklyn returned from the bathroom and took their seats. "I'm not going to be able to eat it all," Brooklyn complained.

"Why not?" I asked.

"Because I've reached that stage of pregnancy where there's not a lot of room. What with the baby rearranging my organs."

"Leftovers," Sutton said. "Or if you don't want to take your leftovers, I'll eat them."

"I've never seen anyone eat as much as you," Willa said to Sutton with a laugh. "It's impressive."

"I have the appetite of a baby T-rex," she said. "Especially when the food is as good as this."

"You guys come here often?" I asked.

"We try to come once a week," Mia said. "Whoever makes it, makes it. It's rare that all of us are here at one time. What with the differing schedules and everything."

"How's your food, Darcy?" Rach asked her friend.

"Good," Darcy replied. She took a sip of her drink, and in a great show of pretending to eat her untouched food, she picked up her fork.

Darcy's gaze lifted from her plate and met mine. She raised her brows as if silently daring me to say something.

I looked away from her.

"Waverly's obsessed with you, by the way," Willa said to me. "Hot sauce?"

Allison handed her the bottle and Willa shook it.

"Obsessed with me?" I asked with a grin. "Why?"

"You gave her some good advice, apparently," Willa said.

"You're not upset, are you?" I asked. "I didn't mean to overstep, I just—"

"Not at all," Willa assured me. "Sometimes they need to hear it from someone who isn't their parental figure."

"What's going on with Waverly?" Brooklyn asked.

"She and Dylan are having a disagreement," Willa said.

"Those two?" Sutton raised her brows. "I don't believe it."

"What's the disagreement about?" Mia asked.

"Dylan might not even apply to Harvard—even

though he's a shoe-in. He doesn't want to leave Waverly behind. Waverly thinks he's being foolish. She says they can do long distance and then she'll follow him when she turns eighteen," Willa explained.

"I don't think any of us doubt their feelings for one another," Mia said. "But I don't understand Dylan's thought process. It's Harvard. *Harvard.*"

"That's Waverly's feeling on the subject too," Willa said. "Anyway. It's between them. They'll figure it out."

"Maybe it's not really about Waverly," Brooklyn said. She leaned back in her chair and rested her hands on her stomach.

"What do you mean?" Willa asked, looking at her.

"Well, yes, I'm sure Dylan doesn't want to be parted from Waverly. But he's a smart kid. Really smart. He knows what this could do for his future. What if he's afraid?"

"Dylan? Afraid?" Willa asked. "He's stood up to big scary bikers without trembling. Why would Harvard scare him? What does he have to be afraid of?"

"You don't just go to Harvard for the education," Brooklyn said. "You got to Harvard for the connections. The families you're going to meet. Dylan hasn't grown up in that world."

"What world? The world of crew and sailing?" Willa demanded.

"And dinners with four forks, galas, and winter vacations in the Swiss Alps at private chalets," Brooklyn added. "Yeah, he doesn't get flustered around a bunch of bikers because he's grown up around grit. He didn't grow up around gold."

Willa blinked. "I never even thought about it like that."

Brooklyn shrugged. "I worked at The Rex in New York. I've seen wealth, you know? It's a different world. And it's different when you're born into it versus earning it.

Dylan will have to earn it, and even when he does, he'll always be *new money* to them. Maybe he's more comfortable here, where he knows what to expect and how the streets work."

The table was silent after Brooklyn's speech.

"Just something to think about," Brooklyn added.

"I'm thinking about it," Willa said. "Men have pride. I wonder if that's how he really feels about it. Using Waverly as a convenient excuse not to go to Harvard."

"Relationships are never simple," Mia said. "And they only get harder the older we get."

"Yeah, why is that?" Sutton demanded. "Just when I think I've got Viper figured out, he does a complete one eighty."

"A one eighty about what?" Willa asked.

"He went back on his word," she explained. "I said I wouldn't marry him until I was pregnant. Well, now he won't get me pregnant until *after* we're married."

Joni raised her brows. "Viper wants a wedding?"

"Yeah, I think Viper wants a wedding," Sutton said. "I don't get it. Why can't we do things the way we agreed to do them?"

"Neither of you guys had normal childhoods," Brooklyn said. "Maybe he wants something traditional for once."

I marveled about how open and honest the Old Ladies were being about their struggles. They spoke with candor and there was no hesitation about baring their souls. Though I had Tavy and we spoke the same way to each other, I'd never seen a large friend group be so close-knit like this before.

Keeping Cash entertained proved to be a struggle and most of my time was spent moving silverware and pepper shakers out of his reach.

Doc polished off the rest of her burrito and hopped up from the table. She scoured through her purse and grabbed some cash and hastily threw it down near her empty plate. "Sorry, guys. I have to go. Sutton, I want to know if you decide to have a wedding. And Willa? Keep me posted on Dylan and Waverly."

"Better than a soap opera, right?" Willa asked with a grin.

"It goes toe to toe with even the best telenovelas." Doc waved and all but ran from the restaurant.

"This was a bad idea," Brooklyn moaned. "Now I want a nap."

"Slash would love it if you finally took a break," Rach said with a smile.

"Yeah, he would," Brooklyn agreed. "However, I've got a wedding cake to bake before I can head home."

I wanted to get to the grocery store—and why did I want to get to the store? So I could buy ingredients to cook dinner for Smoke.

"You okay?" Rach asked as she wiped her fingers with a napkin.

"Yeah, fine."

She took Cash back from me. "You don't look fine."

"It's nothing."

"What's nothing?" Sutton asked.

All eyes turned to me.

"This is why I didn't want to come out with all of you," I said in exasperation. "I knew you were going to ask me about me and Smoke."

Mia raised her brows. "No one said anything about you and Smoke."

"But if you want to tell us things," Joni said, adjusting Everett. "We'll listen."

"It's stupid."

"Doubt it," Allison remarked. "Share. You're among friends."

Among friends. Wow.

"I'm making him dinner tonight," I admitted.

"Special occasion?" Mia asked.

"How can they have a special occasion?" Willa asked. "They just started going out."

"More like staying in." Sutton sniggered.

"No, it's not a special occasion. I'm making him dinner just because. And I know how that sounds."

"It sounds nice," Willa said.

"It sounds domestic," Rach added.

"No, what's domestic is that he already has a toothbrush at my place," I admitted.

Silence reigned at the table.

"And you're *not* his Old Lady, right?" Sutton asked.

Darcy swirled the ice around her glass and took a healthy sip of her margarita.

Cash began to have a meltdown, interrupting the conversation.

"And we just became those people," Rach said with a sigh. "Sorry guys, I've got to get him out of here. Darce? You ready?"

Darcy nodded, chugged the last of her drink, and then rose from the table.

At least Darcy had carpooled with Rach and she wasn't driving. I wasn't sure how she was even standing at this point, considering the amount of tequila she'd ingested without touching most of her food.

"See you guys later," Rach said.

"This weekend," Mia said.

"Yes, this weekend," Rach agreed.

Darcy followed Rach and a screaming Cash out of the Mexican restaurant.

"What's this weekend?" I asked.

"We're getting together at my house for my informal baby shower," Brooklyn said.

"I thought your shower was supposed to be a surprise," I said in confusion.

"I spilled the beans by accident," Sutton admitted, looking guilty.

"Brielle and Jazz are taking care of the food," Brooklyn explained. "The girls are doing the rest."

"No one sent me the link for the registry," I said.

"There's no longer a registry." Brooklyn laughed.

"Why?" I looked at around at the amused faces of the other women.

"Because Slash already bought her everything she could possibly want," Willa said with a giggle.

"Crap, I've got to pee again." Brooklyn rose from her spot and grabbed her purse. "I might as well leave too. The sooner I leave, the sooner I bake the cake, the sooner I bake the cake, the sooner I get to go home."

"And have your hottie husband rub your swollen feet?" Joni asked with a knowing smile.

"Yeah, rub my swollen *feet*." She grinned like the Cheshire cat. "See you guys later."

"Is she gone?" Mia asked a few moments later.

Joni looked in Brooklyn's direction and nodded.

"Good," Mia said. "So, there's no registry, per se, but we're getting her a couple gifts that are just for her. A gift certificate to her favorite seafood restaurant and a spa day."

"That's sweet, and thoughtful," I said. "Can I contribute?"

"Sure thing. We'll put your name on the card." Mia winked.

"I'm not sure I know how to say this, or even if I should, but…Darcy?"

Mia sighed. "Yeah…"

"Rach is kind of fielding that one," Allison said. "Because she knows what Darcy's going through. Darcy lost her husband recently."

"Word of advice?" Sutton asked. When I nodded, she went on, "Don't confront her about her behavior. I tried and…well, it didn't go over well."

"We're all just trying to be here for her," Mia said. "In whatever way we can."

"Sometimes it doesn't feel like enough," Joni added. "But what can you do?"

Heaviness settled across the table, bringing down the jovial mood we'd enjoyed the last hour.

Willa cleared her throat and looked at Sutton. "Do you really hate the idea of a wedding?"

Sutton grasped the conversation thread like a lifeline. "I don't know. The idea of planning one doesn't sound so fun."

"It's actually really fun," I said. "You get to taste a bunch of food, try a bunch of cakes."

"Fork over a lot of cash," Sutton muttered. "Just seems like a ridiculous way to spend a lot of money when you could be spending it on something else."

"You don't have to spend a lot of money," I pointed out. "A small wedding can be very affordable."

"Was yours going to be affordable?" Sutton demanded.

"Ah, no," I said, my cheeks turning pink. "Mine was going to be borderline outrageous. It kind of got away from me."

"Were your parents helping you? Financially, I mean?" Sutton asked.

"They were, yeah."

She nodded. "I don't have any parents. And even if I did, they wouldn't be the type to hand over a credit card for my wedding."

"Have you talked to Viper and told him how you feel?" Mia asked.

"Willa, will you dig through the diaper bag for the nursing blanket?" Joni asked as she unstrapped Everett from his sling.

"Sure thing," Willa said.

"Continue talking," Joni said. "I'm listening."

"I haven't talked to Viper about it yet," Sutton said with a frown. "I'm not even sure what my aversion to the wedding is all about."

"So, it's not about him," Allison said.

"Oh, *God no*. Not even a little bit," Sutton assured her. "I just…it doesn't seem practical."

"It's just money. There will always be a time to make more money," Mia said. "For a day of fun memories? To marry Viper in front of your friends? Seems worth it to me."

"It's *just* money," Sutton said. "I've never had any money. I don't have any money now, either. We're saving for a house. Viper's got a little nest egg, but I have nothing. It doesn't feel right asking him to spend money on a wedding, no matter how small, when every penny we make should be going to the house fund."

"You deserve a wedding," Joni said. "If that's what you really want. Forget about the money for a second. What do you actually want?"

Sutton paused for a moment and then she sighed. "I want a white dress and a tiara with a veil. I want to look like a fairy princess." She looked around the table and sighed. "Damn it."

Chapter 38

"You idiot," I muttered.

I looked at the meal I'd prepared for Smoke as it sat on the kitchen counter. It was past nine o'clock and the food had long since gone cold. There had been no word, no phone call, no text from him.

Idiot, idiot, idiot.

I'd worn my leather pants because after dinner, I was going to ask him to take me for a ride on the back of his motorcycle. I'd styled my hair and put on a full face of makeup. I was completely ready to satisfy him in every way.

Then I waited.

I'd taken the boots off an hour ago.

With a sigh, I got up and went into the bedroom to change. Once I was in a pair of pajama shorts and a threadbare T-shirt, I went into the kitchen to clean up the meal.

I felt like a fool, but I wasn't angry. Disappointment blasted through me, deflating my mood—and my self worth.

Why did I do this to myself?

Why did I place my happiness and enjoyment on things outside of my control?

It was time I did something about this. Maybe I needed a man cleanse. I should've been spending time with myself, doing yoga, meditating, reading a bunch of nonfiction self-help books so I could get really clear about who I wanted to be and what I was willing to do to make my life the life I truly wanted.

I thought Smoke was different. But he was just like Knox. Careless with my emotions. Dismissive of my time.

I was wiping down the counter when there was a knock on my door.

With a glare, I went to answer it.

I was prepared to level Smoke with a tirade, but when I opened the door, I gasped.

"What happened?" I demanded, immediately rushing to him so I could examine his battered face and black eye.

I wrinkled my nose and stopped.

Cheap perfume. And is that—

"Why the hell is there glitter on your neck?"

Before he could muster up a lie, I attempted to shut the door in his face.

"It's not what you think," Smoke said, putting his hand up to stop the door from closing. "And if you give me five minutes, I'll tell you why I didn't call, why I have a black eye, and why I smell like another woman."

"You missed dinner."

"I know."

"I sat around waiting for you." I winced at how pathetic I sounded.

"I'm sorry." His expression was contrite. "Please, Logan. Let me explain."

I reluctantly stepped aside and let him come in.

"Ugh." I put a hand to my nose. "That perfume is making me nauseous."

He closed the door and then bent over to take off his boots. He reached into his cut and pulled out a pistol in a holster and set it on the counter as he started to take off his clothes.

"What are you doing?" I demanded, stepping away from him.

"Getting naked," he said. "So I can wash my clothes."

"Stay dressed," I commanded. "I don't want to be vulnerable right now."

"Cupcake, the last thing I want to do is hurt your feelings or take you for granted. You did a nice thing for me by making dinner. I've been looking forward to it all day."

I crossed my arms over my chest and dipped my head. "Continue."

"Can I sit next to you?" he inquired.

"No," I said, pointing to the chair. "You can sit there and explain. Start with the black eye."

"I like this commanding side of you," he joked as he took a seat. "All right." He pointed to his eye. "Bones did this."

"Bones? What the hell?" I demanded.

He sighed. "I told you I was going to The Ring this morning?"

I nodded.

"Well, Bones and I got into the ring and sparred."

"Why?"

"Because we had to settle some shit between us."

"Shit? What shit?"

"Just had to come to an understanding," Smoke said.

"What kind of understanding?"

"That he's no longer allowed to pursue you. But try not to worry, black eyes come with the territory. There's no bad blood here, we were just blowing off steam like brothers do."

He smiled and instantly winced when his lip split open.

"Does it hurt?"

"Yep."

"Want some ice?"

"A steak would be better," he said.

"You should have told me while I was at the store." My tone was snarky. "I would've bought an extra steak for your eye."

"You made steak?"

"Yes." I leaned back against the couch. "I cooked it in cast iron on the stovetop, and then I finished it in the oven. Black peppercorn encrusted, by the way."

"Damn it."

"I made a bleu cheese butter to go with it. Olive oil mashed potatoes and blanched green beans."

"Aw, cupcake."

"Don't *aw cupcake* me. Why do you smell like another woman? And why didn't you call?"

He scrubbed his jaw. "I was at the strip club."

"*You son of a bitch.*"

"No, for the club," he explained quickly. "The Tarnished Angels recently took over a strip club. It's part of a thing we've got going on."

"The club owns a strip joint?"

"Yes. I was with the boys."

"So which one of them put on the cheap perfume and gave you a lap dance?" I asked.

"It's not like that." He sighed. "We were having a meeting in the back. One of the strippers collapsed on stage and had a seizure. I carried her to her car and drove her to the hospital, but in the chaos of the moment I accidentally left my phone at the strip club. I don't have your number memorized. Otherwise, I would've called and let you know I was running late. I didn't want to send a prospect to explain why I was late because then they'd have to explain about the strip club and I wanted to do that in person."

The vein in my temple began to pulse.

"Say something," he stated.

"I don't know what to address first. The fact that the club owns a strip joint and that I didn't know about it until now, or that you blew me off and got the shit beat out of you."

"I didn't lie about it," he clipped. "And for what it's worth, I didn't lose the fight either. The eye is just part of what happens when grown men get into it."

"It's called lying by omission. You never volunteered that the club was involved in the stripper business, so later you can say you didn't lie. Is that how the club is planning on helping the community? What happened to rescuing women in need and all that shit? Huh?"

"Watch it," he said, his voice low. "The strip joint is part of the club's holdings. I don't owe you an explanation."

"Apparently not." I glared at him. "But I'm not going to stick around and let you cheat on me like Knox did."

"How the fuck did you make that leap?" he demanded.

I rolled my eyes. "*Please*. I'm young, not an idiot. I know what goes on in strip clubs. I know *stripper* is just another word for prostitute. Everyone knows what happens in the VIP rooms. You think I want to be with a man who is regularly around young naked women who have sex for money?"

"I promised you fidelity and I meant it. My word should be enough for you."

"Right. Your word. You were also the one that said

men cheated simply because they wanted to, even if they had something really good at home."

"You could just as easily cheat on me," he pointed out. "You're fucking hot. I see how guys look at you when we're out."

"Don't." I shook my head. "You don't get to do that. You won't be able to convince me this isn't a big deal."

"Christ, woman. You didn't bail when you found out the club was involved with the cartel, but you balk at the club running a strip joint?"

Internally, I recoiled.

How was a strip club my line in the sand, but finding out the club was involved with a cartel wasn't?

He has a point.

"The cartel is in the past," I stated. "The strip joint is in the present. You said you were done with shady shit…"

"By *shady shit*, I meant illegal. The club is legit now. Everything for the strip joint is on the books. Fuck, we even pay taxes."

I shrugged.

"Our club has to make money. This is how we make money. We're bikers, Logan. We're not going to run a fucking ice cream parlor."

"That's no longer a good enough explanation. For Christ's sake, Smoke, you have a daughter. What if it was Tavy on stage? How would you feel?"

"I'd lose my shit. But you have to understand something; these girls have a choice. They choose to make their money this way. They could easily get a job as bartenders or waitresses. Not everyone is a victim. So I'm telling you this is how it is. Take it or leave it."

Blood roared in my ears. "Okay."

"Okay?"

"Okay," I said again, rising. "*Get out.*"

"Logan—"

"*Out*, Smoke. I won't sit here and be disrespected. I won't sit here and pretend that I'm ever going to be okay with a man I'm dating frequenting a strip club, even if it is for business. Not when I know the kind of shit that goes down in them. I don't want any part of it."

He stared at me with glittering brown eyes and then stood. "You're not part of it."

"I *am* a part of it, because I know about it." I crossed my arms over my chest in a signature move of defense. "You said the club was trying to shut down human trafficking. Why would you get involved in another form of the skin trade? It's outright exploitation of women."

"It's not the fucking same. Not even a little bit." He stood taller, his face paling. "We don't exploit them. No one is being forced to be there. Women want to make money, they can do it the way they see fit. And for the record—"

He took a step toward me, and I instinctively took a step back.

Smoke's jaw clenched and he stopped in his tracks. "For the record," he repeated, his voice lower this time, "we don't allow any drugs in our club, and we don't allow prostitution. It puts everyone at risk so we keep security tight. A girl could whisper and our guys would be in the room in a heartbeat to ensure she's safe. They're not whores. We're in the business of making money, not exploiting people who can't protect themselves."

We stared at each other. My ribcage was tight with tension as my heart threatened to leap out of my chest.

"I've told you how it's going to be. Now you have to decide if you're going to trust me or not."

Without another word, Smoke turned, grabbed his belongings, and left.

Chapter 39

I WOKE UP PISSED OFF.

My sleep had been erratic, along with my thoughts.

I glanced at the clock. It was just past seven. I hoped the bakery rush was over because I needed caffeine, and to talk to Brooklyn.

In no way did I feel like I'd over-reacted. How did the Old Ladies deal with their men running a strip club and spending time there?

I got out of bed and quickly brushed my teeth and splashed cool water on my face. It did nothing to make me look better. I was pale and my eyes were bloodshot.

There was only one customer ahead of me when I got in line. Jazz's smile was bright and perky.

"Whoa," she said in way of greeting as I got to the register. "You look like you were up all night. Please tell me you and Smoke had an all-night boink-fest."

Her good nature prickled my already frayed nerves. "No," I clipped.

Jazz's smile dimmed. "Are you okay?"

I shook my head. "Is Brooklyn here?"

"She's in the back," Jazz said. "Want me to bring you a vanilla latte?"

"That would be great. Thanks."

"I'm here if you want to talk."

I found my first smile of the day. "I appreciate that, but this is kind of a club thing."

"Damn," Jazz said. "I need to get with a biker just so I can be privy to the gossip."

"You don't want a biker. They're nothing but trouble," I said before I could stop myself.

I headed to the back kitchen. Brooklyn had a blue apron printed with a strawberry design tied around her bulky middle and she was rolling out dough. She looked up, and when she saw me, she smiled.

"Morning," she greeted.

"You've got flour in your hair," I said.

"I'm not surprised. A bag of flour exploded on me not too long ago." She peered at me. "You don't look like you slept last night. Did Smoke keep you up?"

I put a finger to my lips and gestured to Jazz. Jazz came into the back and handed me my latte and a biscotti before heading to the front.

"What's on your mind?" Brooklyn asked.

"I was wondering how you're okay with the club owning a strip club?"

Brooklyn stopped mid roll and slowly looked up at me. "Say that again."

I blinked. "The club owns a strip joint. I just found out last night. Smoke told me, and for the life of me I can't figure out how the Old Ladies are okay with it."

She gripped the rolling pin in her hands, her expression tight.

"You knew about this, right?" I asked.

"No," she croaked. "I had no idea." She set the rolling

pin down on the butcher block counter. "Please tell me how you learned about this."

I told her about why Smoke had been late last night. "I threw him out," I said when I came to the end of my story. "I just couldn't believe it. I couldn't reconcile it. It felt like he'd lied to me."

"He definitely lied to you," she agreed, her mouth pinched.

"He claims he didn't. But he told me about the halfway house and the health clinic, conveniently leaving out any mention whatsoever about a strip club."

Brooklyn grabbed a stool that had been underneath the counter and hastily plopped down onto it.

"You look devastated," I said.

"I am devastated," she admitted. "Slash never mentioned it to me either."

"What about the other Old Ladies?" I asked. "Do they know?"

"Let's find out." She pulled her cell phone from her apron and fired off a text.

I didn't expect the replies to come in at such a rapid-fire rate.

"The consensus would seem to be *no*," Brooklyn said, setting her phone aside. "None of us knew."

"That's bad."

She nodded. "Very bad."

Her phone vibrated again. She picked it up and read the text. "You got lunch plans?"

"No."

"You do now."

∼

"Where the hell is Doc?" Willa muttered.

Joni checked her phone. "Stuck in traffic, I imagine."

"Anyone want more tea?" Rach asked, rising from her spot on the couch.

"Fuck the tea," Darcy stated. "We need something stronger."

Sutton shook her head. "The last thing we need is to break out the liquor. I'm ready to rage already. Bourbon will just add fuel to the fire."

All of the Old Ladies, except for Doc, were in the living room at Rach's house. The babies were upstairs, napping. We'd congregated at Rach's because it was private.

"Maybe we should order some food while we wait for Doc," Mia suggested.

"I have zero appetite," Willa said.

"Same," Allison remarked.

Brooklyn's phone blew up with an incoming call. She grimaced. "It's Slash. And I'm so pissed I don't want to talk to him. But if I don't talk to him, he'll call until he gets ahold of me—even if that means calling Brielle or Jazz."

"And Jazz saw us both in a state of anger when we left the bakery," I said.

"Damn," Brooklyn said. "Better answer it." She put the phone to her ear. "Hey."

Willa winced and whispered. "I heard her rage through that one word."

I nodded in agreement.

"Can't really talk," Brooklyn said, her tone brusque. "I'm about to walk into a meeting with a bride. I'll call you later." She paused. "Hmm. Okay. Yeah. Bye."

She hung up and set her phone onto the end table and settled her hand over her belly.

"You didn't tell him you loved him," Sutton said. "Slash is definitely going to know you're mad at him."

"Good," Brooklyn said. "I don't care if he knows I'm mad at him."

The front door opened and Doc strode into the living room. "Sorry I'm late."

"It's fine," Mia said. "But now that we're all here, let's get down to business."

"Before we start, are you sure I should be here?" I asked. "I'm not an Old Lady. I'm not involved."

"You really still think you're not involved, huh?" Joni asked.

"I guess I don't feel like I have the right to be here," I stated. "Smoke and I…"

"Did you break up?" Sutton asked.

"Yeah, I think we broke up last night." Sadness permeated my heart. "He said I was just supposed to trust him and I could take it or leave it. So I kicked him out of my apartment."

"I could kill Duke with my bare hands," Willa stated. "I can't believe he'd go along with this. Especially with my history."

"Your history?" I asked in surprise. "Were you a stripper?"

"No. My mother is, though. And Duke and Savage both how much that has fucked with me and Waverly."

"Oh."

The room fell silent for a moment.

"So what are you guys going to do?" I asked finally.

"Damn fine question," Joni said. "It's not like we can get involved in club business and plead with them about this. That isn't our place, and they clearly hid this from us for a reason. They knew we were going to be pissed if we found out, but they did it anyway."

Brooklyn looked forlornly at her belly as she rubbed a hand across her bump.

"Brooklyn?" I prodded.

"We're having a baby girl. How could he..." She shook her head.

I glanced at Rach. "Are you rethinking your move back to town?"

"Feeling that way," she admitted. "Then again...if my husband were still alive, he'd have been involved in this, too."

"So that's it then? You just have to accept that they're involved in this and that's that?" I demanded.

"Why do you care?" Darcy inquired. "You're not with Smoke anymore, so why does it bother you so much?"

Her tone wasn't mean or even pugnacious, but it had me defensive anyway.

"Because I was hoping for once in my life that I hadn't misjudged a man. I'd hoped that there was a real shot that Smoke and I could do this out in the open and it might actually work."

"So you're not ready to give up on Smoke completely, huh?" Joni asked.

I paused for a moment and then finally sighed. "I guess not. But I don't like that Smoke is involved with strippers. And I won't sacrifice my own self-worth and ignore the red flags. Having grown men around women like that...it's like taking a sugar addict to a candy store. Can they resist? Sure...but for how long?"

"So how do we handle this?" Doc asked. "It's not like we can just go to them, tell them we're uncomfortable with it, and then they'll sell the venture."

"That would never work anyway," Joni agreed. "They love us, but they won't allow us to interfere. Especially when they're trying to clean up the business. Let's face it, a strip club beats the hell out of anything involving the cartel."

There was a rumble of active agreement with Joni's statement.

Joni looked at me. "I wasn't supposed to say that in front of you."

"She already knows about the cartel," Rach stated. "Vaguely, anyway. I accidentally let it slip."

"I've kept my mouth shut," I replied. "And I didn't tell Tavy anything. I swear."

Joni nodded. "Mia, you haven't said anything. Thoughts?"

Mia didn't say anything for a moment and then she looked at Joni. "I already knew."

"You knew?" Joni asked. "About them buying the strip club?"

"Yes. Colt talked to me to before he pulled the trigger."

"Jesus Christ, Mia," Darcy snapped. "How the fuck could you know something like that and not tell us?"

There was a reverberation of disbelief from the Old Ladies, but Mia appeared unruffled. "I get it. I know why you're put off by the idea of the strip club. But come on, the club was involved in illegal stuff. They're not anymore. This isn't worse than that, and you all know it."

The room fell silent. Willa stared at Mia like she'd been betrayed.

"Look," Mia said, her tone softening. "They're not Boy Scouts. They're bikers. And the club took a major financial hit when they walked away from the illegal side of things." She looked at Doc. "You want your half-way house finished and upgrades to the clinic? That costs money." She pinned the rest of the Old Ladies with intense stares, one by one. "We're knee-deep in construction to expand the clubhouse. That costs money too. And I don't know about you, but I want to send my son to private school—and that costs money. Should I go on?"

"I think you've made your point," Joni drawled. "But it feels dirty. Like, is my new car going to be paid for because someone shook their tits and ass on stage?"

Mia was silent a moment and then said, "You want your kitchen renovated? You want to go back to work or do you want to stay home with your newborn? You want Zip to quit the club and get a hard physical job working construction?"

No one said a word for a while.

"But the not telling us…" Brooklyn added.

"It's club business." Mia shrugged. "The guys don't tell us about club business. Why is this any different?"

"Because Colt told *you*," Rach pointed out.

"He wanted me to look at the books to see if it was a good investment, and he knew y'all would find out at some point. It took me time to digest the idea, but here we are. The strip club turns a profit and will eventually fuel other ventures. It's time to dig deep. Do you want the lives you've grown accustomed to, or do you want out of the club completely?"

"She's right," Joni said with a sigh. "We can't pick and choose what we're okay with. We're either Old Ladies or we're not."

Chapter 40

The cool autumn air did nothing to ease the heat of my skin as I stepped out of the gym. I'd pushed myself hard, hoping it would quiet my mind.

It had been two days since Smoke had left my apartment; regret and sadness lingered.

I hadn't heard anything from the Old Ladies about the situation with the strip club, but it didn't feel like my place to ask.

I walked back toward the bakery, my mind attempting to move away from thoughts of Smoke and the club to focus on other things. On a whim, I decided to go home to visit my family. I needed to get out of Waco for a few days. I needed to clear my head. I hadn't been thinking straight since I met Smoke, and that had to change.

He'd turned my upside-down life right-side up again. But now he was gone and I was mourning the loss of him already.

I didn't know how to handle what was going on. With Knox, the decision was easy; leave. I just picked up and moved on, changed everything about my existence. But with Smoke, I didn't know what to do. Even though I'd only known him a short time, he'd slowly wormed his way into my heart against my will.

I rounded the corner, and like a vision I'd conjured, Smoke was leaning against his motorcycle, his sunglasses shielding his eyes.

My heart soared in excitement, but it was quickly replaced by annoyance. Leave it to the man to show up when I was red-faced and glistening with sweat from my workout.

When I was within ear shot, he said simply, "Hey."

"Hey," I said flatly. Silence fell between us. "What are you doing here?"

"Can we talk?"

"I think we've said everything we needed to say to each other."

His jaw clenched. "Please, Logan."

Smoke's raspy tone reminded me of how he sounded when he was inside me, whispering words of passion in my ear.

I wanted to pretend I was strong and unmoved, but the way he leaned against his bike so sure of himself, so confident in his mere existence had me thawing immediately.

"Okay, we can sit in the bakery and talk."

"Upstairs."

I raised my brows. "You don't get to dictate where we talk."

"What we have to discuss requires privacy. I'm not having this conversation with you out in the open."

In our battle for dominance, curiosity was my downfall. Finally, I nodded. "Fine. We can go upstairs."

He pushed away from his motorcycle and took a step toward me. "I missed you, cupcake."

Smoke speaking my nickname in a sensual purr was nearly my undoing.

I snapped my spine straight. "None of that. Let's go."

Smoke's lips flickered with a smile. "After you."

When we got up to my apartment, I set my keys and phone onto the counter. I whirled to face him. "Okay. We're in private. Talk."

He'd removed his sunglasses, giving me a clear view of his face. His jaw was bruised and his split lip was healing, but the black eye was still visible.

"Mia spoke to Colt about the Old Ladies' concerns. It's been decided that brothers with Old Ladies will have limited involvement with the strip club, except for Colt, who will deal with the books with Mia's help. Everything else, from hiring, cash drops and security will all be handled by prospects and brothers without Old Ladies."

"Oh." I nibbled my lip.

"This way everyone wins. The club still makes money, but the Old Ladies aren't stewing in anger and worry."

"Not everyone wins," I pointed out. "Not the women who work at the strip club."

"They have a choice. They can leave at any time. We've told them if they want out and need our help, we'll help them. They can quit the strip club and stay at the half-way house we're setting up and start a new life."

My resolve softened.

"I know this is hard for you." He paused. "The last few days, I've had a lot of time to think about what this is all really about."

"It's about the strip club."

He shook his head. "No. It's not really about that. I mean, maybe a little, but this is really about your relationship with Knox. You're worried that every man you meet is just like him. You're worried I'm going to lie to you, sneak around, and eventually cheat. But I'm not that guy. I've *never* been that guy. I'll never be that guy. I know you don't trust me—"

"I do trust you," I negated.

He raised his brows.

I sighed. "Okay. I don't trust you, but it's not because of *you*. It's just that my breakup with Knox is still so recent, and you're right, he did a number on me. It's still so fresh…being cheated on."

"I know you don't want to get hurt, but Logan, you have to look into my eyes and know that I'll never do that to you. The idea of hurting you…" He dropped his head. "The idea of that kills me."

Smoke lifted his gaze to mine. "You're the first person I want to talk to in the morning and the last one I want to talk to at night. You make me laugh. You're loyal and resilient. You're passionate, and you make me feel…"

"I make you feel…what?" I prodded gently.

"You make me *feel*. I'm alive when I'm with you, Logan."

"Oh," I whispered.

"Please don't end this before it has a chance to really start. Give me time to prove to you that I'm not going anywhere, that you don't have to be afraid."

The last two days had been pure agony. Every deep breath hurt, every thought of him made tears leap to my eyes. I'd been pushing Smoke away because I felt like I was falling for him too fast, but nothing good in life happened if you let fear win.

It was time to listen to my heart instead of my head.

It was like we were being pulled together, and then suddenly our mouths met in a forceful release from logic and reason.

My head spun and I drowned in the taste of him.

The strength to say no drained out of me and we sank to the floor. I clawed at his clothing, wanting—*needing*—to feel his bare skin against mine.

He grabbed a condom from his wallet and sheathed himself as soon as he was naked. Our reunion was fierce, combustible. My nails raked down his back when he thrust into me. We kept our eyes locked on one another, moving as one, coming together in a blaze of passion and heat.

He slid out of me and I quivered.

Smoke gathered me close and held me as our hearts beat in unison, beat for each other.

∽

The next morning, I was awakened by Smoke's tongue between my legs.

"Smoke," I moaned.

"I'm making up for lost time." He lifted his head to stare at me, his mouth glossy with my pleasure.

"You did that last night. Twice," I reminded him.

"So, you want me to stop?" he asked as he slid a finger into me.

"God no." My back bowed and my fists clenched the sheets.

"Didn't think so." He chuckled, his warm breath fanning my skin. "Come for me. Let me see you fall apart."

He curled his finger inside of me at the same time he flicked my clit with his tongue. I shattered, screaming loud enough I was sure everyone in the bakery could hear me.

As I gently floated back down to reality, Smoke eased his finger out of me and then crawled up the mattress to settle next to me. He took his finger and traced my lips.

"Open," he commanded. "And suck."

I cleaned his finger, tasting my own release.

"You're the most gorgeous thing I've ever seen," he growled. "Flushed and sated. Knowing I made you that way feels so good."

His erection nudged my leg.

I rolled over and hoisted my body on top of his. His hands immediately grasped my hips.

My brow furrowed as I gently traced the smooth lines of his chest.

"What's got you frowning?" he asked.

"The last thing I want to do is shatter this moment, but there's something we didn't really talk about last night."

"Oh?"

I took a deep breath. "You mentioned that brothers with Old Ladies wouldn't be directly involved with the strip club. But you—ah—don't have an Old Lady, so does that mean you'll be involved?"

"No," he announced. "I guess I didn't make that clear."

My stomach unclenched. "But the Old Lady part?"

His hands slid up my back and urged me forward, so I was leaning on his chest, our mouths close.

"One day, I'll ask you to be my Old Lady."

"One day?"

"When you're ready. We've got plenty of time, cupcake. Let's enjoy this, knowing we're moving toward that. Okay?"

"You're really serious about that?"

"Yeah, I am. Not trying to freak you out, but that first day driving to Waco with you I knew you were it for me."

"Smoke," I whispered, brushing my lips against his.

He clasped the back of my head with his hand and our mouths fused together. His tongue slipped into my mouth, robbing me of thought.

When he finally released me, I leaned over toward the bedside drawer.

"We have a problem," I said as I turned over the empty box of condoms.

"Fuck."

"I could take care of you another way…"

"Yeah?"

I nodded and slid off him. I wormed my way underneath the covers and grasped his erection to glide my thumb across the crown of his shaft. A bead of precum leaked from his slit and I needed to taste it.

With my free hand, I flung off the covers and scooted down the bed. I released him, but only long enough that I urged him onto his back and then straddled his lower legs. I bent over and took him into my mouth, far enough that he filled my throat.

Smoke groaned in pleasure and I sucked harder. I nearly choked on him, but it wasn't enough. I wanted to swallow every bit of him.

"Fuck, Logan." He fisted my hair and kept the strands away from my face. I bobbed my head and used my hands, clenching his shaft, changing my pace so he never knew what to expect.

When he was primed, I released him with a *pop*, and then I scooted up his body and settled on top of him. His erection was sandwiched between us, resting hard against his belly.

I ground against his skin. I was still wet from my release, so I slid against him.

"Dangerous game you're playing," he growled.

I nodded and lifted up so I could reach between us and angled the head of his shaft toward my entrance.

As I rocked against him, the tip of him slipped in.

"Oh, shit," he moaned. "That feels amazing."

I was playing with fire. I knew that. But the idea of Smoke inside me, with nothing between us, made my core throb.

His hands held my hips, but he made no move to urge me down. He waited, seeing what I'd do.

I sank further down onto him and we both let out a tortuous groan. I controlled the pace, squeezing him between my thighs, drawing out both our pleasure.

Smoke gripped my waist and rolled, so my back hit the mattress. He thrust into me hard and deep.

I gasped as pleasure ripped through my body. And while I was in the throes of my orgasm, Smoke drove into me a few more times before completely pulling out and coming all over my stomach.

"*Fuck*," he muttered as he collapsed onto the bed next to me. He grasped the back of my neck and thrust his tongue into my mouth.

My body quivered with renewed pleasure.

"Stop, you deviant." I laughed against his lips.

"You like it," he teased.

"True." I pecked him one last time and then climbed out of bed and headed to the bathroom. After I did my business, I pulled on a pair of underwear and a discarded T-shirt before padding into the kitchen. My cell was resting on the counter and it began to vibrate.

"Tavy's calling," I yelled.

He paused for a moment before he called back, "Answer it."

I bit my lip and debated all of five seconds. "Good morning," I greeted.

"I didn't think I'd get you," Tavy said in surprise. "It's early. And you sound coherent."

"Not the norm, I assure you," I said with a laugh.

"I have five minutes. Tell me all the things."

"What things?" I averred.

"Things. Like, how's your life, how's your website, how's everything else?"

I quickly darted a look in the direction of my bedroom where I had a very naked man in my bed.

"Hmm. Well, not much happening with the website yet. Willa's doing a mockup with a couple of designs."

"That's it? That's your entire life? Please tell me you've been going out, doing fun things with Brielle and Jazz. Anything so you're not sitting at home cuddling the remote."

"Am I so predictable?" I demanded.

"Well? Have they taken you clubbing?"

"No. Why would they take me clubbing?"

"I don't know. It gives you an excuse to wear a short sparkly dress and have strangers grind up on you."

"That sounds not at all fun."

"Then you're doing it wrong."

I laughed. "Not much is happening here, honestly. I had lunch with the Old Ladies the other day."

"And?"

"And...they're a good group. They're eclectic, but they all really care about each other. They're honest and open, and even though they hardly know me, they talk to me like they've known me for years."

"Sounds nice."

"It is nice," I assured her.

"So, nothing else?" she prodded.

"Not really," I lied.

"Oh. Okay then."

"What about you? How's your patient?"

"Easiest job in the world," she said. "We alternate between playing backgammon or cards and then they sleep in the afternoon."

"Sounds pretty chill."

"It is. I better go," she said. "We're still on for Saturday night?"

"Yup."

"Good. Oh, guess what?"

"What?"

"My dad called my grandfather."

"Yeah?" I asked in surprise.

"Yeah. My grandfather left me a voicemail. Maybe there's hope for my family after all."

"Maybe," I joked.

"Okay, bye for real."

The line went dead and just as I was about to set my phone aside I got a text from Rach.

> **RACH**
> Hey, are you doing okay? Haven't heard from you in a few days.
>
> **ME**
> I'm good. Smoke and I are going to be fine. You probably won't see me for a few more days... ;)

I set the phone down and walked back toward Smoke.

"So, you called your dad?" I asked as I entered the bedroom.

"She told you, huh?"

I nodded.

He patted the bed. I crawled onto it and settled next to him.

"How'd it go?" I asked.

"It was like talking to a stranger."

I winced.

"It was awkward as fuck. Not a lot of yelling, which wasn't what I was expecting."

"You expected your father to yell?"

"No. *I* expected to yell." He shot me a wry grin.

"Why didn't you?"

He sighed. "I don't know. Suddenly all the shit between us didn't seem to matter as much as I thought it did. He sounded…old. Frail."

"Not the man you remember."

"Not the man I remember." He nodded. "Maybe he has changed."

"What did you guys talk about?"

"We didn't talk for long. It was mostly superficial shit. The weather, where I live. I mentioned the club and he steered the conversation away. Like it's still a sore subject for him about how I choose to live my life."

"Some things never change," I said quietly.

He scrubbed his jaw and I noticed he was already in need of a shave. "He asked me to come and visit. And he asked me to bring Tavy."

"Oh."

"I'm considering it," he admitted. "I'll talk to Tavy and see how she feels. I mean, it's her grandfather, right? I don't have the right to keep them apart if they want to have a relationship."

"Sounds like you're figuring it out."

He stared at me for a long moment.

"What?" I asked.

"Would you go…with me? I'd like to introduce you to my parents."

My heart fluttered in my chest. I reached out and gently ran a finger across his jaw. "Yeah. I'll go."

Chapter 41

"This is a terrible idea. This is the worst idea we've ever had. What the hell were we thinking?" I demanded, shooting Smoke a panicked look.

He settled his hand on my thigh. "It's not gonna get any easier. We said we were going to tell her, and we're telling her. Today. We're planning a future together…we *have* to tell her."

The last few days had sped by in a daze of sex and talking. Our walls had come down and now it felt like we were inseparable. He'd left for just a few hours to deal with club business and my chest had ached until he came back.

I was completely enamored with Smoke. The intimacy between us was drugging, and despite the swiftness of our relationship progressing, I didn't have any anxiety about him wanting me to become his Old Lady when the time was right. It was surreal, but every time I thought about spending my life with him and being part of the club family, it made me giddy.

Now it was D day. The day that would live in infamy. The day we'd tell Tavy her father and her best friend were in a serious relationship.

"It's gonna be fine," he said. When I raised my eyebrows at him, he grinned. "Okay, maybe not *fine*. But when she realizes this isn't just a fling she'll come around. It's going to be tough, but she has to know how important you are to me."

Despite my nerves, the smell of barbecue made my belly rumble. "I need to use the restroom," I said.

Smoke slid out of the booth and I got up. He placed his hand on my hip and leaned down to kiss me. "Only way out is through."

"How comforting." I snorted.

He let me go and I followed the signs to the bathroom. I didn't have to use the restroom, but I needed a moment alone to compose myself.

But Smoke was right. This wasn't going to get any easier, so facing it tonight was the only way to move forward. We couldn't hide any longer. Not only was it disrespectful to my best friend, but it was disrespectful to Smoke and I, and what was blooming between us.

I splashed some cool water on my heated cheeks and took a deep breath. I could do this. I could face my best friend.

The restaurant was starting to pick up for the rush and I had to dodge out of the way of servers carrying plates of food on my way back to the table. It wasn't until I approached that I saw Tavy had already arrived.

Her dark hair was thrown up into a messy ponytail and it looked like she'd driven to the restaurant straight from her out-of-town patient.

She looked at me, a quizzical frown marring her face. "Hey. What are you doing here? I thought we were meeting for dinner tomorrow night?"

Smoke grasped my hand and pulled me down into the

booth next to him.

"What's going on?" Tavy asked, her gaze bouncing between me and her father.

"I'm dating Logan," Smoke said without preamble.

I whirled to glare at him. "Jeez. Ever heard of bedside manner?"

"Won't change the truth," Smoke said.

"You're...you guys are *dating*?" Tavy looked perplexed, like the words hadn't yet permeated her brain.

I nodded. "Yeah. We're dating."

"But how? *When*?" She glanced at Smoke, but her gaze settled on me as realization set in. "You lied to me, didn't you? About the extra toothbrush in your bathroom?"

"Yes." I winced. "I did lie about that. I wasn't ready to —we didn't know if—" I sighed. "Let me start over. We weren't even sure this was going to be anything other than something physical, so we didn't want to tell you until we knew."

"*Ew*. Physical? Seriously? This is insane." She stared at her father. "How could you do this?"

"Tavy," he began.

She shook her head. "No. *I* talk now."

"But you asked me a question. I was going to answer," he replied. His tone and expression were calm, but my heart was pounding so hard it threatened to beat out of my chest.

"She just got out of a three-year relationship!" Tavy snapped. "You took advantage of her!"

"Tavy, no," I jumped in. "It wasn't like that. I swear it wasn't like that."

"Then what was it like? And when did it happen? Have you guys been hooking up," she made a disgusted face, "the whole time we've been in Waco? Or did it start sooner? Oh, God...it was on the road trip..."

I had the grace to look ashamed.

Smoke put his hand on my thigh. "You want the truth, or do you want the answer that'll make you feel better?"

Tavy's mouth clamped shut and her lips whitened. "This is twisted. My father and my best friend…"

"We didn't mean for this to happen," I said softly.

She glared. "Right, you just got naked and fell on his dick."

"*Hey*." Smoke's voice rose. "I get that you're upset and that this is a bit of a shock, but you don't get to speak to her that way. She's going to be my Old Lady one day."

I winced and let out a low moan.

"Old Lady? *Old Lady*? What the ever-loving *fuck*?" Tavy hissed. She stood and grabbed her purse. "I've got to get out of here."

"Tavy," I pleaded.

"You were supposed to rebound, not fall for my fucking father." Her expression was tight with pain and betrayal. "Enjoy your dinner. I've lost my appetite."

Tavy stormed out of the restaurant, nearly taking a server down in her haste to get away.

I sighed. "What a mess."

"She'll come around."

"Will she? She's pretty fucking pissed off, Smoke."

"I still think I should've told her alone."

I shook my head. "At least now she can't call me a coward."

"You're not a coward."

"Aren't I?" I played with a corner of my paper napkin. "I lied to her directly…about your toothbrush."

"What were you supposed to say in that moment?" he asked. "The timing wasn't right."

"It wasn't just about the toothbrush. She asked me to be honest with her when I was ready to start dating because she wanted to make sure the guy was good enough for me."

"We'll give her a few days to cool off and then we'll see."

"Why do you sound so blasé about all this?" I demanded.

"Are you going to leave me because she's upset?" he demanded.

The gangly male server approached our table. "Hi, would you like to put in any appetizers?"

"The cheese biscuits, the onion brick, and we'll share a full rack of spareribs with collards and corn on the cob," Smoke rattled off.

"Regular butter or the spicy butter?" the server asked.

Smoke looked to me. "Spicy?"

I raised an eyebrow. "How can you eat at a time like this?"

My stomach rumbled.

Smoke grinned at me and then glanced at the server. "Spicy butter. And I'll take another pint."

The server gathered our menus and took off.

"You didn't answer my question," I said.

"You didn't answer mine," he pointed out.

With a sigh, I shook my head. "No, of course I'm not going to leave you, but we just emotionally clobbered Tavy in public. We should've done it at my apartment."

"Nah," he said. "A restaurant is neutral territory. There was no good way to tell her how serious this is, cupcake."

Frowning, I nodded.

"What?" he asked, tucking a strand of hair behind my ear.

"I just—what if she makes me choose. You or her?"

"Look at me."

I lifted my eyes and met his intense gaze.

"Tavy might be pissed as fuck right now. But she'd never put you in a position where she'd make you choose."

"How do you know?" I asked.

"How *don't* you know?" he fired back. "You've known her for years. Is she the type to do that to her best friend?"

"No." I swallowed my feelings stuck in my throat. "She'd sooner cut off her own arm than hurt me. And until today, she thought the same of me."

∽

"You ordered too much food," I said as I took the to-go bag off the table.

"No such thing." Smoke put his credit card back in his wallet and then grabbed my hand. "Barbecue is better the second day anyway. Something about the spices and marinades settling in the fridge overnight."

We stepped out into the autumn night and I breathed in a deep lungful of air.

"You drive," I said to him, rifling through my purse.

"You sure?"

I nodded and tossed him the car keys.

He opened the passenger side for me and I slid in. A slight headache had begun to form at my temples.

We drove with Smoke's hand resting on my leg, my hand covering his.

"You think I'm kind of heartless, don't you?" he asked.

"What makes you even ask that?" I demanded.

"Because I started dating you even though you're my daughter's best friend. It's not lost on me that I'm trying to reconnect with her after years apart. But you have to understand something—Tavy will forgive me when she realizes what you mean to me, but if I let you go, you might be gone forever. I can't risk that. I love Tavy more than anyone will ever know, but if she loves me at all, she won't want me to miss out on the best thing that's ever happened to me."

"Yeah, that right there—you're the exact opposite of heartless. The timing sucks though. I mean, what are the chances that we fall for each other right when you're trying to get to know her?"

"But we did. You're important to me, and that's what she has to realize. She just needs time."

He brought my fingers to his lips.

Smoke parked outside the bakery next to his motorcycle.

"Hey," I said when he closed the car door. "I know you were supposed to stay over, but…"

"You want the place to yourself."

I nodded. "In case she calls. In case she wants to come over and yell at me in person."

"Let me walk you to your door, at least," he said.

"Oh, that's not—"

"Logan." He cradled my face in his hands. "Let me walk you."

"Okay," I whispered.

He walked me into the bakery and up to my apartment. I unlocked the door and turned to him.

"Thank you," I said, leaning in and kissing his lips.

"For what?"

"For understanding."

"I hope she calls you. I hope this shit gets settled sooner rather than later."

"You and me both," I said.

"I'll see you tomorrow," he promised.

I nodded. "Tomorrow."

"Want me to set the alarm before I leave?"

I shook my head. "I'll do it. There's a piece of pie

waiting for me in the walk-in downstairs. I'll set the alarm after I get it."

He kissed me one final time.

I walked him to the door and watched as he headed down the stairs. Sighing, I put the food in the refrigerator and then went into the bedroom to change into a pair of sleep shorts and a T-shirt. I grabbed my phone and keys and headed downstairs into the bakery kitchen.

The girls had made a routine of leaving me slices of pies or cobblers in the walk-in. Smoke and I had eaten a few of them the last several days since he'd been staying at my place.

Sharing space with him was easy—and not just because I was used to living with a man. But because he was just an easy person to be around. The apartment was small, but I never felt crowded by him.

I liked him there.

I was closing the walk-in fridge when my phone buzzed on the prep table. I set the slice of chocolate cream pie down and reached for my phone.

My heart leapt thinking it might be Tavy.

But it wasn't.

It was a text from Willa. I relaxed a bit and read the message.

> **WILLA**
>
> Just reminding you about the baby shower tomorrow. I know it'll be hard to tear yourself away from Smoke now that you two are back together. Word spreads fast through the Old Ladies' grapevine.

I typed out a reply, grinning at the thought of getting to have some quality girl-talk about my reunion with Smoke. My smile slipped when I realized I wouldn't ever get to gush to Tavy about how gooey I was over my new relationship.

I took the pie upstairs and stood at the kitchen counter to eat it.

Loneliness enveloped me. My best friend wasn't speaking to me and I missed Smoke.

I set the empty plate in the sink and then picked up my cell to text Smoke and then just as quickly put it down. The last thing I wanted to do was appear needy.

"Fuck it." I unlocked my phone and dialed his number. It rang twice before going to voicemail.

I hung up in frustration.

And then I called Rach.

"Hello?"

"Thank God you answered," I blurted out.

"What's wrong? Are you suffering from dehydration from all your physical activities with Smoke?"

"Ha-ha."

"Oh come on, we're dying for the story."

"I'll tell you at Brooklyn's tomorrow."

"So, what's up? Why did you call?"

"I just didn't want to be alone with my own thoughts."

"Been there," she said with a laugh.

"Is this a bad time?"

"No. I'm enjoying a cup of tea and contemplating watching a new show. But I'm not sure I'm ready for that kind of commitment."

I sniggered.

"What's going on?"

"Smoke and I met Tavy tonight. And we told her."

"And how did that go?"

"She's not talking to me. But at least she didn't throw a cocktail in my face."

"Thank heavens for small mercies."

"Right?" I shook my head.

"Smoke isn't there with you, is he?"

"No. I sent him home in case Tavy decided to come by and yell at me in person."

"So, there was no drink throwing. Was there yelling?"

"Kind of. We were in public so that kept everyone's behavior in check." I paused. "She accused Smoke of taking advantage of me."

"Ouch."

"He didn't," I hastened to assure her.

"I know he didn't. That has to hurt, though."

"Yeah." I bit my lip. "I'm not sure how this is going to shake out. I hope with some time she'll come around. But even if she does, it's not like I can sit and gossip with her about him. That would be weird."

"So, you'll go to other friends for that. What are you doing now? You want to come hang out? There's a Turkish drama that looks really good. I'll wait to start it."

I smiled even though she couldn't see me. "Nah. I think I'll go to bed. Clearly, Tavy isn't coming over to yell at me. Might as well try and get some sleep."

"Okay, but the invitation stands. Even if you come over at two in the morning—which I'll probably be awake because of Cash."

"Good to know. Thanks, Rach."

"Anytime."

We hung up and even though my mind wasn't completely at ease, at least it was lighter.

A knock on the door stole my attention.

Smoke!

I rushed to the door and threw it open, smiling widely.

"Hi, honey. You miss me?" Knox's large form filled the doorway, a sinister grin spread across his handsome face.

Chapter 42

I ATTEMPTED to slam the door, but Knox wedged his arm in the doorjamb, thwarting my efforts.

Cold terror filled my bones and my flight instinct kicked in.

I turned and ran, grabbing my cell phone off the counter as I dashed into the bathroom. I locked the door as fast as I could, but the lock was a joke and wouldn't keep an angry man at bay for an extended period of time.

With trembling fingers, I unlocked my phone and called Smoke, praying he answered. It rang and rang, and just as his voicemail came through the phone, the bathroom door splintered off its hinges.

I recoiled in fear and the phone slipped out of my fingers and clattered to the tile floor.

Knox's face was red with fury and his fists were clenched by his sides. He embodied the spirit of an irate bull. Irrationally, I expected horns to spring from his head and steam to billow from his nostrils.

He pushed the damaged door aside and it drunkenly

slid out of its hinges to crash to the ground. Knox marched into the small space and blocked my ability to escape.

He reached for me and wrapped his hands around my upper arms and shook me like a rag doll.

"You think you can leave *me*?" he snapped. "You don't leave me. We're gonna be together forever. We're getting married."

"It's *over*, Knox," I yelled, my teeth clacking together.

"It's never fucking over," he hissed.

He bent his head to kiss me, and when his lips covered mine, I bit down hard enough to taste blood.

Knox reared back and roared in pain. "You stupid bitch!"

He shoved me away from him and then punched me in the lower stomach. I clutched my belly in agony as the air left my lungs. Tears sprang to my eyes as I gasped for breath, trying to keep myself from vomiting.

Knox pushed me to the ground and my chin hit the tile floor. Pain ricocheted through my skull and my vision blinked in and out.

"I gave you fucking *everything*," he ranted.

There was a crack followed by the sounds of fracturing glass which rained down from above me and I knew he'd smashed the bathroom mirror.

I pulled what little energy I had together and began to crawl past him toward the living room.

"I bought you a ring!" he shouted as I inched away from him. He was on a tirade and I prayed it lasted long enough for me to escape him.

Wood groaned as it broke apart.

He's destroying the vanity with his bare hands.

"I moved you into my house! I bought you a car! I gave you nice clothes! And now you're fucking some biker?"

Drywall and flecks of paint littered my path as he continued his onslaught.

I'd barely made it out of the bathroom when strong hands clamped my ankles like shackles and halted my escape.

And then Knox grabbed my shoulder and flipped me over.

"We're not done, Logan. We're *never* gonna be fucking done. I've been watching you. I know you've been with him…"

Knox tore at my clothes. My shirt ripped at the collar, exposing my breasts.

I tried to fight, but he grabbed my wrists and clinched them together in one of his large hands and shoved them over my head. He straddled my legs and I didn't have the strength nor the skills to fight him off.

He leaned down close to my face, his eyes lit with excitement. "I'm going to fuck a baby into you before that biker gets a chance to."

Knox licked the tears from my cheeks as his free hand wrenched down my pajama shorts and underwear.

I couldn't breathe, I couldn't scream, I couldn't feel.

My mind slipped away.

I heard the sound of his zipper and turned my face to the floor so I wouldn't see him destroy me.

A bellow of rage split the air, and Knox took a boot to the face. His heavy form was suddenly thrown off me.

I was free.

The force of the kick propelled Knox into the coffee table. It collapsed and crunched beneath the weight of him. Smoke wasted no time and jumped on top of Knox immediately and began to pummel Knox in the face.

The sound of flesh meeting flesh turned my stomach.

I rolled over and hastily dragged up my pajama shorts

and attempted to pull the ruined pieces of my shirt together to cover my breasts.

"Logan!" Smoke yelled. "Get the fuck out of here!"

"You son of a bitch! I know you're fucking her!" Knox roared as he began to wrestle Smoke for control.

Fists flew, connecting with skin. Blood splattered and the scent of unhinged violence was in the air.

Tangy, musky adrenaline and blood.

I tried to stand, but my body refused to move. Somehow, I was able to crawl toward the open front door, but I was too weak to stand. Too weak to scream for help.

If I could just get downstairs to a phone…

Smoke continued to pummel Knox. Panic filled my throat as I saw Knox flip Smoke over using moves he'd learned in mixed martial arts.

How quickly the brawl had turned in favor of Knox. Smoke took an elbow to the face which split the skin of his forehead. Blood began to flow into Smoke's eyes, and he hastily swiped at his face, hoping to see.

They pushed and pulled, elbowed and grappled. One moment Smoke was winning, the next Knox. Time ceased to move.

Finally, Smoke shoved Knox off him again and attacked like a pit bull. Smoke pinned Knox to the ground with a massive arm. Muscles bulged and veins popped, rippling his tattoos so they looked alive beneath his skin.

I watched in mute horror as Knox pulled a knife from his pocket. Smoke screamed as Knox thrust a knife over and over into his lower abdomen. Smoke immediately began wrestling for control of the blade, but he lost his balance and fell backward. Blood spewed from the wounds in his side.

Knox spit bloody saliva onto the floor and then rose to

stand above Smoke. He dropped the knife and watched as Smoke lay in a pool of blood, unable to rise.

Knox looked at me and then back at Smoke, and then calmly said, "The last thing you're going to see before you die is me fucking your whore."

A whimper of fear escaped my lips.

Knox stalked toward me, blocking my view of Smoke.

I stared into Knox's terrifying gaze as I heard the faintest rustling of Smoke moving—and then a gunshot drowned out every other sound in the room.

Knox's body jerked and fell, and blood poured from his head.

Bile climbed up my throat, but I shoved it down. My hands were cold and I shook with fear, but I had to get to Smoke.

"*Smoke*," I cried. I scrambled toward him even as my body screamed in pain.

He was propped up against the wall, his mouth moving, but no words escaping. His white shirt had bloomed red, like someone had taken a paint can and turned it over onto him. His head lolled onto his chest and his hand still held the pistol.

I pressed my hand to his wounds and he lifted his head for a moment and then grunted in pain.

"Help!" I yelled. "Help, someone, *please!*"

It was useless. We were on our own. I had to get someone, but how was I going to leave Smoke long enough to run downstairs and—

The sound of frantic footsteps echoed in the distance and suddenly Jazz appeared in the open doorway of the apartment.

My eyes met hers.

"*What the fuck happened?*" she blurted out as she pulled out her cell phone, her fingers flying across the screen. A few seconds of silence went by, then she commanded, "I need an ambulance at Pie in the Sky. There's been a shooting and someone is badly injured…"

I tuned out everything around me. Jazz's voice faded into the background as she answered questions for the 911 operator. I kept my hands firmly on Smoke's wounds, willing them to close. Willing him to survive. Praying for the bleeding to stop.

"Smoke," I whispered.

His eyes fluttered open.

"Hey," I said, trying to smile. "There you are. Stay with me."

"I'm here." His voice was nothing more than a whisper.

"You came back."

"Missed…you. Didn't…want…you…to…be…" He struggled to take a breath. "Alone."

I was in a vacuum of time and space. My heart pumped like a rabid animal in the wild. My hands slipped in Smoke's blood as I slowly watched his face turn wan.

Voices whooshed near me and suddenly I heard everything around me again.

"Ma'am. *Ma'am!* We need you to move so we can take care of him. We have to take him to the hospital right now."

Firm hands gripped my arms and attempted to pull me away. I screamed and refused to withdraw my palms from Smoke's injuries.

"My hands are going to take the place of yours," the EMT said. "You have to move."

"*Logan.*"

Jazz's voice registered and I reluctantly took my hands off Smoke. They were covered in his blood.

Jazz grasped my arm and helped me to stand. A noise

of distress left her lips. I looked at her and wanted to assure her.

"It'll be okay," I said. "Smoke will be okay."

Jazz shook her head and pointed to me. "You're bleeding."

I looked down and saw the blood on my thighs.

Chapter 43

Beep. Beep. Beep.

My eyelids fluttered open. I was curled up on my side in the fetal position.

The door to the hospital room opened and a nurse came in. Her smile was as bright as the pink and blue patterned scrubs she wore. Her brown ponytail was high and bouncy.

"Good morning, sugar," she greeted. "My name is Sharon. I'm just here to take your vitals. How are you feeling?"

I paused while I thought about the question. I settled for, "Empty."

Her eyes saddened. "Aww, honey."

I was too numb to cry. Even after I'd been brought into the hospital the night before and had an exam where they told me I'd miscarried, I hadn't cried. It was as if the faucet of my feelings had been shut off in a trauma response.

They'd wheeled me into a recovery room where I'd met with the club attorney—Vance Raider—who stayed with me while I'd given my statement to the police. I'd told them about Knox's history of violence and anger, about how I'd left him, and how he hadn't taken no for an answer. About how he'd been about to rape me and that Smoke had saved me.

It was a miracle I'd slept at all last night, but they'd given me a powerful sedative.

"Smoke." My voice came out a throaty growl. "Where is he? What happened to him?"

"He went into surgery last night while you were having your exam."

"And is he…"

Sharon smiled and touched my shoulder. "You must be important to him. He's been asking about you since the moment he woke up."

Tears finally began to flood my eyes. "Can I see him? I need to be near him."

"Let me pull some strings and see what I can do. He's talking with the police right now and I don't think you're allowed to be in the room with him."

I nodded in understanding.

She handed me the TV remote. "Can I get you anything?"

"A chocolate pudding?" I asked hopefully.

Sharon chuckled. "That, I can do."

I ate my chocolate pudding while I watched daytime television. I kept glancing at the door every so often, hoping the nurse would return and tell me I could see Smoke.

At some point, I dozed off with the TV still on in the background. I came to as the door opened and an orderly with a wheelchair entered behind Sharon. "The police left and you can see Smoke now."

They helped me out of bed and eased my abused body

into a wheelchair. They wheeled me down the hallway and stopped in front of a door. Sharon opened it and the orderly pushed me through.

Smoke was laid up in bed, his face different shades of purple and blue, swollen almost beyond recognition.

"*Oh my—*" Tears welled in my eyes.

"Hey," he said gently. "I'm okay."

I reached for his hand but he was too far away. The orderly wheeled me closer and I grasped Smoke's fingers, lacing them with mine.

"We'll leave you both for a bit," Sharon said. "Not too long, though. You both need to rest."

"Thank you," I said.

The door closed softly and we were alone.

I swallowed. "You talked to the police?"

"Yeah." His one eye that wasn't swollen shut was cloudy with pain medication, but he was alert. "They told me about your ex's past."

"I swear I didn't know," I said. Nausea brewed in my belly, threatening to send up the chocolate pudding. "If I'd known, I would've never—"

"His record was sealed," he interrupted. "It's not your fault. I know you didn't know."

At seventeen, Knox had been convicted of date-raping a freshman high school girl at a party. His parents had been able to keep the records sealed since he was a minor at the time of conviction, but the law in Texas allowed for them to be released during a criminal investigation after his death.

"There's no charge against me, Logan. Not only was it self-defense, but with your statement about how he tried to…"

"Rape me," I finished for him.

He nodded slowly. "There won't be any charges. Raider assured me of that."

"Vance was nice," I said softly.

Smoke's lips quirked into a tiny smile, but he winced when his lips split. "Damn."

Without thought, I leaned over and gently brushed the bead of blood from his skin.

"What?" I demanded. "He is."

"Vance isn't *nice*. Vance is a motherfucking shark in a suit."

"Well, he was nice to me."

"Good."

"Smoke, how did Knox find me? I got a new phone; I did everything I could to disappear."

"The bakery."

"What?"

"When you moved, you forgot to change the address on one of your credit cards. The police found a credit card statement with all your purchases in the rental car he was driving. Name of the bakery was right there. As soon as the statement arrived in the mail, he put two and two together. Logan, security cameras show him in the parking lot last night. He watched us both and waited until I left. He didn't know I'd come back."

I looked at our entwined hands. "Smoke, I have to tell you something…"

"I already know," he said softly. "I heard what Jazz said…about the blood on your thighs."

"Oh." My heart leapt into my throat. "I thought you'd passed out."

"I came to just as they'd put me on the gurney. Just long enough to hear."

"They told me—the doctor told me… Smoke, the baby wasn't yours."

His hand tightened on mine. "I'm sorry for your loss, cupcake."

I swallowed and nodded. Neither of us said anything more, we just continued to sit in shared silence. Smoke couldn't put his arms around me, but I felt them anyway.

∼

I was back in my hospital room, replaying my conversation with Smoke over and over in my head. There were things I wanted to say. Things I wanted to ask.

But it hadn't been the time.

The time for all that would be later. Later, when we were recovering outside the hospital.

Later, when I had time to feel through the mountain of pain I had to deal with.

The hospital door opened and Sharon came in. "You up for some visitors, sugar?"

Not really.

"Sure," I said. "Who is it?"

My parents strode into the room and my jaw nearly dropped open.

"Mom, Dad? What are you doing here?" I asked in surprise.

"What are we doing here?" my mother repeated. "Tavy called us. We hopped on the first flight we could."

Sharon moved toward the door. "I'll leave you three alone for a bit. Holler if you need anything."

"Thanks, Sharon," my dad said.

The door closed and I was alone with my parents, who were supposed to be in Idaho.

"Tavy called you?" My gaze bounced from my father's weathered face to my mother's strangely line-free complexion.

"She called us from the hospital," Mom explained. "She gave us no details—she said she didn't know what happened, just that you were in the hospital and that we needed to get down here right away."

"Is she—did you see her?" I asked.

"Of course. She's in the waiting room. She doesn't even look like she's been home to shower," Mom replied.

I burst into tears and hastily covered my face with my hands.

My parents brought chairs to my bedside and took their seats. Mom reached out and set her hand on my leg which only made me cry harder.

Only when I was hiccoughing and my eyes were swollen did the tears finally abate.

My parent's watched me with tacit patience and understanding.

I opened my mouth and slowly told them what happened.

"I wasn't completely honest about Knox," I said quietly. "He was cheating on me, but that's not the only reason I left."

When I paused, my dad said, "Take your time. We're not going anywhere."

I nodded. "He had begun to get physical…"

"That bastard hit you?" Dad seethed.

"*John*," Mom warned. "It's not the time."

My dad took a deep breath and nodded.

"It was moving in that direction. If I'd stayed, I know it would've gone that way."

I had the bruises on my back and stomach to prove it.

"Last night, he showed up at my apartment. He said we weren't over, that we'd never be over. If Smoke hadn't come in when he did…"

I watched understanding dawn on my parents' faces.

"Who's Smoke?" Dad asked. "Does he belong to the biker club Tavy's father is in?"

"Smoke *is* Tavy's father…he's also the man I'm dating."

Dad stood up from his chair. "He's *what?*"

"John, take a walk," Mom commanded.

"Stella—"

"*Now.*" She threw him a pointed look.

"No," I insisted. "It's okay. Dad has the right to be… Dad."

My father's expression softened ever so slightly.

"Knox stabbed him. Smoke was rushed into surgery, but he's in recovery."

"And Knox?" Dad asked. "Is he in recovery?"

I shook my head. "He's dead. Smoke shot him." I rubbed my temple. "I know this is a lot to take in, and I'm sure you have a ton of questions. But can I answer them later? I'm really tired."

There was still so much I hadn't told them…Knox's criminal past. My miscarriage. I just didn't have the bandwidth to talk about it. I barely even had the bandwidth to think about it.

"We'll go down to the cafeteria and get something to eat," Mom said. "And give you time to rest."

"We'll be back before visiting hours are over." Dad leaned over and kissed the top of my head.

Mom gently tucked a strand of hair behind my ear before she let my father guide her out of the room.

I rested against the pillows and closed my eyes. I didn't think I'd be able to fall asleep with my mind whirling, but somehow, I did.

When I woke up, both my parents were sitting in the chairs next to my bed. Mom was reading on her e-reader and Dad was watching TV on mute.

"Hey," I croaked, struggling to sit up.

Mom rose from her chair and set her device aside. "Easy there. What can I get you?"

"Water, please."

She went to the bedside and picked up the plastic pitcher of water and poured it into a plastic cup with a straw. Mom held the straw to my mouth and I didn't protest. I sucked the water greedily, quenching my parched throat.

I leaned back when I'd had enough. "Thanks." My hand searched for the call button.

"What do you need, LoLo?" Dad asked.

"I'm calling the nurse," I explained. "So she can help me to the bathroom."

"I'll help you," Mom said. "You don't need to call for the nurse."

"It's fine," I insisted.

"I've changed your diapers, I can help you to the bathroom," my mom said.

Her words hit me straight in the heart. She didn't know that a throwaway comment about a baby could hurt me, and I hadn't expected to feel the sharp pang of loss, either.

"Okay," I wheezed.

I held out my hand and Mom gingerly helped me off the bed. I hobbled to the bathroom, hunched over like an old crone.

My dad's softly spoken expletives echoed behind me.

He must've seen the bruises on my back from the split in my hospital gown.

Mom flipped on the garish bathroom light and closed the door behind us.

"I can hold my gown, but can you…" I gestured to my underwear.

"Sure can," she said, gently easing them down my legs.

Once I was comfortable and settled back into bed, my parents looked at each other and my dad nodded.

"What's the look for?" I asked in amusement.

"Look? What look?" Mom asked.

"You guys share looks. You can communicate without words."

"Comes from years of marriage," Dad said.

"Hmm. Yeah."

"We spoke with a nice young man in the waiting area," Mom said. "Tall, dark-haired, seems to wear a perpetual scowl."

I frowned. "I don't know who you're talking about."

"He's the president of the Tarnished Angels," Dad said. "Colt, if I remember correctly."

"Oh, yeah. Colt." I had to hide a smile. I was sure the biker president would love to hear that my parents had called him a nice young man.

"Well, we talked to him about Smoke's care. It seems Smoke lives at the clubhouse," Mom said.

"Right," I said in confusion at the direction of their conversation.

"And your apartment is on a second floor," she went on. "Neither of you are in a position to be able to climb stairs for a while. So, your father and I…"

"We got two attached suites at the Donovan Hotel. Your mother and I will stay in one, and you and Smoke will stay in the other," Dad said. "So we can be there if you need anything."

I blinked, unsure of what to react to first. "Wait…You got Smoke and me a suite? Together?"

"Two queen-sized beds," Dad said with a pointed look.

I rolled my eyes.

"Colt agreed it was an excellent idea," Mom said. "His wife thought so too. She's so sweet."

"Mia? Sweet?" I snorted. "She's great, but she can be awfully blunt at times."

"They all really care about you," Dad said, rubbing his beard. "The bikers and their wives, I mean."

"How do you know that?"

He looked at me in confusion. "Because they're all in the waiting room. And every time we see them, they ask how you're feeling."

Tears flooded my eyes.

The hospital door opened and Sharon came in. "Sorry to break up the party, but Logan needs to rest."

"We'll see you tomorrow," Mom said. "Bright and early."

"Not too early," Dad said with a wink.

The hospital door shut and Sharon looked after them. "Nice family you got there."

"Yeah. They're the best."

And then I thought about the people in waiting room. "The very best."

Chapter 44

"Is he sleeping?" I asked Sharon.

She closed the blinds on my window so the parking lot lights wouldn't shine through. "He's awake."

"Can I see him?"

"Visiting hours are over."

"Please?" I begged. "I won't stay long. I just need to see him. Ten minutes?"

I watched her expression waver until finally she nodded. "All right. I'll take you to see him. But you both need your rest."

Slowly, I swung my legs over the side of the bed and made a move to stand.

"What are you doing?" she demanded.

"Walking to Smoke's room."

"Sit." She pointed to the bed. "You can barely make it to the bathroom on your own. I'm getting you a wheelchair."

I smiled.

"What?" she demanded.

"You're bossy. But really sweet."

"Hush, now." She grinned. "I'll be right back."

We had to pass the nurse's station to get to Smoke's room and there was another nurse on duty.

"It's past visiting hours," she said.

"I know," Sharon said. "But love doesn't have visiting hours."

The rule-abiding nurse unbent and her expression softened. "I know nothing."

"Don't lie. You're secretly a big soft marshmallow," Sharon teased.

She wheeled me into Smoke's room. The lights were already off and his eyes were halfway closed.

"Just a few minutes," Sharon said. "And then I'm coming back for her."

I squeezed her hand in gratitude and then she left us alone.

"Hey," I said softly.

"Hand," he commanded.

I set my palm on the bed next to his and he laced his fingers with mine.

"Met your parents," he said.

"Oh?"

"In between your father glaring at me, your mom explained that they're taking us to the Donovan Hotel so they can take care of us while we recover. That sound about like what they told you?"

"Yeah." I nodded. "I told them about you—sorta, I mean. I didn't have the energy to answer the bajillion questions when they found out you were Tavy's father."

"Do they know about the miscarriage?" he asked softly.

I shook my head.

"I've been thinking about it. A lot," he said.

"You have?"

He nodded. "And I just want to say—"

The hospital door opened and the rule-abiding nurse came in, interrupting Smoke.

"I'm here to take you back to your room," she said to me.

"Where's Sharon?"

"She went to the cafeteria."

Smoke released my hand and I looked at him while the nurse turned the wheelchair and wheeled me out of his room.

I wish I knew what he was going to say, but it would have to wait.

The nurse—for all her brusque attitude—was gentle when she helped me into bed. I wasn't due for pain meds for another hour or so, and my body hurt, reminding me of what I'd lived through.

What I was still living through.

Knox had killed my baby.

Smoke had killed Knox.

I waited to weep until I was alone.

It seemed all I was doing was vacillating between tears and numbness. Maybe that was grieving.

The hospital door opened and I hastily swiped at my cheeks. Sharon stopped when she saw me trying to compose myself.

"Did Beth make you cry?"

I let out a watery laugh. "No. I'm just crying because... *life*."

"She wasn't supposed to bring you back to your room yet. I stopped off at the cafeteria to bring you these." She held up two plastic spoons and chocolate pudding cups. "Thought you could enjoy them together."

I started to cry again.

"Aww, sugar." She came toward me and set the pudding cups on the swiveled wooden table.

"I'm fine," I blubbered.

"Yeah, I know," she said, but she gently took me into her arms and let me cry some more.

"When will the tears stop?" I asked through a sniffle.

"When there's nothing more to cry about."

∽

The next morning, Sharon and my mother helped me into sweatpants and a shirt I could button up instead of having to lift my arms over my head. My dad was downstairs in the cafeteria, grabbing a quick cup of coffee before I was discharged.

"After we get you settled at the hotel, I can run to your apartment and pick up some of your clothes and toothbrush and things," Mom said.

"No, that's okay," I said. "I don't want you to have to go over there and see the mess." I glanced at Sharon, who was tidying the bathroom and gathering up my hospital gown.

"It's been taken care of," Mom said. "That's what he said."

"Who?" I asked with a frown.

"The biker with the scar." She pointed to her forehead. "I forgot his name."

"Slash," I supplied with a smile. "Hard to believe you forgot his name."

"Well, there's so many of them," Mom stated.

"All handsome too," Sharon piped in.

"Right?" Mom agreed.

"Like, if they did a hot biker of the month calendar, I'd pay good money for that." Sharon grinned.

"Shut up and take my money," Mom said.

I sniggered while the two of them continued talking about Smoke's brothers. I couldn't wait to tell the Old Ladies about this conversation.

"I'll get you those discharge papers and be right back," Sharon said, heading for the door.

"Sweet woman," Mom said.

"Very." I paused. "So, the apartment has been cleaned up and everything?"

She nodded. "Slash said that some *prospects* cleaned the entire apartment. What are prospects, anyway?"

I smiled. "Men who want to be fully patched in brothers, real members of the club, but they're going through the grunt phase."

"Ah." She nodded. "They found your phone. I have it in my bag. Slash's wife—what's her name?"

"Brooklyn."

"Yes, Brooklyn. She said she's having the place painted."

"That place needs a lot more than a clean and fresh paint. It needs an exorcism."

Mom brushed my hair off my shoulder. "I wouldn't want to live there after what happened either."

Sharon returned with my discharge papers and I quickly signed them. An orderly came with a wheelchair and they got me situated.

The orderly wheeled me into the hallway and my mom trailed behind us. She called my dad to let him know I was being discharged.

Smoke was outside his room in a wheelchair as well, talking to a man in a white doctor's coat. "Normally, I'd want to keep you for at least a week due to the severity and placement of your wounds…but legally I can't stop you from being discharged. It appears you…people, will have a private nurse on hand. If she notes any changes other than slowly improving health, I've asked her to bring you back to the hospital. Eat simple, bland foods for the next week. Single ingredients. Lots of fiber. Scrambled eggs with nothing on them, plain pasta. Broths are good. And drink plenty of water."

"Doc, I'm on a lot of pain meds and I don't know if I'm going to remember all this. Can you write it down?"

"Don't have to," Mom announced. "We'll take good care of you."

The doctor touched Smoke's shoulder before walking down the hallway.

"Hi, Smoke," Mom greeted.

"Mrs. Monroe," he said respectfully.

I met his gaze and raised my brows. He blinked his one open eye at me.

"Did you just try and wink at me?" I asked.

"Yeah. Pathetic, huh?"

My smile wobbled. "Super pathetic."

The orderlies wheeled us toward the elevator and pushed our wheelchairs close enough that Smoke reached over and took my hand in his. We had to let go when the doors opened.

My father was waiting for us in the lobby. He smiled when he saw me, but the moment he looked at Smoke, his expression hardened.

Smoke and I sat in our wheelchairs while my dad went to get the rental car. I shivered despite it being warm. I looked at Smoke. Was he cold? His complexion was pale and he had sweat at his temples, but when he caught me looking at him, he gave me a smile.

I returned his smile and forced back the tears that seemed to be right at the surface the past few days.

My dad returned with the car and he climbed out of the driver's side.

"Smoke should take the front seat," Mom said.

"No, Logan should," Smoke insisted.

"Don't be a hero," I quipped.

"Too late," he teased, causing me to giggle. "And I can't strap the seatbelt. It'll press against my incision. I need to be in the back."

The orderlies helped Smoke into the car and I winced while adjusting into a comfortable position. Mom buckled me in and then went and sat behind the driver's side.

"You okay, Smoke?" Mom asked.

He grunted. "I'll live."

"Take it slow, Dad," I said.

"Will do." He put the car into gear. "We'll stop off at the pharmacy and get your prescriptions filled. Then we'll head to the hotel. Sound good?"

"Yeah." I leaned my head against the seat and closed my eyes.

An hour later, Smoke and I were settled into the hotel room, propped up against pillows in our own beds. The nurse had set up an IV to keep Smoke hydrated and medicated while we rested.

The door between the two connected suites was closed and we had some measure of privacy.

"I don't think your father likes me very much," he announced. "Not that I blame him. You being with a biker has to be a real shock to the family."

"Yeah, well, he'll get over it. You saved my life. I didn't thank you for that by the way." I looked at him. "Thank you, Smoke."

"You're welcome. I'm just glad your father didn't bring his shotgun."

"How do you know he has a shotgun?"

"Doesn't he?"

I grinned. "Yeah…"

"Thought so. I like that he's protective of you." He sighed. "I'm just going to have to win him over with my charm."

~

"Are you awake?" I whispered into the dark.

Smoke grunted. "Yeah. Unfortunately."

"I made a mistake—not taking the sedative."

"I took some heavy-duty painkillers, but they make my heart race. But it's either that or pain every time I breathe."

I fell silent for a moment and then I asked, "You came back that night. Why?"

"I didn't want you to be alone," he said softly. "And stew."

"I called you twice."

"I know. I missed the first call, but I answered the second. I didn't understand what was going on right away. There was a lot of noise, you were crying, Knox was yelling. I was only a couple of blocks from your place and I drove like a bat out of hell."

"Oh," I said in realization. "I was in the bathroom and he kicked the door in. My phone slipped out of my hand to the floor. I didn't realize the line was still connected."

"Christ, Logan. I've never been so fucking scared in my life."

"You and me both." I swallowed.

"I never should've left you alone. I should've stayed. I should've—"

"This isn't your fault," I interrupted. "Knox was unhinged. And he was clearly waiting for me to be alone and unprotected. How were you supposed to know? And even if you did, I can't have you with me every second of every day." I took a deep breath. "I thought it was you at the door. That's the only reason I answered it. I think I forgot to set the alarm."

"You told me not to blame myself. Well, then you're not allowed to blame yourself either."

"Okay," I whispered. I bit my lip, not wanting to address what needed to be addressed. But I forged ahead anyway in a new act of bravery. "I didn't know I was pregnant, Smoke. If you don't want to be with me anymore because—"

"Stop."

I clamped my mouth shut.

"Let me say a few things before you continue, okay?" Smoke asked.

"Okay."

"It doesn't matter to me, Logan. I don't care that the baby wasn't mine. I would've stayed. I would've been there for you through every craving, every doctor's appointment, every hormonal breakdown. I would've been there because I love you, cupcake. Baby or no baby. Mine or not."

I began to cry, loud enough for him to hear.

"Fuck, Logan. Don't cry. I can barely move and all I want to do is hold you."

"What if I move?"

"Come here."

I gingerly got up out of bed and went to Smoke. I gently settled down next to him.

"Where can I touch you that won't hurt?" I asked.

"My pinky."

I felt around in the dark for his hand and stroked his pinky. "I love you, too, Smoke."

"Yeah?"

"Yeah."

"Good. Everything else we can figure out later."

~

The door creaking had my eyes flipping open. When I realized it was the connecting suite door and it was only my mother, I settled immediately. And then I realized I was in the same bed as Smoke and my anxiety spiked.

Weak morning light attempting to filter through the curtains gave me just enough illumination to see my mom place her finger to her lips and then step into the room. She approached the side of the bed and crouched down next to me.

"Dad went to the hotel gym to work out," she whispered. "I was thinking you could come into our room and I could order us breakfast while Smoke sleeps."

I glanced at Smoke who was still dead to the world. Nodding, I gently eased the covers off me. Mom stood by but didn't offer any help until I reached for her hand.

She helped me stand.

"I'll meet you in there. I need to use the restroom," I said.

"You're okay on your own?" she asked.

I nodded and hobbled toward the bathroom. I quietly closed the door and flipped on the light. My hair was lank and I wanted to shower, but I wasn't sure I had the energy to stand long enough to get clean.

Maybe I could call down to the front desk and ask for a stool to be brought to the room.

After I did my business and changed the pantyliner—I was still bleeding lightly—I lifted my shirt and turned so I could get a look at the bruises Knox had left on me. They were dark and obvious—and it was a miracle that Knox hadn't broken my ribs. He'd shaken me like a dishrag and abused me enough for my appearance to reflect his violence.

Bruises would disappear, pain would fade.

Hopefully it will be the same for the memories.

I flipped off the bathroom light and quietly padded to the connecting door. I looked over my shoulder to make sure Smoke was still asleep. His chest rose and fell.

Mom was sitting on the edge of one of the king-sized beds near the nightstand, looking through the room-service menu.

"I know what I want," she said as she handed me the menu.

I gingerly sat down on the edge of the bed and winced.

"Should I ask for a bag of ice when I call down for food?" she asked.

I shook my head. "I'll be okay." I looked at the menu and gave her my order. She phoned the restaurant attached to the lobby and then scooted over and propped against the headboard.

She patted the side of the bed next to her.

It took me a few minutes to move and get situated, but eventually I was comfortable.

"How'd you sleep?" she asked.

"Okay," I admitted. "Not great. But not terrible either."

"Hmm."

"Aren't you going to make a comment about finding me and Smoke in bed together?"

"I'm not your father," she said with a soft smile. "I assumed you'd want to be near one another."

"Ah."

"So, he was the one, then?" my mother asked.

"The one?"

"The one you were determined not to talk about on the phone with me."

"You knew, didn't you?"

"That you'd met someone? Yes. Whether or not it was serious? I wasn't sure." She patted my thigh. "You were trying to talk about him in such a roundabout way, I figured there was a man in the picture."

"There is definitely a man in the picture," I agreed. My gaze strayed to the doorway.

"He's a good one. And not just because he saved you. I see the way he looks at you. That one is completely head over heels in love with you."

I smiled. "The feeling is mutual."

"Does he want kids?"

Her question blindsided me. Not because I hadn't thought of it myself, but because it only reminded me of what I'd lost. It was an innocent question; one she didn't realize had triggered an emotional landmine.

"I'm not sure," I said slowly. I knew what he'd said last night—and I believed him wholeheartedly. That didn't mean that he wanted to make a baby with me and have a family.

"Tavy's grown, you know?" I said quietly, momentarily missing my best friend. "He might be done with that portion of his life."

"Is that a dealbreaker for you?"

I looked at her. "Going for the easy questions this morning, I see."

"Just curious. No judgement either way. Though I

would like for one of my children to give me a grandchild one day. Your brothers don't seem inclined to want to settle down."

"So, all hope rests on me?" I arched a brow. "No pressure or anything."

"None whatsoever. I'm happy if you're happy."

"I know." I reached over and grasped her hand in mine. Sadness swelled inside me. "Mom, I have to tell you something."

Chapter 45

She listened without interrupting as I told her about my miscarriage. And then she held me while I cried.

"I don't know why I keep crying about it," I sniffed.

"Oh, honey. Of course you're going to cry about it. You're mourning a life you don't get to have. A future that was taken from you. We don't know why certain things happen, but they do. So you just feel how you feel and don't fight it. That's all there is to it."

"I didn't even know I was pregnant." I lifted myself out of her arms so I could grab a tissue from the nightstand.

"Doesn't mean you wanted it any less."

"Smoke, he—he said it didn't matter to him. That if Knox hadn't come back and done what he'd done, and we'd found out I was pregnant, he would've stayed. He would've raised the baby with me because he loves me."

"He said that?"

"Yeah."

She paused for a moment and said, "If your father tries to give him any more grief, I'll—"

"You can't tell Dad," I interrupted. "He can't know about the miscarriage."

"Why not?"

"Because."

"That's not a reason," she said gently.

"Getting involved with Knox might've been a mistake. My pregnancy might've been an accident. But it's still…I wanted it."

"And you don't think your father will understand that?"

"It's too raw. Maybe I'll tell him one day. But for now, can this please stay between us?"

"Of course, LoLo. Whatever you need right now."

I blew my nose. "You didn't guess? At all?"

"How would I have guessed something like that?"

"You helped me to the bathroom and saw I was wearing a pad."

"I thought you were you on your period and didn't think anything of it."

"Oh." I nodded.

"Is that the only thing bothering you?" she asked.

"No. I've been thinking about Knox, too. About Smoke protecting me. It's all wrapped up in this big 'ole mess I don't know how to unravel."

"It's a lot," she agreed. "Just take it one moment at a time. One feeling at a time."

It was good advice. It might've been hard to live it, but I'd try.

There was a knock on the door and Mom got up from the bed to answer it. It was room service with our food. The attendant came in and asked if we'd like the trays on the small table in the corner.

"On the bed is fine," Mom said.

The attendant placed the trays on the bed and then left.

"Well, bon appétit," Mom said as she lifted the lids off the plates and then handed me the quiche.

My mother was mid bite of her poached eggs when her cell phone rang. She went to the small table where it rested, plugged in, and looked at it.

"It's your brother," she said.

"Which one?"

"Grady."

I swallowed. "Did you tell them what happened?"

"They were there when we got the phone call from Tavy."

Tavy.

I hadn't had time to think too hard about what was going on between us because of my overwhelming grief at the events of the past few days.

Mom's cell went silent and then a moment later started buzzing again.

"Might as well take the call," I said with a sigh. "He'll just keep calling."

"Yep." She pressed a button and put the phone to her ear. "I'm with your sister and we're having breakfast." She paused and then said, "Okay."

She unplugged the phone and walked to me. "He wants to talk to you."

"I'm eating," I said.

She arched a brow.

With a shake of my head, I took the phone. "Hi, Grady."

"Logan," he said, his tone gruff but soft. "Are you okay?"

My big brother had never been the terrorizing sort. He'd left that for Harlan and Chase. He'd been my protector, making it incredibly difficult to date in high school.

"I'm okay," I said.

"Is Smoke with you?"

I frowned in confusion. "He's sleeping."

"Oh. Right. Well, when he wakes up, tell him I said thanks."

"For what?"

"For killing the fucker and saving me the trouble."

I bit my lip to stop my laugh. "I'll tell him."

"He sounds like a good one."

"High praise, coming from you," I joked.

"Can't be too sure until I meet the guy in person."

"Which won't be for a while."

"Not really…"

"Grady?" I pressed. "What do you mean *not really*?"

"Don't worry about it."

"*Grady*," I snapped.

"Gotta talk to Killian. See you soon."

He hung up and I lowered the phone from my ear.

"Mom?"

"Yeah?" She wouldn't meet my gaze.

"Grady just said *see you soon*."

"I heard. The volume was turned up so loud it might as well have been on speaker phone."

"*Mom!*"

"They're catching a flight later this afternoon," she admitted.

"They? A flight? No…"

"Yes."

"All of them?"

"All of them."

"But, they can't."

"They can, and they are." She gestured with her chin to my half-empty plate. "Finish up."

I groaned. "They're coming to Waco."

"We've already established that they are."

"But I don't want them to."

"Doesn't really matter what you want, love. Grady got the idea in his head and the rest of them agreed. They want to see you and they want to meet Smoke."

"No," I protested. "This is bad."

"This isn't bad. They'll like Smoke."

"Do they know he's seventeen years older than me?"

"They know."

"Great. They'll wait for Smoke to heal and then kill him. Wonderful."

"Have a little faith." She smiled. "Smoke did save your life. That counts for something."

"And yet Dad can't stop glaring at him every time they're in the same room."

"Hmm. You have a point."

∽

"You had breakfast without me?" Dad asked Mom as he closed the hotel door. "Morning, LoLo."

"Hi, Dad."

"Sorry, I couldn't wait," Mom said. She tilted her face up for a kiss and Dad obliged. "I'll order you whatever you want while you shower."

She handed him the menu.

"What did you have?" he asked.

"Eggs Benedict and the quiche," I replied.

"Hmm. That's not at all what I want. Chocolate chip pancakes sounds better."

I laughed. "You do know the chocolate chip pancakes negate the entire workout you just did, right?"

"You gotta live a little," he announced.

My dad had always been in good shape. His gray T-shirt was damp with sweat, so I knew he'd gotten a decent workout.

"Smoke awake yet?" Dad asked.

"I don't think so. I was just about to go check on him though." I eased off the bed and kissed my dad's cheek. "Do me a favor?"

"What's that?"

"Try not to glower at him when you look at him."

He sighed. "Am I that obvious?"

"Yes." I smirked. "I know you're just being a dad, but he doesn't deserve your dad glare."

"I'm supposed to just ignore the fact that he's old enough to be your—"

"Don't finish that sentence," I said lightly. "And yes. You're supposed to ignore all of it. He saved my life." I glanced at Mom. "You talk to him. Please?"

"I will."

I went to the connected suite door and gently pushed it open.

"You don't have to tip toe. I'm awake," came Smoke's raspy voice. "I called for the nurse. She'll be here in a few minutes to help me to the bathroom. I gotta piss."

"Lamp?"

"Yeah."

I turned on the bedside lamp and the room lit up in an amber glow. There was a soft knock and I slowly went to answer the door.

The nurse entered and helped Smoke with his IV bag to the bathroom. She got him back to bed as I was hanging up the phone.

"I just ordered you some scrambled eggs," I said to Smoke.

"Thanks. That took all of my energy for the next two weeks."

The nurse left with the promise that she'd come back within the hour to administer more pain meds and his antibiotics.

"You already ate?" he asked.

"With Mom. While you were asleep. She came in and got me." I shot him a look. "She found us in bed together…but don't worry, she won't tell my dad."

"I respect your father's need to protect you," Smoke said. "And if he wants to give me shit to make sure I'm the right man for you, then I'll take it."

"You might feel differently when I tell you what I'm about to tell you."

"Oh?"

"My brothers are flying in this afternoon."

"All of them?"

"All of them."

"I'm a dead man."

I sniggered, which caused Smoke to grin. "Something tells me you can handle them."

There was a soft knock on the door, followed by my mother entering.

"Good morning, Smoke," she greeted.

"Good morning, Mrs. Monroe."

I held back a smile.

"How'd you sleep?" she asked with straight face.

"Like a baby." His eyes darted to mine as soon as he said it.

"It's okay," I said softly.

I would have to get used to people saying things that would hurt for a while. That was my own issue to handle, and I couldn't expect people to edit decades of common phrases out of their vocabulary.

"How are you feeling?" Mom asked.

"Logan ordered me some breakfast and I'll take some pain meds after that."

"Good. Doc called," she said. "She and Boxer would like to visit, but only if you're up for it."

"Doc called you?" I asked.

Mom nodded. "I'm the point of contact. If you're too tired or not up to it, you let me know. I'll keep the doors barred."

Smoke grinned. "You would, wouldn't you?"

"Yep. Oh, your president—Colt—texted. Asked if we were settled and needed anything. He's so thoughtful."

"Thoughtful," Smoke repeated. "Right."

"So I can call Doc back and tell her you're up for the visit?"

"Fine with me. Logan?"

I nodded.

"Great." She left the room and closed the door.

"Colt…thoughtful," Smoke said with a wry grin. "Not the word I would've used to describe him. But I'm glad he's showing the best side of himself to your mother. We're not used to parents."

"I've missed my family. It's been too long since I've been to Idaho. I'd like to spend Christmas with them."

"You want to spend Christmas with your family, then we'll spend Christmas with your family."

I bit my lip in worry.

"What?"

"My mom will be offended if we don't stay with them."

"Well, I'm not in the business of offending people."

"No?"

"No." He rubbed his jaw. "They might live to regret it though."

"Oh. Why?"

"When we have the kids. It'll be noisy."

"Kids? What kids?"

He looked at me, his gaze soft. "Our kids, cupcake. We're gonna have kids. You know that, right?"

I sighed. "Smoke…"

There was a knock on the door, interrupting our talk of the future. I got up and went to answer it.

The room service attendant placed the tray on the bed next to Smoke and asked if we needed anything else before leaving.

I took the chafing dish off the plate and grabbed a fork.

"How many kids are we going to have?" I asked as I took a seat on the edge of the bed.

"Two. That sound good?"

"Two? You told Edith you wanted a big family," I teased. "Open." I lifted the fork and fed him a bite of food. He didn't even protest.

"How about we start with two and take it from there?"

"That would be okay with me. Can I ask another question about our future?"

"Sure." He opened his mouth as he waited for another bite of food.

I grinned and fed him. I was glad his appetite was present. "Do you have a timeline for these kids?"

"Whenever you're ready for them," he said quietly. "Take as much time as you need to heal. There's no rush."

"There's a little bit of a rush," I said.

"Why? Because of my age?"

"Kinda."

"Cupcake," he said softly, "that's not a factor. And let me answer another question you haven't asked yet—this isn't because I missed out on Tavy's childhood. I'll always regret the hell out of that, but I want kids with you because I want kids with *you*. No other reason."

I sighed. "You're perfect."

"Tell that to your father," he joked. "Speaking of which—we should probably get married before any kids arrive on the scene. No sense in tempting fate with your father's shotgun."

"That wasn't your proposal, was it?"

"Give me a little credit. Proposing while you're spoon-feeding me eggs? No, that wasn't it. You deserve a better proposal than that."

"If you say so." I leaned over and brushed my lips against his. "Smoke?"

"Yeah."

"When you do ask me to marry you, I just want you to know I'll say yes."

He grinned. "You must really want babies with me."

I stroked a finger down his cheek. "More than you know."

Chapter 46

Doc and Boxer arrived, and they didn't come empty handed.

"I'm not much of a cook," Doc said. "So I brought you both some things that will make your stay more comfortable."

She pulled out two travel neck pillows, eye shades, and velour blankets.

"These are the best," Doc said as she reached into the bag and took out two pairs of fuzzy socks.

"I'm not wearing those," Smoke stated.

"Dude, you don't know what you're missing," Boxer said.

"You own a pair?" Smoke asked.

"I own three."

"If we were the same size, he'd steal mine," Doc said with a smile.

"Thank you so much for this," I said. "And thank you both for coming to visit. I know you're busy with the clinic."

"Always," she agreed. "But you have to prioritize, and you guys are a priority."

Tears prickled my eyes.

Boxer sat at the edge of Smoke's bed and the two of them began to chat. Doc and I were on the other side of the room, sitting in the chairs at the table by the window. The curtains had been drawn back. It was a murky, gray day that hinted of rain.

"How are you getting around?" Doc asked, pitching her voice low.

"Are you asking as a friend or as a doctor?" I teased.

"Both."

"I'm sore. This morning was a struggle to get out of bed—I feel old. My bones hurt. But once I'm up, I do okay. I tire easily, though."

"You think you can make it down the hallway?" she asked.

"Probably. Why?"

Doc glanced at Smoke and Boxer who were deep in conversation and not paying any attention to us.

"I want to talk to you. Alone," Doc said.

"Oh. Okay." I rose slowly from my chair.

"Logan and I are going to walk the hallway," Doc announced as she strode over to Smoke's bed. She placed her hand on Boxer's shoulder, her engagement ring glinting in the amber hotel light.

He grasped her hand and brought it to his lips for a kiss.

Smoke looked at me and I nodded.

Doc held open the heavy door for me. We took it easy in the opposite direction of my parents' room, and Doc didn't speak right away. We were on the third floor and the hotel wasn't fully occupied so it was quiet.

"So, how are you?" she asked.

"A little better each day."

"What about emotionally?"

I paused and looked at her. "A little better each day."

She nodded slowly. "It's hard for me to turn off the doctor part of my brain, but I'm going to try. This is me talking as a friend now, okay?"

"Okay."

"Have you thought about seeing someone…professionally? To talk to, I mean."

"Like a therapist?"

She nodded.

"I haven't thought about it," I admitted.

"You've gone through a lot. Really intense stuff. Physically and emotionally. Watching Smoke, well you know…I don't need to say it."

"No, you don't," I agreed.

She absently touched her right hand that was riddled with scars. "I went through something very intense a while back. And I was resistant to talking to someone at first. I guess I didn't want to admit that I needed help coping. Processing. Whatever. But I see a therapist now. Once a week." She sighed. "Sometimes twice a week."

I tried not to let the shock at her honesty flash across my face. "And is it helping you?"

"Seems to be. Progress is slower than I want it to be. But it's progress."

"Is that why you work all the time? So you don't have time to stop and think?"

Her lips pulled into a grin. "Smart cookie."

"What happened, Doc? Or would you rather not tell me?"

"I'll tell you," she said. "But not now. You'll come over

and I'll tell you about it when we're sitting down, a cocktail within reach."

I nodded. "I'd like that. I mean, not swapping war stories, but I appreciate your willingness to be open about it."

"I don't like to talk about it, you know? Talking about it makes me feel like I'm back there, in that situation. It keeps my past very much in my present, and my present is pretty damn good unless it's shadowed by darkness. That's something I'm working on with my therapist." She rolled her eyes and grinned.

"Is your therapist—is she—"

Doc nodded, urging me to go on.

"Is she taking new patients?" I finished.

"She's not," Doc said. "But she might do me a favor if I ask for you."

I took her hand and gave it a squeeze. "I'd appreciate that. Thank you."

The elevator chimed and I heard the doors open. Hope filled my chest at the thought that it might be Tavy coming to visit me. A moment later, Slash and Brooklyn rounded the corner. Slash held a casserole dish.

Damn. Not Tavy.

"Hey," Brooklyn greeted. "What are you guys doing out here?"

"Just having a chat," Doc said. "I didn't know you were coming today."

"I called Logan's mom and she said to come on over," Brooklyn said.

"We brought vegetarian lasagna," Slash said. "For Smoke's bland diet."

"Your hotel room has a fridge and microwave, right?" Brooklyn asked. "I just assumed."

"It does."

"Can I hug you or will that break you?" Brooklyn asked.

"I won't break," I assured her.

Brooklyn hugged me gently and then Slash gave me a one-armed hug.

"How's Smoke?" Slash asked as we all headed back in the direction of my room.

"In surprisingly good spirits," I said. "I wonder how long that'll last though, being cooped up in bed."

"That won't bother him nearly as much as not being able to ride for a while," Slash said.

Brooklyn and I lagged behind, both our speed naturally slower since she was heavily pregnant.

"How's Jazz?" I asked her.

"She's okay. Walking in on that mess really screwed with her head. But she's glad she was there."

"What was she doing at the bakery?" I asked.

"She left her wallet in the office."

"Good fortune, then."

Doc knocked on the hotel door and a moment later, Boxer opened it. "Changing of the guard?" he asked.

"Something like that," Slash said.

"Brooklyn made a casserole?" Boxer asked as he filched the dish from Slash and lifted the aluminum foil. "No way. Lasagna? What do I have to do to get a lasagna?"

"Get stabbed," Smoke drawled.

The bikers laughed but Doc, Brooklyn and I didn't.

"Too soon for stabby jokes," Boxer said. "Got it."

"Logan, sit," Doc commanded.

Smoke patted the side of the bed and I went to him. I got comfortable, the both of us propped up against the pillows.

"They're cute together, aren't they?" Boxer said to Slash.

"Very cute," Slash agreed.

"Aww shucks, you guys are making me blush," Smoke ribbed.

The connecting door to our room opened and my parents joined the party. I didn't even bother trying to get up out of bed.

What was my father going to say when he found out Smoke had all but proposed to me?

I was giddy at the thought.

∾

Everyone left when it was clear Smoke was failing to keep his eyes open. The pain meds were doing their job. I brushed a kiss to his cheek and then followed my parents into their room.

"Everything all right?" Mom asked.

I nodded. "I was wondering if you could head over to my apartment and grab me a few things. My laptop, for starters."

"Why do you need your laptop?" Dad asked. "You should probably talk to your boss and take a leave of absence."

"Yeah, about my boss," I said. "I guess I didn't tell you. I quit."

"You quit?" they said at the same time.

I held up my hand. "I quit so I could open my own design business. So I've talked to myself and I've agreed not to be overly hard on myself while I take some time off."

"You started your own business." My mom smiled. "Well, it's about time."

Dad nodded. "We've been wondering when that would happen."

"Oh." I paused. "Thanks for the support."

"So, if you're your own boss," Dad said, "why do you need your computer?"

"Because I need something to occupy my head space. Sitting and watching TV at low volume is not really what I want to do for the next several days."

"You should rest," Dad said.

"I am resting," I insisted. "I can rest from my bed, but still get some work done."

"It's called screen addiction," Dad said.

Mom put her hand on his arm. "She's right, though. She can't just sit in bed and not have anything to occupy herself."

"She can read a book," Dad insisted.

"On what? Oh, wait, my phone with a reading app. But that's a screen."

"I'll buy you some paperbacks," he grumbled. "Write down some titles and I'll go to the bookstore for you."

Tell my father I read reverse harem? Yeah, how about no.

"You won't go to my apartment? Fine. I'll go."

"You can barely walk down the hallway without getting winded," Dad protested. "How are you going to walk up a flight of stairs?"

"Sheer force of will. I'm pretty sure it's part of my DNA. Wonder where I got it from?"

My dad's expression softened and then he looked at my mom. He sighed. "I'll bring around the car."

He grabbed his keys and wallet and headed for the door.

When the door shut, I looked at my mom. "Whatever you do, don't let him near the top drawer of my dresser."

"What's in the top drawer of your dresser?" she asked with a knowing grin.

"I've officially died," I said with a sigh.

"Relax, honey. I know you have a healthy sex life."

"Okay, *you're done*. Scrub this conversation from the record."

"It's scrubbed," she promised. "Keep your phone close in case I call."

"Where is my phone?" I asked.

"It's charging on the table."

She hugged me goodbye and left.

I went to the table and picked up my phone. I had several missed calls and texts. I scrolled though them.

None were from Tavy.

In a fit of hurt and anger, I pressed a button. Her phone rolled right to voicemail. "You are a real shit, you know that? Not one call or text? Come on, Tavy. I know you're pissed, but for fuck's sake, your dad nearly died and is laid up in bed from multiple stab wounds and my ex-fiancé turned out to be a fucking psycho and now he's dead. I thought for sure you'd at least reach out to see how we were doing. Guess I was wrong."

I hung up. Fuming, I went back into the bedroom I shared with Smoke.

"Who were you yelling at?" he slurred.

"Shit. You heard that? I thought you were asleep."

"Kind of hard to sleep when you're yelling."

"I was yelling at your daughter. She hasn't called or texted me."

"She's texted me."

I stopped mid-rage. "What? When?"

"This morning." He reached around the bed, his hand encountering his phone. He picked it up and unlocked it. He scrolled to a message and then flipped the cell around.

I peered closer.

TAVY

> I love you. I'll visit soon.

"That's the most lukewarm text I've ever seen, and I've dated college boys," I said.

"And not that long ago. Thanks for the reminder," he drawled.

"Age jokes? Really?"

"If you can't beat 'em, join 'em."

"Hmm. We'll discuss that later. Visit soon? When is *soon*? And why is she texting you and not me?"

"She's sorting through her feelings."

I raised my brows. "You're the Tavy whisperer now? Did I miss something?"

His gaze remained steady.

"Sorry, that was mean."

"Yeah, it was. But you're hurting, so I'll let it slide."

"Thanks," I muttered. "And you're probably right about her. She reacts and then she feels."

"She definitely reacted the night she found out we were dating."

"Oh God," I said.

"What?"

"She's going to flip her shit when we tell her we're going to get married."

"Probably."

"Oh no."

"There's more?" he asked.

"Technically, I'm going to be Tavy's new stepmother…"

"Cupcake, you're making my head pound."

"Sorry." I fell silent for a moment and then I moaned.

He sighed. "More?"

"You're going to procreate twice more. *At least.*"

"That's the hope."

"No, but, she's going to have half siblings at least twenty five years younger than her. We're going to send her to therapy with all this."

"I'll foot the bill." He closed his eyes and promptly fell asleep.

Chapter 47

My dad called and said he was taking my mother out for lunch, so Smoke and I were on our own for a little while. Smoke woke up from his nap a few minutes after I heard from Dad.

"You hungry?" I asked. "I was going to zap some of the lasagna Brooklyn brought."

"I could eat," he said, lifting the covers off him.

"Where are you going?"

"The bathroom."

"Let me call for the nurse."

When Smoke was settled back into bed, I cut a huge piece of lasagna and put it into the microwave.

"How's your pain?" I asked.

"I'll live."

"Good to know."

"So, it's been a few hours…"

"Since I left an angry voicemail for Tavy?"

"Since my proposal."

"You said it wasn't a proposal," I said.

"My non-proposal, proposal. Let's call it testing the waters."

"The waters are suddenly feeling very tepid. And didn't I already tell you I'd say yes when you asked for real?"

Smoke laughed and then he groaned. "Fuck. That hurts."

The microwave beeped and I opened the door. I touched the plate and immediately yanked my hand back. "Hot."

"Microwaves do that."

I threw him a glare over my shoulder.

"So, as I was saying, about the proposal..."

"Hmm."

"You didn't panic."

"You expected me to panic?"

"Maybe not panic, but I did expect you to tell me to cool my jets."

"You'd think I'd be a wee bit gun shy right now." I winced. "Jeez, can we ever have a normal conversation again after all this?"

"Yeah, we can."

I touched the plate again, glad to find it had cooled enough to handle. I grabbed a fork from the silverware drawer and brought the food over to Smoke. I sat down next to him.

"I can feed myself," he said.

"Okay." I handed him the plate and fork.

After he swallowed, he said, "Fuck, that's delicious."

"Yeah?" I took the fork from him and fed myself a bite. "Oh yeah. Super good."

"So, you're not gun shy? About marrying me?"

"No, I don't think I am," I admitted.

"Why not?" he demanded. "We barely know each other."

"We know each other," I protested.

"You just got out of a serious relationship."

"I don't think we can use that excuse anymore, now that he's gone to rot in hell."

We looked at each other and burst out laughing. I laughed so hard my sides hurt and Smoke's laughter turned into wheezing snorts of pain.

When we'd both calmed down enough, I took another bite of food.

"I was supposed to be your revenge fuck," he said.

"True."

"I never saw it going that way," he said.

"No?"

"I knew you were trouble from the moment I saw you sitting in that jail cell. Not gonna lie. Your legs did something to me. All I could think about was having them wrapped around my waist as I sank into you."

"Oh…" A bloom of desire suddenly pierced me between my thighs. All I'd felt the last few days were pain, grief, fear, and anger. Desire was a welcome change—and it reminded me that I was still alive.

That I had something to live for.

Smoke reached out and touched my face. "He didn't break you. Not then. And not now."

The sound of a hotel door opening, followed by voices alerted me that my parents had returned.

Smoke's hand fell from my face and he gave me a lopsided grin. "Always interrupted."

"Always," I agreed.

There was a knock on the connecting door.

"Come in," I called out.

My parents entered and my dad set my gym duffel in the corner. "Something smells good."

"We dug into Brooklyn's lasagna," I said. "Where did you go for lunch?"

"A Mexican restaurant Mia recommended," Mom said. "I texted her."

"You could've asked me for a recommendation," I pointed out.

"You've been here less than a month," she said. "I wasn't sure you knew of any good places."

Less than a month. They were going to flip their lid when we told them about our plans for the future.

"Grady called," Mom said. "They just landed in Dallas."

I blinked. "Just landed? Already? I thought they were flying out this afternoon and wouldn't be here until late tonight."

"Whatever gave you that idea?" Mom asked.

"From what you and Grady told me," I said in exasperation.

"They're renting a car in Dallas and driving. It was faster than a connecting flight to Waco," Dad said.

I loved my brothers, but they were overprotective and they still thought of me as a little kid. And I'd wanted one more day before Smoke was subjected to them.

"Stella?" Dad asked.

"Right." Mom nodded and she looked at me. "How do you feel about going to stick our feet in the hot tub?"

I glanced at my dad who was staring at Smoke. Smoke looked unconcerned, but I knew what was going to happen.

They were going to have *the talk*.

Not the sex talk.

The *what are your intentions with my daughter* talk.

"You should go with your mom," Smoke said easily. "Your dad and I can watch sports."

I raised my brows. "You watch sports?"

Smoke tossed me a teasing grin. "No."

Mom pressed a hand against my hip and urged me toward the door. "See you in a bit."

"Don't worry," Mom said when the door shut behind us. "Your father had two beers at lunch and I drove us to the hotel. He's basically sedated."

I chuckled even though I was a bit concerned that the two of them would never get along or have a good relationship.

Like me and Tavy now.

"You're not really worried about them, are you? Your father is just trying to put up a front, but he's caving fast. He spent most of lunch talking about the two of you."

"Oh yeah?" I asked in surprise.

She nodded and pressed the elevator button. "Don't tell him I told you this, but he's actually kind of relieved."

"Relieved? About what?" I asked.

"That for once in your life, you didn't think before you acted. You just leapt with all your heart. You were always so careful, so methodical. But jumping into a relationship with Smoke on the heels of your ended engagement? It was so out of character, Dad knew it was right."

"Weird yard stick to measure by, but okay."

The elevator doors opened and we stepped inside. Mom pushed the button for the pool floor and the doors closed.

"So, what's on your mind?" she asked.

"Am I that transparent?"

"Yes."

"Tavy. She hasn't contacted me. And I left her a really angry voicemail…"

"Has she reached out to Smoke?"

"Yeah. Just a quick text. Saying she loves him and will visit him soon."

"Huh."

"Right?" I shook my head. The elevator doors opened into the lobby. A family of four with two young children were waiting for the elevator.

I smiled at them as we moved past.

"She looks like hell!" the little boy said.

"*Miles*," the mother hissed. "Oh my God, I'm so sorry!"

My mother's shoulders lurched as she attempted to stifle her laughter.

"Don't worry about it," I called back, my cheeks heating. To my mom, I said, "Might be time for a shower."

"Might be," Mom agreed. She opened the door to the pool room and then held my hand as I lowered myself by the hot tub's edge. Mom impressed me when she nimbly sat down beside me.

"Yoga," she explained. "Keeps me limber."

"Ew."

She bumped her arm against mine. "You made me run interference with your top drawer. I think that makes us even."

I laid my head against her shoulder. "I love you, Mom."

"I love you, too, LoLo."

I took off my flip flops and rolled my sweats up to midcalf before sticking my feet into the hot water.

"I need a pedicure," I announced.

"Yeah, you do."

I laughed.

"We'll go sometime this week when you're feeling up to it."

"How long are you guys staying?" I asked.

"As long as you need us to."

"But the hotel—we can't stay here indefinitely. Even a week here carries a hefty price tag."

"Don't worry about it."

"But Mom—"

"Smoke took care of it."

"He what?"

"Well, not Smoke exactly. His club. They're good people, aren't they?"

∽

Smoke was asleep and my dad was back in his room when we returned. I couldn't wait until Smoke was awake so he could tell me what he and my dad talked about while Mom and I were gone.

I checked my phone. No messages from Tavy, but the Old Ladies had blown up my cell. They were wondering when they could come by for a visit, but they didn't want to intrude if we were resting.

I told them they were welcome to come in stages tomorrow.

Jazz and Brielle had reached out too, and I desperately wanted to see Jazz to make sure she wasn't completely traumatized, and to thank her for what she'd done.

I set my phone aside, dug through my duffel for clean clothes and laughed to myself when I saw that my mom had grabbed my most unattractive-time-of-the-month granny panties.

I trekked quietly to the bathroom and closed the door. I eased off my clothes, wrinkling my nose when I dropped them in the corner.

The water felt heavenly, but I didn't have the stamina to stay in the shower too long. I washed quickly, wincing when my hands encountered bruises. I shampooed and conditioned my hair with high-end hotel products.

By the time I was finished, I was wrung out and didn't even have the energy to comb my hair. I slid into clean clothes and then immediately climbed into bed.

I woke up to the sounds of several masculine voices that did not know volume control.

"I think your brothers are here," Smoke said.

I sleepily looked at him. "Yeah. I think so too." I closed my eyes again.

"Mom, just let me open the door and see if they're asleep," Harlan said.

"Incoming," I warned Smoke.

The door opened and Harlan popped his head in.

"We're awake, you animal," I said without any heat. "You might as well come in."

Harlan entered first, followed by Chase, then Killian, then Grady. My parents brought up the rear.

"That God damn son of a bitch," Killian said as his gaze raked over me.

"I don't look that bad," I protested.

"No, you don't," Smoke said in defense. "And you're more than your looks anyway."

Four pairs of eyes turned to look at Smoke, taking measure of him. My brothers were a healthy mix of both my parents, but they'd all inherited my father's protective streak.

Smoke, laid up in bed, completely at their mercy, didn't appear at all concerned. Grady shoved through the group of them and went to Smoke's bedside and stared him down.

"You're Grady," Smoke said.

My brother nodded. "Yep."

"Uhm, hi, Grady," I said with snark. "Thanks for coming to see me."

Grady's expression softened and a slight smile appeared on his face. He walked over and sat down on the edge of the bed and then very gently embraced me.

"Dog pile," Harlan announced.

"*Harlan*," Mom warned.

"Chill, chill. I won't do it." Harlan rolled his eyes, but then he got on the bed. Killian and Chase quickly followed and before I knew it, I was in the middle of a sibling hug.

I closed my eyes and let out a sigh. There was nothing like family. My brothers drove me crazy, but they were there for me when I needed them.

There was a knock on the hotel door and I eased out of my brother's arms. "Who is that? Did you order food?" I asked Smoke.

"No," Smoke said.

"I'll get the door," Mom said as she walked to the exit.

"I don't understand how you can live here," Killian said to me. "Does this place have seasons?"

"Yeah, it has seasons," Smoke said. "Hot and hotter."

Mom was talking to someone by the front door and a moment later, she returned and Rach was with her, carrying a wicker gift basket with a big red bow.

"Rach," I greeted in surprise.

"Hey Logan." Her eyes bounced from me to Smoke. "I just wanted to drop this off—I wasn't going to stay, I'll come back tomorrow."

"Hey, Rach."

Rach turned in the direction of the voice and her eyes widened in surprise. "Chase. Hi."

I watched my brother practically melt in front of her.

The room suddenly went quiet and Rach was the first

to come out of the trance. "Sorry to interrupt family time. I'll leave."

"We should all go," Mom said. "And give Smoke and Logan time to rest."

One by one my brothers hugged me goodbye and left the hotel room. Rach followed suit.

"We're going downstairs to have dinner with the boys," Mom said. "You guys going to be okay on your own?"

"Yeah, we'll be fine," I said. "We've got food."

"Don't let your brothers try Brooklyn's lasagna. They'll eat it in one sitting," Mom warned.

"I'll have my cell. Call if you need anything," my dad said, but his statement was directed at Smoke.

My parents left and I got up to peruse the gift basket. "Chocolate covered cherries, caramel corn, toffee, chocolate covered espresso beans…"

"The cherries," Smoke said. "Definitely the cherries."

"You can't have any of this for a while," I said. "Doctor's orders."

"You're not really going to eat that shit in front of me when I can't have any, are you?"

"I'm not that cruel," I said.

"You're not cruel at all." He sighed. "But you're trying not to eyeball those cherries and failing. You have my full permission to dive into them."

"You really do love me." I picked up the bag of cherries and brought them to his bed. "So, what did you and my dad talk about while you were watching sports?"

"You, of course."

"Of course."

"He asked me what my intentions with you were. So, I told him."

"Yeah?"

"Yeah."

"And…"

"I said I was going to ask you to be my Old Lady and then he wanted to punch my face because he had no idea what an Old Lady is."

He reached out and took my hand, lacing his fingers with mine. "I told him it means you're my woman. It means I'd die to protect you. It means the club would take care of you if anything ever happened to me. It means you never have to worry about anything ever again."

"You said that all to my dad?"

"Yeah, and then he asked if that meant I was going to marry you. I said I was. Then we watched sports."

He grinned at me.

I grinned back.

"I'm gonna make you so happy, Logan."

I sighed. "You already do, Smoke."

Chapter 48

"Wake them up," Harlan stage-whispered.

"You wake them up," Grady rasped.

"You're both too chicken shit to wake them up," Killian said.

"Then you do it," Chase added.

"How about the four of you shut up and let me go back to sleep?" I demanded without opening my eyes.

"You're sleeping in Smoke's bed," Grady stated.

"It's where she belongs, fucker," Smoke snapped.

I finally opened my eyes and let out a squeak of surprise. My four brothers were leaning over the bed, looming, terrifying, and way too alert for the time of day.

I looked at the alarm clock on the nightstand. "It's seven in the morning."

"I wanted to come in at five," Grady stated. "They wouldn't let me."

"No one is awake at five. It's an ungodly hour," I sniped.

"Chase was just getting into bed at five," Harlan ribbed.

Chase glared at him.

"What were you doing out until five in the morning?" I demanded.

"I was—we're not here to discuss me," Chase said, standing tall. "We came to discuss the situation."

"What situation?"

Killian pointed between me and Smoke. "*This* situation."

"Smoke and Dad have already had this discussion. This doesn't involve you."

"Let them have their say," Smoke said. "Won't change a damn thing. I'm still going to marry you. Even if they hate the idea."

Grady and Killian looked at each other. "You want to marry her?" Grady asked.

"Yeah. I want to marry her," Smoke said.

"And I want to marry him," I added.

"You don't want to marry him," Killian said.

"*Yes*, I do," I insisted.

"You barely know each other," Chase protested. "How the hell can you guys want to get married?"

"And you were *just* engaged. Don't you need, I don't know…a mourning period or something?" Harlan winced. "Bad choice of words. Sorry."

I looked at Smoke. "Two kids, max. And they'd better both be girls. Boys are a pain in the ass."

Smoke grinned. "I'll see what I can do."

"Kids? What kids?" Grady demanded.

"You're not ready to have kids!" Killian announced. "I'm not ready to be an uncle."

"Okay, look," I said, finally scrambling up out of bed, forcing Harlan and Chase to back up. "Grady, you haven't been on a date in ten years. Kill, you only do one-night stands."

"Jeez, keep it down, will ya?" Killian looked over his shoulder at Mom and Dad's hotel room.

I glared at him and then turned the force of my anger onto Chase. "And *you*…"

He raised his brows. "What about me?"

"You're still pining for Rachel, and you're kicking yourself for ever having let her get away in the first place."

"Me next," Harlan stated with a devilish grin. "Do me next!"

"This isn't a game," Grady snapped.

"And Harlan sleeps with a ferret," I announced.

"A ferret?" Smoke asked. "A real one?"

"No." I smirked wickedly. "A stuffed one. From when he was a baby."

Harlan's eyes widened. "How did you—you know what? Never mind."

"She's right?" Killian inquired. "You sleep with a stuffed ferret?"

Harlan straightened his spine. "His name is Mr. Winkie. Excuse me." He marched toward the hotel room door. A moment later, it opened and closed.

"Why don't you guys go after him," I stated.

The three of them exchanged glances and then visibly deflated as they left the room.

"You were ruthless," Smoke said lightly.

"Yep." I nodded.

"It was hot."

Laughing, I leaned over and gently kissed him. "You can still get out, you know. My family is showing you that they're crazy and we're not married yet. You still have time."

"I might be nuts, but I kind of like it. Your family is protective and they love you. It shows. Go easy on them."

"You're the one who is laid up in bed recovering from

stab wounds after saving my life. They should be going easy on *you*."

"I can hold my own."

"Hmm, yeah."

"I gotta use the bathroom. Call the nurse, would you, please?"

It still took Smoke a lot of effort to get up, but each time was a little less labor intensive. I hoped that meant he was healing. He never complained either. Not about the pain, and not about my family.

"I'm surprised your parents weren't involved in your brothers' early morning inquisition," Smoke said after he was back in bed and the nurse had left.

"I'm pretty sure they're down in the hotel gym. I think that's why my brothers waited. To make sure the parental units were out of the way so they could go completely rogue."

I kissed his forehead and wrinkled my nose. "Uh. Don't take this the wrong way, but your hair is getting a little…"

"Disgusting? Greasy?"

"Yep."

He rubbed his stubbly jaw. I'd missed his stubble, actually, so that was a welcome sight to behold.

"Not that I want to admit this," he began, "but I don't have the stamina."

I raised my brows. "I should say not."

He rolled his eyes. "I meant about standing on my own long enough to wash. I'd ask for your help, but if your father found out we showered together, he'd geld me. I'll have the nurse clean me up later."

There was a knock on the connecting door and a moment later, my parents strode into the room. They were both in gym clothes and my mother's face was pink from exertion.

"Morning, kids," Mom said.

Smoke snorted, but he smiled.

"We wanted to run an idea by you," Mom said.

"Shoot," I said, sitting down on the edge of my bed.

"We figured you'd be getting a lot of visitors today," Mom said. "The club and their…Old Ladies."

I nodded. "My phone is blowing up with questions about when they can come over."

"Thought so," Mom said. "Well, your father and I were thinking of exploring the town. Getting out of the hotel for the day. Would that be okay with you?"

"We'll stay if you need us to," Dad offered. "But we're getting a little squirrelly."

"You and me both," Smoke said.

"Go, with my blessing," I stated.

"Are you sure it's okay that we leave?" my mom asked.

"Absolutely," I insisted. "We have food, we have the front desk if we need anything. I'm getting around better anyway. We have the nurse on speed dial. We'll be fine."

"I'd hug you, but I'm gross from the gym. We're going to shower and then get out of here," Mom said.

They headed back to their room and closed the door.

"Guess I better get cleaned up," Smoke said with a wink. "Buzz the nurse for me?"

∽

"Well?" Smoke asked once the nurse left again. "How's my hair?"

"Looks a lot less greasy," I assured him with a smile.

"I feel better," he admitted. "I could get used to a woman bathing me."

"Oh you could, could you?"

He flashed me a flirty grin. "For the record, I'd much rather it be you bathing me than a nurse."

"Hmm." I sent him a droll look and then shook my head. "How can you be this charming even while you're recuperating?"

"One of my natural gifts."

I grinned. "You hungry?"

"Not for lasagna. It's too early, even for me."

I handed him the room service menu and while I waited for him to choose, I texted everyone who'd contacted me about visiting.

And then I sent a text to Rach.

ME

> I heard Chase didn't climb into bed until 5 AM...

"Pancakes," Smoke said, setting the menu aside. "With extra butter and extra syrup."

"That's exactly what I want, but you're supposed to eat bland food, remember?"

"You're killing me slowly." He sighed. "Boring scrambled eggs it is."

While we were in the middle of eating our breakfast, there was a knock on the door. I got up and answered it.

Colt, Mia, Zip, and Joni stood at the threshold, sans children.

"Hey!" I beamed.

"Hey," Mia said, quickly looking me over. She held a plate of chocolate chip cookies and Joni had brought chocolate pudding.

"Come in, come in," I said, backing up.

They hugged me, mindful of squeezing me too hard. I waved Joni and Mia over to my bed.

"Hope you don't mind," I said, as I picked up the fork and continued eating.

"Not at all," Joni said. "But damn, that looks good. I had oatmeal and it just didn't do the trick."

We chatted while Zip and Colt laughed and conversed with Smoke. We didn't dwell too long on my situation—I didn't want to talk about it. And with each day, it was moving further into the past. I still mulled over what Doc had shared with me and I planned on talking to a therapist. But I didn't want to bog down my friendships with the intensity of what I'd been through. About what Smoke had been through.

There was another rap on the door and Mia jumped up to answer it before I could even think about moving.

Allison and Torque joined the visitor group. Torque placed a covered glass dish on the table, along with the food Joni and Mia had brought before nodding at me and then joining the men on the other side of the room.

"You guys spoil me with food," I said, hugging Allison when she sat down on the bed.

She placed Tank in the middle and he crawled across the bedspread. Joni grabbed him before he could get away. She tickled his belly which made him giggle.

My heart saddened when I thought of what I'd lost, but when I glanced at Smoke, I saw him watching me. He sent me a smile of understanding and we shared something in that moment that let me know it was all going to be okay.

My heart cracked open even more when Tank took a sudden interest in me by crawling into my lap and falling asleep.

"That was unexpected," I said with a smile. I brushed my hand across his head. "But very welcome."

"Tell her the news," Joni said to Mia.

"News, what news?" I asked.

Mia looked at me. "Boxer and I want to formally ask you to design the bar."

I blinked. "Seriously?"

"Seriously." Mia smiled. "When you're feeling up to it, you'll come over to the space and we'll tell you our vision."

"Oh, also..." Joni pulled out her phone. She unlocked the screen and scrolled through her photos before flipping the cell toward me. "We no longer have a wall."

"You're going to love it when it's done," I said.

My phone buzzed with a text from Rach.

> **RACH**
> We stayed up all night just catching up. Nothing happened.

I frowned. That wasn't a good enough story. Chase had never gotten over Rachel and Rachel was a widow with a son who deserved to find love again.

"What's wrong?" Mia asked.

"What? Oh. Nothing. Just thinking." I set my phone aside, but it buzzed immediately.

"Lady of the hour," Joni teased.

"Jazz and Brielle are on their way," I announced.

"Should we go?" Allison asked. "There won't be enough room for all of us."

I pouted. "I don't want you to go, but yeah, for the sake of space."

It was a good thing they cleared out because on the heels of Brielle and Jazz arriving, so did the South Dakota boys.

"Are you okay?" Jazz asked me.

"I should be asking you that," I said, taking her hand. "I haven't had a chance to thank you or ask how it's been for you since—"

Jazz waved her hand away. "Nothing a little tequila couldn't fix."

Brielle shot her a look.

"What?" Jazz demanded. "She doesn't need to know I have nightmares."

"You're having nightmares?" I asked softly.

Jazz winced. "There was a lot of blood. And a…body." She slid off the bakery box's string and opened it. "We brought biscotti."

"Can I get one of those," Bones called out from the other side of the room. "I didn't have breakfast."

"I brought them for Smoke and Logan," Jazz said.

"You can have one but you have to save at least one for me and Smoke," I said to Bones. I looked at Jazz and said, "We have cookies, a gift basket, left over lasagna, chocolate pudding, whatever Allison brought. We'll never get through all the food without help."

Bones and the other South Dakota boys dove into the biscotti.

"I could do with a nice cappuccino," Kelp added.

"For dunking," Raze explained.

"There's a coffee bar in the lobby," Bones said.

"Just call room service," I stated. "It's easier."

"Coffee and biscotti," Bones said. "I'm becoming domesticated."

Brielle whispered, "But not house trained."

"I heard that," Bones called out.

"How?" Brielle demanded. "I said it quietly."

"I've got hearing like a bat, babe," Bones touted, reaching for the phone.

Brielle rolled her eyes but smiled before turning back to me. "So, you and Smoke…"

"Yeah." I nodded.

"You didn't tell us." Jazz pouted.

"We didn't tell anyone," I said.

"But we all knew," Raze announced.

"Have your own conversation," I stated.

Raze shrugged.

"Wait," Jazz said. "You all knew? But Brielle and I didn't find out until we saw Smoke coming out of the bakery apartment?"

Bones spoke into the phone and placed a massive coffee order, said thanks, and then hung up. Then he addressed the room. "We all knew because Smoke couldn't stop staring at her ass and Logan got really awkward every time they were in the same room together. So naturally, we did what we had to do."

"Which was?" Brielle asked.

"I pursued Logan to piss Smoke off. Finally, we had it out in the sparring ring and we came to an agreement. I was going to back off and Smoke got his head of out of his ass and locked her down," Bones said. "Can I get another one of those biscotti?"

Brielle held out the box to him.

"You mean you backed him into a corner so he was forced to make a declaration," Jazz said.

"Something like that," Bones said with a grin. "It worked. They're together and shit."

"We're not *together*," Smoke said, finally joining the conversation. "She's my Old Lady."

"When the fuck did that happen?" Kelp asked.

"Yeah, when the fuck did that happen?" I demanded.

"Oh, like just now," Smoke said with a grin.

Bones whooped loud enough to rattle my ear drums. "I knew my plan would work!"

"You're a regular matchmaker," Brielle drawled.

There was a knock on the door.

"Not the coffee already," Kelp said even as he went to answer it.

It was Sutton and Viper.

"Just in time for the party," Kelp said to them.

"Party?" Sutton asked. "There's a party? Good thing I brought food."

Chapter 49

"Your friends are exhausting," I said, my head on the pillow next to Smoke's.

"Not as exhausting as your friends." He held my hand as his eyes closed. "Savage and Duke haven't come by yet."

"I think they're coming by later," I said. "Tavy hasn't shown up yet…"

He paused for a moment. "She came by."

I sat up quickly. "When?"

"When you and your mom were down at the hot tub."

"Why didn't you tell me?" I demanded.

"Because I didn't want to hurt your feelings."

"So, you let me believe my best friend was a selfish asshole who didn't even visit her own father?"

He frowned. "Wait. Are you mad at her because you thought she didn't visit *me*?"

"Of course, I was mad about that. I'm also mad that she won't call me back or talk to me, and she and I will have fighting words when we're finally face to face. But the idea that she didn't even see you? Made me livid. She really came to visit?"

"She really did. She didn't stay long." He arched a brow. "Apparently she didn't want to run into you."

"This is ridiculous," I muttered.

"I agree."

"Do something," I commanded.

"Do something? Like what?"

"I don't know. Ground her. Tell her she can't go to the concert unless she talks to me."

"I think I'm about a decade too late for that kind of fatherly punishment."

I sighed and got out of bed. "I need a cookie. And pudding. Did you tell her what happened?"

"I told her about what I walked in on with Knox because that involved me. She knows how that part went down."

"Not the...not the miscarriage?"

"No. That's for you to share. If you want to."

I wanted to. Not talking to Tavy was slowly killing me. Ever since we'd bonded in college, we hadn't gone this long without speaking.

The idea of never talking to her again had me crying over my plate of cookies and pudding.

"Ah, cupcake." Smoke patted the bed and I settled down beside him, setting my plate on the nightstand.

"I need my best friend," I blubbered. "Even if she is being a little shit."

I cuddled into his side and he wrapped an arm around me.

There was a knock on the hotel room door.

"Who now?" I demanded. "Can I cry in peace?"

"Apparently not."

With a groan, I got up and went to answer the door.

Tavy stood at the threshold with a vase of white mums, looking nervous.

"You're a butt munch," I snapped at her.

She blinked. "And you're a backstabbing father fucker."

We stared at one another for a moment and then both of us suddenly burst into laughter.

"Oh, God, Logan, I'm so sorry I—"

"No, I'm sorry that I didn't tell—"

"But you couldn't right away. I understand why you—"

"It was killing me lying to—"

"I know," she said, her tone earnest. "I wanted to see you sooner, I just didn't know how to—"

"And then I yelled at you over voicemail and—"

"I deserved it."

"You didn't."

"I did," she insisted.

"Well, maybe a little," I agreed. "But you never left the hospital. And you called my parents for me and—"

"I should've come in to see you while you were admitted."

"It's okay that you didn't. I was a mess."

"Why don't you come in now?" Smoke called from the bed.

"Right, come in, come in," I said, stepping back. My heart lifted at the sight of my best friend.

She set the vase of flowers on the table, trying to find space among the food. "The Old Ladies?" she guessed.

"Yep." I nodded.

No sooner had she put the flowers down than she held her arms out to hug me, but then she quickly dropped them in a moment of uncertainty.

I wouldn't let her linger there. I embraced her. "Don't hug me too hard," I warned. "My ribs are sore."

"That son of a bitch," Tavy muttered. "If Dad hadn't already killed him, I'd do it."

I pulled back and stared at her. Tavy's expression was fierce and determined. "I appreciate the sentiment, but it's over."

She nodded, her eyes glistening. Tavy looked at Smoke. "Hi, Dad."

"Kiddo," he said.

She rushed over to him and gave him a gentle hug.

"I think you guys need some time to catch up," Smoke said as he reached for the remote. "Why don't you go down to the hotel restaurant. Grab a cup of coffee and shoot the shit."

"But I came to see both of you," Tavy said.

Smoke cracked a grin. "You came to see Logan. It's okay, Tav. Go. You'll come back up for a quick visit before you leave."

"Okay," she said.

I went to Smoke. "You have everything you need within reach?"

"I've got your plate of cookies and pudding and the remote. I'm good."

"No cookies," I warned. "The pudding is gentle though." I leaned down and kissed his lips.

"Ew. That's gonna take some getting used to," Tavy said with a shake of her head.

Once we were seated in a corner booth of the restaurant, our coffee orders placed, we looked at each other.

"Who's going first?" I asked with a rueful smile.

"I should go first," Tavy said.

"If you want," I allowed.

She let out a sigh. "I wasn't mad about you and my dad getting together." Tavy made a face. "That sounds so weird to say."

"I know. It's still kind of a shock to me, too. You weren't mad about us getting together? Really?"

She shook her head. "Not when I calmed down enough to really figure out the heart of the problem. It was…well, I felt betrayed because it was a secret. You lied to me."

"We didn't mean for it to be a secret. But we didn't want to tell you if it wasn't going to be anything. Neither of us wanted to jeopardize our relationship with you for a fling that would've run its course."

"Yeah." Her brow furrowed. "When I came to see my dad yesterday—" She looked at me.

"He just told me about you sneaking a visit in." I tried not to let hurt permeate my voice, but I didn't do a good enough job.

She winced. "I wasn't ready to see you. And then you left that angry voicemail."

"Sorry about that."

"No, you're not." She grinned.

"No, I'm not," I agreed with a laugh. "Continue though."

"My concern was about you. You had just gotten out of an engagement. And Dad is like, *a lot* older."

"You didn't really think he'd take advantage of me, did you?"

She shook her head. "No. Not really. I was just… thrown. And confused. And out of the loop. I don't like being out of the loop."

"I know. Tavy?"

"Yeah?"

"I'm his Old Lady now."

She nodded. "Oh, wow…"

I bit my lip.

"There's more?" she asked.

"There's more."

"Well, spit it out."

"He said he's going to ask me to marry him. And I said when he does, I'll say yes."

She didn't say anything for a moment and then finally she asked, "Where's the ring?"

I blinked. "Well, he hasn't actually asked me yet. He just said that he *would* ask."

"So, you're not officially engaged?"

"Not technically."

"I'm going to ask you a question and you're going to be completely transparent with me. Okay?"

I nodded.

"This is not me being a brat or trying to sabotage anything. I see how he looks at you. I can't believe I missed it." She rolled her eyes. "We can scratch detective off the list of potential jobs in case the nursing thing doesn't work out."

I smiled but said nothing.

"Are you ready for this?" Her eyes were concerned. "You went through a lot of shit with Knox. And now there's all this...*baggage*. I just want to make sure you're not rushing into something because you're afraid of being alone or Dad's a crutch. Okay?"

"Okay." I reached across the table and took her hand. "I can't thank you enough for being willing to ask the hard questions. This is why I need you in my life. This is why you're my best friend."

She squeezed my hand. "So?"

"So," I began, "Smoke is not a crutch. Smoke is not—I'm not transferring feelings for Knox onto Smoke. I've never felt like this about anyone. I think I wasn't ready to admit things to you, or to anyone publicly, because I *knew* this was different. It didn't matter how it looked on paper or that the timing of it was weird. I just knew he was special. And every moment I was with him, I just wanted more."

"What else?" she demanded. "What else do you want to say, because you seem like you want to say something else but you won't."

"It's about our sex life," I said dryly.

"Never mind then. I never want to know about that."

"I promise I'll never tell you," I agreed.

"That would just be too weird." She shook her head. "I mean, you're going to be like, my stepmom. Wait, can I call you step-monster?"

"If it pleases the court," I joked. "Tavy, he wants more kids…"

Her eyes widened. "What?"

I nodded. "Yeah. He wants more kids."

"And you?"

"Yeah. I want them too."

"So, my best friend is about to become my step-monster and be the mother of my half-siblings? This is too bizarre."

"How about you just call me your best friend and leave the rest of it to shake out how it will?"

"Yeah." She nodded. "A healthy dose of denial that you and my dad are gonna get frisky and make little Ember and Cole."

I raised my eyebrows. "Baby names?"

"Just my two cents. I think that would be really cute. Besides, you owe me."

"I owe you?" I said with a laugh. "How do you figure?"

"Aside from sleeping with my dad?"

"Ah," the server announced at the table. "Sorry about the delay. We had an issue with the cappuccino machine."

I shook my head as I felt my cheeks heat.

Tavy glanced up at the server and smiled. "Thanks."

The server ducked his head and hustled away from the table.

"You're going to make it your mission to embarrass me every chance you can, aren't you?"

"You know me so well," she joked. "But honestly. If you guys are happy, I'm going to be happy too. It's just going to take me a little while to get there. Once I get past the shock of it all, I think it will be okay."

"Fair enough." I reached for my decaf cappuccino—my second for the day—and wrapped my hands around the cup. "There's more."

"More? What else is there. Oh God, you're already pregnant, aren't you?" she screeched.

The few other customers looked in the direction of our table.

"Tavy," I hissed.

"Sorry," she muttered. "But are you?"

I paused and then shook my head. "I'm not. But I was."

She looked at me in confusion. "I don't understand."

"I was pregnant," I said slowly. "But I had a miscarriage. It wasn't Smoke's, Tavy."

I gave her a moment to process what I'd said, and when it registered, her eyes widened. "You mean, you were pregnant with Knox's…"

I nodded.

"Oh. Oh, wow." She swallowed. "Why didn't you tell me you were pregnant? Did you think I'd be upset because it was Knox's?"

"I didn't know I was pregnant."

"What happened? How did you miscarry?"

"It was probably the punch to the stomach that did it," I said, wincing as I remembered the pain, the agony, the terror of Knox brutalizing me.

"Dad told me what happened," she said gently. "About Knox trying to…"

"Yeah." I swallowed and took a deep breath. "Thank God for Smoke."

"Thank God."

"He knows about the miscarriage, Tavy. And he—if things had been different and Knox had never come back, he says he would've stayed with me and the baby."

"He said that to you?" Tavy asked, her eyes glistening with tears.

"Yeah." I swallowed.

"Damn. No wonder you're in love with him."

I let out a startled laugh. "Yeah, no wonder. Look, I don't know when he's going to propose or when we're getting married, but when I do, you'll be the first one I call."

"You promise?"

"I promise."

"What do your parents think of all this?" Tavy asked.

"Mom knew something was going on," I said. "I called her, trying to talk around the fact that I was seeing someone new so soon after ending my engagement, but she was onto me from the beginning. She doesn't care about our age difference. Dad and my brothers on the other hand…"

I quickly told her the story of that morning, waking up to my brothers standing over us and trying to intimidate Smoke.

Tavy laughed so hard tears streamed from her eyes. "If they had any idea how much of a bad ass my dad is, they wouldn't have even tried that shit."

"Are you telling me I fell in love with a bad boy?"

"A bad boy biker," she agreed. "Although, you might reform him."

Fire & Frenzy

"God, I hope not. I love him just the way he is."

"Aww, that's sweet. Nauseatingly sweet, actually." She took my hand and gave it a squeeze. "But you guys deserve your happily ever after."

"What about you?" I asked.

"What about me?"

"Are you dating anyone?"

"Me? Dating? Please," she said hastily. "Where are your parents?"

"They went out. They wanted to explore Waco."

"So where did they go?"

"I don't know. I guess I'll find out when they get back."

"And your brothers? Where are they?"

I frowned. "Don't know, actually. Once I kicked them out of the room, they went radio silent. In fact, not one of them has called or come to check in on me. I don't trust this…"

"Logan's over there!"

Tavy and I both turned in the direction of the voice and saw Waverly bounding across the restaurant toward us.

"More visitors," I said with a smile.

"And they brought a casserole," Tavy said. "Can we dig into it? I'm kind of hungry and they're not serving food right now."

"I've done nothing but lay in bed and eat the last two days." I reached for the fork at my place setting. "What's a little casserole going to hurt?"

Chapter 50

"Are you sure you're up for this?" I asked Smoke.

"I'm sure. If I don't get out of this hotel room, I'm gonna go insane," Smoke said. "I want to eat breakfast in the restaurant even if that means being taunted by your brothers."

We paced ourselves, and by the time we got to the elevator, Smoke was pale and grimacing in pain. I'd brought his medication in my purse, just in case he wanted to take it at breakfast. He was no longer attached to an IV and the nurse had begun allowing him to move about without her help.

Smoke and I had both been asleep by the time my parents had gotten back to the hotel last night, though we had gone to bed early, tired out from all the visitors. Darcy and Crow had showed up for a brief visit, but Willa and Duke and their crew had stayed for a while.

I'd woken up to a family text asking if Smoke and I wanted to meet them downstairs for a meal.

Everyone was already at the table waiting for us, menus down in front of them.

Fire & Frenzy

I kissed my mom's cheek and took the chair next to her. Smoke lowered himself into the empty seat next to me.

The server came by while we made small talk and asked what we wanted to drink. He left and then we sat in awkward silence, Grady and Killian looking uncomfortable. Chase appeared exhausted and I wondered if he and Rach had spent any more time together, and whether or not they were going to continue to lie about what was actually going on between them.

"As much fun as the palpable tension is," Harlan said, "someone better start talking."

"You just did," I pointed out.

"No, I'm breaking the ice." Harlan reached for his glass of water. "There's a difference."

"I vote for Grady," Chase said. "He's the oldest."

"Second the motion," Killian said.

Grady tugged at his collar. "We're sorry about how we were yesterday. LoLo, you're an adult."

"Barely," Killian muttered.

"Hey," I snapped.

"Sorry. Force of habit." Killian grinned.

"As I was saying. We're sorry, and to make it up to you…" Grady pulled out his phone and scrolled through his screen. "We went house hunting."

I frowned. "House hunting. You're not all moving here, are you? I love you guys, but—"

"If I had to live in this humidity, I'd kill myself," Grady said. "No, the house is for you two."

I looked at Smoke and then back to Grady. "For us?"

Grady slid his phone across the table to me. "We were out all day yesterday looking at places. Mom and Dad came with."

The phone went untouched. "I don't understand."

"Mom said you didn't want to live in the apartment

above the bakery anymore," Grady said. "And I can't say I blame you. So, we found you a place. For you and Smoke."

"Look at the photos," Chase urged.

"It's got a big backyard," Harlan added. "In case you guys want a dog. I think you guys need a dog."

"And a great tree for a tire swing," Killian said. "Or a treehouse. We can come down and help build it. You know, for the kids."

"What kids?" I demanded.

"The kids you're gonna have one day. Obviously," Harlan said. "Mom wants grandbabies, and as you pointed out, the rest of us are too emotionally stunted to think about procreating."

"Be nice, you're talking about my children," Mom said.

Smoke said nothing, but he picked up the phone and began to look at the photos.

"Well, isn't this just like you guys," I said, my tone acerbic.

"Uh oh," Killian said.

"Told you she'd yell at us," Harlan mumbled.

"You guys can't help yourselves, can you? First you butt into my love life and attempt to intimidate Smoke."

"They didn't intimidate me," Smoke said absently as he continued scrolling through the photos.

"I know they didn't," I said. I turned my attention back to my brothers. "And then you do something incredibly sweet so I can't possibly stay mad at you."

Harlan blinked. "Wait, you're not mad?"

"I'm not mad."

"Then why are you yelling?" Harlan asked with a smirk.

I opened my mouth to reply, but I quickly clamped it shut.

"Look at the photos," my dad prodded. "If there's

something you don't like, the boys and I will fly down here and fix it ourselves."

"It's nice having a contractor in the family," Smoke said. He leaned over toward my father and showed him the phone. "This backyard situation isn't going to work for me. It's not a good use of the space."

"Agreed." Dad pointed to the screen. "If you remove that structure and—"

"Wait, can't I see the house?" I asked in exasperation.

"Maybe you should've been looking at the phone instead of yelling at us," Chase reprimanded as he reached for his cup of coffee.

"We did all the dirty work for you guys," Killian said. "You can't imagine how many shitty houses we saw in a single day."

"It's ten minutes from the clubhouse," Mom said. "And it's in a good school district."

"Ember and Cole are going to private school," I muttered.

"Who and who?" Smoke asked.

"Don't worry about it, it doesn't concern you," I said with a shake of my head.

Smoke handed me the phone and I scrolled through the photos. Out of the corner of my eye, I saw the server approach and my dad gestured that we needed another minute.

The house was gorgeous. Four bedrooms, three baths. Huge kitchen. Aside from needing new paint and our own personal touches, I couldn't wait to see the space in person.

"What do you think?" Smoke asked.

"I think it's a miracle the place hasn't sold already," I admitted.

"It's not on the market yet," Killian said.

I looked at him. "It's not?"

"Slash and Brooklyn gave us their realtor's number," Mom said.

"Oh," I said quietly.

Smoke settled his hand on my thigh underneath the table. "Well? You want to see it?"

"I—" Words lodged in my throat. Nodding, I gave Grady his phone back.

"I can make a call right now, if you want," Grady said. "You can see it this afternoon."

"Okay," I agreed.

Smoke lifted my hand to his lips and kissed the back of it.

Mom let out a sigh.

"God, they're staring at each other like they want to eat each other whole," Harlan groaned. "Looks like you guys will have grandkids within a year."

"There's no rush," Dad said, looking panicked.

"There's a little bit of a rush," Chase said with a wide grin. "Gotta get a move on before Smoke is eligible for the AARP discounts at the buffet."

"Or needs a hip replacement," Killian added.

"Or needs his prostate examined," Dad said.

The entire table went silent.

Smoke looked at my dad and grinned. "Good one."

My dad smiled.

"If we're trading insults, can we at least do this over a pitcher of mimosas?" I asked.

"Mimosas? So, we have to trade intelligent insults?" Harlan asked.

"Intelligence isn't your strong suit, is it, Harlan?" Smoke asked.

Dad slapped Smoke on the back. "Welcome to the family, son."

"You're taking Smoke's side? Over your own flesh and blood?" Harlan asked. "Rude."

Dad looked at Smoke when he said, "The man saved my daughter's life. As far as I'm concerned, he is my own flesh and blood."

Epilogue

A week later

SMOKE

I watched Logan toss the bean bag and it landed in one of the holes in the old painted wood. She whooped in excitement and Waverly hugged her eagerly.

Across the lawn, Tavy and Sailor glowered and went to gather the bean bags. Sailor tossed the first bean bag and it landed on the wooden plank and slid off into the grass.

Logan started heckling Tavy and Sailor until Tavy lost her temper and began to march toward Logan. Logan immediately began to retreat, laughing as she did. But Tavy had a good arm and beaned her in the back.

I laughed when Logan turned after being hit and went on the offense.

Logan and I had seen the house and agreed it was the

right one for us. I'd put in an offer and it was accepted immediately. But closing paperwork was going to take weeks to work its way through the banks, so we were crashing at Willa and Duke's for the time being. We were staying in the guest house because it was only one floor, and climbing stairs wasn't in my immediate future.

We'd displaced Waverly and Sailor who were now sleeping in a spare room, but neither of them minded because they both had become low-key obsessed with Logan and wanted to do her the favor.

It was a full house, people coming and going constantly, and Savage stayed with them more often lately than at the clubhouse.

"She seems happy," Savage said as he lifted the bottle of beer to his lips.

"She is happy," I said.

"She sleeping okay?"

I shrugged. "On and off."

"She jump when you touch her?"

"No."

He nodded.

Logan would start therapy next week, but that was her shit to share only if she wanted to. I could talk to her, but there were things she'd need to discuss with someone who did that sort of thing for a living.

"So, the club going legit…" Savage began. "You as bored as I am?"

I cracked a grin. "Looking for trouble?"

"Always." He looked at me. "You're not bored?"

"Nope. Not even a little."

"That's because you got a woman."

"A good woman," I clarified. "Maybe you should find a good woman."

He looked in the direction of Tavy.

"Don't you *fucking* dare."

Savage laughed. "I might be crazy, but I'm not *that* crazy."

"Good."

Tavy was off limits, especially to my brothers. They were the kind of men who'd have your back. In battle, there were no better warriors than my brothers. They were family to the end. But that didn't mean I wanted my daughter to get caught up with one of them.

Even though we weren't into illegal shit anymore, these were men who lived by different rules and trouble had a way of finding men like that, whether they liked it or not.

My phone chimed in my pocket and I fished it out, a smile drifting across my face.

"You look like a dope," Savage teased. "What's got you smiling?"

"The ring came in," I said.

"No shit. You picked out a ring already?"

"I didn't pick it. There's a jewelry store in Sandpoint—a local artist. Logan's mom sent me a photo of the ring Logan always admires when she's home for a visit."

"How are you so fucking thoughtful and shit?" Savage asked.

"I want to make her happy." I shrugged. "Everything I do, I do for her. It's easy when I think about it from that point of view."

"Huh." He shook his head. "I'm not ready for that kind of commitment."

I laughed.

"What? Why are you laughing?"

"Because you don't have any fucking control over it. When the right woman comes along, it'll hit you like a Mack truck. You'll fall hard, you'll fall fast, and you won't be able to do a damn thing to stop it."

"This is depressing." Savage took a sip of his beer and stood up. "Excuse me. There's a woman out there who hasn't met me yet, who I'd like to meet, and seduce—just for the night."

He walked into the house and disappeared out of sight.

I opened my phone and shot a text off to Bones.

ME

Go time.

A few minutes went by and he replied.

BONES

On my way.

"You're grinning," Logan said as she plopped down in the chair Savage had vacated.

"Am I?" I lifted my arm and grasped the back of her head, dragging her lips toward mine.

"Ewwwww get a freakin' room!" Waverly yelled.

Logan laughed and pulled away, her face flushed with excitement.

"No, don't tell them that," Tavy said. "That's my dad and my best friend. Yuck squared."

"Need anything?" Logan asked.

"I'm fine."

Logan hopped up. "I'm gonna see if Willa needs help inside." She looked at me with raised brows.

"I'm good, I swear."

"Even if you weren't, you wouldn't tell me," she accused.

"Nope."

She dragged a finger across my jaw and then she turned and walked away.

"Tav!" I called. "Come here a second."

Tavy tossed the beanbags to Waverly and then bounded over to me. "What's up?"

I pitched my voice low and said, "It came in. Roman signed for it."

Her eyes lit up with excitement. "Really?"

"Yep. Bones is on his way over. I'll need your help distracting Logan so I can get out of here."

"You can count on me, Captain." She saluted.

∼

Two hours later, Bones pulled into Willa and Duke's driveway. Logan stood on the sidewalk, barefoot, her arms crossed over her chest and a glare across her gorgeous face.

"Your woman is pissed," Bones said with a laugh.

"She won't be in about ten minutes." I unlatched my seatbelt, hating that I had to ride bitch. "Thanks for your help today, brother."

"Anytime. We'll have to celebrate when you're up to it."

I got out of the car, holding in a wince of pain. I walked up the driveway and headed toward Logan who hadn't lost her scowl.

"You're beautiful when you glower," I said in greeting.

"Don't try to flatter me," she snapped. "I can't believe you left without telling me where you were going! And you didn't answer your phone! I was worried sick about you."

"You weren't supposed to notice I was gone," I drawled. "Tavy was supposed to distract you."

Her gaze narrowed. "I know. She enlisted the aid of Sailor and Waverly and they first gave me a pedicure, then a face mask, and then we all talked about Dylan and Waverly's relationship. By the time I'd realized what was going on, I figured you'd given me the slip."

"I had to run an errand," I said. "Can we sit?"

Her glare melted. "Yeah. Let's sit."

We sat down on the front porch and I casually rested my left hand on her thigh.

She looked down. "What is that?"

"What's it look like?" I asked, trying to keep the smile out of my tone.

"It looks like you got a tattoo of a cupcake entwined with a vine on your ring finger…and the vine seems really familiar, but I don't know why."

I lifted her chin so her gaze met mine. "Reach into my inner cut pocket."

She did as I said and pulled out a black velvet jewelry box. She stared at it for a moment and then opened it.

Her breath caught in her throat. "Smoke," she whispered. "How'd you know?"

"Your mother," I said. "She knew it was your favorite."

It looked nothing like the gargantuan, gaudy piece of shit her ex-fiancé had bought her. This ring was elegant, but unique. The band was a rose gold vine, a diamond nestled among the leaves. The vine pattern matched the one I'd had Roman tattoo on my finger.

"I love you, cupcake," I said. "I thought about waiting to propose until I could actually get down on one knee without moaning in pain…"

She hastily covered her mouth but couldn't conceal the giggle that escaped.

"But I can't wait, cupcake. I love you."

Her eyes shined with unshed tears.

"I was yours the moment I saw you," she said softly. "I just didn't know it yet. And I don't care if you get down on one knee."

I grasped the back of her neck and pulled her toward me. "Marry me, cupcake."

"On one condition."

"Name it."

"You tell Edith and Harry the truth. They're going to have some questions when they get our wedding invitation."

"I can handle Edith and Harry." I laughed and slipped the ring onto her finger. "Kiss me, Logan. Kiss me like you can't live without me."

Her gaze softened. "I can't, Smoke. I can't live without you."

I cradled the back of her head. "You'll never have to."

Additional Works

The Tarnished Angels Motorcycle Club Series:

Wreck & Ruin (Tarnished Angels Book 1)
Crash & Carnage (Tarnished Angels Book 2)
Madness & Mayhem (Tarnished Angels Book 3)
Thrust & Throttle (Tarnished Angels Book 4)
Venom & Vengeance (Tarnished Angels Book 5)
Fire & Frenzy (Tarnished Angels Book 6)
Leather & Lies (Tarnished Angels Book 7 - preorder)

SINS Series:

Sins of a King (Book 1)
Birth of a Queen (Book 2)
Rise of a Dynasty (Book 3)
Dawn of an Empire (Book 4)
Ember (Book 5)
Burn (Book 6)
Ashes (Book 7)
Fall of a Kingdom (Book 8)

Additional Works

Others:

Peasants and Kings

About the Author

Wall Street Journal & USA Today bestselling author Emma Slate writes romance with heart and heat.

Called "the dialogue queen" by her college playwriting professor, Emma writes love stories that range from romance-for-your-pants to action-flicks-for-chicks.

When she isn't writing, she's usually curled up under a heating blanket with a steamy romance novel and her two beagles—unless her outdoorsy husband can convince her to go on a hike.

Made in the USA
Columbia, SC
05 May 2024